M000165783

ARSALAN THE MAGNIFICENT

Copyright © 2023 Jason E. Tolbert

Cover illustration and design by Jason E. Tolbert. All rights reserved. No part of this book may be reproduced in any form or by any electronic or mechanical means including information storage and retrieval systems, without permission in writing from the author. The only exception is by a reviewer, who may quote short excerpts in a review.

Second Publication January 2024, Curlicue Press.

ISBN 978-1-0881-9193-4

CONTENTS

CHAPTER 1

Resplendent was the age of the magical architects of long ago. It was the age of the magical engineers of pillar and stone who could command rock to float in the air and could compel metal to bend at one's touch, and the age of sorcerers who could make crystals glow to light great plazas and could enchant castles to revolve on their bases to face the sun and moon. The likes of these gifted women and men—angels and demiurges, some say, possessing wondrous and wizardly crafts over their materials—have not been seen since the end of that distant eon. Only echoes of their accounts remain with us as fables and fairy tales told by grandparents to children.

Most everyone has heard the stories of Ubaldini the Ingenious and his courtyard of lapis lazuli tiles that conveyed astonished visitors from one side of the court to another, or of Sigrid the Lucent, who erected the Inverted Pyramids of Vaduz and possessed the secret of imbuing stone and metal with translucent qualities. Likewise, many are familiar with the legends of Conrad's Castle, which hovered, unsupported and untethered, over Lake Starnberg while lit from all sides by luminous lobes of ensorcelled amethyst. And of course, few are ignorant of the tales of Arsalan the Magnificent, the creator of the World's Leaf, once humankind's tallest and most sophisticated structure before it came crashing to the ground.

The lives these magical architects had lived in those days of unfettered royal demand and patronage, of opulence and renown, those years of rivalry and passion and jealousy over each other's genius. Historians are uncertain when that era began its gradual and intractable decline, but many of them agree in pinpointing the collapse of the World's Leaf at that point.

Arsalan the Magnificent was the greatest and most famed of all the living magical architects of his day and enjoyed their enduring envy and admiration. Well into his career, he had been commissioned by Sultan Muhteşem to realize a dream the sultan had had one breezy summer night while vacationing in his pearl tower on the shore of the sapphire seas. Muhteşem described a vision of a single, green stem sprouting from the earth, and from this stem a single, wide green leaf hung perpendicularly and waved in the wind. In his dream, the sultan said, the plant functioned as a building large enough for thousands of people from all over the world to occupy, and that building would function as a university that would work for the peace and education of all humankind. Such a lofty ideal surprised Arsalan and inspired him, for until then, he had heard nothing like it. Arsalan had constructed strong and splendid fortresses for kings and queens that would intimidate their rivals. He had built impenetrable vaults and banks and dams and dikes with walls yards thick that could not be toppled or breached by man or wind or tide. Arsalan had constructed towering temples of one religion or another that adherents would occupy to pronounce fiery edicts against heretics. He had built dazzling boulevards and glittering opera houses for decadent royals. But the idea of a university for peace that was shaped like a simple leaf truly had taken him with its simplicity and beauty. Arsalan bowed to Muhteşem and promised its construction and immediately received his commission.

The hull of the structure was a continuous surface of emerald-colored steel, without seam or rivet, whose metallurgy was a mystery to the other magical architects, and some say even to Arsalan's fellow guildsmen. The dimensions of the structure's stem were comparable to those of other buildings except for the stem's sheer upward reach; it soared so high into the azure sky that it seemed to caress the clouds. Inside, it was sunlit and airy, and occupants could stand inside the stem's many rooms and could walk its many spiraling stairways without feeling constrained by the tower's tubular curvature. Holes in the building channeled wind currents from outside to cool the interior. A small, mobile chamber of enchanted metal, as large as a wardrobe, would transport occupants up a chute to the highest point of the stem, and then sideways into the leaf, which was honeycombed with many classrooms and lecture halls and library rooms, with windows facing outward over the vast expanse of the dazzling desert province and its electric blue sea. The leaf itself was designed to yield slightly to the great winds of that altitude, absorbing their force such that the building would not crack, and yet its occupants would not be conscious of its swaying.

No one had beheld such beautiful and otherworldly architecture. Gleaming in the blazing sun on the sparking shores of the Red Sea, it was singularly the greatest achievement of any of the magical architects. So far was it beyond anyone's imagination that indeed some began to doubt that it was more than a façade. Perhaps it was from astonishment, or fear, or jealousy, or some other source, but the murmuring began. Nonetheless, Arsalan ignored the grumbling din and continued with his work until the day of the grand opening.

Royals and prime ministers and sultans and emperors from around the world attended the unveiling, and they sat at a distance from the base of the building in a great semicircle facing the sea, looking like mere grains of sand beneath the immensity of the structure that sprouted before them on the shoreline. Beneath the fierce sun they sweated as they waited, in their wigs and makeup, their plumages and hats, their epaulets and corsets and robes and headdresses, and all beneath their parasols and tents. All those who had been involved in building, financing, and overseeing the construction stood at attendance to one side, and the building was ordered to be vacated so that Sultan Muhteşem himself would be the first set foot in the World's Leaf at the opening. Finally, the time arrived when the horns were sounded, and Muhteşem's speech was made, and the ribbon was cut, and the doves were released and flew into the air like a great, fluttering sail unfurling. But the crowd's cheer was cut short by the sudden, ominous screeching and creaking of metal from above. Everyone looked upward and saw the great leaf drooping downward toward them, and they knew they were in danger. All of them, royal and common, commander and servant, panicked and began to run in every direction that led outward from the base of the moaning monstrosity before them. The stampede was unstoppable and chaotic. Like a parade of pageantry gone mad, all forgot their regality and scrambled for their own safety, running over each other's feet and hands, over one another's dropped hats and turbans and umbrellas. The tower veritably deflated and fell backward into the azure sea, roaring and squealing like a fatally wounded man and kicking up a plume of dust and dirt and mist so high that it lasted the rest of the day and was visible for miles around. The beautiful, slender sculpture that once had shone malachite under the desert sun now was replaced by a crooked, mangled tendril half-submerged into the seawater and a column of plain brown dust that lingered like a ragged ghost.

Arsalan, who found himself standing among the dazed and wandering crowd covered in dust, was summoned to Sultan Muhteşem's tent which had been erected nearby. The magical architect, who had just that morning stood so proudly by the sultan during the speech, now kneeled prostrate before Muhteşem. Tears streamed down Arsalan's face as he petitioned for forgiveness from the great, young sultan, who glared at Arsalan from within a mask of cold, deep fury.

"Your greatness," implored Arsalan, "you know that I did not intend for this to happen, and that I poured every ounce of my soul into this project, and that the failure of the structure feels like the collapse of my very own soul. Please forgive me and spare me. Although I cannot say how, I believe that my building was sabotaged!"

Muhteşem stared at the magical architect for a long while, and then out a window to the desert's horizon where the sun was setting. Though his unwrinkled face was stern, tears escaped his eyes and ran down his cheeks.

"You have cast my dreams asunder and have humiliated me in front of the most powerful people in the world, all of whom have spared no expense to travel here for the unveiling. They all nearly died here today. What kind of catastrophe would it have been if all the world's leaders perished here? How can I face them? What do I say to them? How do I recover my honor? How do you think this will affect my diplomatic relations with their governments? Was anyone killed in that building? Hopefully not. The only reasons I do not have you executed is your reputation, longstanding and worldwide, and the sincerity of your contrition and remorse before me. Of course, we cannot ignore the fact that you could use your formidable magical powers to resist detainment and execution, and there would no reason for you to submit to such sentences willingly. For this reason, I ask you to return your commission in full to me, and to issue a formal apology to the world for whom you attempted to build this university. In addition, I ban you from erecting any more buildings in my kingdom until such a time as you ascertain the reason for the building's failure. Perhaps that day will come, or perhaps it never will," said Muhteşem.

Although Sultan Muhteşem's mercy was merely a formality in Arsalan's case, the sultan's fury and disappointment were successful in shaming Arsalan deeply. Arsalan, once robust with pride, was now terribly wounded, and gathered himself and stood in a sickly and stooped way, seeming to hold something small and crumpled in front of himself. Shakily, he bowed to Muhteşem and retreated from the tent, not daring to turn his back on the sultan, who, tall and calm with anger in his white robe, had turned to stare again out the window at the dying sun.

Back in his workshop, Arsalan transformed into an altogether different character. He screamed and ranted fierily at his terrified journeymen and apprentices, five in all, whom he had employed to help him build the structure. He performed a veritable inquisition with each one of them in the presence of the others. He grabbed them by their hair and their chins and shook his pointed finger at their noses and slapped their faces. Each one kneeled and pleaded and implored to Arsalan their ignorance at the cause of the failure and maintained that they had followed his instructions to the letter in constructing their individual portions of the structure. Some of his journeymen grew tired of receiving his vicious blame, and they protested. They began to argue with him, venting their pent-up rage, against which Arsalan defended himself with apoplectic exasperation. Dishes and tools were thrown against walls, and neighbors peered nervously out their darkened windows at the ruckus. Long into the night the roaring continued, until several journeymen and apprentices quit and stormed away down the street. Arsalan the Magnificent was exhausted and sent everyone else away and retreated to his palace bedroom. There, he wept and drank himself to sleep on his canopy bed behind his silk curtains while his distraught wife caressed his forehead.

Arsalan's assistant and old friend Doruk, along with a crew of investigators, helped the famous magical architect examine the rubble of the downed World's Leaf. The mutilated wreckage lay all around them like the aftermath of some great war. The workers were dwarfed by the tremendous hulls of metal that lay crumpled like the dissected carcasses of whales. The wreckage started from the building's former base many yards inland and extended to the lapping, soapy surf and beyond into the water. The investigators tread carefully among the garden of sharp rubble and steel beams strewn at their feet. Although Doruk's powers were not as potent as Arsalan's, he was still wise and prudent, perhaps even more so than Arsalan himself, and Doruk was able to determine the general cause of the structure's compromise. Doruk raised his eyebrows, wrinkling his forehead in his slightly bedraggled way, and rather blandly issued his initial finding.

"Magic depletion," said Doruk.

"Magic depletion?" pronounced Arsalan. "Where did the depletion take place?"

"Universally throughout the structure," said his old friend Doruk, waving his fingers in the general direction of the wreckage.

"Impossible!" barked Arsalan. "Those magic spells were sure to last two thousand years!"

"Unfortunately, and for some unknown reason, they simply didn't," said Doruk, as he stared with frank thoughtfulness down at a block of stone lying at his foot.

"Sabotage!" cried Arsalan. "Someone must have drained the magic intentionally! I'm sure of it!"

Doruk touched the stone at his foot with his instrument, and the stone glowed from within with a lavender light. A white stain appeared in the corner of the block.

"This is where your magical charge entered the stone," said Doruk, pointing to the stain, "and there is no exit mark indicating a focused drain of the charge."

"Maybe the saboteur drained it at the point of charge entry," surmised Arsalan, "to make it less obvious."

"If someone did, the point of charge entry would glow twice as brightly," commented Doruk.

Arsalan and Doruk proceeded to inspect all the blocks that were strewn immediately around them. These all yielded the same result. They then continued, long into the day, to examine many more of the blocks beyond that, including the ones that were now nearly submerged in the sparkling, azure waters, but none of their results differed. After this, Arsalan had not much else to conclude. Though the investigation would continue, he trusted the judgment of Doruk, his loyal associate of many years, who always had proven himself to be unfailingly factual, if not a little laconic. Indeed, after some weeks, the official findings of the investigation were no different from Doruk's initial assessment. The structure had suffered from a rapid, universal depletion of magical energy. No cause was known.

Such an extraordinary case had no precedent in the long history of magical architecture. The study concluded that all protocols to ensure safe construction were followed by Arsalan's team, and that no one had fallen short of his or her duties. Yet this did not explain the building's spectacular and immediate failure. Having no real hope of a firm explanation, Arsalan did not let the investigation drag into befuddling inconclusiveness. A man of his word, Arsalan assumed full responsibility for the failure of his structure and repaid the sultan's commission in full. This put a sore dent in his immediate finances, but he could survive it. He also wrote his long and formal apology, which he read from a ceremonial scroll in the court of Sultan Muhteşem in front of the dignitaries of the world, with a straight and unerring posture. What he found most difficult to stomach, however, were the consequences for his career; his reputation had become sullied. His agent Bayram visited him to tell him that, try as he might to encourage business, Arsalan was now losing the chances for future commissions. Potential customers were afraid to ask him to build anything lest it was to crumble in front of their eyes as famously and as dramatically as the World's Leaf. And since Arsalan's sizeable wealth had made him blind to the benefits of sound investment, his profligate lifestyle, which he found difficult to restrain, began to drain his coffers ever so gradually and without his noticing. His horse-racing, his elaborate parties, his visits to the opera, his donations to the local temples, his drinking, and his gambling, all caused his finances to shrink. An intervention by his very own personal accountant shook Arsalan awake to the reality of his situation. With elegant deliberation and rectitude, the tall, thin, old accountant drew a chair up to a counting table and tallied Arsalan's expenses and his earnings over the prior year down to the coin. Arsalan only could sit in a chair by the counting table, with his shocked wife by his side, and he looked down at his embroidered house shoes. Arsalan realized that he had to sell many of the prized possessions he had acquired throughout his career: his robes, his bejeweled coats, his furs, his set of mechanical clocks, his ivory globe of the world, his silver sextant, a few of his horses, many of his crystal chandeliers, and a few tapestries. After the sales, it was as if a cold winter morning had dawned on Arsalan Ozdikmen's palace; it was grayer and emptier, joyless and bare.

These worsening circumstances his wife, Teodora, Lady of Brzeg, found intolerable. Arsalan had met lively Teodora during a project in Silesia to build the Levitating Bridges, which rose into the air to make way for boats when they passed through town. She was twelve full years his junior, was blond and buttery with irises like topaz disks, and had all the aspirations of a princess but sadly none of the temperance. She had been captivated by Arsalan's abilities, his fame, and his elegant poise, and she contrasted beautifully against his swarthy skin and black hair, his flashing dark eyes and his majestic nose shaped handsomely and evenly like quarter wedge of a circle.

"I can't bear this anymore!" she screamed one day, trembling with wrath and indignation in her robe of sky blue. She was still gorgeous as she stamped on the marble floor and shook her fists at her husband, but Arsalan also became frightened, as he often did, at the ability of her snowy face to turn crimson with rage like an octopus. "I'm a Lady! I deserve better than this! I will not be married to a pauper! I'm returning to Silesia where I can live the life of real royalty, not to a dissolute gambler or an overblown artisan who can't manage his gold!"

As she spit her words at Arsalan, she threw Yuan vases and bottles at him, and they shattered on the wall behind him as he dodged them. After this firestorm, she sent a letter to her father, packed the last of her precious things that had not been sold, summoned a great caravan of horse-drawn carts, and left for Silesia. Arsalan the Magnificent had neither the funds nor the power to stop her, so from a high turret window he watched her depart.

Teodora already had given Arsalan three fine, healthy children. None of them inherited Arsalan's magical powers, but this did not bother their father, who knew that such powers were a gift from the heavens and not an expectation. Arsalan loved them as much as any father could love his children. In fact, many would say he spoiled them as liberally as any grandfather. By this time, they were already young adults who largely could fend for themselves. Nevertheless, they still had not learned from their wealthy, famous father the valuable lessons of financial acumen and independence, as they still depended on him for their income.

Their son Omer, the oldest, was as extravagant a gambler as his father. Many considered him handsome and intelligent but useless, as he had not devoted his natural assets to much else other than women and horse racing. He was deeply in debt at the time of his father's bankruptcy, and it was not long afterward that Omer was pursued by his creditors. In fact, so deep were his arrears that Omer chose to flee the country rather than to face the collectors, and Arsalan found himself in the awkward position of having to fend them off and telling them he did not know Omer's whereabouts. Of course, this was a white lie, and Arsalan hated lying, even if to protect his son. Arsalan secretly received letters from Omer overseas, first from a monastery in Cyrnos, and then from Urgell, where he was dwelling in the mountains among the unintelligible Basques and spoke of sailing to the New World to regain his former riches. At this time, however, the letters abruptly stopped, and Arsalan, even after his repeated written urgings to Omer, could not encourage his son to write again. Now what was formerly a white lie regarding his ignorance of Omer's whereabouts became a confessable fact, and this saddened Arsalan even more.

Their second son Asker was much like his older brother, except that he was cleverer and more upstanding. It was true that he had accrued significant debts through his frequent visits to gambling halls, as well as through his expensive tastes in horse-carriages and smoking-pipes. Upon learning of the bankruptcy, however, Asker, instead of fleeing, enlisted in the Imperial Navy, where he was given the rank of Officer Cadet due to his elite education. There, he agreed to four years of military service during which he would send his pay to his creditors. Asker soon donned the stiff blue and red coat of a Naval serviceman and went off to war. He served valiantly in skirmishes all along the kingdom's borders against marauding nomads, pirates, rival kingdoms, and revolutionaries, at one time receiving a leg injury and a medal. Arsalan loved reading Asker's letters, which came regularly. Their descriptions of places and events were at times so fantastic that Arsalan, despite his own worldliness and wizardry, thought he should be more skeptical of them. But he could find no reason to doubt Asker, for this son always had proven himself to be the most forthright of his three children.

Their daughter Defne was just a maiden at the time of the bankruptcy. Everyone loved her intelligence and lovely features, her reddish-brown hair and hazel eyes. She was so young that she had few vices to mention aside from a taste for books and embroidered shoes. Despite her now being associated with a discredited family, her beauty had caught the eye of an angelic young Prince Ergin, a boy with a brilliant smile and gallant manners, who asked for her hand in marriage. Defne and her father thought that accepting the offer would be her best way out of fiscal insolvency, but just before accepting the offer, Prince Ergin was discovered to be cruel and jealous toward his women. Defne became afraid and thought of fleeing, but this effete but sinister prince revealed to her that he would hunt for her and would find her wherever she fled. The night after this terrible discovery, Defne sat on her bed for a long time, feeling persecuted and power-less. She stared out the window at the moon, lost in terror and thought, and the next morning she left a loving letter bidding farewell to her dear father. She then vanished, utterly. She disappeared so completely that not even the suspicious prince could find her, and again Arsalan found himself in the uncomfortable position of having to fend him off along with Omer's debt-collectors. But one day, Ergin became menacing and persistent toward Arsalan at his doorstep, and Arsalan lost his patience. The seasoned wizard used his powers to lift the prince far into the air, placing him atop the tallest tree in a nearby grove where Arsalan could hear the prince curse and scream for help for hours. Arsalan watched Ergin from his turret window, secretly using his powers to keep the prince safe from any true harm as the Royal Guard scrambled and fumbled with ladders and rope to retrieve the screeching, gesticulating prince from the treetop. When Prince Ergin finally was rescued, shaken and weak, he angrily brushed pine needles and sap off his fine satin suit, glared up at Arsalan's turret, and shook his fist.

This was the final undoing of Arsalan the Magnificent. The prince's father, Lord Kadir, was angered, and requested Arsalan's immediate presence in his court. Kadir knew that magical architects were too powerful to be detained by force, but he also knew that they were governed by certain rules of civility and that Arsalan would come on his own. And indeed, Arsalan did arrive at Kadir's court, which was regally bedecked in banners and tapestries of violet and gold. In its midst Arsalan stood before Lord Kadir with a straight back and an iron face.

"I am sorry to hear of your recent series of misfortunes, my dear Arsalan, and I am sorry to trouble you, but I understand you and my son have come to a confrontation recently," said Kadir calmly. "Please explain yourself."

"Yes, Lord. More correctly, your son Prince Ergin chose to start a con-frontation with me," said Arsalan. "Your son threatened to kill my daughter if she did not accept his offer for marriage."

Kadir, taken aback, turned to his son, who stood nearby, and stared at him. "Is this true, my son?" he asked.

Ergin looked at Arsalan in petulant irritation and anger, then looked ner-vously at his father, and back again at Arsalan, who only returned the prince's gaze unblinkingly. Finally, seeing that he could not escape to the penetrating stares at the two older men, Prince Ergin succumbed to his conscience and looked at the ground and held his hands together.

"Yes, Father," he said.

"You and I will have a talk, Ergin. I knew you were looking for a bride, and I would have helped you had you asked, but this is not how I taught you to act, and this is not the behavior becoming of a true prince. When a maiden does not give her your hand willingly, you do not deserve it," said Kadir. He stared for a long time at Ergin, who only continued to hang his head. Kadir then turned to Arsalan again. "And what happened next?"

"My daughter became so afraid for her life that she disappeared and is now hiding where not even I can find her," said Arsalan. "Prince Ergin then confronted me at my own doorstep, demanding that I produce my daughter for him, and that's when I decided to place him at the top of the tree, to defend myself and my daughter, but without hurting him, though I could have hurt him."

Kadir thought for a long while in front of Arsalan, who stood and waited. Finally, Kadir said, "I understand your actions, Arsalan Ozdikmen, and I apologize for my son. It seems my dear son has much to learn yet about what it means to act as a noble. But the law is clear in this land that threatening or endangering the life of a noble is an offence punishable by imprisonment or death."

"My lord, then I respectfully submit that this law is unjust," said Arsalan. "Your son endangered my daughter's life on my own doorstep, and this is something I will not tolerate from any man, noble or common, old or young. All the same, Lord Kadir, you know as well as I do that you have not the power to detain a magical architect even if the law says you must, especially since I am the one who built the prison in which you would like to detain me. So, allow me to extend an offer that might ameliorate this situation between two powerful but wise and civil men."

"Then what is your offer?" said Kadir.

"I offer to sell my palace to you for five hundred thousand lira," said Arsalan.

Kadir looked at Arsalan in astonishment. "Your palace?" said Kadir. "You are offering to sell it? At that price? Why, that palace must be worth at least three million."

"Three and a half million, more precisely, Lord Kadir. I had it appraised recently. If you are willing to purchase it at my reduced price, it will be yours, and hopefully our issue will be settled," said Arsalan.

"And what makes you offer your palace at such a low price, besides wanting to make peace with me?" asked Kadir.

"I wish to retire, and I want to move where it is peaceful and quiet, where I will not trouble anyone else," said Arsalan, gazing at the ground in front of him. "Or, rather, where I will not be troubled by anyone else. And five hundred thousand lira worth of gold, I estimate, is all that my horses and cart can carry, even using magic."

Kadir looked at him with a smile barely suppressed.

"Then I accept your offer, my wizard friend," he said. "And the agreement will be the resolution of our dispute. After the purchase, you will be gone from here, as you have said, and I will bid you good luck."

Arsalan thought that he should have asked Lord Kadir for his help locating Defne, but he still did not trust Kadir's ability to restrain his own son from harming her once she was found.

So, the purchase was arranged. At the broad marble steps in front of Arsalan's ornate, pink palace, the personal accountants of the two men—Arsalan's tall and thin and old, and Kadir's short and stout and bearded—sat at a counting-table. Secretaries and assistants were in attendance as the two accountants counted stacks and rolls of gold coins. Arsalan munched despondently on the few pastries that were served to ameliorate the seriousness of the affair.

"Dear sir," said Arsalan's accountant to Lord Kadir's accountant after an hour of counting, "I believe we have received from you an excess of fifty thousand lira."

"That is correct," said Lord Kadir's accountant. "Lord Kadir has decided that the price offered by Mr. Ozdikmen was a little too modest, and humbly bids him to accept this nominal increase, that is, assuming his horses can pull it."

"I accept," said Arsalan, slightly taken aback. Now he was forced to think of a few more spells he would need to cast to lighten the heavier load his poor horses would have to pull.

Arsalan signed the purchase agreement with a flowery quill, and the two parties gathered their respective belongings, bowed to each other, and went their separate ways. Arsalan made sure to bid his accountant a thankful farewell for his flawless service of many years. Finally, Arsalan loaded his gold and his last possessions onto his large, plain coach carriage, which he had bought for his servants to transport wine from the vineyards to his cellar. The carriage was tied to the only two horses of his seventeen he had not sold, which were his favorite steeds Solmaz and Aysel, two enormous, gleaming auburn draft Malakans with bellicose heads like those found on chess pieces and limbs rippling with muscle. But as strong as Arsalan knew his horses to be, the load was now beyond their maximum, so the wizard cast the spells necessary to make it much lighter for them to pull.

Before his departure, Arsalan the Magnificent, while sitting on the driver's seat of his carriage, took one last look over his shoulder at the grand, pink, ornate chateau, with its turrets and balconies and grand windows overlooking a distant view of the sea. He remembered presenting the palace to his bride for the first time, and how she kissed him. He remembered the sound of his small children as they ran through the echoing hallways with laughter and play as the servants chased them. He remembered his grand parties with friends and their families. But now the inside of this dwelling, for the first time in the decades since he had built it, stood dark and empty and spiritless, and it pained him to look at it.

"How tacky it was," blustered Arsalan to himself, though he knew he was lying, and he was momentarily ashamed.

"No," he then added, as if apologizing to the castle. "How grand you were. I'm sorry for leaving you, but I must go now."

Arsalan turned back around, flapped the reigns to Solmaz and Aysel, and they were all off, trotting down the road that spiraled up to the treed hilltop on which the palace sat. Arsalan was now determined to leave his life of excess behind him, even down to his clothes. He made certain to wear his plainest clothing, with no silk or embroidery, so that no one would bow to him as he passed or would recognize him as Arsalan the Magnificent. It was a simple outfit made of brown linen, and only the most attentive would notice the slight hint of fashion that still adhered to this attire.

Arsalan then spent the next two weeks wandering through the city that had been his home for so many years, Kirklareli, with its spires and arches and minarets and domes all decorated with stonework of pink or tan or green or white. He regarded the architecture poignantly, as he himself had built some of it, such as a post office, the public bathhouse, two churches, and a theater. None of it was particularly fancy, as he had built them closer to the beginning of his career, and the customers he attracted at that time did not command large budgets. Arsalan passed the café he used to frequent before his ignominy, and he recognized all his business associates sitting at the same tables as before, drinking coffee and smoking and discussing business. Arsalan lowered his head, hid his face, and rode on, hoping they would mistake him for a common merchant.

Discreetly, Arsalan stopped every so often to ask unfamiliar store owners and passersby if they had seen his daughter Defne. He had a small, realistic portrait of her drawn by a skilled royal artisan, although it had been produced when Defne was younger and slighter. The portrait was nestled inside a brass locket that was shaped and opened like a book, and Arsalan kept this locket inside his shirt pocket. He would step down from the carriage and would show a stranger or a familiar acquaintance the picture and would inquire. The person would try his or her amicable best after being interrupted during some daily task to recall if the girl had passed their way.

"No," said the stout, bent old woman who was hauling a bundle of kindling on her back, after squinting and straining her neck backward to see the picture clearly.

"No," said an elderly shopkeeper with ears like wings that wobbled when he shook his head.

"No, I don't believe so," said a fat, squinting smith with a dirty face and smock while scratching one ear.

"I'm afraid not," said the bearded fruit peddler. "But would you like to buy some pomegranates? They're fresh!"

"Yes! I've seen her!" said a passing schoolboy. "No, no. I'm sorry. I was thinking of my friend's sister."

"No, and a girl like this shouldn't be out on her own at all," said a policeman, who later invited Arsalan into his office for a description. There, for an hour, five or six burly policemen with nothing else better to do listened with calm and factual gazes to Arsalan's heartbreaking story while leaning heavily on chairs and tables as if watching the events of a play.

Constables, priests, clerics, nuns, and professors all said no. Taxmen, bankers, buskers, landlords, vendors, street urchins, and artisans all said no. Cheery noblemen stopped laughing among themselves long enough to think but said they had not seen her at any social functions. When the librarians and the shoemakers also said they did not recall seeing Defne, Arsalan knew, inwardly and weightily, that she was truly nowhere in the vicinity.

The days were hot and dry, and the roads were haunted by tufts of floating dust, and the glaring sun shone onto everyone's faces, causing them to grimace, half-blinded, in the noonday heat like sneering theater masks of bright, melted platinum, showing their every crease, wrinkle, and worry and mundane and distant concern, none of which had anything to do with Arsalan's runaway daughter.

Arsalan did not stay in any hotels or inns but stopped near their stables for a small fee, and he slept nights in the carriage, thinking of his sons, his wife, and his daughter, while watching the moon float by the window and peek inside at him. On certain nights he would light a lantern and would reread the letter that Defne had written to him.

My Dearest Father,

How sad that fate has brought us to this point. How well you had tried to raise us with your wealth and fame, and how swiftly and mercilessly fate has snatched this material fortune away from us. I do not grieve the loss of these worldly treasures, for I knew I always had my family to surround me with love and kindness under any circumstances. But now it seems that fate, so cruelly, has proven me wrong and has blown these close bonds to pieces. How could this have happened? I believe, dear Father, and do not be angry with me when I say this, that your wealth and success has blinded you and has confused you and has led you astray. You loved us, Father, and you also loved magical architecture, and you loved Mother, and you loved your horses, and your gambling, and your parties, and your drink and food, but many times you were uncertain which you loved more. You were too wild with material happiness to teach your sons and daughter prudence and strength. Now that these material treasures have disappeared, I feel my father is adrift and helpless.

Now a new threat is menacing me. Prince Ergin has promised to take my life if he cannot take my hand in marriage. I am terrified of him, Father, more terrified of him than of anything else in my life, because I no longer feel that I have my brothers or parents to protect me. You may be able to protect me, Father, but perhaps at the cost of prison or death or destitution, at which time I will have no one. What I do next, Father, I do for you as much as for myself. I have decided to go into hiding. Tell Prince Ergin you do not know where I am, because you will not know, because I will not tell you. Once Prince Ergin is convinced that I am unreachable, I feel that he will abandon his passions. Spend no expense to protect me. Just defend yourself. I now will know what it means to protect myself as a grown woman. Just know that I will be safe, and perhaps I will return when I am a full woman, confident and brave.

I love you, dear father. I love you, I love you, I love you. You are my sun, the sun to my mother's moon. Please do not be angry with me. Know that I will be alive, I will be well, and I will be good.

Your Daughter,

Defne

Arsalan, as he usually did, read the last two paragraphs through swelling and rolling tears, while a pain impaled him like a javelin. It was clear that Defne had taken her fate into her own slender hands, but Arsalan wished it were not in this way or under these terrible circumstances.

"I'm a failure," he whispered to himself in the small cabin. "Arsalan the Magnificent is a failure."

Chapter 2

I will use my powers to harm neither man nor woman nor child, nor will I allow harm to come to them through willful neglect. I will not use my powers to cause deliberate pain in any living thing. I will use my powers to construct dwellings and structures for the benefit and protection of humankind and toward a society prosperous, peaceful, and wise.

This was one of the magical architects' vows, which Arsalan had taken when he was accepted into the Magical Architects' Guild a lifetime ago in his youth. He had adhered to these vows absolutely, even throughout all the vicissitudes that a life of fame and wealth and fortune would bring him. He was proud of this unswerving adherence to his principles, and admittedly even rather surprised. Violations of this vow resulted in disbarment from the Magical Architects' Guild and the loss of one's right to practice the profession. But now that his profession had died a sudden and tragic death due to an anomalous magical depletion, and now that his wealth, his marriage, and his family life collapsed along with it, he came to wonder if such strict observance of any principle at all had been worth the effort. Still, it made him feel good to recall how well he had maintained such professional integrity for so many years, even if his enamorment with wealth and fame had been more than moderate. Now Arsalan felt it would be better to shrink into seclusion and exile where the sting and the stench of his disgrace would evaporate over time while he pondered the reasons for his building's magical depletion. Perhaps in doing so he safely could unravel himself and then could reassemble himself into some other man, some innocuous, humble, peaceable stranger whom no one could recognize and would not bother.

Arsalan decided to head for the destination he had imagined when he first announced his intention to retire, which was in the countryside up north, among the mountains and pines, in the rough, stony wilds just inside the borders of the kingdom ruled by Sultan Muhteşem, or perhaps even just outside them. He thought of the Balkan Mountains, which was the setting for so many of the fairy tales Arsalan had spun for Defne at night by her bedside. These tales had inspired a particular fascination in Defne of those cold, misty mountains filled with foreboding precipices and silent pine forests filled with secrets and spirits. She often asked her father to tell her stories involving this land, and she owned many geography books involving the Balkans. For this reason, the idea occurred to Arsalan to continue his search for Defne there, for it seemed reasonable, perhaps even promising, to consider it one of her possible hideaways.

In any case, Arsalan was eager to leave Kirklareli and sought to escape all the tormenting memories it harbored for him. He directed his carriage onto the main road that led northwest out of town. Once on it, Arsalan rode with his head down, hoping for the last time to avoid seeing anyone he knew so that he would not have to explain himself or to say goodbye. Poignantly, his home of so many years now was diminishing behind him and into his past. In a melancholy daze, he watched the road pass beneath his horses' hooves and scarcely noticed how the road's reddish-brown surface roughened as he ventured away from the city. He was in no hurry, as he had only a vague plan of where to go, but many skills at hand to use when he arrived there. Gradually, buildings shrank into dwarven versions of those found in the city, and houses became simpler and more modest and grew apart from each other, separated by deep groves and copses. Finally, houses became rare and timid, and the thickets aggressed to command the landscape all around Arsalan and became forests as deep and silent and sacred as cathedrals, with trees like columns and leaves like stained glass and golden shafts of sunlight that shimmered intimately onto velvety beds of emerald moss through which Arsalan's path wended its way.

Along the road he passed peddlers driving donkey carts wishing to sell him their goods, and he met lean pilgrims on foot who bid him blessings. He passed farmers with faces red and creased who observed him with passive distrust as they led their livestock and carts loaded with mounds of golden wheat. He met itinerant workers with bags on their backs who sang and talked with each other in such a lively manner that they scarcely noticed him. Arsalan hailed each of these folks to ask them if they had seen Defne, but to his inquiries the passersby invariably responded with peering, confused eyes, slackened jaws, and wiggling shakes of their heads. When there were no other travelers, Arsalan occasionally saw foxes and deer crossing the road far in front of him, but by the time he reached the spot where he saw them stealing across, they already had fled and had vanished into the deep, silent greenness.

Somewhere amid his reverie, Arsalan suddenly realized that although he had spent several days purchasing supplies before his journey, he had not taken a careful inventory of them in his eagerness to leave unseen. He also felt in need of rest. He parked his carriage in grassy clearing among some tall trees and proceeded to drag out his boxes and crates, opening them one by one, and scanning their contents. After some time, Arsalan was standing amid an unruly, makeshift store yard of boxed possessions stacked in the grass, and he was holding a pencil in one hand and a list in the other, muttering to himself while making notes and calculations like a shopkeeper. The busywork distracted him from his sorrows and the heavy task of leaving his old life behind, and the listing and counting gave him a new, if tenuous, sense of peace. But after a long while at this, his businesslike flow of activity was interrupted when he was visited by a stray cat.

The cat was ugly and bedraggled. Its coat was reduced to tufts of sparse, scraggly orange fur, missing in patches here and there, and it was frightfully emaciated. Arsalan noticed the animal from the corner of his eye. The cat peered at Arsalan through the grass with eyes of cool, gleaming jade, and it walked cautiously toward the busy man on footsteps of sublime, expert silence through the green blades and leaves, occasionally sniffing at the ground. The next time Arsalan noticed the vagrant cat, it was already flirtatiously brushing itself against his legs as he sat in the door of the carriage and worked at his notes. Arsalan recoiled at this, stood stiffly with notes and pencil in hand, and he glared with cool disgust at the cat from over his reading spectacles.

"Go away," he said. "I haven't time for a pet, especially one as wretched as you who is sure to give me fleas or mange. Besides, I've nothing for you to eat. Shoo!"

The cat retreated, and Arsalan sat again and continued with his serious business of listing and counting. But the cat returned and continued its feminine dance of ingratiating itself to the human. As Arsalan tried to work, the cat wound itself around Arsalan's legs with its vertical tail. It crawled around one of Arsalan's legs and behind the other, over his foot and then under his thigh. The feline forced its face against Arsalan's pant legs as it did so, purring and mewling in aggressive advances for endearment. Arsalan slowly and impatiently contorted to avoid touching the pitiful and possibly diseased creature as it sought his attention. He squirmed, lifted his legs one after another, stood uncomfortably again, and brushed off from his clothes whatever sickening hair or parasites the cat may have given him.

After a time, the cat, as if sensing how little of its affection was being duly reciprocated, relented somewhat and sat in the grass nearby, where she watched the old man focus on his fastidious rifling. Arsalan was sorting through some small boxes, stacking them here and here on a large crate while muttering to himself. He stopped to examine one of the boxes. It was a jewel case, carved with a particular serpentine ornateness. Glancing briefly up at the cat with a guarded look, he opened the box, revealing a soft, indigo velvet cushion in the center of which sat a small, smooth white sphere of featureless marble, like a moon in the night sky. Arsalan inspected the stone orb and carefully brushed its surface with his fingertips before closing the box, locking it, and putting it aside. He then turned his attention to his list, which he updated with marks from his pencil. This seemed to attract the cat's curiosity. While Arsalan's back was turned, the cat leapt silently onto the crate, approached the mysterious jewel box, and sniffed at it. Arsalan noticed and waved the cat away with fierce annoyance.

"Shoo!" he said. "This definitely is not for you."

The cat jumped away into the grass again. Arsalan hurriedly put the collection of little boxes away in a larger crate, as if the cat had been able to espy some private matter of his. He felt the desire to kick the animal, but Arsalan was not so heartless. He simply stared at the sickly creature, wishing it would tire of its own annoying ballet and would leave.

"I suppose it makes sense for a creature as unlovely as you to be starved for affection, or maybe food," said Arsalan. "You must be the lost pet of some poor farmer, missing for days in the forest, and you've crossed paths with me here in this godforsaken field. But you should know better than to be approaching strange men like me who could hurt you. Away with you. Go!"

The cat sat a few feet from Arsalan and stared at him with eyes beguilingly green, demonstrating a coyly knowing air. It sat in the demurely regal way well-bred cats sit, like a rare vase, wrapping its tail around its compact base, and regarding him as if pretending to withhold some valuable secret.

"Well, now suddenly you look like you have something to say to me," said Arsalan, having found a possible source of amusement in this distraction. "So, what is it? Tell me."

The cat only returned his gaze with a mute and coquettish stare. Although Arsalan was impressed by the poise of this strange cat and the eerily sentient way it watched him, he still was not so easily seduced.

"I'm going on a long journey," said Arsalan, "to a place perhaps far away from here, in the countryside, to find someone I am missing. It may be dangerous. There may be wild animals that wish to eat creatures like you, that is, assuming there is anything about you that is worth trying to eat. Are you wanting to come with me on this journey?"

The cat answered by sneezing. One of its lower eyelids became half-closed, and the cat was seized by a fit of violent sternutation until chartreuse snot shot out of its compact little face, and the cat shook its head in disorientation. Arsalan was aghast and grimaced in disgust.

"Oh, for the love of heaven, never mind," said Arsalan. "If you're still here by the time I'm finished, then maybe you can share my carriage. If not, then good luck to you."

Arsalan began reloading his crates and boxes into the carriage, making sounds that were loud enough to startle the poor creature. Each time Arsalan slammed a container into the cabin, the cat flinched and cowered in the grass, its ears reverted, as if ashamed that it had offended the man. Arsalan, done with his coarse work, finally leapt onto his seat and flipped the reins quickly and rumbled off the grass and onto the rocky road, taking one last glance at the cat as he did so. The cat, fearful of the power and might of Arsalan and the horses as they passed, fled a short distance away and took shelter among the tall vegetation, staring at the departing carriage from between the green blades with wide and vigilant eyes.

Arsalan drove the horses into a lively trot down the road for a short time, as if to flee the cat. Gradually, he and his horses emerged from the forest, and he slowed them to a casual walk, and he thought only of his next rest in a few hours when the sun would be approaching the horizon. The sky was broad and bright and was carpeted beneath with rolling farm fields of green crops on reddish soil. The occasional donkey cart passed, and to its drivers Arsalan waved in kindly acknowledgement. Far away on either side, low mountains lounged like sleeping oxen in the blazing sun, and on their balding surfaces trees grew like countless short hairs. Eventually, the dome of the sky grew darkly orange, and he parked his carriage off the road onto a small field to take supper. A pleasing breeze was blowing over the fields and cooled his brow as he prepared a fire and produced his cooking pot and kettle of water. The horses chewed at the thick, verdant grass now dotted with evening dew. Arsalan sang softly to himself as he boiled his stew, and the fire was painting his face every shade of gold and ginger. All was fine for that moment, until Arsalan heard another meow.

Arsalan looked up and around him, but he could not see what had squeaked the new noise. The day had been replaced rapidly with the black curtain of night while he was paying attention to his cooking, and the curious new sound was now outside the small radius of his fluttering firelight. After a moment, though, he spotted the source: two gleaming green eyes staring at him from the shadow beneath the carriage chassis. As the animal emerged, Arsalan, to his shock, saw the same red, scabrous cat he thought he had left behind in the forest. The wretched thing stared at him with a strange insistence fueled by fear and desperation, and it shivered in the cooling night temperature, meowing pleadingly once more.

"What are you doing here?" whispered Arsalan.

Arsalan came closer to the cat, then inspected the carriage above and around it.

"You little stinker," he said. "You stowed away on my carriage like a rat."

Despite Arsalan's words, the cat displayed a certain determination in its supplication. One of its paws was extended toward Arsalan on the ground, as if about to reveal a gift from beneath it, and the cat met his gaze with glassy, fishlike eyes. For a moment Arsalan was unnerved, and he glanced behind him to make sure the cat was not reacting to something more dangerous than himself. Seeing nothing but the starry night sky, Arsalan came to his senses and looked back at the stowaway. His initial disregard for the creature finally gave way to some degree of pity, so he stood tensely still as the starveling approached. At last, the cat was at his side, brushing its face again against his shirt and pant leg. Arsalan found himself carefully touching the bumpy pelt of the frightful little thing, checking it absently for disease or injury, or for fleas or lice or mange, in the dim firelight. Oddly, though he was no expert, he could find no such ailments. He could see only that the cat was starving. He then examined the rest of the cat, finally determining that it was female. Around her slender neck was a thick collar of tightly woven linen clasped with a small, plain, rectangular buckle of brass at her throat.

"Damn you, you pathetic creature," chuckled Arsalan. "It seems you've adopted me more definitively than I ever would have adopted you. Perhaps you can be my company as I venture into my new life, if you wish. If not, then you are free to go whenever you like. If you had a previous owner, then to hell with them for neglecting you like this. We can be two miserable rejects together, you and me, and I will name you Kizil."

Arsalan produced from his stash of food some dried jerky, ate a bit, and gave a small amount to Kizil. He placed the piece on a box in front of him and allowed the cat to sniff at it. It only took an instant for the desperately famished cat to learn that it was smelling edible meat before its primal instincts took command. The meat was swept swiftly from existence before Arsalan's eyes, and soon Kizil the scraggly, bony cat was chomping and swallowing the tough shred of meat in frantic and exaggerated spasms as if choking.

Arsalan could not help regarding this behavior with pity laced with antipathy. He wondered how much of his own cache of food he was to spare for the poor animal, who seemed to eat as if she had no bottom. Nonetheless, he gave Kizil a few more pieces of meat, and then many more, all which she devoured in a similarly ravenous fashion. He reasoned she must be thirsty after ingesting all that rigid, briny meat, and he poured a small bowl of water for her, which she lapped up with great, coarse slurping sounds. In hardly any time at all, Kizil was lying by the fire, stretched out on a rock with all four limbs pointing outward, immobile and engorged with food and drink, and with not a whit of regret visible on her. Her ribs protruded visibly from her body as she breathed like the curled fingers of a fist. She seemed limply exhausted from the simple act of eating. As blissfully content as she seemed, the cat was still an awful sight and scarcely discernible from a hawk's kill.

"Dear God in heaven, what am I going to do with this little ogre?" he said. He sat and leaned against the wheel of the carriage and watched her eyelids succumb to heaviness and close. He smiled wearily until he, too, fell asleep and dozed beneath the stars.

A few hours later, Arsalan awoke to the barking of a dog in the distance, and he looked at the cat by the fire. She had not moved an inch, but the fire was dying, and he threw a few more pieces of kindling and wood onto it. For a long while he examined the black horizon for possible danger but could see nothing, especially with the glare of the campfire in his eyes, which enclosed him and the cat in a spherical room of shivering orange light. It was chilly that night, and he exhaled plumes of vapor that glowed and swirled in the air before him before quickly vanishing. After a time, he fell asleep again, and he awakened several more times that night until he noticed the silvering horizon of twilight. Kizil was curled into a gray ball and the fire was out, and a column of wispy smoke ascended languidly from the ashes. Finally, Arsalan caught one last doze before the hot, shining, metallic pink light of dawn poked his eyes, awakening him one last time. He certainly was not used to sleeping outside. His body ached from lying in an awkward position all night, and his clothes smelled of smoke and his pants were covered in dust, and he wondered if he had subscribed unwittingly to a type of life that he would not be able to stomach.

Kizil awoke and stretched each of her scrawny limbs in turn, shaking the sleep off them. She blinked her eyes, yawned, and shook her head, and her ears for a moment were turned in two odd directions on her head. She looked as drowsy as Arsalan felt, but otherwise seemed rested.

"Well," said Arsalan, "at least someone got a good night's sleep last night."

Kizil responded to his voice by staring at him again with her green, jew-ellike eyes.

"I suppose you would like breakfast, too, eh?" teased Arsalan, and he started another fire to brew some tea. In a pan he stewed more meat, some of which he fed to Kizil, who was startled at the scalding food at first, but quickly overcame her pain and fear to consume her breakfast as voraciously as she had finished her supper. Arsalan gently laughed as he chewed on a piece of bread and drank his tea.

"So, heat is not as painful as hunger, it seems," said Arsalan. "You'd burn your little tongue before you go another day without food."

After breakfast, Arsalan packed his cooking utensils and mounted the carriage, reigns in hand. He then looked down at the cat, who stood on the ground watching him with curiosity and anticipation.

"Well? You still want to come with me, don't you? I mean, you might as well, seeing as how you've hitchhiked all this way already," said Arsalan. He cast a gentle spell that slowly and delicately lifted Kizil and placed her on the seat beside him. Kizil panicked a little at first, but then simply allowed herself to be lifted, although it was clear that she still was not sure what was happening to her. Arsalan made sure to place her soft feline body in the middle of the carriage seat, where she gathered herself and lay. Arsalan sat to her left, where he addressed her firmly with a finger.

"You sit there and come no closer to me," he declared. "I don't want to catch anything from you. Also, don't jump off the carriage as we're moving, or then you'll be in even worse condition than you're in now."

Perhaps the cat had listened and had understood Arsalan, or perhaps in her underfed state she was too weary to move. In either case, as Arsalan flipped the reigns and the carriage began to wobble, she panicked again in her attempts to stay still and level on the flat carriage seat, and Arsalan briefly had to hold her in place with one hand. After the carriage was stabilized on the relatively level ground of the road, she gradually felt safer lying there on the seat next to Ar-salan, wrapping herself into a ring while keeping watch with her wary, coinlike eyes. As time passed and the sun warmed the carriage seat, she grew calmer, and her eyelids blinked contentedly. Arsalan still made sure not to touch her and to keep his distance, as he was still concerned about fleas or lice. How crazy he thought himself to be to befriend such a forlorn creature. What would anyone say upon seeing the two of them?

After some hours, Kizil seemed to squirm and to become sleepy under the heavy sunlight, and Arsalan coaxed her to sit in the shady cabin of the car-riage, where she immediately discovered a comfortable hole between three boxes and hid herself between them quite contently. He left her a bowl of meat next to her in the cabin and continued along his journey with her ensconced there.

After a time, Arsalan's road took him into another forested area, where he encountered a patrol of the colorfully armored Royal Guard who stopped him for questioning.

"Ho there!" they cried. "A moment with you, old sir."

Arsalan stopped his cart and wordlessly regarded them and their fine, shining black stallions who huffed in the heat.

"Are you alone?" asked the head guard.

"What does it matter to you?" asked Arsalan.

"We only ask for your safety. We hear reports of bandits on this road," the head guard said.

"If I say I am alone, will you leave me alone?" Arsalan said.

"You can trust us, sir. We are the Royal Guard," the head guard said.

Arsalan said nothing to this, as he really trusted no one on this road, but after a time, he reluctantly said, "Yes, I am alone."

"Are you safe? Have you seen any suspicious characters?" asked the head guard.

"Not yet," said Arsalan, not counting the men in front of him.

"What is in your carriage, sir?" the head guard asked.

"My belongings. There is not much of which to speak. I am a simple man finding a new farm on which to live," he said. Arsalan did not wish even to hint of the piles of gold he was hauling, lest they begin asking for bribes.

"May we look?" the head guard asked.

Before Arsalan could answer, one of the guards trotted forward on his horse and peered into the windows of the carriage, looking this way and that while the long, blue plume sticking up from his hat wagged and wiggled in circles like the dance of a praying mantis. During the guard's inspection, the man saw only the cat looking back at him from among boxes covered in cloth; she had been busy cleaning her hind parts with her own tongue, as cats do, and realized she had been spotted. Contorted and frozen into a most undignified position while having her privacy breached, Kizil stared back at him with a look of indignant horror, until it was the Royal Guard who looked away with a smile of mild embarrassment and disgust. He turned to the others, shook his head, and shrugged.

Arsalan used the pause in conversation during the search to speak to the lead guard.

"I also happen to be searching for my daughter. She ran away from home. Have you seen any young maidens traveling this way?" said Arsalan, who showed him her picture from his locket. The guard peered at the portrait with a thoughtful frown.

"I can't say I have seen any," said the guard. He looked to the other guards for confirmation, and they all shook their heads, their own plumes wiggling ridiculously. "In fact, I can't say that a lone girl on his road would survive very long if not rescued by us. I don't mean to sound grim, sir, but these roads are perilous."

"I understand," said Arsalan. "Thank you, but I am grasping at any chance I can find."

"Of course. In any case, you also must be careful with your belongings on this road," the head guard said to Arsalan, "especially if you are an old man who is riding alone yourself. Whatever you have, even if it's a simple as a cooking pot, bandits will feel the need to rob you of it, and perhaps to kill you with it."

"That I understand. too. Thank you, gentlemen. I am capable of defending myself in most situations anyway," said Arsalan.

At this, the guards looked at each other uneasily. "Good luck to you, old sir, and be careful," commanded the heard guard. They then roared off on their beautiful steeds and their gleaming hind legs, their horseshoes kicking up clods of red dirt behind them.

Arsalan stroked his graying beard. "I am not yet an old man," he muttered over his shoulder after they were gone.

But indeed, later that day ageing Arsalan did encounter the bandits.

Arsalan had heeded the advice of the guards and had enchanted the carriage to project a weightless, invisible wall of force around it that protected him from attack, one of the many self-defense tactics he had learned at the Magical Architects' Guild. At a certain hour, Arsalan heard a sound on his left and saw several arrows hanging in mid-air for a moment and then falling to the ground, apparently arrested by the magic wall he had cast. Arsalan stopped the carriage and saw a gang of about ten men emerge abruptly from behind the trees at his left. The men surrounded him, sporting all sorts of shining, bladed weapons. The gang was dressed in refined but mismatched clothing, as if what they wore had been stolen from traveling wealthy folk.

A man who stood directly to the left of Arsalan rudely said, "Give us what is in your carriage, traveler, and we will consider sparing your life."

"You wish to kill me?" asked Arsalan.

"Only if you don't give us what we're seeking," said the ruffian.

"Then kill me," said Arsalan, "because I won't give you anything. You'll have to take what I have by force."

The lead ruffian looked at the others incredulously and laughed, shaking his head, and then began to move toward Arsalan. But the bandit then stopped, as if frozen in place. The other men did the same. Their heads craned forward, their hands rotated and flapped back and forth in their sleeves and cuffs, but they remained rooted to their spots and strained to move.

"Well? What's the delay?" said Arsalan. "I'm waiting to die, and you're disappointing me."

"What sorcery is this?" said the ruffian. "I can't move! My clothes have turned stiff!"

"Then perhaps you should consider washing them once in a while," said Arsalan. "You are the filthiest killers I've met in my life."

Arsalan raised his hands, and all the stiffened bandits, soldered into their poses like metal figurines, levitated into the air and began to float off the right side of the road. The brigands screamed and pleaded in panic as they drifted through the air against their will, unable to bend their bodies or to see where they were being directed. Arsalan moved the men down a slope, toward the bank of a nearby stream, and then dropped them squarely in the mud, where he made sure to soil everything they wore in the muck. There they lay, screaming and cursing and emptily promising revenge as Arsalan spoke to them.

"Who have you robbed?" he interrogated. "Who have you murdered?"

"We know no names," said the lead bandit. "And if we did, we wouldn't tell you."

"Have you encountered any young girls?" he demanded.

"Go to hell," said a bandit.

"Maybe your willingness to confess will depend on how long you stay in this frozen state," said Arsalan. "Maybe it will be hours. Maybe it will be days. Maybe weeks."

"Let us go!" said another bandit.

"Tell me," Arsalan said. "I am a wizard. I am capable of many great and terrible things, of which this is the least."

"No girls," said a bandit. "We never encounter any girls here. Who would bring them to such a remote and dangerous place?"

"We don't touch girls!" pleaded another bandit. "We only threaten and steal! Let us go! We are not killers!"

"Then I suppose those arrows you shot at me were made of cloth?" asked Arsalan.

The bandits were silent.

"The spell I cast upon you will wear off at sundown," said Arsalan. "But I swear to you, if you ever see me again, turn around and run in the opposite direction as fast as you can go, because then I will not be so cute and playful with you, especially if you are lying about your treatment of innocent folk, and especially of children."

Arsalan marched back up the bank, mounted the carriage, and continued at the same speed as before he was stopped. For a moment, he regretted vaguely that he had not killed all the bandits, but then dismissed such a thought as too savage and against his creed. How could he think that? He had never hurt anyone in his life, and, assuming they had not hurt Defne, he saw no reason to start now. They were just local folks facing poverty, perhaps, and trying their best to survive in a harsh environment. Arsalan tried hard to find any reason in the encounter that justified his refusal to hurt the men to the same degree they were threatening to hurt him. Arsalan, until now, had lived a cultured and civilized life, graced with protection and privilege, and he was not used to these types of encounters. He trembled with rage from then on. In fact, it took Arsalan all evening to wait for his anger over the incident to abate, which it did eventually as he sat by the campfire that night, staring into the dancing flames and petting Kizil at his side as they both dined on cured meats and water.

For the next few weeks, Arsalan became somewhat of a nomad. He traveled generally northwest, through one city, village, or small town to the next, procuring provisions and sending letters to his sons from local post offices, which in this area were administered by the Austrians rather than the Royal Post. The Austrians proved to be more reliable. Arsalan in his wandering was looking for a parcel of land large and secluded and wooded, and this desire pushed him away from the shimmering, populated, sunlit coast in the east and toward the mountains drenched in snow and mist to the west. By day he rode unhurriedly and in deep thought, and by night he and Kizil took their supper by a campfire in the wilderness and slept in the cabin of the carriage, which Arsalan secured with a locking spell. Solmaz and Aysel worked tirelessly but contentedly throughout these days, and whenever Arsalan felt sad or uncertain, he found encouragement in watching energy and strength course softly through their hulking musculatures as they strode. Such fine horses, he thought to himself. On certain days he would reward them with rest in a sunny meadow where he would allow them to roam for a few hours, free from their chafing reigns, to feed on grass. Arsalan and Kizil would sit beneath a nearby tree, where they watched the horses and had lunch. He began the habit of buying Kizil fresh lamb and chicken from the markets, which they ate together. Kizil continued to partake of her meals ravenously, but with a tad less desperation. Arsalan was impressed how Kizil would not allow her feline curiosity to get the better of her; she would not venture off into the weeds looking for prey, getting lost or killed. Perhaps it was because Arsalan was a source of food and care and that staying with him was better than scrounging in the woods, or perhaps somewhere in her feline heart she experienced the animal analog of gratitude, but she stayed by his side always, like some sort of benevolent familiar.

Arsalan's attitude toward Kizil changed during these relaxed times.

He viewed Kizil's ailments and symptoms with lessening disgust and growing empathy. Oftentimes the cat would explode into a salvo of coughs, sometimes producing vomit or a slimy hairball, and whereas before Arsalan would roll his eyes, curse his fate, and scold the cat with angry and testy remarks, now he was increasingly comfortable with petting her with his bare hand and soothing her with friendly words. Eventually he responded to her sicknesses with honest worry. Over time, it appeared that Kizil's health improved; her frame had started to fill with weight and vigor, her fur became a little fuller and glossier, and a sparkle of life seemed to come to her already mesmerizing eyes. She became playful and affectionate, even more so than she had been, and her loving advances were met with less and less of Arsalan's squeamish revulsion.

Otherwise, it was difficult for Arsalan to think of a time when he had enjoyed the smaller and more immediate comforts of life as contentedly as he did now, although he wished he could bathe more often. Each week he would spend a copper coin to bathe in a public bathhouse where he would talk with the local men to hear the latest news. Whenever he was in the absence of such luxuries, Arsalan would resort to bathing and washing his clothes in a secluded stream, which he at first found to be a cold, miserable, and humiliating experience, but after a time also uncovered its purifying and invigorating aspects, which he found strengthening. After those frigid baths, he would sit naked beneath the bright sun or by a warm campfire to dry himself, closing his eyes and thinking of nothing. What would his family and friends do if they saw him like this? Oh, they would laugh and laugh, but Arsalan did not care. No one was here but the sun, his horses, and his cat, and for the first time in a long time, or perhaps ever in his life, he now experienced stretches of deep and simple bliss and contentment.

What Arsalan missed often was a good, solid drink of beer or a sip of wine. He had brought a few bottles of valuable wine with him but had sold the rest to pay his debts. What remained was so precious to him now that he dared not waste it on anything but some special occasion that he could not foresee. For now, he had to survive with tea, which was cheaper and more plentiful, only without too much sugar. He did try the local liquors, but often found them atrocious. This new dimension of asceticism, too, had its purgative effects that Arsalan slowly learned to appreciate. These extended bouts of sobriety kept his wits about him as he negotiated the long journey through the lands that were less familiar to him than they should have been. The last time he had come these ways was many years ago in large caravans navigated by servants and assistants, and he was often sleeping or hungover in the cabin as they rode. Arsalan knew he was unusual among his folk to drink so much. He had acquired the rather foreign habit while traveling abroad in Europe on all his commissions, and his wealth had enabled these exotic and extreme tastes that his countrymen regarded with distaste. But now he realized how foolish he was that he could not have remained soberer in his younger years, at least to savor the extravagant distances he had traversed in his lifetime.

CHAPTER 3

To My Dearest Asker,

It has been two weeks since I last wrote, and my travels have led me to the feet of the Balkans, where I have located a reliable Austrian post office, an outpost for their own official use, so they say. I have determined that they will serve me as well if I pay them enough. It seems even their upright clerks are impressed by the officialness of silver. I am doing well. I am still on the search for suitable land for my retirement, but in any case, this post office box shall be your point of communication with me. Write me here, and every few weeks I will come to see if you have written me a letter. I do look forward to each one.

Defne is always on my mind and in all my prayers. I never found her, and it pains me so. Please do tell me if you have heard from her. Be a good son and do not hold secrets such as these from me, if you keep them. The threat from Prince Ergin is long over. I am nowhere within striking range of the young brat and his remarkably magnanimous father. When Defne reveals herself again, I will do everything I can to reunite with her.

I miss Omer and your mother very much, though neither of them returns any communication. I imagine Omer is far away or unable to write, indisposed somehow. Only heaven knows where he is, but I hope he is alive and well. Your mother is probably still angry at me. Perhaps I do not recall the address to the Duchy of Brzeg, or maybe my letters have not been arriving there, or perhaps her father burns my letters as soon as he sees them. If you know her correct address, which I suspect you do, send it to me. Also tell me if Omer has contacted you. You are my only link to the family I once had. I am sorry for the troubles I have presented to us all. I am proud of you for uncovering opportunities concealed in adversity, and that you are doing well and serving proudly in the navy. You did not run away from our troubles like everyone else did, including myself. You faced them, truly and squarely, like an adult.

Please be well. I was pained to read of your injured leg in your prior letter. Please take care of it. Write to me as soon as you see this. I love you.

Your father

Arsalan sealed the letter, addressed it to Asker's command base far away in Mitsiwa, and delivered it through the Austrian post office in Sliven, where he now rented a post box. The serious, blue-eyed postal clerk wore a trim moustache and a high, cylindrical cap with a stiff little brim. The clerk said nothing as he executed the small transaction for Arsalan. Time would tell if the letter would arrive at its faraway destination. And time did tell. Fate was kind, as several weeks later, Arsalan received a reply.

Dearest Father,

I have received your letter. Although I do not see much sense in your retiring so far away from civilization, from the standpoint of the heart I suppose I can intuit an understanding of it. You are weary, and you wish to simplify your life and to subtract from it all those things with which you had burdened yourself previously. I suppose I will understand more clearly when I am older and more burdened with the consequences of my own actions. But I assure you, Father, that I will have few, as you have taught me more than your share about what it means to be a man in this world. You may have been busy as a celebrated builder of fantastic structures, but I was watching you the entire time, Father, and I loved you each minute I observed you. Even when you were acting foolishly and extravagantly, I know that your actions did not come from hatred or fear but from love of the world and all its promises, and your only confusion was that you did not have enough time and energy to devote all your love to all its treasures. Even when you became angry, you loved the object of your anger.

I fear that I do not hold the secrets you so desire. I, too, have written Mother and with no reply. Perhaps it is too soon, and her heart must cool. I also have not received a reply from Omer. I fear he is lost, Father, perhaps in mind as well as body. I do not make a jest of him. His words about traveling to a new world troubled me, especially after they were followed by silence. Please know that I will send you word as soon as I receive any communication from them.

Recently our duty here in Mitsiwa has been to conduct surveillance and reconnaissance to determine how easily we would retake the Straits for the Sultan if he so desired. The information we have gathered is not promising. We would need a greater naval complement than has been apportioned to us to conduct a successful battle against the Iranians, and we do not believe our navy has such resources.

It is so ungodly hot here, Father. I wish I were in the cool mountains with you. Here the sea is so dazzlingly bright under the sun that it hurts one's eyes to look at it. The glare is formidable through our telescopes. Our uniforms are not appropriate for this heat. They are too stiff and heavy, and often our men fall ill and faint on the hottest days.

Nonetheless, the people of Mitsiwa are good people. The very dark skins they have protect them like iron from this sun, and they are serious and noble and accommodating. I have been making a concerted attempt at learning their language, which is very unlike ours.

Do take care of yourself, Father. Do settle down somewhere and make friends. You were always a sociable one. Your problem was that you had so many friends that you had none whom you could say you loved the best.

Write again. I will be waiting, and I will keep myself safe.

Your loving son,

Asker

Arsalan noted that his son did not mention his leg. Perhaps my poor son did not want me to worry, thought Arsalan.

"Good afternoon, sir," said Arsalan as he strode into a butcher shop.

"To you as well, sir," said the butcher, a large, burly man with a thick beard and dense, curly hair on his shoulders. He was so much larger than Arsalan that Arsalan felt relieved the butcher had such gentle manners. Arsalan ordered a side of lamb and a chicken, which the butcher retrieved from hooks and cutting boards at the sides of the butchery. Arsalan watched as the butcher's bearlike hands and arms manipulated the globs of pink flesh, cutting them with decisive yet graceful thuds and slices and finally handing the meat to Arsalan in brown cloth.

Upon receiving the payment and staring at it for a moment with one eye, the butcher asked, "Please forgive me for prying, sir, but we do not see too many folks like yourself up here. I am assuming you are from the south."

"Indeed, I am," answered Arsalan.

"What, pray tell, brings you to our humble village up here by the mountains, if you don't mind my asking?" continued the butcher.

"I worked as a builder for many years," answered Arsalan, "and now at my age I am retiring. I am here to seek a plot of land on which I can spend my retirement."

"A builder, you say, ay?" said the butcher, "And retirement."

The butcher was rubbing his chin, slightly impressed, and apparently feeling an inkling of professional kinship with Arsalan. But Arsalan did not wish to elaborate on the nature of his building skills or of the fortune he was carrying with him.

"Why would you want to live so far away from where you lived?" asked the butcher. "Don't you have family there? It seems an awfully long way to come for one's own retirement."

It was a forward but fair question, for which Arsalan had a prepared answer.

"My wife left me," he said, "and my sons are both grown and live in different parts of the world. I am afraid I am alone, and my old place is empty and cheerless, and I wish to find a new life elsewhere. In fact, I came here because my daughter also has run away from home, and I believe she may have come to these parts."

"Oh, I see. Such an unfortunate set of events. I'm sorry, sir," said the butcher politely in despondent confusion as he measured the gravity of Arsalan's story. The hulking butcher looked down in thought for a moment and said, "But I haven't heard tell of any young runaways to come across these parts these days, and I know everyone."

"Thank you," said Arsalan, "but I shouldn't trouble you with such things so soon. Right now, my concerns are slightly more immediate. I need to find a place to live. Do you know of any land in the forests on the mountains that I could purchase where I could start a farm?"

"A farm in the mountains, ay?" said the butcher, who inadvertently had wiped a swath of dark lamb's blood on his chin and jaw, "Well, as a matter of fact, there is a farm up in those parts. I buy meat from the farmers and shepherds around here, and they tell of a farm that was abandoned many years ago. I wouldn't say it's purchasable, mind you. I don't know who owns it. I don't think anyone does own it now that I think about it. I do know no one wants to live there."

"Why not?" asked Arsalan.

"The plague!" said the butcher. "It came through here in my grandparents' time and the family that lived on that homestead all perished, every one of them, I hear. Since then, many people think it's still tainted by the illness, and they won't set foot on it."

"Not at all?" asked Arsalan.

"Oh, maybe some shepherds graze on the fields here and there, but no closer," said the butcher. "The house stands there still, dilapidated and such. The folk just have the habit of not approaching it. I may be wrong, but I don't think anyone has bothered to own it since."

"Do you think it's still tainted by the plague, as they say?" asked Arsalan.

"Oh, I'm not sure," said the butcher. "I don't think I believe it. It's been two generations since then. How long can a place be tainted by illness when there's no one living there? It's rather funny when one considers it."

Arsalan asked the directions to the plot of land, and the butcher began to tell him, gesticulating upward with his tremendous forearm while hunching his head and furrowing his brow in thought. But then he began to scratch his large balding crown and realized he could not recall the entire way, since it had been so long since he had been anywhere near there. At that point, the butcher's daughter walked in carrying a basket of giblets. She, too, was a tremendous person with a red face, yellow hair, massive forearms, and a feisty, forthright personality. Hearing the conversation, she began to supply the missing information, but in the middle of answering she stopped short to ask Arsalan what the devil he was doing going to a place like that anyway. When Arsalan and the butcher began to explain, she blurted. "So far away? Are you in trouble with the law?" The butcher laughed heartily at this, slapping the butcher's block. Arsalan tried hard to conceal his impatience while explaining to her that his family had dispersed and he wanted to start life anew while looking for a lost loved one, an explanation that the daughter found slightly incredulous before beginning to give directions anyway. Attracted by the raucous laughter, the butcher's wife burst in, asking what the ruckus was all about. She was another towering woman, scarcely distinguishable from the daughter except for the color of her black hair. She was holding a bucket of raw sausages. The whole process of peppering Arsalan with the same questions was repeated, and then a third time when the butcher's brother strolled in, and then a fourth when a petite, old customer wandered into the shop to chat, until all five them were arguing and talking over each other and gesturing in every direction, trying their best to recall the way to a place they would never consider going themselves. Arsalan stared and sweated in mortification, then, when he was able to formulate a generally accurate picture of the route to the cursed house, he bowed to them and thanked them profusely and politely while walking backward out the door. The five locals wished Arsalan good luck as he was leaving, but not without interjecting at the last second to make certain he remembered one last bit of crucial information about a bend in the road or a tree where he should turn left. At the doorway, they watched him trudge away, and as soon as he was out of sight, they all shook their heads and muttered to each other in confused exasperation.

"Turks!" they sighed.

Arsalan made his way back to his carriage with hunched shoulders, fuming with irritation and embarrassment. He had hoped to conduct all his transactions with locals as discreetly and as innocuously as possible, reducing his relations with them to a bare minimum, and now these plans were in tatters. Arsalan resolved never to return to that butcher shop, though he knew such a decision would make it more difficult to procure meat.

Arsalan, Kizil, and his two horses left the town and ventured on into the surrounding forests where they followed the way described by the five arguing strangers. The way was up a mountain path whose entrance was indeed hard to find among the trees at first. From then on, it was a dark, narrow, difficult road, filled with rocks, ruts, and puddles of mud, and several times Arsalan was forced to pause and to make sure he was on the right road. Once he was sure, he then looked around to make certain he was not being watched. He held out his hand, palm downward, and used his powers to press the rocks into the ground, to flatten the mud, and then to tamp it down, until the road in front of him was as smooth and as flat as any of the empire's causeways. Continuing upward, he passed several dwellings with roofs of large tiles like fish scales, and he saw blue smoke languidly meandering out of the tops of stone chimneys and loitering there in the humid air like regret. Some dwellings were sound, tidy, and comfortable cottages while others were mere shacks or hovels, slumped to one size and composed of jumbles of rotting gray wood, cobwebs, and shadow. Short, stocky folk in linen and wool stood in front of their abodes, engaged in some sort of slow and nameless work or another—perhaps to empty buckets of bilge into the mud or to sharpen a knife. Upon seeing Arsalan trot by in his carriage, they stopped whatever they were doing and stared at him with slack jaws and expressions of almost offended disbelief until he was completely out of sight.

The air became cooler and drier as Arsalan ascended, and the woods deeper and more welcoming. Arsalan enjoyed the freshness of the air and the comfortable sense of darkening isolation. The road was longer than he had imagined, and after most of the day, it seemed he and his animals had climbed to such an elevation that the forest began to thin, yielding clearings and revealing the sharp white peaks of mountains all around them like a hound's teeth and groves of spruce and pine trees pointing heavenward like barbed spearheads. The pure, arid breeze sang within Arsalan's lungs and was charged with an inexplicable electricity, as if a splendid winter were possible at any time.

At last, Arsalan had reached the end of the road. He could ascend no further before confronting the rugged, grassy feet of the barren peak. The route to this spot had not been as enigmatic as folk in the butcher's shop had characterized it, yet Arsalan could see why no one felt possessive of this desolately lofty area. Arsalan found himself on a rounded, meadowy plateau hidden among peaks and spruce trees all around him and capped with the eternal blue void. He knew, according to the butcher's family's directions, that nearby should sit the old house, abandoned and forlorn. Arsalan looked around, and indeed he saw it, there on his right, in front of a grove of spruce and pine trees and behind a wild meadow. The dwelling had two floors, the upper floor paneled in vertical wooden slats and the lower floor composed of stone. It was primitive, but in its day would have been a fine house. However, as Arsalan approached, he already could determine that the house was so dilapidated that he may not be able to use it as it was. Part of the thatched roof had caved in near the chimney, exposing the rafters. The slats of the second-floor walls were withered and gray, such that daylight shone between them. The front stoop was in shambles, and the front door was ajar and hanging on one hinge. Arsalan climbed up the crumbling front steps and opened the front door as carefully as possible without breaking it. Inside, the house was silent and gray, covered in dust, and it smelled of mold. Cobwebs graced every corner of the rooms. Old, broken pieces of furniture were left behind, askance on the hardwood floor. There was evidence of termites and mice, and there were stains of moisture from leaks. Plaster and dust were everywhere, and it crunched underfoot as Arsalan crept inward. Arsalan found the stairway to the second floor. He carefully inspected the stairsteps for possible weak spots before he stepped on the first stair and committed his full weight to it, and then the second one, and then the third. They creaked painfully beneath him as he gingerly climbed. Eventually, he came to the second floor. In one bedroom on the left was the hole in the roof with its riblike rafters laid bare and black against the electric blue sky. In the thickness of the thatch exposed by the hole there were the nests of birds and their white fecal stains dripping downward to rotten reeds of thatch on the floor.

From the way the folk in the butcher's shop had spoken of this place, Arsalan was expecting a crypt filled with human skeletal remains sprawled across the floor in ghastly poses, but he found no such thing. It was simply empty, evacuated. It certainly stood as a shrine to death and decay to a degree but evoked more sadness than fear and demanded more somber respect than silent, tense trepidation. Arsalan felt humbled standing there in the ruins of someone else's history. He saw the structure as a testimony to the human lives that once called this place home before a faceless nature commenced its program of gradual and inevitable reclamation.

Arsalan confirmed to himself that indeed the house was uninhabitable in its current state. Half the structure was rotten and crumbling. The other half of the house's material—mostly the frame made of sturdy timber, the stones from the foundation, the ground floor walls, and the chimney—were in fact usable with some replacements. Judging by its remoteness, abandonment, and dilapidation, and by the butcher's statement that the property was unwanted and unowned, Arsalan decided the property was safe simply to claim as his own. This act was not without risk, as there was a chance that some distant legal owner could come to contest his claim. Even in this case, Arsalan felt confident he simply could purchase the property with a few of his gold coins, settling any argument. For now, though, he resolved to begin his repair work on the house the very next morning. The sun was setting already behind the high peaks, illuminating those craggy summits to the east with a ruminative, fiery orange glow. Arsalan had failed to anticipate how early the sunset would chime in the mountain dells with their narrow apertures of the sky, and, accordingly, how precipitously the temperature would drop once the sun absconded. He was forced to rummage through his boxes for his warmer clothing and quilts, and for the horse-blankets for Solmaz and Aysel. That night he lit a campfire by the door to the carriage, as he often did, and prepared and ate his dinner. It had been a long time since Arsalan had witnessed the celestial dome above him in such clear detail. It was as pure and sublime and perfectly round as a ball of glass and filled with clouds of glimmering crystal dust that glared downward with frightening silence. Crisp, frigid winds seemed to blow in directly from the swirling constellations. Arsalan sat and stared at the bejeweled universe for a long time until the campfire started to dwindle, and Kizil began to fall asleep on his lap, and eventually he retired to the cabin to sleep with his cat curled next to him.

The next morning's tasks began in earnest. The gray morning air was clear and chilly and distilled. The western peaks blushed a deep pink in the gaze of the rising sun's opening eye. Arsalan stood in front of the old dwelling with his arms raised like the musical conductors of Vienna, and he began to move his hands slowly up and down, and to the left and to the right, and in circular motions. On command, the house began to come apart, but carefully and slowly like clothing, as if being disassembled by some giant, invisible, and elegant mechanism. With a groan or rip or snap or puff of dust, each of the house's constituent sections removed themselves from the main body of the dwelling one by one and from top to bottom, floated to one side, and then placed themselves on the ground in tidy and organized piles. Even the old plaster's powdery billows were contained, like candle smoke in a glass vial. The roof's thatch skin rose upward in one discrete unit and was placed down on the grass to the left where it lay, flat and shapeless. The sections of each of the four walls of the second floor were lifted and stacked on their broad sides next to the roof. The wooden slats of the floorboards of the second floor rose in a single, graceful wave like a windchime blowing in the wind, and the separate slats were stacked in neat, rectangular stacks on the ground to the right. From the first floor Arsalan removed only the wooden floorboards and the plaster walls, until just the foundation, the outer stone walls on the first floor, the timber framework branching upward from it, and the chimney all remained.

Arsalan then briefly examined the chimney. It was rather crudely assembled, and Arsalan decided that he wanted one that was neater. He raised his arms again and the stones began to quit the structure of the chimney, popping out in rapid bursts and forming a gently progressing queue that led to several pleasingly organized cairns of rock that rested to his left. With his magic force, Arsalan extracted from the wooden framework some of the nails, and then he plucked the dilapidated rafters, struts, joists, and posts out of their positions. He commanded them to progress in a gentlemanly fashion to the left, where their long wooden bodies lay in neat rows on the ground. The extracted nails, which had been suspended in mid-air, now streamed into a small pail next to Arsalan's feet. He then picked up the pail and peered inside; some of them were rusty, but most were usable. He had planned for this and had brought many more fresh nails with him in his carriage.

The noonday sun was directly above him, and Arsalan took his tea and his lunch while petting Kizil, who had watched the entire performance from the top of the carriage with that type of feline observance that switches abruptly from boredom to curiosity to sudden terror and back again to boredom.

Arsalan then resumed his work, moving to the foundation. It was disheveled and cracked to his professional eyes, and he spent nearly an hour healing the fissures and fusing crumbled rubble back onto the main body of the foundation. He then adjusted the positions of the constituent rocks, even as they still were embedded within the mortar, such that the foundation became a geometrically perfect rectangular prism. He followed a similar program for the ground-floor walls, using an odd stone from the chimney to fill a gap or missing piece here and there. Then he rebuilt the chimney, and it turned out to be as pleasingly sturdy and square as he had envisioned it. In fact, it was now a dual chimney, with fireplaces for both the first and second floors.

By now, Arsalan felt somewhat tired and began to consider his plans for the second floor. He wanted to build the second floor's walls from logs rather than slats, but he knew he would not be able to finish that stage in the remaining daylight of the mountains, so he rested until morning.

The next day, Arsalan wandered into the nearby woods to look for a good set of trees to fell. He sought ones that were tall and straight and could yield sound beams. The wind soughed through the branches of the tall spruces and pines as he strode among them at their bases, and the trees swayed peacefully and mightily as Arsalan looked up to estimate their heights. Finally, he identified a suitable specimen, and he patted the side of the tree like a farmer assessing a workhorse. It was a good, sound tree.

He held his left hand up to cast a spell for bolstering the tree upright, and with his right hand he mimicked a cutting motion toward the base of the tree, and a loud cracking noise filled the small forest dell. The tree was separated at its base but did not fall. Arsalan rotated his left hand and the tree turned sideways until it was suspended horizontally in the air, several feet above the grass. In this way, Arsalan then walked back toward his camp, towing the whole, mighty, wavering tree along with him using a magic force.

Arriving at the camp, he continued to hold the tree aloft, and with the fingers and thumb of his left hand formed a circle, and he swung the arm of that hand forward and away from his face in a quick motion. Suddenly, all the branches of the tree snapped off the trunk and fell to the ground. Then, pointing a finger at the tree, Arsalan caused the bark of the tree to split along its length, then, with a circular motion of the finger, he commanded the bark to separate from the inner wood like a rind being peeled from a melon and then to fall to the ground like a disrobed coat.

Arsalan cut the bare trunk into many equal lengths with more cutting spells, notched their ends with linkable notches, and stacked them to make the walls of the upper floor. He commanded the sap to seep from the logs' interiors and to migrate to the spaces between the logs, and he blended the sap with mud and silicate dust that he had extracted from rocks. He then heated the mixture with a magic spell to harden it into a type of mortar. Arsalan then harvested more trees that he used to make more beams to repair the house's frame and to build the upper floor's vaulted ceiling with many rafters.

Arsalan hiked up the hill that led from his house toward the nearby mountain peak that towered above his little clearing. On the side of the bare hill, he found several boulders, which he compelled to roll gently down the hillside toward the house. There they stopped like docile cows. He looked at the layer of old thatch that lounged on the ground next to the house. Arsalan was not partial to thatched roofs; they were too primitive for him. Rather, being from warmer climes, he preferred a roof assembled from hard tiles, and so from the boulders he used his powers to carve many such tiles, large and square and uniform. These he assembled into a beautiful roof with its high, sharp peak that rose into the sky like the armored helmet of a general.

Arsalan then held his hands in front of another boulder, and there was a loud report as the enormous rock abruptly cleaved in two, and then into four, then eight, and then multiple fragments. Arsalan continued reducing the boulder into smaller and smaller shards until it became a pile of sand, from which he extracted a long stream of white, sugary silicate dust with a high twirl of his index finger and directed the dust to settle in its own pile nearby. He then gathered globules of the silicate to float before him, and with his powers, he heated the globules until they glowed like persimmons in the desert sun and melted into orbs of lava, which he shaped into flat rectangles. Steam quickly rose from them and Arsalan was glad to see that he had created thick glass windows, which perfectly fit the openings he had made for them within the walls of his house.

Arsalan then went on to fashion an outhouse, several paces away from the house by the edge of the grove, and for his horses, a cozy, sturdy stable, with its very own fireplace and a corridor connecting it to the main house for cold, snowy days on the mountain. Also connected to one side of the house Arsalan built a small, crude bathhouse, with an earthen tub over a small oven. Lastly, beneath the floorboards of the first floor of the house Arsalan made sure to hide his stacks of gold. Although it was merely a fraction of this prior wealth, it was still more than most folks in or near Sliven ever would see in their lifetimes.

At last, after only four days' time, the house was complete. To an experienced magical architect such as Arsalan, the house was hardly any effort at all, yet he found himself as pleased with the outcome of his new homestead as he had been with the Levitating Bridges of Brzeg or the Diamond Dams of Rotterdam or the Budapest Royal Opera House. He ran his thumb over the tight, hairline seams between the rock and mortar of the dense walls of the ground floor. It was a job well done—a cottage tightly and expertly crafted—solid. succinct, insulated, and impregnable. No, this structure would never collapse. It would never disappoint him. It would never crumble in front of a crowd of all the world's dignitaries to make a fool of him. Even if a giant boulder were to roll down the mountain peak to strike the house, Arsalan was certain the structure would be so resilient that, at most, it simply would roll onto its side like a ball, fully intact and uncrushed, while laughing at the boulder in defiance.

CHAPTER 4

No sooner had Arsalan unloaded all his belongings from the carriage and into the house than he had his first visitor, a large man driving a crude, jostling cart loaded with layers of wobbling meat and the hooved legs of animals jutting out from beneath a canvas tarp. It was the butcher from town.

"Ho, Mr. Turk!" cried the butcher jovially from his carriage seat. "So, you are here after all!"

"Yes, hello, Mr. Butcher," said Arsalan with bemused circumspection. "I certainly am. I see you now remember the way here. What brings you all this way?"

"Yes, it was just a matter of asking directions. I was up hereaway on business, buying carcasses from the shepherds and farmers and whatnot," said the butcher, "and I thought I'd stop by see if you had made it up here alright, and..."

The butcher stopped and stared at Arsalan's newly rebuilt house.

"Is that the old house that was said to be cursed by the plague?" asked the butcher. "I don't recall if I ever did see the house with my own eyes, but I never imagined it looking as new and as well-built as that."

"Oh, that," said Arsalan, modestly. "It was just as desolate and ruinous as you said it was, but I rebuilt it."

"You rebuilt it?" said the butcher. "Why, what kind of craftsmen did you bring all the way up here to make a house like that?"

"No one, sir," said Arsalan. "I rebuilt it myself. As I said, I am a builder."

"My, indeed you must be," said the butcher. "You must be stronger than you appear to be! I mean, not that you look small and weak by any means, sir, but it usually takes five to ten men to lift stones and beams like that. You must be some sort of magician!"

"I have my ways," said Arsalan.

"Truly," said the butcher, who had dismounted his carriage and was facing the house. He had one arm under the other and was rubbing his chin.

"Say, do you also do repairs? My brother has a barn that needs fixing, if you're not averse to the idea, you know."

"Well, I suppose," said Arsalan, "But first, perhaps formal introductions are in order."

The butcher laughed, admitting that he had forgotten his manners, and after a few embarrassed and self-deprecating mutterings, he introduced himself as Lyubomir. Arsalan likewise introduced himself, and they shook hands.

Arsalan had not anticipated company. In fact, had he the choice, he would have preferred none, and this was his primary reason for relocating to the top of a mountain far away from imperial city life. Yet he could not help but be charmed by Lyubomir's guileless affability. He even found himself offering Lyubomir a tour of his cottage, an offer which the butcher graciously accepted. The butcher wandered through the house with Arsalan like one led by a docent through a museum, and he expressed amazement at the detailed workmanship of the rafters and mortar and wood flooring. The burly man tested the solidity of each element of the house with a soft pound with the meaty side of his ursine fist. It was this hand that also found Kizil wandering around Lyubomir's ankles as the big butcher reached down to pet her. Arsalan was momentarily afraid that the man's giant paw would break the cat's back, but the butcher's hands proved as graceful in the act of stroking a cat as they had been while slicing fat from meat or while dispensing small change at the counter. Lyubomir was not even squeamish toward Kizil and her ailing appearance. Perhaps all cats up here looked no better than that, thought Arsalan.

They talked long into the afternoon. Arsalan remained polite and demure in his speech, and Lyubomir gaily voluble, such that Arsalan learned practically everything there was to know about the butcher within a half hour. He learned that Lyubomir had lived at the foot of this mountain at the edge of town all his life with his family and was particularly close to his brother, who was a farmer. Arsalan also gathered that Lyubomir had watched his town undergo many changes in his life and had heard many stories about events in the outside world that he had not witnessed himself. The butcher did his best in his daily business to comprehend all the news there was to gather but formulated no judgement about it. Lyubomir gave the impression of a man who lived his life with simple and honest goodwill and who could find happiness and comfort in the mere sufficiency of tangible goods and the presence of friends and relatives. Arsalan sensed that it simply was not Lyubomir's nature to find fault in others. Affairs of the soul that were subtler and darker, such as self-doubt, regret, jealousy, or ambition, appeared to be alien to Lyubomir, and this innocence Arsalan discreetly found endearing, yet also somehow touchingly sad.

Lyubomir, pausing for a moment, read this momentary preoccupied sadness on Arsalan's face, and he felt concerned enough to ask, in the politest of ways, about Arsalan's missing daughter. Arsalan, though initially reticent to address the subject again, nonetheless felt an unusual trust in Lyubomir, and he shared with the butcher an abridged version of the story involving the evil Prince Ergin. Lyubomir was visibly shocked at Arsalan's descriptions of the nefarious prince's bold behavior and the complicit coddling he received from Lord Kadir. The butcher shook his big, thick head and, leaning against the doorframe, reacted with huffing and empathetic indignance.

Seeing Lyubomir in such an agitated state, Arsalan felt encouraged at having found such empathy for his travails, but he assured Lyubomir that he was determined to find Defne and that he had just started his search. Lyubomir was then heartened at Arsalan's air of quiet determination and optimism and, embarrassedly recognizing his own worked-up state, laughed at himself a little. The big butcher then brightened fully and stood upright, like a sun rising over a hill, and he promised Arsalan that he would put a word out to all his friends and relatives to keep watch out for a missing girl who might be in the area. Arsalan was moved at this gesture and thanked him with a firm handshake.

"Oh, my heavens," said Lyubomir finally, "It seems I almost have forgotten that I must deliver my carcasses back to my workshop. It was good to talk to you and to see you are well, all the way up here. If you need anything, come to visit! I know everyone."

"Of course," replied Arsalan.

"Although, I know my brother really will need someone to repair his barn, if you don't mind the idea," said Lyubomir.

Arsalan agreed tentatively to the repairs, but under the condition that no one watches Arsalan perform the repair work, as his techniques were trade secrets. To this Lyubomir laughed jovially and shook Arsalan's hand again in agreement and was off down the road. Arsalan stood in his doorway for a long while and stared at the faraway peaks. Lyubomir's goodwill and heartfelt offer echoed in Arsalan's mind, and then his thoughts drifted with wordless tenderness to Teodora and his three children.

After some time, Arsalan decided to spend the rest of the day tilling. There was a rather large garden he wanted to dig next to his house. He walked outside and, after some careful estimation, pointed his finger at the ground and commanded the soil to mix itself. He added the rotting straw from the removed thatch roof into the mixture. In the tilled ground he planned to plant turnips and cabbage for a fall harvest, but he paused and wondered if he really needed to use his magic powers to perform tasks so simple. So, in the middle of his operation, he took out his shovel and began to dig, whereupon he discovered that he had depended on his magic powers so extensively throughout his life that he was now unaccustomed to the physical exertion of using his own hands and arms, and he felt ashamed that he had led Lyubomir to assume he had built his house with his own bodily strength.

To combat this woeful effeteness in some small way, Arsalan resolved to till the entire rest of the garden by hand. He found a shovel and began to use it. He sweated and grunted and stumbled and panted, his heart pounded, and several times the shovel fell from his hands when he stepped on it the wrong way, and he cursed at himself. He soon saw that manual labor was another type of engineering altogether, an intuitive one, and that he had to learn how to use the force and balance of his own weight to pry the soil loose and to toss it aside, like a strange, lurching dance. It was disorienting, but he discovered that handiwork had its own unusual elegance in which he used the laws of nature against themselves in clever, circular ways rather than bypassing them altogether with magic spells. If one found just the correct set of movements, the work would achieve a pleasing efficiency. In time, Arsalan saw the magic in ordinary work, and he uncovered a newfound respect and empathy for laborers who were forced to use this ungainly but ingenious sort of magic every day of their lives.

Arsalan wondered what his family would think if they saw him toiling like this in a garden, and if they would feel proud, disappointed, or simply puzzled. Arsalan guessed that Defne might be fascinated, that Asker and Omer would stand at a distance and would laugh at him from their bellies, and that Teodora would be horrified. No matter, he thought; he had to feed himself in the way he had planned on this mountaintop, and his family should be much gladder to see him farming than living out of a horse carriage like a wandering Roma.

Next came the planting of the turnips and cabbages, and he found himself enjoying the act of burying seeds into the moist, glistening soil like an artist with clay. He looked at his fingers and realized he could not recall the last time since childhood he had had brown soil all over them and under his fingernails. The stained mess evoked a primal, childlike, inner joy that he could not explain.

In time, the day arrived to repair the barn of Lyubomir's brother. Radimir was his name, and he lived at the bottom of the mountain, just outside the town. The brother owned a small but fertile tract of land bordered on all sides by tall, dark groves. The land bore the advantage of abundant sunlight, and at certain spots the ground was terraced. Lyubomir introduced Arsalan to his brother, whom Arsalan recognized from the butcher's shop; Radimir seemed like a mildly differing replica of Lyubomir, only slightly stouter and with black hair rather than brown. Still, both towered over Arsalan, and it was clear that most other attributes Radimir shared with his brother, including his heroic laughter and his crushing handshake.

The brothers brought Arsalan to the barn, which sat under a tree on one side of the tract of land. There were many holes in the roof, including one large one near a corner, that Radimir simply had not had the time or the ability to repair, as his knees hurt when he used the ladder. Arsalan, upon assessing the state of the roof, promised complete repairs within three days. Here, the two jolly brothers patted Arsalan on his back and took their leave to let him perform his work. Arsalan listened to the two brothers speak to each other in their own language as they stomped away beyond the trees. They spoke a guttural tongue full of consonants occasionally interrupted with bursts of raucous laughter, and Arsalan realized then that without the two of them in front of him he could not distinguish their voices.

He then turned his attention to the barn and inspected it. It had two stories, the second being a loft. The structure had the familiar, motionless, and stiflingly sultry ambiance of a barn in the summer. Diagonal beams of dusty sunlight streamed between the slats of the walls onto piles of musty hay. Barbarous, dirty tools hung on the walls, and flies buzzed everywhere. Arsalan realized to his dismay that the barn needed far more repair than to patch a few holes in the roof. The wooden slats were old and shriveled, and several doors hung on one hinge and no longer fit their doorways. If it were Arsalan's barn, he would have rebuilt it entirely. It was obvious that the barn was inherited from his parents and that Radimir had had it for so long that he was accustomed to its state of dilapidation. It was also clear that the funds to pay for a wholly new barn was an extravagance he never considered seriously.

Arsalan looked around him to make sure he was not being watched. Only Kizil was there to witness his labors. Like an Egyptian princess, she lounged on the roof of the carriage under the sultry shade of the tree, flipping her tail here and there. It was a humid day full of sweat and flying insects. Summer had swollen to its full, corpulent apex and oozed honey-colored sunlight from every pore. Birds' cries echoed from afar as if from a daydream, the cicadas chattered into perpetuity, and tree branches hung still and low as if burdened under the syrupy air. Arsalan, however, heard and saw no one else. Assured, he went about casting the necessary spells to repair the hole with his replacement materials. As Arsalan had predicted, it was difficult for him to make the surrounding material hold the patch, and he ended up replacing much of that as well. In fact, Arsalan found himself replacing almost a third of the roof, but made the decision to stop there, as his stated task was complete. But just to make certain, he cast a spell on the roof to make it last another fifteen years, and another to make it waterproof. He decided he would not tell Radimir about his additional efforts and would charge him only a dozen copper para. Arsalan then spent the next two days visiting the site briefly and inspecting it for any other chinks or leaks, but otherwise doing nothing else to it. Arsalan was now certain this barn, as old and shoddy as it looked, would not collapse into a heap, and certainly not in front of all the world's nobles.

After three days, Radimir returned to the barn and saw Arsalan there having completed the repairs and petting Kizil. Radimir proceeded to walk semicircles around the corner of the barn beneath the part of the roof that had had the largest hole. He peered up at the repair this way and that, adjusting the brim of his hat several times to guard against the sun's glare that shot through the trees, and he squinted and muttered to himself. "Hm!" he said, "Huh!" Radimir grabbed his ladder and placed it against the barn's wall, climbed halfway up, craned his bulging neck left and right to stare at the roof, climbed back down, and then plunged into the barn and looked at the roof from inside. After a few minutes, he emerged again.

"Not bad!" he said to Arsalan, laughing. "In fact, better than it ever was!" And he clapped Arsalan warmly on his back again. "Lyubomir! Come and look at this!" called Radimir. Lyubomir walked over and followed Radimir as the farmer pointed to the roof and made comments. Seeing how impressed they both were, Arsalan was not sure if he should feel glad that he had lifted someone's spirits with so little effort or if he was wasting his time on someone who was not able to appreciate how much he was getting for his money. Lyubomir, while craning his own beefy neck to gaze upward, repeated all his brother's previous mannerisms and exclamations. "Hm!" he said. "Huh!" Finally, he turned to Radimir and struck him on the elbow. "See?" he remarked in quiet triumph. "What did I say? I told you he was a professional."

"Penka!" Radimir called to his wife. "Bring the copper!"

Penka emerged from their house. Everything about Penka reminded Arsalan of an apple. She was short and almost perfectly round with red cheeks that jutted from either side of her muffin-like face. Her eyes narrowed playfully as she smiled and approached the barn to inspect it cursorily. Arsalan later would learn that she always would sport this expression just before dropping some humorous rock of truth onto the ground in front of everyone.

"Huh!" she interjected. "The repairs look so nice they make the rest of the barn look like a dung hole!"

Lyubomir laughed uproariously until he doubled over and braced himself with his hands on his knees. Radimir smirked at her and held out his giant hand until she realized what he had called her outside to do in the first place. Amid her own chuckling, she reached into her purse and produced some copper coins and gave them to her husband. Radimir then turned and transferred them to Arsalan.

"Thank you, sir!" Radimir said gallantly.

From then on, Arsalan's reputation as a builder and repairman was established, and news of his accomplishments spread among the locals like the migration of butterflies. The gossip was quiet but unretractable, and it took Arsalan rather by surprise. First, it was Lyubomir's brother-in-law who approached him about rebuilding his chicken coop, and then it was Radimir's sister-in-law and her crumbling well, and then a friend of the sister-in-law with a request for a cellar and, by the way, her broken cart's chassis. Then there were friends and relatives of increasing remoteness from Lyubomir and Radimir who rounded out the population of mountainside community that Arsalan now called home.

Arsalan remained coy over this newly garnered repute. From the standpoint of a wizardly and urbane magical architect, he saw his repair work as hardly worth mentioning, yet he came to appreciate the countryfolk's gratitude. In fact, he felt that any attempts to quash the hearsay about him would disappoint their willingness to define him in some comfortable terms under which they could accept him. Arsalan did not forget the suspicious glares he encountered upon his arrival, and he was grateful for any opportunity to earn their trust. Thus, Arsalan, with feigned self-effacement and reluctance, agreed to their requests for repair, refurbishment, rebuilding, and extensions without exception and without complaint or irritation at being interrupted from his gardening. He invariably professed doubt to each customer in his ability to perform each repair adequately and made it a practice of estimating each job to last much longer than it did. It was this humility that charmed all the locals, and the fact that when the time for the work came, Arsalan performed each repair with such seamless professionalism and sound, durable construction as they had never seen. He charged them appropriately low fees; a few copper para here and there, a silver kuruş at the most. His customers would beam with pleased faces at his work and barely suppressed chuckles at Arsalan's self-deprecating nature, and they later would report their stories about the new builder to a neighbor over a fence or to folks at the market.

At the end of several weeks of such work, Arsalan was surprised at the amount of small change he had accumulated in his box by the window. He did not consider it valuable at all in contrast to the gold he already had in his house, and particularly in comparison to the wealth he already had experienced in his lifetime. He considered these new copper coins playful trinkets of goodwill and paid them little mind. Yet goods here were so inexpensive that he found the little copper coins increasingly useful for purchasing his daily necessities without depleting his own gold, such as when he bought meat from jolly Lyubomir in town or wool from the weaver whose loom Arsalan had repaired. In fact, over time, he discovered that he did not need even to touch his gold.

Arsalan demanded only two strict conditions under which he would perform his work. First, under no circumstances could anyone watch him execute the task. Second, his cat must be allowed to accompany him always. His customers willingly obliged these easy requests in anticipation of the known results. They cleared their children, pets, and livestock away from the work area and let Arsalan be, only to return later to find their objects of disrepair refurbished flawlessly or their new structures constructed wonderfully and Arsalan petting Kizil in his arms. It was for these reasons that the locals joked that Arsalan must be some sort of wizard, and his cat his loyal familiar. Arsalan the Magnificent they called him among themselves, referring to the famous, legendary, and faraway magical architect of the same name, the fabulous sorcerer of immense wealth whom they did not realize was the very same man who was now among them rebuilding their barns and root cellars. None of them took seriously the possibility that he could have been the same Arsalan, and this relieved and comforted him most. For this reason, he guarded his personal life and his real identity with a face of reticence and humility and seriousness that, so far, they had chosen to respect.

Arsalan spent the remainder of his time in his garden, irrigating, weeding, and fertilizing it. He dug a small canal from a nearby stream to the garden, and after it was finished, he leaned on his hoe and watched the sparkling vein of life dance beneath the sun. He made it a practice of using no magic for his gardening tasks, relying instead on his own slow, careful handiwork. He now enjoyed sweating and using his muscles until they were sore. He found happiness in the soil on his hands. He looked forward to being weary at the end of the day such that at sundown he could immerse himself at once into a solid, lightless block of sleep until sunrise. The large rectangle of dry clods by his house slowly loosened and grew dark brown, and he no longer felt intimidated or defeated by it as he felt when he began his manual labors and had to rediscover how to use a shovel correctly. He was master of his garden through his own bodily efforts. The unfolding process of the work fascinated him, and its slowness became an element that appeared to influence the quality of the outcome. Arsalan always had paid attention to details, but now he could observe them and could savor them. Work no longer was done in such a brief, magical flurry that was difficult to appreciate; it now displayed the full flora of its unfurling and interlocking parts that possessed their own strange beauty.

The smell of soil gladdened Arsalan. It was not an offensive stench but one that rang with the fresh odors of minerals and water, and Arsalan observed with a curious adoration the worms that crawled through it. When Arsalan hurt a hand or a finger while working, he cursed like bolts of lightning, but it was a sweet, pink, throbbing pain like an expensive desert, one that eventually melted; afterward, it seemed like a miracle that he was fine, and he found himself newly glad at his own wellness. Each day Arsalan looked forward to returning to the garden to witness what new developments had taken place there and what new treasures had sprouted, and to busying himself with the meditative act of pluck-ing weeds and churning the rich, brown soil. Arsalan was fascinated when he discovered the first tender, chartreuse sprouts of the turnips and cabbages, and he devoted all his time to nurturing the tiny fetal coils. After some of them had matured into thick, crisp turnips, he marveled at the soil's benevolence, the fact that the earth had given birth to food for him to eat. They looked like a child's playthings: round and sporting a white bottom and a purple top on their rubbery skins. They reminded him of his own children's toys as they sat at the bottom of their toyboxes. The turnips were of differing sizes, and they tumbled playfully around the bottom of the basket in which he collected them, leaving clods of dirt wherever they rolled. Arsalan felt a vague loss at not engaging his children in gardening when they were small. All his gardening had been performed by servants, working distantly and dutifully, whom he saw only from inside his windows. He saw now that Omer, Asker, and Defne would have loved the work, and even Teodora would have tolerated it if she saw they were having fun at it.

Arsalan developed a new love for the weather atop the mountain. It was always dry and cool, burning under the lone sun but chilly in the shade. He fell in love with the warbling birds and humming bees and waltzing butterflies whose home was the meadow by his house. He loved to hear the broad wind sing its symphonies through the treetops, prompting the trees to engage in mysteriously swaying dances. The weather was cooling for autumn, and abrupt-ly there would occur a downpour, a thunderstorm, or even ephemeral flurries that quickly evaporated. Banks of gray clouds piled against the peak above his house, sometimes shrouding it, sometimes producing snow, sometimes creeping outward from the peak to hover over Arsalan's house like a looming parasol. But what startled Arsalan most was the thunder. He had never known what it was like to be just under a bellowing thundercloud. It was so explosively, roaringly loud that it seemed to infiltrate his insides, and those times he spent in his stable calming his horses who whinnied nervously, his cat who clung to his shoulders, and himself. It reminded him of the nights he spent comforting his children and coaxing them to sleep during violent storms in Kirklareli, and he reminisced about the rainy nights he spent with Teodora. He spent hours listening to the baroque whispers of the rain against the walls of his new dwelling, the trillion droplets silently requesting admittance but never entering. But on the days when the weather was clear and the sky was a flat, brilliant azure, Arsalan took notice of how the peak above his dwelling, depending on the angle of the sun, could glow with gold or red or pink or violet like the towers and minarets of raucous, bustling Istanbul, in hues that shifted like the hands of a clock through the hours of each infinite, jewellike day.

CHAPTER 5

Among the many routines he established for himself at his new home on the mountain, Arsalan also conducted regular searches in the surrounding area for Defne. He would wake early in the morning to harness his horses to his cart, and he and Kizil would trundle down the mountainside in a plume of dust, riding far and wide around Sliven in his search that sometimes lasted for days at a time. He would ask everyone he met in the countryside if they had seen the girl whose likeness was in the locket that he showed them in front of their noses. All the farmers, blacksmiths, peddlers, housewives, priests, monks, and woodsmen he asked peered and squinted at the portrait, shook their heads, and replied in the negative. No one had seen the girl. No one even gave the impression of lying about having seen her, and Arsalan was quite skilled at detecting duplicitousness. In fact, Arsalan could not help but notice the strange looks they sometimes gave him in their replies, as if to suggest that he was looking in the wrong place altogether, judging by the ornateness of the locket and the foreign appearance of both Arsalan and his little portrait of Defne.

Weeks passed, and the hope in Arsalan's heart of finding his daughter dimmed. Even his regular encounters with Lyubomir in his butcher's shop yielded no reports of Defne. Lyubomir looked at Arsalan with increasing sympathy, one that grew more pained each time he told Arsalan no one had found her. At each of these times, Arsalan would look away in attempts to conceal his despondency at his loss and his guilt at having Lyubomir undergo such an increasingly fruitless exercise on his behalf.

Then came the time of the harvest festival, which occurred all over this region among the Bulgars and Roma, including on Radimir's farm at the foot of the mountain. Lyubomir and Radimir's family organized festivities there, and all who were invited were their friends and kinfolk. The two brothers thought they would be mistaken if they did not invite their shy, lonely new friend Arsalan the Magnificent, the seemingly magical Turkish carpenter who could fix anything, to their celebrations. It took Lyubomir much pleading and smiling to convince Arsalan to come. Arsalan spent fifteen minutes behind his own half-open door trying to decline Lyubomir's invitation with the most anguished and tactful hand-waving. Eventually, Arsalan succumbed, but only on the condition that he bring Kizil, who would be lonely without him.

The festivities were not as uncomfortable as Arsalan had imagined, at least at first. On a field under the warm sun and cool breezes there stood many tables on which people were preparing food. Arsalan spent the chilly, sunlit day among cheerful crowds watching lines of women link arms and dance in a green field while wearing embroidered vests and skirts of vivid red and black. Later, men and boys stood together and sang choral pieces while wearing black suits laced at the collars and sleeves with scarlet brocade. He did not understand what was being sung or the significance of each dance or song, but he watched in polite silence. His attention eventually wandered to the trees behind the crowds of revelers. The groves' leaves had been burnished to warm, rusty hues. The lowering sun mingled with the ragged edges of cottony clouds of marigold and salmon. The aromas of bread and fruit and smoked meats blended with the blazing colors and invigorating breezes in a way that Arsalan found intoxicating. Kizil lounged dutifully across Arsalan's shoulders as if on a throne, watching everything around her with lethargic aplomb. When he idly approached the tables of food, celebrants who recognized him cheered and offered him a seat and a plate. The table was already seated with elderly folk whose kind, wrinkly faces smiled with mouths only partially full of teeth. Arsalan had arrived bearing a gift in exchange for the hospitality: a basket of turnips, which the younger women accepted with gracious and appreciative remarks.

The cat lying across Arsalan's shoulders like a miniature regal tiger quickly became the initial topic of conversation among the old folk at the tables. No one could resist extending a gentle knuckle to pet the mangy fur of the slothful red cat who looked back at them with silent, jade eyes. No one mentioned how rough the cat still looked, whether out of politeness or because no one had seen a cat that was any healthier. Questions as to where Arsalan had acquired his pet swiftly led to talk of gratitude for all his repair work and direct inquiries as to his past and where he had learned his trade. Arsalan answered their questions in a way that was not entirely untruthful but minimized the facts of his prior wealth and success and revealed nothing about his magical powers. He presented himself as a common laborer who had enjoyed some success in the construction trade and had learned some architecture and engineering but now was retiring. Some then quietly leaned toward him and expressed their sorrowful regret at hearing the story of his missing daughter, adding that they had not come across anyone matching her description. Arsalan thanked them but did not allow the subject of conversation to dwell on himself for long, redirecting the subject of their conversation to themselves and their relatives and the festivities at hand.

Eventually, Lyubomir and Radimir made their way to Arsalan's side and bellowed their familiar greetings, perhaps wishing to embarrass Arsalan in the most festive of ways, which Arsalan found warmly irritating. Lyubomir made a point of slapping Arsalan on his back and yelling, "Everyone, this is the man who's getting rich off of us!" and then laughing while shaking hands with him. One can imagine how this might have startled any other cat that had been lying across Arsalan's shoulders at that moment, but Kizil, to her credit, simply and calmly looked up at Lyubomir. "What a brave, tough cat!" said the giant man with smiling eyes and a few strokes from his enormous finger. "Here's a cat who has seen some danger and hardship. A man's cat! She fears nothing." Radimir, who rather suddenly appeared flanking Arsalan's other side, asked him if he had eaten enough, which reminded Arsalan to look at his food on his plate, realizing he had not touched it yet. "Eat! Drink, then!" commanded Radimir merrily. "In fact, there's good ale at yon table for just a copper, sold by Widow Grozda."

There was a twinkle in Radimir's eye as he said this and turned away. Lyubomir and Radimir then walked away together, Lyubomir slapping Radimir across his back and laughing at something.

Arsalan's curiosity was mildly piqued. He was not certain of the nature of Radimir's playfully suggestive tone, but he knew that by going to get any ale from the person known as Widow Grozda he would be falling prey to one of the many mischievous but good-natured jests with which he already had begun to associate with the two guffawing brothers. But it had been a long time since he had had any good liquor that he no longer could resist the temptation of such cheap fare, and he reasoned that whatever further embarrassment lay ahead was probably worth the trouble. He kept the idea in his mind while he finished his food, which, admittedly, with its breads and meats and gravies and cabbages and greens, was quite gratifying. He then wiped his mouth and beard, stood, thanked his tablemates for their food and conversation, and gave them a copper coin for their hospitality, which they of course initially refused once and twice out of propriety. Arsalan then began to walk, in the way one waddles when one is freshly full of dinner, in an indirect path toward the table where Radimir indicated there was ale. He meandered among many inebriated revelers who spat droplets of saliva while telling raucous stories to each other, children holding flowers and sticks while running from each other below Arsalan's waist, and dogs searching for scraps on the ground, which was strewn with hay. The sky was beginning to darken to a smooth, somber navy blue studded with peeping stars, and folks were beginning to light lamps and torches, signaling that the party's end was in no way nigh. Men produced accordions, hurdy-gurdies, and fiddles and began to play, and women began to dance in circles again, and secretly Arsalan was devising plans and times for a discreet escape to his cozy house.

The festivities reminded Arsalan, quite against his own will, of his own luxurious functions and balls he used to organize in his own pink chateau, where everyone from high society drank crisp champagne from elegant crystal glasses that gleamed under his ornate chandelier while musicians played fine, thoughtful melodies beneath tapestries. There were nobles, statesmen, generals, philosophers, artists, bankers, merchants, and of course other magical architects. There were games of billiards and cards played by fat, waistcoated diplomats smoking pipes while telling tales of international travel and intrigue. They sat around Arsalan's dark oaken table with its high, mirrorlike shine which was obscured only by the endless satin tablecloth of violet and red draped along the table's exaggerated length. It was festooned with glittering silverware, crystal, and china, which even after having been used and casually pushed aside in a mess was one of the most beautiful arrays of objects one could see. It pained Arsalan to think that he had sold all those sumptuous items, but after his reputation as a magical architect had plummeted, their utility to him had evaporated, and their stacks and piles then stood in despondent mockery of his former prosperity.

All those important personages who had sat at those tables had vanished after the debacle of the World's Leaf. The disaster alone had rendered any continued association with Arsalan a cause for embarrassment, and his subsequent loss of fortune had cemented it. Arslan was all too keenly aware of the social protocols among the supremely wealthy. When one of their own faced a sudden financial difficulty, the proper and socially accepted course of action was a charitable one, but beneath their magnanimous exteriors stewed an implicit revulsion toward poverty and low social status, particularly when it was perceived to be in any way self-inflicted, as it was in Arsalan's case. So, to spare themselves the trouble and Arsalan any further indignity, they chose to avoid the matter altogether by avoiding Arsalan himself. They shook their heads in pity in private, wished him the best of luck in public, and continued their carnivalesque lives of worldly and significant affairs without him, and Arsalan wished to spare himself further humiliation by avoiding them as well. He wanted them to forget about him utterly and not to worry where he was, even if it was in the rural Balkans, sitting on unvarnished wooden stools and eating farm food from benches among hounds and shoeless children and toothless, elderly countryfolk.

Arsalan found himself standing at a pair of tables in front of a row of trestle stands holding barrels turned on their sides. The barrels were pierced with spigots from which the barrels' contents were drawn. One table was laden with emptied mugs, which a girl was gathering into a large basin. The girl walked away without offering any greetings, as she was merely a child occupied with a heavy load in her thin arms. A woman also was standing there, occupied with wiping one of the other tables with a cloth. She turned her head to look at Arsalan, and then her full body. She gave Arsalan a quick and frank look up and down. She was stocky and muscular, and her serious face, framed by the cloth wrapping her hair, was very round but with a small, straight nose that pointed downward. In her forties, she gave the impression of a woman who had experienced too much of life to be swayed by nonsense.

"Excuse me, madam. Are you still selling ale?" said Arsalan.

"I am," she said. "You must be the builder from Kirklareli who fixes things."

"Yes," said Arsalan. "I have obliged many friendly requests to conduct repairs, you can say."

The woman grabbed a clean mug and placed it on the table, directly in front of Arsalan, and she began to fill it from a pitcher.

"What brings you all the way here?" she asked.

"Retirement," said Arsalan. "I am growing old, and I feel I have enough to live on, and have had enough of building, and this is a nice place."

The woman looked at him for a moment. "You'll have to forgive me if I'm not understanding your idea of retirement, for no one here retires until they're too feeble to work and their grown children must take care of them, and even then, it's difficult to keep old people from their previous work. What do you do for your retirement?" she said.

"Well," said Arsalan, "what I've been doing so far is gardening."

"Gardening," said the woman. "You came all this way just to garden?"

So, she is teasing me and challenging my story, thought Arsalan. He could see this person was on a more equal footing with him in terms of mind, so he had to be careful with his words.

"Well, no, if you must ask," he said. "I faced a crisis in my life, and my daughter ran away from me. I believe she fled here, but I have not found her yet."

"I'm sorry to hear that," she said. "I believe I have heard rumors about that, but I didn't know how much to believe. You know how rumors go. Anyway, I hope you find her."

"Thank you," said Arsalan, sipping his ale.

"Would you mind if I asked you what kind of crisis that was that caused her to run away like that?" she asked.

"Well, it's a complicated affair," said Arsalan. "But I can say that it was a—how to say—a professional debacle that caused myself and my family significant financial losses."

The woman furrowed her brow as she wiped a cup with a cloth.

"Did one of your buildings fall?" she asked.

Arsalan found it difficult to breathe for a second.

"I'd rather not say," he said, looking down at his drink. "What I can say is, after the financial failures, we found it difficult to stay together anymore. My daughter eventually was courted by a rich prince who turned out to be nefarious and threatened her life. She fled from him and from everything that had led up to that point. So, I'm here to find her. I also feel this country is a suitable place of exile from my troubles for the time being."

"Well, I don't like to think of our land as a place of exile and disgrace, mind you. This is a home, after all, where people live. But I think I see what you mean," she said. "Either that building, or whatever it was that failed, was of some extreme importance, or your life must have been built on foundations shakier than you previously had realized, if it can be capsized by one single adversity like that, if you don't mind me saying. Typically, with sound family and friendships, one can survive any number of setbacks."

Arsalan was quietly astounded at the woman's insightfulness, as if the wind were taken from his lungs, and he had to sigh.

"You are not wrong about any of that, madam," he said, and he consoled himself with another drink from his mug.

"In any case, I'm sorry to hear it," she said. "Now it does make more sense, and I understand why you would want to keep it a secret. I'm sorry to drag it out of you."

"These are mere facts about one's own life that one must accept," he said. "But tell me. Are you the one to whom others refer as Widow Grozda?"

The woman became irritated and flustered for just an instant and then recovered.

"Yes, but just call me Grozda, if you will," she said. "I dislike the moniker they give me."

"I'm sorry," asked Arsalan.

"But it's true. The consumption took my husband," she said, "But I still have my children, a grandchild, and my cattle and sheep. My husband used to make ale. I continue the hobby with his methods and recipe. I make it with the help of my family."

"That is good that you still have that much. It is to be cherished," asked Arsalan. "But tell me, in your religion, do you pray to your deceased beloved?"

"In a way, yes," she said. "We are Orthodox."

"Then the next time your pray to your husband, please extend my respects and compliments to him for the ale. It was particularly good," said Arsalan, placing the empty mug on the table in front of him.

"Thank you," said Grozda.

"How much for the cup?" asked Arsalan.

"One para," she said. "But you needn't bother."

"I insist," said Arsalan. "It was quite good. Perhaps I'll return to have more, madam."

"There's much more to you, builder," said Grozda. "Perhaps you can return and can tell me about it all, and your cat, who looks as if it has as many stories to tell as you have."

Just then the girl returned with the basin and gave Arsalan a searching, puzzled glance before going about her tasks again. She was accompanied by a boy who tugged at Grozda's apron, pestering her with a question or complaint about the girl. Grozda's cool poise was compromised, and she immediately became distracted by a petty dispute between the boy and the girl and set about mediating it like a judge. Arsalan tactfully took this opportunity to slip away, leaving behind on the table not one but two copper para.

The night grew late, and Arsalan knew it would be a long, cold ride up the mountain. He did not bother to find Lyubomir to say goodbye, for he knew the good man would go far as to offer his own bed to sleep in for the night. Arsalan would see him on his next visit to the butcher's shop. Arsalan would not have minded a longer conversation with Grozda, but her frank, probing questions annoyed him, and frightened him at least a little, and he was relieved to be away from them.

But no sooner had he decided all this than he was accosted by Lyubomir in a bid to join in some dancing. "Hey, Arsalan!" the huge man bellowed, "It's time!" He hooked Arsalan by one arm, and veritably dragged him to an open area where revelers already had begun their clapping and their twirling to the accordion music. They held their arms out to each side and snapped their fingers while they performed some sort of nervous jig with their feet that Arsalan could not follow. Before he could think of escaping, they formed a circle and rotated around a middle, where laughing Lyubomir had captured Arsalan. The old Turk waved his hands in imploration, insisting he could not dance, but the cheering crowd refused to believe his excuses and demanded that he join them. Lyubomir's giant daughter took Kizil from Arsalan's shoulders, and the cat looked around in mild panic before the girl began to pet her while swaying to the music. Finally, Arsalan realized there was no polite way out, and he smiled resignedly and relented to the merrymaking. He imitated their dance. It seemed that the Bulgars' style of dance was not too different from his own, and he did quite well at first, before adding some exotic flourishes from his home country, such as bowing down here and there and whirling on one foot, which delighted the crowd immensely. At length, confident that they had absorbed Arsalan into their abandon and revelry, they began to form swirling streams of motion, where they exchanged partners in swift, cyclical succession. Arsalan found this pattern hard to follow as well, and several times he bumped shoulders with others, who excused his clumsiness with loud laughter and smiles and slaps on the back.

Lyubomir danced particularly well. He was graceful and energetic and performed some sort of hopping duet with his brother Radimir that illustrated their vigorous fraternal bond, linking arms and gamboling with bent knees and outstretched feet while frequently changing directions, first clockwise, then counterclockwise. Everyone gave the two dancing giants a wide berth and clapped their hands to the music's rhythm while cheering.

Eventually the crowd converged again and continued their gyrations, and Arsalan noticed the throng had become larger, and even Grozda had joined. Even though she was some distance away, he could not help noticing her each time she happened to face his direction in her twirling. Her visage was like the gleam of a lantern that shot into his eye. Unexpectedly, he found her directly in front of him, staring at him with the same intent expression but with a sly smile on her face. She, too, was a good dancer, and he saw he had much to learn from her. In fact, their encounter here, although lasting only a few seconds or more, seemed to extend into an intoxicating interlude for Arsalan. After this flirtatious interval, she tilted her head appreciatively and smiled broadly toward him before spinning away and becoming lost in the shuffling.

The currents and eddies of the river of cavorting people eventually deposited a tired Arsalan to the shores of the activity, where he caught his heaving breath and watched the frolicking from a distance. He laughed gently to himself and decided he had had fun, but now it was a good time to decamp while unseen. Arsalan found Kizil being held and petted by a crowd of little girls sitting under a nearby table and thanked them for their care of her. The cat leapt immediately into Arsalan's arms, and they were off. He found Solmaz and Aysel at their posts, readied them, mounted his carriage, and left.

The forested road was as black as a tunnel, with only the eye of the moon above him lighting his path. It was as dark blue as the bottom of a sea. He lit his lamp, which served to illuminate only his horses' haunches, so thick was the darkness. Kizil slept on his lap as they climbed, and it was late when they reached the house, and the next day he and Kizil slept till the noon sun was high and was casting calm, parallel beams on the floor through the shutters. Once he awoke, he lay in bed for a long time and wondered with some regret whether he had confessed too much to the woman who had sold him the ale.

CHAPTER 6

The next few weeks proceeded according to the predictable routine that Arsalan had developed for himself. All week, Arsalan would garden, which at this time of year meant weeding and harvesting the newly matured vegetables. He was not entirely prepared for all the produce his sizeable garden would yield. The fruits of his labor were so plentiful that he was forced to dig a root cellar in which to store them. He built the cellar below his house, accessible from a small wooden door outside that leaned against the wall. One opened it by grasping an iron ring in a hinge, and a set of stairs led downward from the door to the small underworld of the basement where one was met with walls and flooring made of an array of cobblestones the pale, bulging ends of which protruded from gray mortar. There were fixtures on the wall for lanterns or torches. One corner of the cellar was occupied entirely by a heap of turnips, and the other, heads of cabbage. Assessing the size of his yield, Arsalan determined he was prepared for the winter, although he admitted he would ensure greater variety next season.

At the end of every week, Arsalan ventured into town to buy his other necessities, which typically would be meat from Lyubomir's butcher shop, clothing from the tailor, or tools from the smith. Occasionally, Arsalan would find some small luxury item, such as lotion or soap, imported from Istanbul or some other more cosmopolitan part of the empire. The local shopkeepers, not knowing exactly what to do with these exotic novelties, tended to place them on the shelves next to their ordinary produce like curios. Newly laden with supplies from the shops, Arsalan would venture outward into the surrounding countryside to resume his exhaustive search for Defne. These searches would last for a day or two, or sometimes three, and they were executed with a hand-drawn map that over time grew embellished with slashes, strikethroughs, and notes. Through this conscientious probing, Arsalan eventually would become familiar with every village, town, mountain, and lake around Sliven. None of these, though, yielded any hint or sign of Defne, and Arsalan wondered whether he had committed a grave miscalculation in coming to the land of the Bulgars to look for her.

At Lyubomir's shop, Arsalan absorbed all the local news and chatter. He was not interested in gossip for its own sake but analyzed it to navigate the politics of the local area so that he would not run afoul of it. Arsalan was selective in telling Lyubomir any critical news about himself. Arsalan knew his divulgences would become everyone's news, not because Lyubomir had a taste for gossip either, but because the butcher was so egalitarian in his conversation. Lyubomir was not the type to discriminate between hearsay and objective news or between those who did not care for grapevine prattle and those who eagerly sought it as a valuable commodity.

Several days after the harvest festival, Lyubomir asked Arsalan, "I heard you partook of the Widow Grozda's ale. What did you think of it?"

Arsalan was not certain how to respond to this, but eventually said, "Well, to be honest, I thought it was quite tasty. It seemed she put some sort of spice in it that I could not identify."

Lyubomir said, "She's good at that, she is. Her husband made the best ale. Secret recipe."

"Yes, and so it seems, it does," Arsalan said, tapping gently on the counter and looking idly at it. "I'm wondering, though. Does she sell the ale regularly?"

"Not that I know," said Lyubomir, rubbing his chin and leaning on his counter. "I hear she makes it only for her family and for gatherings and festivals and such. Would you be looking for more? If so, I can tell her to leave a batch here and I can keep it for you."

Arsalan was not prepared for Lyubomir to offer the idea so quickly but decided to go along with it.

"Oh, well, that wouldn't be a bad idea," said Arsalan. "Thank you."

"But I tell you, if you don't come buy it when it's ready, I might drink it myself!" said Lyubomir, laughing.

And that was that. The transaction was arranged, and Arsalan received the ale from Lyubomir a week later. Lyubomir gave no indication of having interpreted any subtext from Arsalan's inquiry. No free or innocuous inroad was exposed by which Arsalan could ask where Grozda lived that could not be interpreted by everyone as burgeoning personal or romantic interest, one that Arsalan would refuse to admit even to himself.

Grozda left no note or message with the delivery. Arsalan returned home that day with nothing but a whole keg of ale in his carriage. While he drove, he shuddered with relief.

"Thank the heavens," he said to himself. "Then that settles it. Don't get involved. Just keep to yourself. Don't be a fool. You'll just cause trouble. You are here for two reasons only, and those are to retire alone and in peace and to look for Defne."

Winter approached, and it proved a mounting challenge for Arsalan.

However difficult he had depicted wintry life to be in the Balkans in his fairy tales to Defne, he was unprepared for its real and eventual extremes. Snow arrived early toward the end of autumn in sleepy, dusty falls, dissolving from the gray roof above like fine sawdust from incessant carpentry work. As the weeks passed, the snowfalls grew in intensity and their snowflakes in size until vagrant, marauding drifts blocked the only road leading to his house and blanketed everything within sight of the windows in blindingly white icing. On a day when the deluge ceased, Arsalan discovered he could open his front door only partially. He peeked outward with one eye and saw the door was blocked by a snowdrift piled against it. He cast a spell to blow the fine, dry, sparkling dust away from his stoop. The tiny motes of crystalline ice swirled in every direction, including into Arsalan's eyes, beard, and mouth, where they melted into a steely taste. Frigid air slinked onto the floor inside and surrounded his ankles like snakes. Eventually, he was able to open the door fully, and there he discovered an astonishing sight. Arsalan's house was cloistered within a large, ashen hall of low clouds, walls of mist, plush carpets of thick snow, and a strange, muffled silence. Everything existed in a calm, milky twilight resting somewhere outside of time and removed from earth or heaven. The sun was reduced to a wan rumor of light existing somewhere above the glacial roof of clouds, imbuing everything with a pearly luster. From some unfathomable distance, a wind roared, raw and ruthless, and caused the tall spruces to sway in place and to drop from their hoary, drooping boughs shapeless pillows of snow that burst into clouds of cascading dust. All else seemed to be dormant, frozen, and brightly asleep.

Arsalan knew at once what he must do. He dressed in his warmest clothes, which were not so warm by themselves but were so in many layers, and stood outside, facing the ocean of snow in front of him. He held the palms of his hands outward and parted the snow from the path that led from his door to the road. Snow whirled furiously before him as if in protest at being disturbed from its slumber. Miniscule bits of ice glinted here and there. Arsalan's breath rose like smoke from his bearded face. Eventually, the snow was organized neatly to one side and the other. Arsalan had carved a neat wound in the white icing from his front door to the road, revealing the dry, pale grass hibernating beneath.

Arsalan then went about plowing a similar path all around the perimeter of his house and stable, and then from the stable to the road. He then looked behind him and realized it would be best to remove the snow from his rooftop as well. Arsalan cast a spell, and the snow slid down the roof and poured onto the perimeter of the house he just had cleaned.

"Dragon's farts!" he cursed, before plowing it again.

Kizil appeared in the doorway in her curious fashion, sniffing with distaste at some of the snow that was still on the threshold.

"Don't come out!" said Arsalan. "You'll get lost, and you'll freeze to death!"

Kizil, whether deciding from her own reasoning or through comprehension of Arsalan's human words, complied and smoothly retreated inside.

Arsalan then carved a path from the house to the outhouse, and then all around the outhouse for good measure. He then went back inside his cabin, ate a sound breakfast, and spoke to Kizil.

"You must remain here," stated Arsalan at the breakfast table. "I will take the horses and I'll plow the road as far as I can go."

Kizil answered by caressing his shins with her fur, and Arsalan petted her.

"I will return," said Arsalan. "I promise you."

Arsalan locked the door behind him and said goodbye through the window to Kizil, who sat behind the glass on the sill as cats do, imprisoned in her terrarium. She stared at him with a gaze one might interpret as worried. Arsalan then hitched his horses to the carriage and guided them to the road. Here, he began his operation, blowing snow off the road and seemingly in every direction like a mad steam engine. Arsalan then turned his horses to trot down the road. From his seat on the carriage, he conducted his plowing and parting, creating a tumultuous series of powdery explosions before him as he progressed.

When he reached the first other house along the road, Arsalan decided he should not cause such a wild ruckus but should be more discreet about his snowplowing. He did not see any of the house's occupants outside; the languid blue haze of smoke emerged from their little chimneys. Arsalan cast his spell toward the ground in a way that would contain the dry clouds of ice as he merely shifted the snow to the right and left along the ground. He went forth, quietly cleaving the snow to either side before him, packing it neatly, and leaving openings near the paths from the doors of the other houses. Arsalan proceeded swiftly but quietly, such that those watching from the windows of the houses would see only Arsalan riding past on his carriage.

At length, he reached a point near the bottom of the mountain where the snow was no longer thick and did not need plowing. He had escaped the heavy mountaintop drifts. He no longer felt trapped, and his cause for indignant panic was ameliorated. He also hoped that the lives of the other occupants of the mountain road were made easier by his efforts, though he was glad that he had not encountered any of them on his way down.

However, once he had stopped, he did see a dark shape moving along the white road toward him, up its gradual slope. It was a mother and her children in a small cart pulled by two hearty donkeys exhaling gray steam from their flaring black nostrils. When the family arrived at Arsalan's side, they stopped and looked. The figures were black against the snow, bundled in countless, tightly wound swathes of wool, revealing only their pale faces from which their white breaths smoked. It was Grozda and her five children, and presumably one of her sisters.

"My, sir, I have never seen the snow cleared like this before," said Grozda. "Do you know who did this? We were all prepared to shovel our way up."

"Perhaps it was the work of the district governments finally caring for its people," said Arsalan.

"I haven't heard of anything like that, but I did notice the roads were flattened and paved last summer," she remarked.

"It's a fair guess to think it's the same workers," said Arsalan.

"Mr. Arsalan, the builder, you are," said Grozda. "I haven't seen you since the festival. I trust you received my shipment of ale?"

"Oh, yes, I did, madam, and it has succeeded in keeping me warm on these cold nights," he said. "Thank you. Have you been well these days?"

"Yes, I have, and thank you for asking," said Grozda. "Those are two majestic horses you have there. Where does one get horses like that?"

Arsalan patted the haunch of Aysel, brushing some snow away. The horses' nostrils and clumsy black lips fumed with white steam. "Oh, I purchased them some years ago from the army, who planned to replace them," he said. "Horses were a hobby of mine. These are my two darlings."

"Well, it's getting cold, Mr. Arsalan," said Grozda, "and we must be on our way to deliver some goods to an elderly friend of ours. Perhaps we could come to visit you on the top of the mountain there now that you've scared away any fear of lingering plague."

"If you can brave the long way there," said Arsalan, "you would be welcome."

Grozda flipped her reins, and the donkeys trotted up the road. After they had passed, a daughter turned around in her seat and stared at Arsalan with the transparently suspicious and inquisitive glare with which children seem to regard all strangers. Arsalan waited until they were out of sight before he turned around and went in the same direction. He knew they would be turning somewhere, and he wanted to grant them plenty of time to do so before he ventured back up the mountain at full speed.

What a foolish thing for me to say, thought Arsalan. He was bound by the rules of propriety to say that Grozda was welcome to come to his house for a visit once she mentioned the idea, but he was now terrified at the prospect of her taking his invitation seriously. He briefly considered the possibility of hiding inside his house and not answering the door if she made the significant effort of going to the top of the mountain to see him. But no, that would be the epitome of rude buffoonery, and now he knew he was obliged to greet her at the door. Damn me, he thought, why couldn't I think of an excuse?

The brief, drowsy, gray days, compressed between extended nights, began to take their toll on Arsalan's mind. To him, it seemed more like a continuous night that at certain regular times grew notably paler, offering views out his windows of slush and mud puddles and melting icicles. On certain warmer days when snow thawed and trickled down the side of the house, it seemed damp enough for fish to swim through his dwelling in midair, and he lit many fires to dispel the humidity. He had nothing left to do in his garden. It lay fallow and frozen beneath the snow but was prepared for next spring. He found wood in the forests and split it into logs, which he kept in piles next to his house. He was loath to fell any live trees for fear of thinning the lovely forests. Rather, he relied on dead wood and brambles and the occasional newly fallen spruce or pine. Reducing a whole tree to sections by hand with an ax proved much more taxing than shoveling a garden, so here he relented and just used magic again. He used much of the firewood in the hearth in the stable to keep the horses warm, and he spent many evenings there comforting them with talk and soft caresses on their faces while the fire crackled and with Kizil circling their feet.

As the winter progressed and the nights expanded and plunged into colder depths, Arsalan began to talk to himself. At first his speech consisted of small gatherings of mumbled words that periodically surfaced from his continuous inner monologue. But soon his ruminations flowered into fully comprehensible discourses on his own life. He spoke from morning to night, as if dictating his memoirs to an unseen writer, about his own life, his youth, his family, his fears, his regrets, and his prides. He spoke to his horses, the fire, the walls, the snow, or anything nearby that could hear him. He spoke to Kizil at the table while he had his meals. The cat sat on an overturned bucket placed on a chair, and she stared at him with listening eyes like two pools of reflective pondwater. Arsalan spoke to Kizil of Omer, Asker, and Defne and how proud he was of them, even though he did not know at any given time their whereabouts or states of health. He grieved the fact that Omer did not write and feared his son was dead. He took Asker's latest letters from a chest and repeatedly read them aloud, then began to write responses to them while reciting his own writing. He would write no further than the first paragraph of a letter to Asker before placing his face in his hand and moaning in anguish in his worry that Asker would be killed in action before he ever would know about love, marriage, and children.

Each night after dinner, cloistered in his cabin, Arsalan would pace around his table while he delivered entire soliloquies, spontaneously and without ever writing them, regarding his love for his daughter Defne and his grief over her disappearance. Is she still in hiding? Did she marry someone? Is she in another country? Is she even alive? Arsalan realized that he must gird himself for the possibility that Defne could be dead. Solid leagues of distance and silence separated them and prevented him from ever knowing. He knew his only choice was to trust her own assertions that she would keep herself safe and healthy. She was a woman now, he thought, and he must respect her decision to take her life into her own hands. However reasonable this sounded, though, it still did not bring him the peace for which he yearned.

Arsalan thought of the time when his children were small. He missed their grubby toddlerhood. They were round and adorable and full of love, and he treasured the sweet odor of their heads and hair as they embraced him and lavished him with sloppy kisses. Omer was a particularly affectionate one and demanded the most attention. Asker was also loving but in a more self-assured and teasing way. Defne was observant and calm. He recalled how he and Teodora would soothe their children's tears after their many squealing fights and made them reconcile and laugh again. He remembered the wide eyes with which his children regarded him when he conducted his thaumaturgy, with his hands held high above him and blocks of material floating through the air. Omer would hide behind a curtain, Asker would laugh, and Defne would stare in complete mystification. Arsalan would make his children laugh with delight by making their toys move by themselves like magical puppets, all the while assuring them of the properties of magic so that they were not afraid. Arsalan remembered the way his children looked at him from behind half-open doors and curtains when he was speaking with famous nobles and businessmen about commissions and permits and other matters. As a child, Omer would gaze at his father with looks of awe. As Omer grew older, however, these looks dimmed into ones of bored incomprehension, an expression that suggested a notion that his father's world of concerns was inaccessible to him. Arsalan realized that he probably spent too many nights like this, paying more attention to his enterprise than to his children, while allowing them to witness him at his most indulged and preoccupied.

Arsalan thought of Teodora and remembered how beautiful she was. She was so gorgeous to him that she made him tremble with desire, especially when she looked at him a certain way, with her sapphire eyes over her left shoulder, her golden hair flowing down around her face. He changed from a man who wished to possess Teodora to one who was captivated by her. He desired Teodora all over again, and his passion for her turned into anguish and confusion. "Why would you leave me like that?" he said aloud. "I gave you everything your heart wanted. I gave you jewels, carriages, robes, perfumes, everything that a princess could want. I was richer than your whole noble family in backwater Silesia altogether. Only when my riches were removed did you leave. Did you love me just for that?"

Arsalan spent many afternoons and evenings outside in the snow, arguing with Teodora, as if she were right in front of him. He argued his case back and forth, how he was wronged by her leaving him, how he had given her much more than she ever had expected, and the phantasm of Teodora's memory listened and wept and screamed back at him. And finally, Arsalan realized what she must have experienced. He remembered that when he met her, she was just a young, guileless maiden of eighteen with little schooling, and that Arsalan was bold to spirit her away from her Silesian family to the fabulous palaces of the Ottoman Empire. It seemed to everyone, including to Arsalan himself, that he had married her solely for her beauty, though it was not entirely true. Teodora had other qualities that he liked that he found difficult to articulate. But they did not change how their marriage was initially based on physical exchanges of wealth and lovemaking and children. They grew to love each other in this way, but by the time Teodora's heart had matured, she had transformed into a shrewdly observant and intelligent woman with viewpoints and sentiments of her own. She saw Arsalan's immoderate spending and gambling, as he certainly recognized now, as troublingly reckless. She often complained of Arsalan's brooding and short temper, which would flare in the face of adversity. She saw Arsalan's love of business and socializing as distracting his heart from hers, and she learned of his many previous girlfriends before her, and at all these she became particularly jealous and resentful. She felt as if she were kept as just another of Arsalan's prizes, one that he displayed for her exotic yellow hair and jeweled eyes. Worst of all, Teodora saw how Arsalan's exorbitant traits were being passed on to their sons. Arsalan saw clearly now, in the purity of the wintry winds and the drifts of snow in which he stood, that by the time he had gone bankrupt, Teodora's grievances were not novel developments but ones that had accumulated over the years into an unbearable litany. Yes, he had been loyal to her, but business, high society, horse racing, and wine had been his mistresses. When Arsalan realized this, the phantasm of Teodora faded away, and suddenly he felt her invisible presence near him to be realer than the vision with which he was fighting. She seemed to stand by his side, pointing to the vision of his prior familial life that was laid out before him like a landscape from the eyes of a bird, and he experienced a lucid epiphany, a curious mixture of clear insight and distilled sorrow.

At a certain time during this tortuous winter, Arsalan, at night before he slept, became tortured by memories of the Worlds' Leaf collapsing, replete with the unforgiving details of nobles and diplomats screaming and scrambling for their lives in a stampede among the cloudy sands. He recalled how the Queen of Prussia's enormous wig had fallen from her head, and how she held her hands up as she ran rather pitifully, and how her tears caused her black mascara to run down her powdered cheeks like weeping death. On the ground, there was a trifold hat that had been trampled, and an overweight, pink-faced old man in epaulets was being helped to his feet by a man in a fez. A dark-haired little princess cried as she and her mother were being swept to safety by a black dignitary in a green robe. Arsalan rolled back and forth in his bed until he was forced to sit upright, and he attempted to soothe his tormented mind by staring out the window at the lovely, blanketing darkness in which his house was safely ensconced. He was not there anymore at the site of the World's Leaf. He was far away, hidden in the mountains, where there was no one to judge him for the disaster, and where he wished to stay until the world forgot.

Arsalan discovered in himself a deep and repressed rage at Sultan Muhteşem. "Stupid Sultan and his foolish dream of an idiotic tower for world peace," Arsalan spat in the darkness. "There will never be peace in this world among nations, and if it comes, it won't come through a single new school. One would have to fit the entire human population in the school for it to have any effect! And what an imbecilic design for a building! A plant! Plants are crushed underfoot every day or eaten by goats! Why not build a pyramid at least? That moronic young Sultan and his foolish boyhood dreams! I should have seen how stupid they were, and I should have stated it stridently to set him straight! This was all his fault for insisting on his dream, and my fault for entertaining them! And to think how I prostrated myself in front of him to beg for my life out of mere propriety. Disgusting! He should be more grateful that magical architects don't topple his empire!"

In the mornings, however, he would discover that his insolent and violent rage toward Muhteşem had dissipated entirely, leaving behind the dried crust of his own misplaced shame. There it was, unmistakable. How could Sultan Muhteşem be blamed for his vision of peace among humankind? Arsalan recalled with cringing regret how he had blamed his apprentices and journeymen for the magic depletion, interrogating them like criminals until they became incensed, rebelled, and left him. Was it even their fault? Oh, what a monster he felt he had been to them. But if they had not been neglectful in their construction, why did his tower fall?

After a time, his heart grew calmer, and he began to think more objectively about the cause of the collapse. Deep within the rubble the clue to the cause of the downfall was hidden, but he could not locate it. Deep within his memory he searched and searched again like water washing over an impassive rock. He recalled his old plans, his schematics, his tools, his workers, with perfect detail, so familiar was he with them all. There was no errant shred of evidence that could be paired with a previously overlooked hint that could help him make sense of the sudden magic depletion. He and his workers had executed his plans exactly as planned and according to the rules and procedures regarding the safety of magical structures. He rolled this rock of memory over and over in his mind but could find no crack, no fault, no chink in its surface. This he mulled quietly, long into each night, until the very thought of continuing with this rumination made him feel ill, and he pleaded with himself for the chance to occupy his mind with other thoughts. At these times, he often drew out his jewel box containing the white marble sphere that glittered in the amber candlelight, and he stared at it for a time before placing it back where he had hidden it, deeply concealed within his system of boxes and cases.

One frigid evening, when the mountaintop was wrapped in black, howling winds and the candlelight danced nervously in his dim, brown room, Arsalan began to reminisce about his father and mother. This was a random recollection prompted seemingly by nothing. His father was a plain man, a cloth merchant, with broad, powerful shoulders, violent gesticulations, and forceful opinions. Arsalan's mother and father adored Arsalan; he was their only child, and many have said that they spoiled him. His father was astonished and overjoyed when they discovered young Arsalan's talents, which were a miraculous fortune on top of their already modest success as merchants. They immediately arranged for him to study in the Magical Architects' Guild in Florence. There, his magical talents would be honed, and he would be schooled in mathematics, engineering, ordinary architecture, and finally magical architecture. His parents wrote Arsalan many letters and often visited him at the Guild. His father often erupted with abrupt, crashing laughter and his mother gazed lovingly and touched Arsalan's face. Their visits caused him both rejoicing and embarrassment, and both emotions were sweet to him. He would take care of them with his riches in their dotage. They lived with him in his chateau for a time before they died; first Mother of an intestinal sickness, then soon afterward Father of a broken heart. But they had made sure to let him know how proud of him they were. He was still certain his parents had been sent from Heaven to Earth just to give birth to him, and he wondered if they had returned to Heaven and were watching him with the same pride as before or if they now had turned their faces away in shame and pity at him.

Magical architects were so rare that gender or background played no part in the Guild's decision to admit them. Any child with demonstrable skill was admitted at once. At the Guild, he met his guildmate Sigrid, from the far north, who wore her hair in pigtails on either side of her head, which she would cock to one side with her icy gray eyes widened in a slightly disconcerting way while listening to others speak. His best friend was Emilio Ubaldini, with his long, narrow nose and wavy hair and elfin grin, who always played practical jokes on others and then consoled his victims by revealing to them the mechanics of the trick and encouraging fascination with it. Emilio was a few years older than Arsalan and became a mentor to him, and Arsalan learned much from the older boy. There were Fernando from Bilbao, who was excitable but ultimately serious and fair-minded, and his best friend Marcelle of Nice, who sported a calm and poetic soul. Acting like an older sister to them was thoughtful Anastasia, from the Ukraine, with her hair the strange color of copper. As an older brother to them was the warm and friendly giant everyone knew as Irakli, whom no one could anger despite their best attempts. He hailed from the hills of Georgia and could sing like no one else in his polyphonic scales. Mistress Dimitra, from Greece, was their teacher, as was soft-spoken Master Gustav, droll, wry Master Fahim, the reasoned Master Jawahir, and the colorful, laughing Mistress Kirakosyan from Armenia. All the guild masters were professionally working magical architects who once studied at the Guild. They travelled extensively to perform their commissions while attending to their duties as guild masters at the school in Florence. The Guild's school building was a small, enclosed plaza consisting of four solid marble walls four stories high with many beautiful windows and no visible doors. The magical architects entered by casting a spell on the back wall in a rear alleyway; a doorway would form in the wall, complete with a decorated frieze and a column on either side, all of which would disappear seamlessly and immediately behind the enterer. Only the wisest guild masters knew how this was accomplished, chief among them Conrad the Ineffable, born Conrad Scharnagl, hailing from Bavaria. By the time Arsalan had entered the Guild, Master Conrad was already elderly and retired from teaching, apprenticing, and even building, and continued his existence at the Guild as a counsel and as librarian of knowledge. The old man would be seen here and there among the columns of the dark upper floors in the rear of the building on some silent business in his deep blue robe and flaring white beard, and the apprentices were under strict orders not to disturb him. Occasionally he was urged by the other working guild masters to address the new recruits, a task that Conrad would oblige willingly but wearily and with so little volume or breath in his voice that all would lean forward, straining to hear him. Yet it was known that behind closed doors, Master Conrad was vigorous and argumentative and sported a brittle temper, often disputing fine points with the guild masters and throwing them out of his office.

Aside from times when Master Conrad would address the new apprentices, Arsalan saw him only from afar, behind the colonnades on some higher floor of the ambulatory, exiting one old, oaken door and entering another. Arsalan otherwise had no meaningful encounters with the elderly man, except perhaps one. One day, Arsalan and Emilio were in a corner of the building playing a game of balancing rocks, which was a common pastime among the apprentices at that time, in which two or more players would take turns using their powers to place small stones, one by one, in a tall stack before the whole thing would collapse. The game was encouraged by the masters to sharpen the young apprentices' magical skills but was strictly prohibited from the walkways in front of the doors where Arsalan and Emilio nonetheless were playing that day to avoid the hot sunlight of the plaza square. They were making such great progress in their game they did not notice Master Conrad himself emerging from some shadowy recess behind them, his arm full of books, gazing intently at his feet as he trundled. The old man, upon encountering the two boys, stopped suddenly, startling them. Arsalan felt the old man's watery but keen blue eyes burn into him for a few prolonged seconds before turning to look at Emilio with deep, sour suspicion. The sheer unpleasantness of that look disturbed Arsalan so much that he never forgot it. Arsalan was certain he and Emilio would be punished, but then Conrad's gaze quickly flitted to the stack that the two boys had built, which reached to twice the height of a man. Arsalan then thought he had caught a glimpse of wonder and begrudging astonishment in Master Conrad's glare at the stack, but before the boy could be certain, the old man looked down again and continued walking as if nothing had happened. Arsalan watched the old man shuffle down the length of the arcaded, columned balcony then turn and vanish again into one of the sable oaken doors. Emilio was shaken and tense, but he then found it within himself to turn to Arsalan with the bright, relieved, and mischievous grin of a robber having escaped a bank with all its money.

Arsalan and Emilio loved each other as brothers, and yet perhaps for this reason developed into the fiercest of rivals. Arsalan's skill at balancing rocks impressed everyone at the Guild, most of all Emilio, who despite his outward graciousness watched Arsalan's progress with increasing concern and envy. So rapid was Arsalan's advancement in his crafts that he became a journeyman at the same time as the older Emilio, a fact that was not lost on the older one. This was probably why the older boy's public congratulation of Arsalan, as gracious as it was, seemed somewhat cooler than it should have been. But Arsalan was certain that his best friend had not been too injured by the fact, as after a time Emilio's mood improved and they appeared to be on normal terms again. In fact, after this, Arsalan found it difficult to keep pace with Emilio's ambitious progress. It seemed that Emilio had devised a new strategy to outdo Arsalan, or at least to avoid direct competition with him. Whereas Arsalan's structures were forthrightly tall and broad and sweeping in scope, Emilio opted instead for elaboration and intricacy, for moving parts and hidden entryways, unusual floor plans, optical illusions, and bedazzling colors. Arsalan observed this development gladly, for he knew that by adopting two distinct stylistic approaches, the chances of their work being compared against each other were mitigated. And indeed, for this reason the two boys were then seen by their masters more as equals.

"Oh, Emilio Ubaldini," Arslan thought before sleeping in bed one night. "My dear friend and brother. I miss you so. What happened to us? Where are you now? Oh, how I'd love to be with you at the Guild again."

Perhaps, Arsalan thought, he was still in Rome or Florence making cathedrals with subtly mazelike interiors that would confuse parishioners and clergy alike for years. Arsalan chuckled to himself at this, for he knew Emilio's sense of humor. Arsalan wondered how Emilio would take the news of the collapse of the World's Leaf. Would he pity Arsalan? Would he laugh in his kindly mocking way? Arsalan loved that laugh of Emilio's. It was a triumphantly lighthearted lilt, one that rose above the rooftops and flew in circles in the blue winds and called Arsalan out of his brooding and revealed his weighty concerns as the mere trifles they were.

Strangely, among all this, Arsalan found Grozda dwelling in his dreams like some sort of ghost. She appeared from the shadows of his sleep with her interrogating brown eyes and grave visage and probing words that poked him like fingers on the sorest points of his soul that he wished to conceal, insisting that he reveal them to her. The sensation of the fingertips of her searching was irritating yet tickling and honeyed and deeply stirring. In his dreams he was afraid of Grozda yet drawn to her, and as her face approached his he felt his breath become hoarse and his heartbeat began to thrum. He awoke and sat up in bed to listen to the dark winds cry. Kizil crawled over to him in the darkness as if to console him, investigating him with her cold, wet nose, and he petted her until they both slept again.

Kizil was responsible for the preservation of Arsalan's sanity that first, long, desolate winter on top of his mountain. He talked endlessly to her. At the height of winter, he took to drinking heavily again. Each evening, beginning after supper and raging on to bedtime, he would become roaringly drunk, swaying in his seat and talking to his cat as if she were a stranger at a tavern, retelling his stories as if she had never heard them before. His eyes would grow bloodshot, and his voice would become slurred, and he would spit as he spoke and paused for breath after each phrase. His comically gesticulating arm would set him off balance in his own seat, and he often would end his tirades with fierce arguments and insults levied at unseen opponents or with jags of weeping and sobbing into his own sleeve.

After many days of this, it was as if Arsalan's drunken self, as distinguishable from his sober self as another man, became lucidly aware of its own behavior and predicament. For the first time, on one night of drunkenness that in all other ways resembled all the others, Arsalan stopped talking, and his eyes focused on Kizil in a gaze of wonder laced with suspicion. He pointed his finger in the air with his wavering arm and then, slowly, unsteadily, eased it down to point at the cat.

"You can talk," said Arsalan seriously. "I swear you can talk. You sit and stare and listen to my words every day, and for that I am grateful, but it seems you have thoughts and ruminations of your own you do not express to me. You don't say anything to me. Maybe it is simply because you have a feline mouth and not a human mouth. But you can talk. Oh yes, I swear you can talk."

Of course, at this Kizil said nothing and just blinked her lustrous green eyes at him. Then, gently, tactfully, spontaneously, she tiptoed over the table's surface toward him, looking at him in his face. Arsalan responded by petting her, as he always had done. "You have become such a beautiful cat now, but now with such a disgusting, slobbering old man like me. Why do you stay? And if you must stay, why don't you talk to me? I am in obvious and dire need of a conversationist."

Kizil began to paw at her collar, pulling at it from below her chin as if wanting to remove it.

"Oh, my dear cat," said Arsalan. "Your collar is irritating you. I never removed it. It probably has been chafing your neck all this time. Here, let me unclasp it, and you can go without it for some time."

It was a challenge for Arsalan in his inebriated state to fetch his reading glasses and to unlatch Kizil's collar in the dim light of a lamp. He mumbled to himself as he tried to work the clasp, taking great care not to hurt his pet in any way.

"It would be easier if I wasn't drunk," muttered Arsalan, before bursting into laughter, and then, after a few minutes, recomposing himself well enough to resume his knotty task.

After some moments, Arsalan found himself with the unclasped collar in his left hand, and the cat cleaning and grooming the fur on her neck in unusually wild gestures of glorious relief, licking her paws and smoothing it all down, and then rolling around on the tabletop on her back. Arsalan could not recall how he had removed the collar, but he was glad Kizil was happy. He noticed something odd about the clasp. In its mechanism, there seemed to be an object hidden, a small piece of paper, folded into a tidy and compact rectangle and inserted there. Arsalan removed it and unfolded it. Peering by the low, orange light of a candle, he saw lines of Roman script written in neat and clear penmanship, but he could not read it. Not only was it in another language, but it was a language he could not identify by sight.

"Oh, dear me," said Arsalan. "I'll have to look at this again tomorrow morning for it's too late and I'm too drunk and I can't recall my languages. Maybe it's some form of Latin." And with this, Arsalan went to bed.

The next morning, after he had recovered from his hangover, he observed the mysterious note with fresh though slightly blurry eyes in the snowy morning light.

"I still can't determine the language, my dear cat," said Arsalan, "but I am guessing it is a set of instructions on how to return you to your previous owners if you are lost. Perhaps your owners were foreigners, and this is the only language they knew. Well, if that were the case, it's too late now, because now here you are in the Balkans with me, and you are my cat, and I have named you Kizil."

"Of course, I can't be certain," added Arsalan, "and I am intrigued by this note. So, I'll refer to my books."

Arsalan had made sure to bring with him on his journey a small library of his most essential tomes: reference guides on structural engineering and magical spells, books on geography, astronomy, myth, culture, language, and religion, historical biographies, and a few anthologies of poetry. With the cat standing on his shoulders, he leafed through all of them but could not find any references to the language that was printed in tiny text on the note. Latin, High German, Catalan, Polish, Greek, Flemish; none of them matched. After several days of intermittent research, he gave up and placed the little note in the clasp that held Defne's portrait.

Arsalan carefully placed his books back on the shelf and went outside to chop firewood. Kizil stayed inside, and by the time Arsalan returned, he noticed that the cat had dragged many of the books off the shelf and onto the floor again, where they were opened. The cat sat in front of the books, staring at them curiously with a cocked head, and pawing at the pages. Seeing Arsalan standing over her, the cat looked back at him with a steady gaze and issued a meek, kitten-like mewl from the rear of her throat. Arsalan stood and thought for a long while, before stooping down to pet her.

"My, my, what is this?" he said, "My cat is so intelligent that she reads books, or at least she thinks she can read them and is imitating me. What is going on here? Don't worry. I am not angry."

Arsalan rearranged the books on the floor so that Kizil could continue her play of reading them. He then sat on a chair and watched, but Kizil seemed to revert to more feline behavior, that of licking her fur and then lounging on the open books instead of pretending to read them.

"Why do you disappoint me this way, Kizil?' asked Arsalan quietly, "You attempt to deceive me. Do you playact at being an ordinary cat, or at being more than one? I cannot tell. When I expect you to be a cat, you act as if you are a familiar. When I expect you to be a familiar, you act like a demure cat. Please choose one to be. Maybe just be a cat and stop teasing my expectations! I guess I shouldn't be so cruel, though. I will love you either way. I rescued you when you were just a rotten, flea-bitten rag. Now look at yourself. We both should be glad you are so healthy." Arsalan petted Kizil a few times and walked back out the door to cut more wood.

After a time, it became dark, and Arsalan returned, and this time he noticed his door was slightly ajar. What was more, Kizil was nowhere to be found in the house.

"Kizil?" called Arsalan. "Kizil!" But the cat did not come. Arsalan wandered back outside and looked at all the drifts of snow behind which stood the dark and tangled trees and brush. "Kizil!" he shouted. "Kizil!" He looked around the perimeter of the house. He looked in the stable. He looked in the cellar. He even looked in the outhouse and around the woodpile, and the snow bore no trace of her. His cries for her became hoarser, deeper, more desperate, more commanding, angrier, as he hurried this way and that, in a radius wider and wider, farther from his house in every direction. The wind howled around him, and the moon glared down at him in cold accusation. He held a lantern whose flame threatened to be extinguished in the gales. Finally, he reached the woods by his house and looked within their impenetrable depths with a severe and sudden horror. She was lost, he thought. She wandered off like an idiot, he thought, or because I was impatient with her. "It's my fault!" he cursed out loud. "I didn't cherish her that one moment when I spoke to her last. I took her for granted. I had contempt and derision in my voice, even if just a little. Curse me to hell! Kizil! I'm sorry! Where are you?"

In his panic he raced back to his door, though he could not remember why he was headed there. His mind was spinning, and he paused to collect it, and at that moment, he saw her fur halfway in the door. Kizil peeked out of the doorway at him, and tears came to Arsalan's eyes as he ran to her and stooped down to embrace her.

"Kizil! Where did you go? Why did you leave?" asked Arsalan. But then he noticed a small, dark object lying before her feet: a dead mouse, frozen in agonized sleep.

"Oh," said Arsalan, "you brought me a little gift! I guess you just were being a cat after all!" And he laughed, and his laughter turned to cries and sobs as he sat and hugged the soft, boneless body of his dear Kizil long into the night in the light of the doorway, weeping into her fur. "I'll love you always and I will never leave you unguarded again! I promise! Never leave me like that. Oh, my dear Kizil!" The windblown mountains probably had never heard such pitiable sobs and pleas and promises from such a mature, ageing man since the years when the plague came to seek its victims on this very same plot. But there he was, a lone man secretly broken and defeated several times over, thanking every star above him for this desperately good fortune and promising to devote his last strand of life for the simple love and companionship of a mute, stupid, staring cat.

CHAPTER 7

Several days after a long snowfall, the small plateau around Arsalan's house was a continuous ocean of undulating snowdrifts that appeared to span from mountain peak to mountain peak. It had softened under the warm sunlight of a previous day and then had refrozen overnight into a rigid, shimmering glaze on which one could march without leaving footprints. The open, polar sun shone downward as if through a thick lens and glared painfully off the smooth, glassy ice and colored the wintery desert shades of watery blue and orange, and the remorseless winds swept over it all in singing, blasting gales, inhibited by nothing. It was not a day when one would expect visitors of any sort. Nevertheless, on this most inhospitable day, Arsalan received one.

Arsalan happened to be outside splitting firewood with an ax when Grozda arrived in her donkey cart. They looked at each other for a few moments before the wild winds prompted Arsalan into polite greetings.

"Hello, Ms. Grozda," said Arsalan. "You've come a long way. Welcome. What brings you here?"

"We've been worrying about you, Mr. Arsalan," said Grozda from her seat. "It's been monstrously cold of late, and everyone at the foot of the mountain has been wondering if you're well."

"Not that I mind you coming, but I'm surprised they sent you and not Lyubomir or his brother," said Arsalan.

"I volunteered," she said. "I had some business delivering some of my ale to a cousin close by, and I dropped by to see if you needed some."

"Having more wouldn't be a bad idea," said Arsalan, "as I believe this winter has caused me to exhaust my supply already. But you did not need to trouble yourself with an unprompted delivery."

"Well, thanks to whomever cleared these roads, the trip was made much easier," she said.

"Either way, you must be freezing," said Arsalan. "You must come in for a few moments. I have stew and tea brewing."

After a miniscule but breathless hesitation, Grozda conceded, "I believe it's too cold out here not to accept your invitation, Mr. Arsalan."

She had taken one donkey with her, and they tied it inside the stable by the fire, away from the two horses but well within warmth. Again, Grozda was taken by the majesty of the two Malakans who stood in their stalls nearby while eating their hay, and she could not help but feel their warm, silken pelts with her ungloved hand. She followed Arsalan into the house, where he had a cauldron of lamb and turnip stew, flavored with onions, brewing over the fire along with a pot of tea. Grozda placed the keg of ale on the floor next to the table, while Arsalan doled stew into two bowls and prepared two cups of the black tea, and Arsalan and Grozda began to partake of it at his table. She thanked him, and they looked at each other cautiously and surreptitiously as they ate. Grozda ate daintily, as if trying to be polite, but probably also because the stew was still rather scalding.

They did not offer much exchange over the food until Grozda finally felt obliged to say, "It's very good, Arsalan."

"Thank you," he said. "It's my favorite dish in cold weather."

"You've been well in this weather alone?" she said.

"I've taken care of myself well enough. I've learned a lot about this climate in the meantime," he said.

"I hope you don't mind me mentioning," she said. "I heard more about your missing daughter, and your efforts to find her here."

"Yes," he said.

"I'm sorry to hear about it," Grozda said. "I don't suppose you've heard of any promising leads."

"I'm afraid not," said Arsalan. He looked down into his soup and stirred it as he shook his head.

"Why here, Arsalan?' she asked. "Why Sliven? Why do you think she would be here from so far away?"

"When she was just a little girl, and I used to tell her bedtime stories, I would weave fairy tales involving the wild lands of the Bulgars and its misty, magical mountains full of sprites and spirits. She loved to hear them. When she fled the evil prince, she kept her destination a secret even from me. I was convinced that of all the places to which she may have escaped she would come here, but I still have not found her here."

"Even if she were anywhere here, Arsalan," she said, "I can't imagine where she would be living now during a winter like this."

"Hopefully someplace warm and comfortable," murmured Arsalan.

"I certainly hope so, too," she said.

"How does one manage this weather?" Arsalan asked. "How do you manage it?"

"I'm used to it," Grozda said. "I've lived here all my life. Please don't mind my saying this, but I've been more concerned that since you're from warmer climes, you yourself might freeze to death here."

"I do appreciate your concern," he said.

"It's more than that, Arsalan," she continued. "I don't know how to say this. It may sound foolish, but even before I learned much about your missing daughter, you've been in my thoughts. I've thought of you ever since we met at the festival last fall."

"Ordinarily, I would ask why," he said, "but I think I can sense the reason. You've been in my thoughts, too."

"What do you think it is?" she said. "What is the reason in your heart?"

"You and I," he said, "we both have experienced loss, profound loss. It was evident in you. I only can suppose it was evident in me, too. We share a loss so deep that it sets us apart from those who surround us. We can sense the loss in each other in ways those around us do not see."

Grozda's eyes became dewy, and she paused, looking down into her bowl as if into her soul. "My husband was the very fabric of my life, the ground on which I walked. After he died, I felt as if I was falling, never reaching the bottom. I felt as if nothing around me came together to make any sense. I have my children, and I love them, but my care for them seems more like the motions of a millwheel than the acts of a mother. At the same time, acting like a millwheel gives me a routine sense of purpose. It's simple, daily. I don't have to think too far forward in time, or too far back. I have the same schedule under each sun. It's numbing, but healing."

Grozda paused. Arsalan quietly sipped his stew.

"And you?" Grozda asked. "Did you feel the same when you lost your wife?"

"Luckily, no one died, but I lost everything else," he said. "At the same time, it had seemed that what I possessed already was becoming less meaningful over the years, and that its removal from my life confirmed some suspicion deep within me of its meaninglessness. I was devastated, but I did not fight it. I waited until the devastation was complete, and I rather proudly decided that I no longer would demand what was denied to me."

"Is it possible to stop wanting what was robbed of you?" she asked. "Can it be that simple?"

"No, I want it back every day," he said, staring down at his own food. "But I try not to see myself as a victim of theft. I now see my previous success, in a way, as having been borrowed from the world and not repaid with my gratitude for it."

Grozda looked at the table, and a flash of insight passed over her eyes, and she turned her gaze to Arsalan.

"What were you?" she said. "What were you before you came here?"

"I told you. I was a builder," he said. "But I admit I was more successful than I let on with the folks here when I first arrived. I constructed many buildings for many nobles and merchants. I was a wealthy man. But I am wealthy no more."

"You gave the impression of an educated man, and I suppose it is not hard to guess your education came from wealth," she said, "but no one wanted to mention it."

"Bless this folk," said Arsalan.

"You say you faced a crisis in your career, and I guessed it was a fallen building," she said. "Was I right?"

Arsalan's eyes wandered from his stew to some undefined point on the table, as if regarding something in a distance, and his eyes, too, welled with tears, and he dried them with his sleeve. Arsalan then shook his head.

"I can't say yet," he said.

Grozda put her hand on his arm. "Don't answer," she said. "I'm sorry."

She then thought for a moment. "Could you show me around your property outside?" she asked.

"But it's freezing outside," he said.

"I'll be fine now with your stew," she said.

They bundled in their woolen cloaks and coats again and ventured outside, where the bright, turbulent winds greeted them and flapped the edges of their clothing. Arsalan proudly showed Grozda everything he had built: the house, the cellar, the stable, even the stack of firewood. He explained their construction in the most general of terms to conceal any mention of his magical powers, but he felt that the more he explained, the more questions were silently evoked, and that his secret would remain one no longer. To change the subject, he talked about some of the more mundane buildings whose construction he had overseen in his previous life: the post offices, the bathhouses, the dams, the churches, temples, and mosques. Grozda, however, restrained her questioning and listened, and when he was finished, she instead talked about life on her farm: her barn, her animals, her parents, her children. They both shivered, partially from the cold, and partially from a peculiar nervousness that overtook them.

They looked around at the rocky peaks that sentried their fortified horizon. Chalky snow on black rock, the peaks resembled pyramidal totems of some distant epoch whose painted glory was now deteriorating. But the sun was turning marigold as it began its descent behind the stony summits, and their westward faces mirrored the splendor of the outgoing sun with a fiery blush.

"As long as I've lived here and ridden up and down this mountain, I've never been to this property at the very peak, and I've never seen how beautiful it is up here," she said.

"Yes, it is quite beautiful," Arsalan said.

After a gulping pause, Grozda touched Arsalan on the arm again.

"Arsalan," she said, "I need to tell you I live life honestly and with open eyes. I don't like to fool myself with dreams and promises."

"Then you and I are very much alike," said Arsalan.

"A man has asked for my hand in marriage," said Grozda, "a second cousin of my husband. He is a good and dependable man. We've known each other all our lives. He is a farmer whose wife also died. He can take good care of me and my family. I'm sure my former husband would approve of it from where he is in Heaven."

"Congratulations," said Arsalan. "Have you accepted?"

"No," she said. "My heart is not sure. I don't think I'm ready to marry him or anyone, for that matter, just for convenience."

"Then why did you come here today, Grozda?" asked Arsalan. "Did you want me to ask you for your hand instead?"

"The thought occurred to me, but no, because I sense it would not work between us either," she said. "I suppose I'm more interested in why it wouldn't work between us. I came here to see what I would be missing."

"I am not a farmer, I am not a Bulgar, and I am not of your old friends and family," said Arsalan. "I am an outsider. I do not wish to come between your family members, disrupting their suggested arrangements for you. More importantly, I am not capable of being a good father to your five children or of being a good member of your extended family. They will look at me with suspicion and contempt and discomfort. I am too different, too old, and I am grieving too heavily for the loss of my own family and career, and a man whose heart is weighed with grief cannot lift the hearts or lives of others. He only can drag them downward in his own anguish."

"Everyone I know loves you, Arsalan," she said. "You are humble, charming, and capable. And they sense you are hiding from something. Maybe we can help you heal from your grief. Maybe we can teach you how to farm."

"Perhaps, but jumping into your family is too sudden, I feel, and not a good way to achieve that goal. Also, I am afraid of disappointing others, Grozda," he said, "and I am afraid of disappointing you."

"There is something more you're not telling me about yourself, Arsalan," she said. "There is one last thing you are concealing. I can sense it's important. Tell me, please, if you can."

"Of course there is something I'm concealing from you," said Arsalan, "and its revelation will ruin everything I have built here. No one will look at me the same way, and I will be forced to go elsewhere to live the life I need, and there will be no one in this world who will be able to stop me."

Grozda grasped Arsalan's hands and looked at him. "We are drawn together through our unbearable pain," she said. "I feel this makes us kindred spirits, and that I have known you much longer than I have. I feel if you tell me, I will never tell another soul."

"You must promise," said Arsalan, looking sternly into her eyes.

Grozda nodded, and somehow Arsalan felt a stirring and uncanny trust in her. Arsalan lifted his left hand, and many yards away the snow on the ground began to crumble and to stir. On its own, it gathered into a growing pile that reached skyward. Up and up, it reached, mimicking a plant sprouting from the ground. Grozda watched, not fully comprehending. The giant sprout of snow grew two stories into the air, and from one side grew a single, elephantine leaf, hanging sideways. The rough, snowy texture of this strange and beautiful growth from the snow diminished and became weirdly smooth and shining. All this startled and disturbed Grozda, who held both of her hands in front of her mouth and looked afraid.

"What witchcraft is this?" she stammered.

"Many folks here jest with me by calling me Arsalan the Magnificent because I can fix their barns," he said, "but what they do not realize is that I am the real Arsalan the Magnificent, Arsalan Ozdikmen, member of the Magical Architects' Guild, and I was once considered the greatest magical architect alive. Ubaldini the Ingenious, Marcelle the Marvelous, and Fernando the Fabulous were my peers. I was commissioned by Sultan Muhteşem to build the World's Leaf, a university, looking like this, but one hundred stories high and devoted to world peace. But fortune was not kind to me then, and for some reason my beautiful structure collapsed to the ground in front of all the leaders of the civilized world. My name now lies in shame and infamy."

Arslan made a chopping motion with his left hand, and his sleek model toppled and exploded on the ground into a cloud of fine, white dust.

Arsalan continued, "The Sultan banned me from erecting any more buildings in the borders of the empire. My reputation disintegrated. My family's fortunes dwindled. My family dispersed. Although I still do not know the reason for the building's collapse, the reasons for the crumpling of my life afterward were all clearly my doing, seeded by my own negligence far in advance. And now I am here, chopping firewood."

Arsalan pointed at his woodpile, which immediately disassembled into a cloud of floating logs whirling in circles around each other and then settling back into place as a pile.

Grozda was shaken, at once full of fear and pity. "You are not one of us," she said. "No, definitely you are not. I am afraid of you, Arsalan."

"You wanted to know my secret. There it is. But also know this," he said. "We magical architects assume the vow never to harm any living human soul with our magical powers, only to use our powers to benefit society. It is in our code, stored in our bones. You have no reason to fear me. I am a civilized man. If I had wanted, I could have used my powers to hold my wife captive, to ridicule and to punish the Sultan, to keep my wealth, even to assume control of the empire. But we magical architects are made to realize in the Guild that we are human beings with the gift of channeling powers that course through us but do not originate from us. We are thankful for this privilege. We accept that we are not gods."

"I don't know what to say," said Grozda. "This is all so overwhelming. I suppose I am just a simple farm woman. I never thought I would encounter anyone like you."

"Yet you are not such a simple farm woman," said Arsalan. "You are discerning, insightful, passionate, and strong, and you demand the truth in things. You already have succeeded in haunting my dreams. You have the power to burrow into my soul and to pull the truth from me like yarn. I have met no woman like you before."

"And I have seen that you are a man of the world, and of worlds beyond. I sense you and the larger world are inseparable. You love it so much that divorcing yourself from it causes you suffering. Just as much, the world loves you and is searching for you, and at some point, it will come seeking you here, and I won't be able to constrain you here. It's only a matter of time," said Grozda.

Arsalan lowered his eyes and was silent.

"Thank you for telling me the truth. Forgive me for what I do now, Arsalan, for it isn't proper for a woman like me, but I feel I love you already, even though we've known each other so briefly and can't be together," said Grozda, and she approached him and held her face close to his. She touched his cheek with her hand, and she kissed him on the face. There they stood, with their foreheads together, as the daylight began to dim, and the dome of the sky was illuminated with saffron fire. Arsalan's terrible fears of being embroiled in yet another tortuous love affair were soothed. Arsalan was filled with a deep sense of relief and bliss, and he rejoiced at the understanding to which they both had arrived. They did not have to marry. Grozda drew her face away from Arsalan's, their breath steaming, and they gazed into each other's eyes for a long time with this inexplicable new pact established between them. Arsalan and Grozda then turned and walked together to the stable, entirely without words or rancor. She readied her cart, mounted it, wished Arsalan goodbye, and was off down the powdery road. Inside his house, Arsalan found the keg of ale on the floor by the table. There were two copper para stacked on it, the very same coins he had given her at the festival.

"That woman," Arsalan chuckled, shaking his head.

That night he experienced the deepest sleep he had had in months, perhaps years. It was dreamless and blissful, as black as the universe, and he arose from it with a renewed sense of exhilaration and purpose in the icy, pink dawn. He laughed at everything, every small thing that evoked the merest sense of joy, every breeze and glimpse of sunlight, for he knew he had emerged from his purgatory and that nothing more could hurt him, and he was grateful for every good and beautiful thing he saw.

As it happened, Grozda did not accept her suitor's offer for marriage, and she kept Arsalan's secret to herself.

That spring, Arsalan attended one of the many festivals marking the return of the long, warm days. There were dancing performances by folks in costumes of horns and fur and bells. Everyone wore red and white threads on their wrists, and they adorned their horses with flowers and ribbons and raced the majestic animals across the emerald fields to Arsalan's great delight. It was during these days when Grozda's wedding would have occurred, and from a distance he was able to catch a glance of her previous suitor, a large and boyish man with reddish brown hair who had asked for her hand. The festivities were lovely and merry, and at each one, Arsalan stood toward the fringes, enjoyed himself quietly, and left midway through with flowers in his hand. He laughed along with their mirthful music as he rode back to his house.

Chapter 8

Three years passed, during which Arsalan's monastic life atop the mountain was thriving in its own quiet way. He was now, of course, a little older and a bit more careworn, his face creased and tanned. Stray hairs, now aberrantly long, radiated from the arched brambles of his eyebrows like the loose plaits of partially woven baskets. But it was his uncut hair that compounded his aged appearance. It was much grayer, but still full and vigorous, and he had grown it long and had bound its white wires into a tail on his nape. His beard was also quite ashen, and it had grown so long he could use it as a small scarf. Among these many strange new growths of his was his definite new paunch, which did not concern him too much. In fact, to him it was a sign of contentment and stability. But one also might notice that his stature had shortened just a tad over these years, although anyone who knew Arsalan well enough would not dare mention it.

This stouter, hoarier Arsalan now had something that resembled a small farm, with a modest barn and a chicken coop and a wide pen where he raised sheep for their wool and chickens for their eggs. He even had erected a trellis on which grew twirling, leafy vines pregnant with the plump green gems of grapes. During the day he took the sheep out to the pastures of short grasses that grew near the foot of the looming peak. Shepherding was easy for him; he contained the sheep in a single area with invisible fences of force that rose from the ground while he sat on a log and looked off into the gorgeous distance steeped in honey-eyed sunlight. Here he petted Kizil as he admired the patchwork quilt of crops and homesteads and miniature villages that were stitched together onto the green fabric of the land, and he looked forward to the faint chiming of the steeples at each hour.

For all the time he spent tending sheep, Arsalan could not bear the thought of slaughtering any of them. Only when they died naturally did he think of butchering them for meat, and even then, he brought them to Lyubomir and paid him for his services. Arsalan and spent many hours there in conversation with the wonderful, laughing, naive giant who was now his good friend. But when any of Arsalan's chickens died, he did not wish to trouble Lyubomir with such a small task, so Arsalan attempted that butchery himself, though it never failed to disgust him thoroughly and to ruin his appetite for the rest of the day. At these times he turned to his colorful garden, whose repertoire of vegetables he significantly expanded to include a joyous eruption of carrots and kale and beans and other verdant fare that took his mind away from the deadening sight of animal blood and gore. He consistently produced a surplus of food that he often gave away to friends or, in some cases, used to trade for goods. The irony was not lost on Arsalan that he had become somewhat of a farmer after telling Grozda that he was not one, but he knew that farming was not the issue; it was his solitude and freedom he treasured, and his desire not to be distracted from the activity of his own mind and heart in their acts of ruminative healing.

For the first time in his life, Arsalan had found some fulfillment in nothingness, or at least what resembled nothingness to others, but was in fact silence, the blue sky, a stark mountainside emblazoned crisply onto it, the sound of rain or wind, the sighing of trees, leaves blown across the ground, the call of a bird, or the sight of an owl flying furtively from one branch to another. Daily connection with these phenomena made up the content of his soul and needed no articulation, no validation from others. He felt a desire for little else, except of course, one day to be reunited with his children. He otherwise no longer felt the need to strive, to compete, or to fret. He needed no fame or adulation, and experiences of jealousy or hatred or shame were becoming increasingly foreign to him. He recalled his previous life distantly and with mild impulses of quiet, bittersweet gratitude. On occasion, an emotion from long ago would return afresh and would soak him in days of melancholy, during which he would drink to excess again and would argue with recollections of people from long ago, but after a time he would return to his new mood of gentle, kindly mirth laced with tristesse. Arsalan's tendency to disappear for days at a time in his search for Defne by now was well-known, though ultimately fruitless. His old map was crinkled, worn, torn, and filled with slashes and marks. He could not find Defne anywhere near Sliven, or anywhere further afield, and this was his one true sadness, deep, solid, and insoluble, and one which he kept to himself under his thickening layers of placid self-possession.

The townsfolk had begun to invent new names for this older man: Arsalan the Merry, Arsalan the Mysterious, who would sit at a distance from others with a fey smile on his lips and a crinkle in his eye and whose frequent commentary to others' gossip was a sad, melodious chuckle. Strangers often shared claims that there was magic behind the eccentricity of the old repairman who lived on the mountaintop, although when those new folks met him for the first time to hire him for a task, they found their tantalizing stories disappointed, as they met only a mild-mannered but taciturn codger who displayed no apparent magical qualities whatsoever.

During those three years, Grozda's hair became discernibly streaked with gray, her face a bit rounder and sagging more around the edges, and her bodice, which before could have been described as buxom, was now thicker with the weight of matronly and grandmotherly concerns. Her eldest daughter had two more children, and a son was newly married. In her expansive matriarchal role, her previous desirous intensity lessened to a more empathic demeanor. However, she found it increasingly difficult to discern Arsalan's moods, which became more inscrutable. Now when they met during their errands, she would gaze at him with concern, wonder, faint regret, and yearning, with the eyes and brow of a mother, or a sister, and a former lover all at once, and she would touch him on his forearm as if to detect a familiar vibration.

"I'm worried about you up there on that mountain all alone, Arsalan," she would coo. "No one is meant to live like that for so long. Are you certain you are well? Are you taking good care of yourself?"

Oh, how Arsalan loved Grozda and desired her even now, as unfeasible as their love was. But to various degrees of success, he had tried to subsume his desires for her into a love and compassion for all people and living things, and he practiced exhibiting an avuncular sagacity. To her kind inquiry Arsalan would offer quick assurances laced with gentle laughter, and Grozda looked back at him as if searching for Arsalan's eyes but instead seeing the eyes of a mystic who had happened upon the secrets of existence. She was vaguely saddened at the possibility that he no longer shared any true concern over the mundane details of daily existence that had been the fodder for so many of their fleeting but cherished conversations.

Luckily for Grozda, though, Arsalan's subtle, teasing beatitude would prove more fragile than it had seemed, and more dependent on circumstances, for what is a serene retirement and seclusion but a process of waiting for something else to occur—whether death, illness, misfortune, or fortune—to try to shatter it?

Such an event happened one day while Arsalan was visiting the farrier to buy new shoes for Solmaz that he heard of a man who had strode through town looking for Arsalan. The smocked farrier interrupted his pounding work in his shop, with a hammer in one hand, to tell Arsalan the news.

"He was a tall man. A Turk he was, with a balding head and an upturned nose like this," yelled thin, spritely farrier, pressing the end of his nose upward with his dirty index finger until it looked like a wrinkled pig's snout. Arsalan for the life of him could think of no one who fit such a grotesque description. But the farrier continued.

"He wore a trimmed beard, like a rich man," said the farrier, scratching this sides of his own hoary jaws with his fingernails, "and what's more, he rode a great, black stallion, as big as a carriage, gleaming with glossy fur, it did. A beautiful thing, with feet as big as my head. I would have loved to make shoes for that horse if I had the apprentices to help me carry them around, so big those horseshoes were."

"Did you tell him where I was?" asked Arsalan.

"Are you crazy?" said the farrier. "I didn't let on. I don't care how rich he was. We don't take kindly to strangers such that we leave ourselves vulnerable to their interloping here. Remember when you first came here? I didn't say anything to him about you. 'I don't know who you're talking about,' I said to him, 'Go on and look elsewhere.' Then he left, with his horse clopping on the ground with those beautiful, shiny shoes. Such craftsmanship!"

The farrier then proceeded to elaborate on the horse's shoes in so much detail that he lost Arsalan's interest altogether, and Arsalan was confused and could not think of who this mysterious visitor was at all. Eventually, the farrier's wife eventually came by to fetch him and to tell him to get back to work.

Then later it was reported by Lyubomir that a man had stopped by the shop asking for Arsalan but did not leave a name. Lyubomir's description of the enquirer matched that given by the farrier, with some intriguing additional detail.

"He had an affected manner, learned, like you, but vaguely—how to say—effeminate. Foppish, you might say. A man of means, but a friendly man, no doubt, and one who could handle a strong horse. The size of that thing! A horse's horse! I would spend a week butchering it! Not that I would want it dead, mind you. A gorgeous beast, it was!" said Lyubomir, leaning against his counter with both huge hands, sweeping a thick arm through the air whenever he described the majestic stallion.

Even Lyubomir, as guileless and voluble as he usually was, felt uncomfortable revealing the location of his friend's Arsalan's abode to the imposing stranger. Thus, for now, Arsalan was safe from unexpected visitors from afar. But still, the stories began to test his sense of serenity, and he chose to venture seldom from his property and found himself drifting into apprehensive moods during which he spied on the outside world from within his windows as if hiding from a rumor of nameless menace. At other times, he chose to take walks in the woods by his house so that the probing stranger would not find him at home. This he could do only for so long until he felt like a coward and a fool for keeping himself out in the cold for seemingly nothing, like someone afraid of ghosts in the house.

In late Spring, after a week or two with no further reports, Arsalan felt safer, and decided to enjoy the chilly morning air. He sat on a log in front of his house one brisk, pinkish gray morning, dressed in a thick brown tunic of coarse lambswool with a high collar while playing his cura.

Arsalan's father had taught him how to play the cura when Arsalan was just a child, before his parents had discovered his magical talents. After this ecstatic discovery, all else was swept aside and forgotten in favor of fostering Arsalan's thaumaturgical skills, everything including the small, quiet evening hours Arsalan's father used to spend with him each week to teach him a chord or a phrase or a technique.

His father had his own instrument and had bought Arsalan the one he now held. Together they sat in the small study after evening prayers, surrounded by shelves of ledgers and papers, where it smelled of freshly varnished wood, odorous and authoritative. Arsalan still could hear his father's voice there.

"Not so stridently on that note," said his father, demonstrating. His fingers were played across the neck of the instrument like a spider while he pointed with the index finger and thumb of his other hand. "Like this. Don't hammer it out. Draw it out. Draw the notes out like a love letter from an envelope, like perfume from a phial." Arsalan at first would look in wonder and incomprehension, and then he would smile, before trying his best to imitate his father's practiced motions.

Arsalan inwardly had regretted the abandonment of these informal lessons with his father, who ordinarily was such a tense and busy man that he could find no other such time for his son. These weekly evening lessons with his father reassured Arsalan that his father could take the time to slow himself and to demonstrate his love for his son in this intimate, calming, and spontaneous way. But nothing was said about the music lessons again after Arsalan was sent to the Guild. However, though he did not play it anymore, Arsalan kept the cura with him, locked in its case and stored somewhere under a bookshelf or in a trunk, wherever he lived. It was a piece of his father's love and attention he carried with him, one he guarded so jealously that he had not given any thought of teaching the instrument to his own children. How terrible I am, thought Arsalan, to deny this to them, and as soon as I find my children again, I will teach them, and if they have given me grandchildren, I will teach them.

In any case, his time on the mountain had been the perfect opportunity to resume practicing. Whenever his mind needed soothing, he brought out the stringed instrument and strummed it, straining to recall the lessons his father had taught him many decades ago in that lovely study. He loved how the cura so anticipated the act of singing that it softly rang while simply being taken from the case. He immediately could sense how it needed to be tuned. Arsalan was somewhat surprised to be able to recover the skills he had cultivated before he quit the cura, but it was a long while before he could conquer his urge simply to repeat his old childhood lessons instead of breaking through with some determination into greater mastery of the instrument. When he finally did so there on Sliven, he felt almost sad to leave his amateurism behind. Now he played a dulcet and wistful ballad. He had heard it somewhere before but could not recall its name, or for that matter the lyrics, or even the whole piece. It was about a god, or a homestead, or a farm. It did not matter. He improvised a new song from the portion he could remember. No one was there to hear it or to judge his performance. While he gently drew the bittersweet melodies from his instrument, he thought of Teodora, Defne, Asker, and Omer, and he wordlessly dedicated the music to them.

Kizil was there as his audience, and what an adorably impolite audience she was; sometimes bored and drowsy and yawning, sometimes restless, and only halfway interested, turning this way and that and strutting aimlessly, and sometimes leaping onto Arsalan's shoulders and draping herself there. Arsalan nonetheless was so lost in his playing and so accustomed to Kizil's antics that he did not notice anything else, not the birds, the wind, the sun, or a stranger who was approaching him on the road that ran up the hillside toward his house.

It was a balding man with a large, pointing nose and a nicely trimmed beard, riding high on his striding stallion. As he neared Arsalan, he commanded his horse to slow its walk, noticing that the ageing man's back was toward him, perhaps wishing to surprise him. Arsalan did not hear the horse's heavy footsteps behind him until it was several paces away. Arsalan then suddenly ceased his music and stared off into the ground in front of him but did not turn.

"Do you know how difficult it is to get hold of you?" said the visitor.

Arsalan turned halfway around and coyly averted his gaze to the grass.

"Have you thought that maybe there's a reason for that?" he answered.

"What in the heavens are you even doing in a place like this," said the man, "with not a bathhouse or a café in sight?"

Arsalan turned completely around this time and gazed up at the visitor. He recognized the man immediately.

"Bayram!" he exclaimed. "I think the question is more pertinent when applied to you! What brings you all the way here?"

"Is that any way to greet your loyal agent after so long?" said Bayram. "And after braving a hundred leagues of dusty roads full of bandits!"

"You're a fool to make a journey like that. But then again, you are a businessman," said Arsalan. "You should be used to bandits!"

The two old men broke their ironically stone-faced playacting and burst into raw and hearty laughter. Bayram jumped from his horse and Arsalan stood, and they embraced like long-lost brothers. Bayram's plain brown cloak opened to reveal a suede outfit that, although not ostentatious, was thick and well-tailored enough to speak of money.

"Look at you!" said Arsalan. "Who is your tailer, eh?"

"Look at you!" said Bayram. "You look as old as I feel!"

"I feel sorry for you!" replied Arsalan. "How did you find me?"

"Well, there's a lot to explain," said Bayram, "if you will have me as a boarder for the night, in your...er...cottage there."

"Of course, my old friend," said Arsalan gesturing toward the house. "Isn't it wonderful?"

"Quite quaint!" said Bayram. "But look, let me get down to business here. I have a job for you."

Arsalan's face turned serious.

"Dragon's dung!" he said. "How you jest. You know I am finished with that life. I told you before I left. No more building! No more magical architecture! I'm done!"

"I'm serious, my friend," said Bayram. "There's potentially a lot of money for this one. You could regain all your fortune. You could have it all back!"

"I don't want it back! It's poison, those riches! It turned me into an insufferable buffoon who treasured nothing real! I want no part of it!" yelled Arsalan. "Be off if that's what you came for!"

"My friend, my friend, calm yourself. It's been a few years. Things have changed. I have to explain it to you," pleaded Bayram.

Arsalan paused, remembered his manners, and assuaged his own agitation with a sharp and heavy sigh and an apologetic bob of his head.

"I'm sorry, Bayram. I thought I'd gone beyond my loss, but I suppose part of me still suffers from it. You've come a long way. Come inside. You must be famished," he said.

Inside, Arsalan served his favorite dish of lamb stew with turnips, this time with chives and radishes. Bayram sat at the rustic, sturdy table and looked around him at Arsalan's small dwelling with its low ceiling and reassuringly hefty rafters.

"I have to say that for a cottage it's very well made," he said. "Quite cozy."

"It was a joy to construct after all those pretentious palaces I had built," said Arsalan, pouring Bayram some tea.

"I wouldn't be too critical of your own work, Arsalan the Magnificent," said Bayram. "Everyone knows it was the best magical architecture in the world."

"Was?" asked Arsalan.

"Something has been happening to the buildings over the past few years. Not only your magical structures, but all of them," said Bayram. "Ever since the collapse of the World's Leaf, all the other magical structures have been falling apart as well. Jawahir's Egg, you remember, the building shaped like an ovum that hovered over its round marble base in a bay? It dropped, slowly, onto its bottom, and then rolled over. The exterior is beginning to chip. Your Diamond Dams of Rotterdam are beginning to leak. One of Marcelle's palaces, the one in Paris supported by a single tree, also fell, and now the tree is in the middle of the reception room, surrounded by rubble. And I won't even talk about the Inverted Pyramids that Sigrid built."

Arsalan received this news with alarm. "Why is all this happening?" he said.

"Magic depletion," said Bayram. "Just like yours. But no one knows why. It's slow and steady, block by block, Gradual deterioration. Everyone is losing faith in magical architecture. I don't know how much you've heard here, but popular sentiment has turned against it. Nobles want less and less to do with it because they don't believe in its durability."

"Huh!" snorted Arsalan. "So, it's not just me! Maybe magic itself is bunk!"

"That's surprising to hear from you, of all people, Arsalan," said Bayram.

"Not so much considering what I went through," said Arsalan. "Now everyone can see why my faith in myself was so shaken that I had to go into exile!"

"Well, it's not universal, Arsalan. There are a lot of people who still believe in it," said Bayram.

"But why should they believe in it?" asked Arsalan, "Maybe the doubters are right! Maybe magical structures aren't necessary! Maybe magic is just some superficial gimmick to make exotic structures that only increase the prestige of a wealthy noble or merchant! Maybe magic is just so much cheap glue that has nothing to do with real engineering principles! Maybe we never understood this glue or how quickly it could dry and could flake off!"

"Arsalan! It's not all lost!" said Bayram. "We can do research into magic to see why it has been failing us! We still have the time and energy to further the cause of magical architecture. There's still a lot of business to be done!"

"With me?" Arsalan said, pointing to himself. "But I have no reputation!"

"No, you don't, except with two people who never stopped believing in you," said Bayram. "Me and your potential new client."

Arsalan was silent and stared at the table.

"When that building collapsed, I wept, too! When your life fell to pieces, I grieved! When you left everything behind and refused to tell anyone where you were going, I understood, but it was like a knife through my heart. I felt I was losing a brother and an era was ending!" said Bayram. "Back then, before the disaster, it was beautiful. I was working with the most talented magical architects in the world. All of us, we were a team, a community. I'm positive we can bring it all back."

"What's the job you have in mind?" asked Arsalan.

Bayram said, "There is a princess of Bavaria whose name is Berthilde of the house of Wittelsbach. She is in line to assume the throne. I don't understand their line of succession entirely. She has an advisor named Siegfrieda Hildburghausen, who is much older and is like an aunt to the princess, but ultimately yields to the princess' ruling. Siegfrieda's counsel to the princess is often sterner and more skeptical. Berthilde is a firm believer in magical architecture since many of Conrad the Ineffable's works lie within her realm and she was raised listening to tales about him. Princess Berthilde sent delegates to contact me at my house. She asked for you specifically. She wants to repair Conrad's old structures, which are beginning to deteriorate as well."

"Which structures?" asked Arsalan.

"She wants to start with The Turret of Fürstenfeldbruck," said Bayram.

"Really?" asked Arsalan. "The twenty-story Turret! How much repair work does it need?"

"The roof tiles need repair, and no one else has the ability to reach the top," said Bayram.

"The roof," said Arsalan.

"Yes! Isn't that grand?" asked Bayram excitedly.

"You want me to travel all the way to Bavaria to repair a roof," said Arsalan.

"The roof of the Turret of Fürstenfeldbruck! Who else can reach the top of that but one with magical powers?" said Bayram.

"Do I look like a crane?" asked Arsalan. "I'm a wizard!"

"My friend," said Bayram, "this will be the first of many tasks that will grow in scope. You start with that one, and then, as you get their trust, you can continue with all the other work she has in store. And then her court can be your exclusive client!"

"I'm not an itinerant roofer!" said Arsalan.

"At least you won't be repairing wheel hubs and barns and donkey carts for farmers in exchange for copper!" yelled Bayram.

"Who told you what I do here?" barked Arsalan.

"Asker," said Bayram, "who also told me where you live."

"You wrote him?" Arsalan asked.

"Yes!" said Bayram. "He is a man, after all, who can correspond with whom he wants."

"Damn that boy! I mean, that man!" chucked Arsalan. "If he doesn't get himself killed in war, I'll beat his bottom."

"You don't belong here, Arsalan," said Bayram. "You can do better than to live here among the Bulgar peasants. You always could have done better than to abandon your life. You could have persevered, but you were so demoralized!"

"They are more than just Bulgar peasants here," said Arsalan. "They've become my family. They are humble people with hearts and minds and histories. When a person is in need, Bulgars don't scatter away like scared roaches. They congregate to offer help."

"That's very nice, I'm sure," said Bayram, "and I'm sure that if I ran away and lived in exile here, or anywhere in the middle of nowhere, I'll discover everything about the hospitable natives. But I wouldn't do that."

"That's because you have no shame," said Arsalan.

"Well, yes, that may be true," said Bayram, pointing in the air, "but you have too much of it. You have too much fragile pride, and too much shame festering beneath it! You must relinquish the humiliation in which you've been wallowing for so many years. It's time to stand up and to reclaim your magnificence! It's time to show the world that magical architecture can rise again!"

"And if I don't accept the job?" asked Arsalan. "Or rather, if I can't?"

"Well," said Bayram, sighing, leaning back and crossing his legs, "there's always Ubaldini. I've heard he may be available. He doesn't live too terribly far from here."

"Ubaldini," repeated Arsalan absently.

"Yes, Emilio Ubaldini the Ingenious, your friend," said Bayram, "and your rival."

"Emilio," said Arsalan, staring into the distance. "What has he been doing lately?"

"Lately," said Bayram, dipping bread into his stew, "he's been terribly busy repairing his own structures. The conveyor tiles in the Blue Plaza have stopped moving, for one thing, and he can't seem to get them working again. The crystal lights in the Cathedral in Turin have gone out. It's a mess, I tell you. But he always can turn around to repair a roof at a moment's notice."

Their conversation faltered, and they both fell into thought while eating. Arsalan stared down into his own soup bowl like a troubled mystic searching for answers in a dark well, while Bayram ate his piece of bread while watching Arsalan patiently, almost predatorily.

After the meal, Bayram softened his tone to calm the conversation. Bayram knew how to manipulate people; he was so skillful at it that he could succeed even when his victim was fully cognizant of Bayram's techniques. The victim, in the natural flow of conversation, simply had no defense. Bayram the agent was like a musician with his listener as the instrument. He was not predatory with his talents but worked ultimately for a mutual benefit that often only he was intelligent enough to foresee.

The two spent the rest of the day exchanging news with each other. Bayram told Arsalan all about the escapades of the colorful magical architects. Sigrid had been commissioned by the Estonians to build a theater hall, but instead built a stadium that could double as one, with a retracting roof. This angered the king in Tallinn, but upon seeing the new creation, he was immediately taken by it and showered Sigrid with praise. Fernando was building a summer house for his Queen with a grand solarium that faced the sea; its framework of windowpanes emitted orange light as the evening sky above the waters turned dark blue. Otherwise, Fernando was sworn to secrecy about certain other accoutrements. And Fahim the Fathomless was hired by the Emperor of India to construct an underground temple in the Himalayas that delved thirty stories into the ground and contained a library, all of which was still under construction.

Arsalan showed Bayram his homestead, with its little barn and coop, its pen of braying, stumbling sheep and clucking, fluttering chickens, and the stable and the cellar. Arsalan showed Bayram the garden and the grapes, in which Bayram displayed most interest before turning his attention to the more stunning view from the plateau. Arsalan presented his farm with a humble, radiant pride that Bayram carefully chose not to mock but accepted with kindly remarks and appreciative nods as he toured the property with his arms linked behind his back. This indicated to Arsalan that the agent was putting forth effort to be impressed with the quaint farm, but inwardly found it difficult to be dazzled by them, especially when compared with the news he had brought of the temples, palaces, and theaters the other magical architects were constructing. Arsalan fell silent and realized he could see no reason why Bayram should be so impressed in the first place. These types of little farms existed everywhere, after all. For the first time in three years, he now saw his house and property, in contrast to the wider world from which he had arrived, as more of the temporary campground it had been, one where he had been hiding while he waited for something else to happen. Arsalan learned many valuable lessons about simplicity and renunciation in his time on the mountains, but now he felt that these lessons had been suitably learned. He could tell Bayram all about his experiences being at peace with silence and nature and cultivating a love for all living things during his reclusion here, but Arsalan knew that he would be simply reiterating his knowledge and that Bayram would not understand the value of it much. Bayram was still an urbane man of worldly society with concerns that flew above the countryside from one city to another like migrating birds, and his arrival was a message that the world was calling for Arsalan's return. Bayram's arrival stoked in Arsalan a certain fresh, new need that surprised him. It was an itch, like skin healing beneath a dried scab. This inkling did not concern so much his past glamour, glory, or envy toward his fellow magical architects as before. No, it was something deeper and more substantial, resembling a desire for the vindication of his namesake, perhaps, but somehow more wholesome, more yearning. This strange new urge mingled with his already dwindled and threadbare hopes of ever finding Defne here and placed him in a deeply contemplative mood. Arsalan now discovered deep within his bones the feeling that he needed to move on from his house on the mountaintop.

At night Bayram slept in the spare bed on the upper floor, while Arsalan stood on the lower floor and looked out a window long into the night. He stood straight with his arms behind him, all the while muttering the same names over and over. "Ubaldini," he whispered. "Ubaldini…Defne…Defne." Arsalan barely moved, such that in the morning, when Bayram awoke and descended, he found Arsalan in the same position.

"You haven't slept," said Bayram.

"My sheep," said Arsalan in a gravelly voice, "and my chickens. I'll need someone to tend to them. And I'll need someone to look after my property while I'm gone."

"And your cat?" asked Bayram tactfully.

"She comes with me," declared Arsalan.

Arsalan did not consider it proper to sell his livestock to his friends; the idea seemed too transactional for him. Instead, he decided to give the animals away to Radimir and to Grozda. Radimir, however, did not think that it was proper to accept a free donation, and insisted upon paying Arsalan, who relented and accepted the small stack of silver. Grozda, on the other hand, knew Arsalan more deeply than Radimir, and accepted the livestock with a warm and knowing smile at Arsalan's plans for departure.

"So, do you see?" said Grozda. "The world is calling you back to it, just as I told you. Your talents will be in demand again, even at your age."

"You were right, it seems," said Arsalan, "but I am restrained as to my expectations of where this will lead. They are only small jobs."

"You and I both know where this will lead," said Grozda. "Back to where you belong. It took longer than I thought. In fact, over the years, I thought it would never happen, and I began to regret telling you that a marriage between us would not work. But now I see that if we had wedded, I might be saying goodbye to my husband today. I love you, Arsalan. I say this without shame or pride, without any plans to elicit love from you in return. I say this as a factual description of my heart. I have loved you ever since I first saw you on the night of the autumn festival. But it didn't feel right, and I had to make a choice, and here we are."

"And I love you," said Arsalan. "I have not met any other woman like you. I loved you so much that I was afraid of you. I regret that we did not meet under more normal and fortuitous circumstances. You make me wish I had been a farmer instead of a magical architect."

"I would not wish that for you," said Grozda. "You are now what you are now. Now go accept your job and recover what you have lost."

She embraced him and dried her tears from her eyes, and she kissed him on the face again.

Arsalan wrote a letter to Asker informing his son of his good fortune and that a forthcoming letter would arrive from Munich. As always, he implored Asker to tell him if he had heard from Defne, Omer, or Teodora, though he knew Asker simply would reply, as he always had during their three years of correspondence, that he had not heard from any of them.

The time came to tell Lyubomir of his plans to depart Sliven for repair jobs in Bavaria, though Arsalan still maintained the secret of its magical nature, as he had done with the entire community. Lyubomir's response to Arsalan's news was one of sonorous laughter of pride and delight.

"So!" he bellowed over his butcher's counter. "Your reputation has gone beyond our little mountain town here, it has, and now even kings and queens want their houses repaired by you! What fortune! Now you can become richer, my friend! Good luck to you! Come back with many tales to tell us! We'll keep an eye on your little abode for you!"

It was difficult for Arsalan to decide what to pack. He honestly did not know how long he would be gone. He decided to take a fifth of his gold wealth, before changing his mind and taking all of it. He packed all his clothes and his small library and his box of papers and letters, and he still did not know if that would be sufficient, or too much. Eventually, he packed everything of value in the house, leaving behind only his box of spare copper and silver coins. He locked his door with a key, and then placed a locking spell on the entire house for good measure to render it impenetrable, and then he cast a spell for inflammability, and another to prevent leaks.

Kizil sat, waiting, on the seat of the packed carriage, to which Arsalan's two fine horses were reined. Arsalan stood in front of his beloved little cottage, silently and poignantly, where he already had spent so many blissful months and seasons. It was empty and dark, and his property was silent, no longer bustling with the stirring, clucking, and braying of livestock. He found it even more difficult to separate himself from this house than it was to pack for the journey. But Bayram was waiting for him at an inn in town, and Arsalan had to leave to meet him. Slowly, Arsalan turned and walked to the carriage and mounted it. A desire tugged at his heart, surprising him. It was a desire to return to his little kingdom of peace and solitude and solace after his labor for the faraway princess was completed. But he thought to himself, don't be a fool, the work may lead you to better things, and you never found your daughter here anyway.

Arsalan, Kizil, and his horses made their way down the mountain road. Some of the folk there, seeing him pass, and hearing of the news of his leaving, made sure to be standing at the fronts of their houses to wave goodbye to him. Arsalan wished they had not done so. It was heart-wrenching and it made him want to cry, especially knowing that these were the very same people who glared at him so blankly when he first arrived three years ago.

Arsalan met Bayram at the inn, which of course happened to be the finest inn in Sliven. Arsalan realized he had never set eyes on this inn, as he had done his best to avoid the world of wealth to the best of his ability, as if all wealthy folk were spies who would report Arsalan's decrepit situation to some central authority. These vague and irrational suspicions had dissipated, and now the old magical architect stood before the inn, gazing upward at it and admiring its elaborate architectural features and wondering if he ever would stay in a place like this again. Eventually, Bayram emerged, carrying his sacks. Arsalan was impressed that a man as old as himself could maintain such a trim and dashing figure and could travel so lightly. But Arsalan recalled that Bayram was a capable and resourceful man for whom nothing was a serious obstacle. Arsalan watched Bayram latch his baggage onto the gleaming black stallion in swift and assured motions. In just a few minutes, Bayram was sitting on the horse and looking back at Arsalan, waiting for the magical architect to flip his reins so they could be off.

"Just like old times, eh?" said Bayram, smiling and adjusting his cloak.

And off they went, toward the city of Munich where a princess awaited them.

CHAPTER 9

It had been a long time since Arsalan and Bayram had spent so much time together, and Bayram used every iota of it to update Arsalan on gossip both old and new. Arsalan, during his time on the mountaintop, had avoided gossip as much as possible among the farmers and village folk so he could dodge becoming its subject, and this caused Arsalan to react guardedly to Baryam's stories. Soon enough, though, he began to warm to the information, reacting to Bayram's accounts with small giggles and chortles, and Arsalan prodded his trusty agent for more. At length, the old man was laughing out loud from mere joy of hearing about his friends again and how their personalities and quirks had persisted into a type of perverse legend.

Irakli Gonashvili was a particularly entertaining topic of conversation. Gonashvili the Giant was his public title. He was known for his imposingly massive but functional structures that lacked any sort of loveliness. It was Irakli's philosophy that form should follow function and that decoration was a waste of time and good material. For this reason, he was often employed to build dams, fortifications, bank vaults, and other impenetrable structures. Plainly cut stone was his material of choice. The King of Sweden made the mistake of hiring him to design a tremendous theater that could fit the entire population of the capital all at once. Irakli built the theater to the king's vague specifications, but to the king's horror it turned out to be a towering volume of flat, featureless stone walls that, although acoustically sound, resembled some sort of cellar. The king was then forced to hire Marcelle the Marvelous to adorn it, at greater expense.

Elsewhere, Dimitra Oroglas the Blue was commissioned by the mayor of Argos to construct a city hall, which she built to look as if it were made of gleaming white porcelain lavished with blue ornamentation that slowly changed over time. Anastasia Chumak the Austere had built a cathedral in Kiev of black lava rock that stayed warm throughout the brutal winters there, and a bridge over the Dnieper consisting of the same material. And Hratchouhi Kirakosyan the Colorful had built a fancy, modern office building for a government bureau in Brussels that dealt with trade, although some felt the teeming ornamental stonework was a bit excessive, especially when it moved. Gustav the Golden had contracted a serious illness before recovering but was able to complete his commission of a causeway, connecting Hamburg to Berlin, that glowed at night with a reassuring yellow light. There were a few new names and faces who recently had become masters but who had not assumed any titles: a man named Ramūnas who hailed from Vilnius, a woman named Majdouline from Tunis, and another whose name Bayram could not recall.

Arsalan and Bayram talked long into each night they travelled together over the roads to Bavaria, through forests and valleys, over mountains and by lakes, through the heat and the rain, through Plovdiv and Sophia, through Niš among the Serbs, and many towns between there and Belgrade populated by hospitable but toughly incredulous folk who regarded the two strangers with cautious accommodation. Arsalan and Bayram stayed in the finest inns in the Balkans, which were not terribly expensive, or, for that matter, especially fine, either. The two men kept to themselves and started few conversations with others while Arsalan made a valiant effort to refrain from alcohol, even at the insistence of boisterously gregarious natives who wanted drinking partners and story-swappers at their tables. At night while he listened to Bayram snoring in the next bed, Arsalan found himself missing his little cottage and worried if it was safe from fire, thieves, and rain. He missed his garden with its vegetables, as he found the fare at the inns too meaty, greasy, and bready. He also did not feel entirely safe in the inns; and often he felt the need to descend to the stables to make sure his two Malakans were treated well and that his carriage was secure.

The two Turks were compelled to take many precautions against burglars and bandits. In addition to Arsalan's magic powers, Bayram concealed a long dagger in his pant leg that he rarely drew, except to inspect and to sharpen. Bayram was always able to negotiate safe passage through each province and each region with flattering words and carefully placed bribes to local police and guardsmen, who would accompany them for a brief time, providing news and conversation for restless Bayram. In this way, the two proceeded all the way to Zagreb, Ljubljana, Kranj, Villach, and finally to Salzburg, where they stopped to rest for a week. They were familiar with this route from their previous travels, and they knew that Salzburg was a good refuge in which to recuperate while listening to music, whose harmonies flowered from every window, cascading onto the cobblestone streets below, especially in the wealthier sections of town. Arsalan was so familiar with the lively and refined city of Salzburg that he knew a few notable statesmen and diplomats who lived here and who surely would recognize him, and for this reason Arsalan kept a low profile. From Salzburg, they make their way rather casually toward Munich, through the Alps with their rolling meadows dotted with flowers of violet and gold attended to by butterflies; snowy, faraway peaks; gabled houses with blossoms at their windows; and small herds of languid cows wearing bells on their necks and chewing cud as they watched with prolonged gazes of boredom and contentment the two strangers passing by them. Here, there was the occasional rainstorm that loomed in gray palls near the horizon before overtaking the two men and just as soon dissipating, yielding again to brilliant skies filled with golden sunlight and ragged, silvery clouds. After a month and half of travel, the two men finally arrived at the outskirts of Munich one evening where merchants and farmers were carting their wares, then through the gates of the central city, hastening to yet another inn with lanterns hung outside and music and conversation burbling within.

After a day's rest, Bayram reminded Arsalan to prepare his best clothes.

"I know it must have been a long time since you've worn your old, luxurious raiment, but please do try to improve your appearance in this regard. She is royalty, after all," said Bayram.

Arsalan looked down at his thick, linen traveling outfit, which was visibly worn at the cuffs and knees. His boots, too, were caked with mud at their bottoms. Bayram, by contrast, already had dressed in a nicely tailored suit of green and blue. It was decidedly Western, almost too much so, with a frock coat embroidered with silk, a vest, knickers, stockings, and black shoes. Bayram apparently wanted to make a good impression.

"Not to worry," Arsalan said. "I have not come unprepared."

Arsalan dug into one of his cases and pulled out an outfit of brown satin and green velvet, and he held it up to the light for inspection. It was characteristically Ottoman, but with some staid Western elements, and Arsalan thought the mixture was a good compromise.

"I hope it's still good," he said. "I haven't worn it in years." And with this, Arsalan donned the outfit. To his dismay, he found it tight around his middle, which caused Bayram to snort with laughter before stifling himself.

"Well," said Bayram, "either you or the suit needs some alterations. Also, it's a little out of fashion. But it should do."

Arsalan wore his embroidered boots, which he thought added a nice touch, but at which Bayram shrugged. The agent was more concerned now with behavior and courtesy regarding the Bavarian nobility and began to lecture Arsalan on its finer points.

"Bayram," interrupted Arsalan, "I'm not a stranger to nobility of the Western persuasion. I have mingled with them on countless prior occasions in my work. I think I will do well."

"But it's been three years," said Bayram.

"Things must not have changed that drastically over only three years," said Arsalan.

"Perhaps," said Bayram, "but watch for my cues. Also, where will the cat stay while we're visiting the princess?"

Arsalan picked up Kizil in his arms, held her to his chest, and began to pet her.

"With me," said Arsalan.

"No," said Bayram.

"Yes," said Arsalan.

"I'm not letting you take an animal into the Bavarian court," said Bayram.

"She's polite, intelligent, and well-mannered, and she will cause no fuss," said Arsalan.

"That's what everyone says about their pets," said Bayram.

"Perhaps," said Arsalan, "but we also don't know what will happen to her if she stays here alone."

"Even this inn has rules against animals that we're breaking right now by keeping her here," said Bayram.

"Correct. So, if the innkeepers find her, they will harm her," said Arsalan. "Therefore, she comes with me."

"You don't understand me," said Bayram. "No one wants a strange cat near them! Fleas! Lice! Mange! This will make a bad impression."

"She has none of those ailments," said Arsalan.

"The cat stays here," said Bayram.

"Then the job doesn't happen," said Arsalan, "and I will go all the way back to my cottage on the mountain among the Bulgars. And you can approach Ubaldini."

Bayram threw his hands up and stifled a groan of impatience, before sighing heavily and helplessly looking around him on the ground.

"Keep her in a bag," Bayram said. "If the princess sees the cat, I'll explain to her that you're an eccentric."

"Fine," said Arsalan. "I don't mind. It's probably true anyway. Now we go."

"All this over a cat!" muttered Bayram, exasperatedly.

Cats, lovers of enclosed spaces, haunters of empty boxes and crates, dwellers of mystery and shadow from which their keen green eyes stare outward like the disembodied gazes of caliginous wraiths—Kizil truly was one of these creatures. Perhaps it should have been no surprise that she did not mind being offered a seat in one of Arsalan's leather shoulder bags, which he carried unfastened so that Kizil occasionally could peek out of its top to relish her delightful sense of encasement. Kizil, upon entering, circled the comfortable hollow within to inspect it before settling into a pleased and watchful position. Arsalan carried this bag at his side with the strap slung over his shoulder, pretending to carry in it only his official documents.

Arsalan and Bayram together took the carriage, pulled by Solmaz and Aysel, to the grounds of the princess' royal palace, which, even despite the two men's previous knowledge of the structure, astonished them when they found themselves amid its sprawling, flowered lawns and its shimmering fountains and its system of wide, flat, graveled roads that wended their way to the main set of buildings that stared back at them from a distance. To approach the Bavarian palace was to approach some sort of dazzling mountainous formation; one could see it from afar, but due to the sheer size of the landmark, one underestimated one's distance from it until the road leading to its base proved unexpectedly long and the monument finally loomed over one's head like an imposing cliff, which in this case was ornamented with a bewildering array of windows and swarms of baroque stonework. The tiled roofs glared with vermillion under the splendid sun, and two enormous wings of the palace extended from either side of the main building such that one had to turn one's head in a half circle to absorb it all. Along the way, Arsalan and Bayram were stopped several times by stations of guards asking for copies of official invitations, which Bayram produced each time. When the two visitors found themselves at the grand front stairs of the entrance, a final team of elite guards asked again with no less sternness than the very first guards until they were satisfied with the paperwork. The stairs where Arsalan and Bayram now stood were two sets that climbed onto either end of a veranda that sat over three arched entrances to tunnels leading to stables and storage rooms beneath the castle. Here, where even the utilitarian stone arches looked majestic, the two visitors were made to wait for a noticeably long time until they were permitted to ascend. When they did, they faced on the broad veranda three expansive doors set with so many elaborate windowpanes that the doors resembled fragile lacework. The central door opened slightly, and guards appeared in it, motioning the two men through, where they were greeted by gently bowing servants in red coats and white wigs and stockings. They led the visitors down a yawning, protracted, echoey hall with high ceilings and walls that were adorned with paintings, statues, and tapestries featuring various generals, ancestors, and scenes of religious and military glory. Arsalan quietly rejoiced at the sight of regal luxury again, much like his old chateau, but at the same time experienced a vague disorientation at its aloof distances, outlandish artwork, and improvident consumption of space and materials to which he was no longer accustomed.

The servants led them to a waiting room, where there was a more senior servant, perhaps a butler, who scrutinized their clothing while leaning on one foot and holding a thoughtfully posed hand in front of him. He told them, in a firm but velvety voice, to await the presence of the princess' advisor Siegfrieda and to show her all due courtesy. He then turned on his heel and silently left the room.

The chamber was sized modestly and was tastefully decorated with red wallpaper and paintings on each wall and a fireplace under one of them. There was sumptuously carved and stained furniture, chiefly a table with four chairs, at which Bayram reminded Arsalan not to be found sitting when nobility arrived. Arsalan impatiently muttered to Bayram that he very well remembered this type of thing. So, there they stood, hands at their sides, with not much to do but to look out the tall windows at the grounds outside, which were nearly vacant of activity except for the odd servant or guard walking past on some soundless errand. The deep red walls made the two men gloomy and anxious, and it irked and confused them to be made to wait for a meeting to which the princess personally invited them.

"Don't fret, my old friend," said Bayram quietly. "It is a sign of noble privilege to keep even the world's most famous magical architect waiting in a small room."

"I'm well aware of that, too, my friend," replied Arsalan. "Besides, it's the least of the many indignities I've suffered thus far."

"That will end soon," said Bayram.

"You are certain that the princess does want to see us" asked Arsalan, "after our traveling so many leagues?"

"Yes, I'm as certain as I've been about anything, according to what her delegates promised me," said Bayram.

Arsalan turned to stare at Bayram in sudden realization.

"You hadn't met her first before bringing me here?" said Arsalan.

"I'm afraid not," said Bayram. "It seems they are very protective of their princess."

After thinking for a moment, Arsalan turned to resume idly studying the carpet beneath his own feet. He sighed thoughtfully and shook his head.

"It might have helped matters if you had met her first, but by now I'm ready for anything," Arsalan said.

A few moments later, the chief servant returned with a woman by her side, an older woman wrapped in a billowing dress of green and white, and a flowered cloth band on her head of dark green satin. Her face was long and somber, and she greeted each of the visitors with a penetrating glance.

"The princess' advisor Siegfrieda," commanded the chief servant.

"We are honored to make your acquaintance, Madam," said Arsalan and Bayram together, bowing like a set of mechanical toys.

"Gentleman," said Siegfrieda nodding stiffly, "Arsalan the Magnificent. I am honored to make yours. But no need to bow so lowly. I'm not exactly the princess herself."

"Our sincerest gratitude in any case," said Bayram, bowing again but with less exaggeration, which Arsalan followed.

"Mr. Ozdikmen, I trust you've been well these years? You'll have to excuse me. I am not a follower of architecture, much less the magical type," Siegfrieda said.

"Oh yes, very well, Madam. Thank you for your concern," said Arsalan.

"Gentlemen, I am grateful for your coming such a long way for the princess' request, but there is something of which I must remind you. Princess Berthilde is a firm believer in your magical architecture. But I implore you that..." stammered Siegfrieda.

"Yes, Madam?" asked Bayram.

As Siegfrieda spoke again she slowly wandered to a window to look out of it. "I suppose what I want to say is," she said, sighing, "please be realistic in your promises. Be sensible. She is very...oh, what is the right word...idealistic in her ambitions, somewhat gullible. Full of ideas, many of which are not always reasonable. None of us in the royal courts wish for her to be disappointed."

"If you are referring to the incident of the World's Leaf years ago, Madam," said Arsalan, "I promise you with utmost sincerity that such an incident will never happen again under my name."

"I didn't mean any unfortunate disaster of that scale," said Siegfrieda. "I am sorry that happened to you, Mr. Arsalan. I have heard you have been in exile for some years after that, so perhaps you have not heard that, since your incident, there has been much more skepticism surrounding magical architecture. There are those who doubt its durability. There are even those who doubt that it is real, that it is some sort of charlatanistic trick using non-occult means. And there are those who have never been close followers of magical architecture, like me, who have never had opinions one way or another, and now, because of all the controversy, don't know what to think."

"Madam," said Arsalan gravely, "I assure you, and I swear upon my parents' graves, that magical architecture is quite real, or else I too am one who has been deceived into thinking that I have such powers. If you wish, I can provide a demonstration of my gifts, and of the general principles of magical engineering. I have based my entire existence on the noble arts of which you speak."

"No need for a demonstration, I believe," said Siegfrieda. "I don't have that much doubt, and no need to put on a show for my sake. I suppose I'm not making much sense, even to myself."

"It is well understood, Madam," said Bayram.

"Well, you both have come a long way and have waited quite long enough. Dietrich," Siegfrieda said to the chief servant nearby, "please show our guests to the reception room,"

"Indeed, Madam," said Dietrich, and turned on his heel, motioning the two mean to follow him.

The four of them emerged from the little red chamber and back into the massive, dim hallway, and Arsalan was quietly invigorated by the fresher air that met his face and nose again as he walked down the corridor. They strode some way, passing large rooms on the left and the right outfitted in various bright colors, until the group arrived at a room not unlike the rooms they just had passed. This one, too, was bedecked in red, but was tempered with the accents of green and blue pillows and vases and other décor. In the middle of the room, there was a large, variegated sofa, flanked on either end with chairs of a similar style, on which neither of the men dared to sit. After a few minutes, Dietrich, who had disappeared around a corner in the back of the room leading to a hallway, returned, stood stiffly at attention, and announced, "Her Majesty the Princess!" He then bowed toward the corner, from behind which the bottom hem of a woman's enormous dress was now emerging. Siegfrieda bowed with Dietrich, and likewise Arsalan and Bayram followed suit before even setting eyes on the figure who was walking into the room.

Before the four of them stood a tremendous, conical dome of gold and white satin, silk, gauzes, and lace in many overlapping layers in which seemed to be trapped a young woman whose oval face seemed nervously stiff. Her eyes were otherwise wide and searching as she assessed the newcomers, and her movements halting and uncertain as she approached them. By Arsalan's astonished reckoning, the princess could not have been older than sixteen years of age, perhaps even fifteen, and no amount of regal garb could conceal this from him as a father of three children of his own. In fact, she reminded Arsalan quite uncomfortably of his own daughter.

Toward Arsalan Dietrich extended a hand, gloved in white and with his palm facing upward as if presenting a small gift, while addressing the princess.

"Arsalan Ozdikmen the Magnificent, Your Majesty, as per your request, and his assistant, Bayram Yaşaroğlu," said Dietrich.

"Your Majesty," said Arsalan with such seriousness that it was almost a hoarse whisper, "it is an honor to make your acquaintance on this glorious morning." And he continued to bow so deeply that he was facing his own shins, and his long, gray hair tumbled down over the back of his head.

Not to be excluded, Bayram, who was not bowing so severely, added, "And to me as well, Your Majesty."

Princess Berthilde clasped her hands awkwardly in front of her, as if not knowing what else to do with them, then she gestured upward with them. "Please, my dear gentlemen, please stand. I want to look at you," she said.

Arsalan and Bayram both arose and stood in a slightly stooped way, with polite, closed smiles, and they looked at the princess, although not directly to her face, except in many shyly surreptitious upward glances as she approached Arsalan. Princess Berthilde stared directly into his eyes, as if studying him, while unable to suppress a look of wonder. Arsalan was not sure how to respond. Eventually, when the princess was right in front of him, her imperceptibly shaky breath belied her practiced composure. Princess Berthilde was apparently more nervous at meeting Arsalan than he was at meeting her.

"Are you the real Arsalan the Magnificent?" she asked with almost the same type of whisper with which Arsalan addressed her. "The magical architect of so many fabulous magical structures? Is it really you?"

"Why, yes, Your Majesty," said Arsalan. "You are not mistaken. I am him. You have gone through much trouble to contact me, and I have heeded your call."

"You built the Diamond Dams of Rotterdam, the Royal Opera House of Luxembourg, the Levitating Bridges of Silesia, the Royal Post Office of Istanbul, the Vertical Gardens of Tripoli, and so many other wonderful structures," she said.

"Indeed, Your Majesty, I did have the fortune of building them," said Arsalan.

"I have studied all your works, Mr. Arsalan, and let me say I find it all fascinating," said the princess.

"My deepest and humblest gratitude, Your Majesty," said Arsalan.

"I hope you do not mind my saying this, but you seem older than I imagined you," she said.

"I'm afraid time has not been completely kind to me and has not spared me its ravages, Your Majesty," said Arsalan, "but I assure you that my powers have not dimmed, as far as I have been able to determine."

"When I read the stories about the World's Leaf, I wanted to cry," she said. "It seemed like such a lovely sight. I wanted it to be real. I wanted to visit it one day."

"I understand, Your Majesty," he said. "Let me assure you that no one shed more tears over its failure than me."

"But it is wonderful to have you here, Mr. Ozdikmen. It is hard for me to believe it is you. I would like to discuss business with you immediately," said Princess Berthilde.

"We are prepared, Your Majesty," said Bayram, "to begin whenever you are ready."

"Perhaps it would be better if we discussed this over tea?" asked Siegfrieda. "Our guests have come a long way."

"Oh, of course!" chirped the princess. "Where are my royal manners? You must come with me to the tearoom if you don't mind."

"Not at all! After you, Your Majesty," answered Arsalan.

Minutes later, the five of them were in the princess' tearoom, which was about as tea green as one would have expected. The walls, the upholstery, the carpets, and the curtains were all the same color of deep sage. The four sat at a round wooden table inset with a green marble tabletop, and after many quiet but forceful commands and gesticulations from Dietrich to the corners and doorways of the room, the lesser servants emerged, producing a complete set of jittery, clinking teacups and dispensers that they presented before the guests and hosts on the table, along with spoons, bowls of sugar, dainty little dishes, and cloth napkins, all of which were decorated with intricate lacework the same shade of green as the room. It had been so long that Arsalan had had tea with Western royalty that he struggled to remember his etiquette but was reminded by furtively glancing sideways at Bayram for cues. Arsalan recalled the instinct to compliment his hosts as to the taste of the tea, which in his opinion could have used much more sugar and milk, if it were not considered excessive among Princess Berthilde's people to add so much. It was only five years prior that Arsalan had had his own loyal servants who had waited on him with such nice, strong, milky tea, although not quite so many servants as Princess Berthilde had now. Her many red-coated servants stood behind the sitters in a circle around the table like soldiers at attention. Their backs erect, their faces ironclad and purposeful, they held their pitchers of water and trays of dishes at the ready like instruments of war, and their tense dutifulness put Arsalan ill at ease.

Eventually, he was distracted from this by the lighthearted discussions about the weather and their experiences traveling from Sliven, through the Balkans, and then through the Alps. Princess Berthilde was rapt with attention; she could not take her smiling eyes from Arsalan and listened to his regaling with fascination regardless of how demurely he spoke. In fact, it was his modesty that charmed Princess Berthilde the most, as it contrasted with the unreal nature of his stories, as if Arsalan were talking calmly about venturing through tropical jungles and wrestling with giant snakes. It became obvious that Princess Berthilde had lived her entire short life thus far confined within the cavernous spaces of the castle in which they were drinking tea, ensconced in the unreal lavishness and insulating privileges afforded to her. Siegfrieda watched her cautiously and issued subtle but unmistakably polite cues and disclaimers to prevent the princess from becoming too starstruck and to cajole her back to reality. Arsalan recognized these small, tactful admonishments for what they were and allowed the two royal women to come to tacit agreement each time before continuing with his descriptions of events. Ever so gradually and courteously, their conversation made its way back to the issue at hand, which was the repair of the roof of the Turret of Fürstenfeldbruck, and how much it would cost the royal coffers of Bavaria. Here, Arsalan fell quiet and allowed Bayram to do the talking. Bayram proved himself to be as adroit and as understatedly brilliant a negotiator as he ever had been, and Arsalan recognized in his agent's dealings with the princess the same tactics and strategies, the same softly muscular force in his haggling, the same deft and blinding persuasiveness and subtle checkmates from which Siegfrieda and Princess Berthilde could find no escape. As Arsalan listened, he busied himself with staring down into his cup of dark tea and gently stirring it, trying his best to hide a lopsided smile, while occasionally and coyly glancing upward at the royal haggling before him. Siegfrieda's realistic and suspecting stare alternated between Bayram and Princess Berthilde, and sometimes the older woman would interject with a factual consideration that would throw a snag into the dealings, slowing their pace. But it was not as if Princess Berthilde was powerless against Bayram completely; her most efficacious weapon against him was her forthright and wide-eyed honesty, which at certain times seemed to disarm Bayram for a moment before he was able to recover. She stared always directly at Bayram, sometimes curiously and confusedly, sometimes laughingly and affably, never seeking to deceive but always trying to understand, which touched Arsalan pointedly and at times made him glance sideways at Bayram to remind him to temper his predatory adult aggressions. But at some length and with the fanfare of smiles and laughter, the two parties settled on a price that pleased both greatly: the royals because it seemed to them such a paltry amount, and the Turks because it was a price that was higher than either of them had expected, making Arsalan's mutedly surprised eyebrows rise like the sun at dawn. In relief that the pain and awkwardness of arbitration was over, the four resumed their previously friendly chatter about the lighter subjects of travel and cuisine and family.

"Your Majesty," asked Arsalan at a certain point, "I couldn't help but wonder what your parents, the king and queen, think of your plans to repair all of Conrad's structures."

Siegfrieda's face became grave for a moment, and Princess Berthilde for a fleeting instant looked down at her table before looking up at Arsalan.

"You probably haven't heard," answered the princess. "My dear parents passed away five years ago of the consumption."

"Oh my, my dear Majesty, I am so sorry," said Arsalan. "Please forgive my impropriety and ignorance. I simply was not aware."

"It's alright. Not all the nations of the world have heard the news yet. We have been quiet about it. But for me it was long while ago when I was a small child," she said.

"So, this means you have inherited the throne of Bavaria?" said Arsalan.

"Not quite yet. Until I am eighteen years of age, I am advised in my ruling by Siegfrieda, our close family friend of many years. She serves as a partial Stewardess of the throne. I am so lucky to have her here to take care of me. She is like an aunt to me. When I come of age, I will inherit the full powers of the throne and will not need a Stewardess, but I will still have her as an advisor," said Princess Berthilde, beaming at the older woman. Matronly Siegfrieda returned her blissful smile before glancing at the two men with perhaps a flash of nervous suspicion, which Arsalan interpreted as fear of being misperceived as taking political advantage of a young royal girl, or of allowing others to do the same. It could also have been her annoyance at Arsalan's broaching of the subject.

"It's obvious, Your Majesty, that you are in good and loving hands," said Arsalan carefully. This perhaps mended the situation for the moment, for Siegfrieda again gazed at the princess lovingly.

Startlingly, the two women gasped, making Arsalan jump. They were staring at a point behind him. Both men turned around to look, and saw Kizil climbing out of Arsalan's bag, which had been placed on the floor by a chair and forgotten. Arsalan looked at the two women in terror. Siegfrieda regarded the cat with a type of horror, leaning backward with her hand to her throat. The princess sat upright and held her hands in front of her mouth and began to scream. "Oh, my heavens!" she exclaimed.

Arsalan stammered, "Your Majesty, I apologize. There was nowhere else to keep her—"

Bayram interrupted, trying to offer a better explanation. "Your Majesty, we're deeply sorry," he offered. "It seems my client here has a few eccentricities he has developed in his time in exile. This cat has been his companion while he was alone in the—"

"Oh, my heavens! I love cats! Is this a gift? Where did you find her?" she cried.

Bayram and Arsalan looked at each other in confusion.

"Your Majesty," stuttered Arsalan, "this is Kizil, my cat, and my dearest companion of the past few years. I found her during my travels in exile."

Kizil was already out of the bag and examining her surroundings with her graceful and furtive motions. She tiptoed to the table, sniffing the ground here and there, and jumped up onto Arsalan's lap. The four humans watched her with breathless wariness and admiration. Kizil's shining orange coat was many times furrier and glossier than when Arsalan had found her, and it contrasted beautifully against the soft white fur of her mouth and paws, and her body was far heavier and stronger and strutted with much more assuredness. She was an altogether different cat from three years prior, and this was the cat that the princess saw before her.

"When you invited us to your castle," said Arsalan, "there was nowhere else to keep her. I did not feel safe keeping her in our inn either. I was forced to bring her with us. I am terribly sorry, Your Majesty."

"Don't be sorry!" said Princess Berthilde. "Such a beautiful orange cat! I have not seen one like this before! Come here!"

The princess rose from her seat, almost flipping her chair backwards, trotted over to Arsalan's chair, and sat in the chair next to him. Here, she bent forwards and began petting the luxurious fur of the exotic feline.

"Oh, dear me! Look at you! Such lovely fur!" squealed the princess. Kizil mewed quietly in reply, as it seemed she took a liking to the princess as well. Princess Berthilde did not ask permission to take the cat in her arms, but did so rather recklessly, and soon Kizil became acquainted with the princess's embrace as she was receiving sumptuous pets from her. Arsalan laughed in retroactive approval, while Siegfrieda regarded the princess and the cat with a mixture of relief and patient annoyance.

"You say the inn will not take her?" said Princess Berthilde. "Then you must board with us, right here in my castle instead of that dirty old inn, so I can see her. I insist! Siegfrieda! Dietrich! Prepare rooms for our guests immediately!"

"Your majesty," said Siegfrieda tactfully, "perhaps it would be inconvenient for them to change their boarding plans so suddenly. And we have no means to care for a cat."

"Nonsense!" said Princess Berthilde, smiling, with the cat fully in her arms. "I'm sure they can manage. Can't you, Mr. Arsalan and Mr. Bayram? Also, there's nothing in Bavaria we can't purchase to care properly for one cat for a short while!"

Siegfrieda's attempt to stymie the idea about the cat failing miserably, she straightened herself and stared out the window with a barely audible sigh and a shake of her head.

"Dietrich," said Siegfrieda, "you heard Your Majesty. Please make the necessary arrangements."

"Yes, Madam," said Dietrich, who again pivoted on his toe and vanished from the room.

The princess' servants accompanied Bayram and Arsalan to their inn to fetch their remaining belongings. They all arrived at the inn in an ostentatiously gilded carriage framed with round, wild curves and covered in delirious filigree, astonishing everyone there. As Arsalan sat inside on the velvet cushions, he regarded this extravagance with fond remembrance of his own days' past, and he chuckled quietly to himself.

"I must say, Arsalan," said Bayram, riding in the cabin with Arslan, "I was afraid you almost lost our deal twice, once by bringing that cat along and then again by asking about the king and queen. But bringing Kizil turned out to be a stroke of brilliance."

"You could have told me about the princess' parents, at least! I wouldn't have asked her!" protested Arsalan.

"Her delegates never told me," said Bayram. "I suppose they wanted to keep it quiet for some reason, which I sense has something to do with the political circumstances surrounding their throne."

"How so?" asked Arsalan.

"They have a sixteen-year-old girl in charge of one of the most powerful kingdoms of the Holy Roman Empire," said Bayram. "Her conditional ascendency and her lack of ruling experience presents a political weakness for others to exploit, don't you think?"

"Are you suggesting that we should exploit her," said Arsalan, "or that others will suspect us of doing so?"

"No," said Bayram. "We want to be in her favor, which we are. We must continue to engender her complete trust with our honesty. Their domestic political intrigue isn't much of our business, but it is simply something for us to keep in mind for the sake of your commissions."

Their rooms at the castle were accordingly opulent, although the décor was admittedly somewhat girlish, with pastel colors and gauzy, puffy curtains. Arsalan's room neighbored Bayram's room such that they even shared a door between them. Both the rooms' windows looked out upon a broad central courtyard where it seemed the princess' guards kept their horses and carriages during the day. The activity there seemed languid and uneventful, almost sleepy. The guards' bleached white wigs glared in the relentless sunlight as they attended to their horses, and Arsalan wondered how much the men must have sweated under them.

The princess had been with Kizil all day while the two guests were away retrieving their baggage. The plans were to meet for dinner that night for further discussions on the work to be done in Fürstenfeldbruck, which was to start in three days. Arsalan and Bayram arrived at the princess' dining room in their finest attire. The room was more like a long hall, its walls paneled with enormous portrait paintings of royal ancestors whose grave, pale blue stares no one in the dining hall could escape. Everywhere there were vases filled with fresh flowers of every hue, and there was an elaborate chandelier that hung from the high ceiling above the heart of the room like a luminous spider. Under this was the extended oaken table that was as long as a pier and covered with gleaming white porcelain dishes and finely translucent wine glasses, all of which filled Arsalan with a certain nostalgic envy. There they met several high officials in charge of public works and civil engineering who greeted Arsalan with wide, genuine smiles and enthusiastic handshakes. Also in attendance was Siegfrieda, who stood alone and in silence while waiting for the princess, and of course stern Dietrich and his team of servants. Everyone stood.

"Her Majesty, the Princess!" announced Dietrich, who bowed in the direction of the door through which the princess was emerging, and everyone in the room followed suit in the bowing and curtsying. In came Princess Berthilde whose dress resembled an ornate yellow church bell. She held Kizil in her arms while grinning broadly, and Dietrich took the cat and placed her on a purple embroidered pillow on a small table, where there were bowls of finely ground and seasoned meat and water waiting for her. Kizil took to this meal immediately but daintily.

"Thank you all for coming!" said Princess Berthilde cheerily, and sat in her seat, after which all in attendance sat as well. Dietrich pulled a chair backward for Siegfrieda next to the princess. Arsalan and Bayram were directed to sit across from them, and to their right and left, the high officials.

"Your Majesty, I thank you for providing such wonderful accommodations for my cat," said Arsalan, smiling, "but I'm afraid you might spoil her so much I won't be able to keep her!"

"I'm sorry. It's been so long since I've had a pet, I can't help myself," Princess Berthilde replied. "Perhaps if our partnership works well, you will be able to spoil her just as well!"

"If you don't mind my asking," said the Chief Official of Public Works, and older man with crisp diction, "where did you find such a pleasant feline?"

"It was the strangest meeting," said Arsalan. "I found her alone in a grassy field outside of Kirklareli and she wouldn't leave me alone. She was starving and sick and scrawny and I thought she had been abandoned by a farmer."

Princess Berthilde gasped, "And you nursed her back to health? How sweet!"

"Yes," Arsalan said, "but around her skinny neck was a collar with a small note hidden in its clasp. I could not read the note. It was written in a language I could not identify."

"Oh, how intriguing!" said the princess. "Do you have it with you? May I see it?"

"Certainly, Your Majesty," said Arsalan. "As a matter of fact, if you have scholars of philology at hand, I should ask your help in translating it."

Arsalan produced the note from his clasp. The princess ordered Dietrich to pass it to her, and she stared at it for a moment before passing it to Siegfrieda, who only grimaced at it in her attempts to make any sense of it.

"I must say, I don't know the language either," said the princess quizzically, "but I am quite intrigued."

The note was passed around the table to the other men. Despite being educated in all matters related to engineering and architecture, planning and preservation, and despite peering at it with pouting and pinched faces through their reading glasses and monocles, they simply and mutedly shook their pink faces and white heads.

"Well!" exclaimed Princess Berthilde. "There's a mystery for us to solve. How exciting! I shall summon my best scholars to translate it!"

Siegfrieda nodded absently, and the high officials at the table nodded and murmured to each other in general accord, trying their best to demonstrate interest in the princess' sudden and parenthetic whim.

"Thank you, Your Majesty," said Arsalan.

"Well, now that that's out of the way," sighed Siegfrieda, "let us enjoy our dinner and discuss our plans for the turret, shall we?"

"Hear, hear, Madam," said the high officials at the table.

The conversation over dinner proceeded smoothly. The diners ate their veal and duck and dumplings while sharing and agreeing upon their plans for the roof of the famous turret. The officials brought maps and diagrams, which they spread out between the tinkling forests of glass, porcelain, and silverware on the tabletop. They leaned toward each other over the table and nodded their heads vigorously in their palaver, and the servants floated about behind them, taking this empty plate or filling that glass with slightly more wine. Princess Berthilde watched the chatter with wide and excited eyes and laughed like a little bell at Arsalan's jokes, while Siegfrieda observed with a more clinical and careful eye, saying little except to offer clarifications or to ask a pointed question, but was otherwise impressed and almost intimidated by Arsalan's passionate and intelligent delivery. Arsalan felt like a hand slipping back into a glove. He felt as if he were in his own palace again, entertaining his own guests and bantering with the world's most important people. All his charming and witty social instincts from long ago returned as if they had never been interrupted, and Bayram regarded him with renewed gladness and confidence, and almost wonder, that the young wizard with flashing, dark eyes and a dashing, triangular smile had returned, ready to reconquer the world of magical architecture.

But ever so gradually, things began to take a turn for the worse. Everyone was relaxed and had had a few glasses of wine and were now comfortable enough with each other to laugh heartily at each other's jokes and stories. Arsalan just had finished regaling this audience with his tales of travel and adventure in Latvia and Lithuania to build the Amber Spire and the Grand Palace of Narva, when one of the older officials, in the spirit of completely innocent and unmalicious inquiry, asked Arsalan forthrightly, "And how was it that your World's Leaf fell? I've always wondered!"

At this Arsalan paused, flustered, as if being thrown off balance, and stammered a reply that the cause was magic depletion, the cause of which never was determined.

"What could cause magic depletion as abruptly as that?" another official asked, to which Arsalan answered that no one could be quite sure, as it could be a combination of causes, such as the interaction of those specific materials or perhaps a larger stress on the structure than was previously known. Arsalan was also careful to add that magic depletion happens naturally over time to all magical structures, just not as rapidly as in the case with the World's Leaf.

"Could the same thing happen to the Turret of Fürstenfeldbruck after you repair it?" asked another official.

"No," said Arsalan. "Although magic depletion has been happening to the Turret naturally over the years, it has done so slowly, and the roof carries less of a load than the World's Leaf."

"Can you be quite certain?" asked Siegfrieda, who seemed to have sensed an opportunity for voiced skepticism. "I mean, you haven't built any major structures since the Leaf, and it's been years! I ask because I don't want anyone walking under the roof to be hurt! And I wouldn't want to spend anything from the royal coffers in vain!"

"Of course, I am certain," said Arsalan. "After all, it's just a roof!"

"A roof over peoples' heads!" answered Siegfrieda.

"Have any of the tiles that have fallen off hurt anyone so far?" asked Arsalan.

"No," said Siegfrieda, "but I think we've been lucky so far."

"I have built close to a hundred large-scale structures in my lifetime," said Arsalan. "The Leaf is the only one that has fallen. Are you all going to judge me for that one?"

"Well, no" said another of the officials. "We just want to make certain, Mr. Ozdikmen. We don't think such a concern or question is unreasonable to voice. It is a question of safety."

"Why was this issue not addressed before?" asked Arsalan. "Why was I invited all this way only to be held in suspicion at the last minute after all the bread was broken and the wine drunk and our plans made?"

No one was certain when the deterioration of relations began to occur or how it could have been prevented. It surely began with one honest question, and then perhaps in teasing amusement among the officials when they saw Arsalan squirm a bit under it. But the rancor seemed to be fed by Siegfrieda's seemingly innocuous questioning between their inquiries, feeding the fire of suspicion and doubt between the two parties of engineers and architects until they began to raise their voices at one another. The more the others questioned Arsalan, the more defensive he grew, and the more he voiced his displeasure, the sterner and more insistent was their questioning. Voices were raised, faces flushed with red and pink, the table was knocked with knuckles and fists, and silverware tinkled frightenedly on porcelain. Eventually, almost instinctively, Arsalan began to slap wine into his glass and then to slam it into the back of his throat before pointing his finger at them and defending himself with less and less coherently sober reasoning. Bayram started to paw at Arsalan's arm, which Arsalan shook off and ignored as he launched into arguments and diatribes. Princess Berthilde watched the breakdown of the talks with horror and dismay, and likewise grabbed Siegfrieda's arm for help, not quite realizing that the older women was the subtle cause of the disturbance. Siegfrieda coldly pretended to be too concerned at the arguments before her to be aware of the princess' pleas. But Arsalan was truly on fire and melting into a pool of drunken lava before them, slightly swaying and slurring his words as he gestured at all of them.

"I did not have to come here!" said Arsalan. "I did not need the wealth! I did not live happily alone on top of a mountain for three years only to be disturbed, compelled here, and mocked in a royal mansion! Jeered for some failure I committed years ago! If you didn't think I could perform this job, you should have left me alone! Like my wife, and my three children who all fled me! And my rich friends who all abandoned me until I had but two horses and a cat to call my companions! I am the most powerful magical architect in the world! I can destroy any building in the world, and I can reconstruct it within days! None of you have any idea of my power! You just think of my one failure! My one failure, and you want to worship me and to shun me at the same time for it. What do you want to hear? You want to hear how magic is unreliable. You know, maybe you're right! Magic is just so much cheap, gimmicky glue that dries up and flakes away! It's nothing. It's paint! It's makeup! It's worthless!"

Now Bayram was holding Arsalan by the shoulders as if holding him back from an altercation, and he begged the magical architect to retreat to his room, while apologizing over his shoulder to the company at the tables for Arsalan's behavior. Siegfrieda wore a face of disgust and ordered the servants to subdue Arsalan quietly. The high officials muttered to each other in shock and consternation. Finally, Princess Berthilde stood and declared, "This dinner is over. Everyone here is dismissed and ordered back to their quarters for the rest of the night! Please, stop your fighting, gentlemen!"

Siegfrieda touched Princess Berthilde's arm and began to murmur some warning into her princess' ear, but the princess swung her arm away and re-buffed her words.

"I want to be alone!" cried Princess Berthilde, and she stalked from the room in tears.

CHAPTER 10

The next morning was a sickly yellow color, blanketed in a translucent gauze of clouds behind which the tawny sun rose, glaring and watery under the haze. It pained one to look at it and cast everything beneath it an indistinct and silty light.

Arsalan woke from his sleep with a rude snort and a weighty headache. He was sleeping on his stomach with his face over the side of his bed. Arsalan vaguely remembered Bayram tossing him into this position to reduce the possibility of his choking on his own vomit. Arsalan's mouth was dry and sandy, and he worked his lips and tongue to summon moisture to them, but to no avail. His eyes were bloodshot and sagging, and he reached for his pitcher of water beside his bed but could not reach it. To his shock, cold water flew into his face anyway, from some other direction, splashing all over his shirt and collar, and Arsalan sputtered and rolled to one side to sit upright. It was Bayram who, having spent the night sleeping in the chair beside Arsalan's bed, now had thrown cold water into Arsalan's face to revive him.

"There's your water. Now wake up," said Bayram sharply. "Get up or I'll drag you out of bed."

Arsalan could say nothing, but only could lurch around on his bed in pathetic attempts to right himself.

"You're not the only one who has come all the way from your mountain to here," said Bayram angrily. "I did, too, after weeks, months of traveling to Sliven to find you and to give you the chance to set your life in order. I did not have to do that, either!"

"Forget about me," said Arsalan. "I am too much trouble. I will prepare my horses and I will leave for Sliven this morning. End of discussion."

"No, you will not," said Bayram. "I'm not letting you make a fool out of me, too, in front of these royals. I have too much invested in you, now. I've made too many promises. If I give up on you now, what an idiot I will seem to them!"

"Ubaldini," said Arsalan. "Go see Emilio. He can fix the blasted roofs."

"I was bluffing," said Bayram. "He's not interested in traveling from

Rome to fix a roof. I just said that to get you out of that cabin."

"You lying cad," said Arsalan, laughing. "And yet, I sensed that anyway. I am the fool."

"I spent all of last night mollifying Siegfrieda's fears," said Bayram. "I had to explain to her that you were still devastated by the World's Leaf's collapse, and that you spent three long years in lonely exile after losing everything you had and everyone you loved. I explained to her that your losses and subsequent prolonged isolation have turned you into a bit of an eccentric."

"So, you used that line after all, yet she was the cause of all this, I'm sure," said Arsalan. "And the princess?"

"You will go directly to her room to apologize to her," said Bayram. "You did not have to become angry. You did not have to start drinking to fuel your rage at your misfortunes."

"The princess," said Arsalan. "Oh, the princess. What will I say to her? Oh, she reminds me so much of Defne. And Teodora. I'm so ashamed of myself in front of her."

"Go now and, for once, face your shame and conquer it," said Bayram. "Dietrich will lead you."

And there was tall Dietrich just outside the door, waiting for him. He stared down at Arsalan from under his white wig with a look of thinly disguised contempt, to which Arsalan reacted with a proud yet resigned huff, a slumped head, and an averted gaze. Dietrich then wordlessly pivoted on his heel to lead Arsalan down the darkened hallways to the princess' room. It was difficult for the hungover Arsalan to keep pace with the energetic and polished gait of the chief servant's white-stockinged calves. In fact, it was apparent that Dietrich, quite aware of Arsalan's condition, did nothing to make the task easier for him.

At last, they stopped at one of the princess' rooms, a sort of small, intimate study also decorated in dull green. The princess primly sat at the edge of a couch, staring out a window at the morning light. Her back was toward him and the door behind him. She had not slept; she was still dressed in the previous night's yellow dress. Long Arsalan stood there, waiting for the princess to say something, until at last offering a phrase in his hoarse, gravelly whisper, "Your Majesty."

Princess Berthilde did not answer but turned to look at him with a blank gaze. There were purplish circles beneath her eyes. She then turned back to the window.

"Your Majesty, if it is of any use for me to say this, I am deeply remorseful for our argument last night," said Arsalan. "I should have conducted myself with far more rectitude and decorum, but I allowed my painful experiences to get the better of me. I offer to pack my belongings and to leave here and not to trouble you any longer."

"Sit," she said.

Arsalan was uncomfortable and was not sure if he should take her offer.

"Please," she said, and finally Arsalan looked around himself and found a small chair on which to sit, and did so on its very corner, as if he did not deserve to occupy the whole seat.

"When I was just ten years of age, as you know," she said, softly, "I lost both my parents to the consumption. I had never been more devastated by anything in my life. My dear, loving parents were both gone and there was nothing I could do to bring them back to me. Fortunately, I had the rest of the court's servants and advisors to comfort me and to care for me, and for that I was grateful. But there was something else that consoled me. I had been an avid reader of accounts of your work from the time I was small, and when my parents were gone, I filled the hole that their death left in me by reading accounts of your buildings and looking at drawings of the structures. They were such amazing and wonderful structures, the types of buildings one only sees in dreams. I used to imagine what you looked like: gallant, dashing, smart, full of confidence and vim. I used to imagine what you looked like when working in your studio or workshop. When you arrived, to my pleasant surprise, you were just like whom I imagined, only older, which did not disappoint me. In fact, your age only made you more intriguing, more approachable. You were so witty, and you made me laugh and believe that anything was possible. But the man I saw late last night after dinner…"

Princess Berthilde paused and began to sob while Arsalan winced and looked at his feet.

"The man I saw last night was utterly the opposite. He was an overproud, angry, hairy, red-faced, drunk old fool. Embarrassing and insecure. It was shocking and horrifying. Maybe it was your drink. I don't know. I didn't know Turks drank so much. I thought they were soberer than that. But I also sensed that Siegfrieda was also to blame for the hostilities. She means well and she wishes to protect me from harm, but sometimes her means are delicate and underhanded. She knows how to get beneath others' skins to expose their true intentions and natures. And last night I saw her getting under yours. You were not prepared for her. Not even the clever group of engineers, with all their degrees and wigged heads full of knowledge, knew precisely what was happening. Please know that I have admonished her for her actions last night. In any case, what I saw when Siegfrieda exposed the dermis of your heart filled me with pity. I did see an old man full of pain and heartache and rage. I heard about your losses as described by Bayram later last night. He pleaded for my forgiveness toward you. He told me your entire story surrounding the World's Leaf, and despite myself I pitied you. I pitied you."

Princess Berthilde wept again, trembling uncontrollably with sobs.

"Is that, your Majesty," said Arsalan quietly, "the reason why you have not dismissed me yet?"

"Partly," she said.

"Then, humbly I do ask," said Arsalan, "what else keeps you from wholly condemning me from your palace."

"It's in the other room," she said.

Arsalan did not understand. Princess Berthilde called Dietrich, who had been standing by the door during their conversation, and she gave him a cryptic command to show them to a chamber. Dietrich produced from his large, red pocket an iron key jangling on a ring and approached a door in the rear corner of the study. With a loud clack that echoed from some hollow interior, he unlocked the door and pulled it open, revealing a long, narrow, bare corridor of smooth stone. High on the wall to the right there was a row of small windows casting light on the wall opposite, showing the way to yet another thick wooden door with intimidating hinges, a round ring of a door handle, and a bulky square lock, all wrought of black iron roughly dented by the hammer strikes of some muscled smith. Unlocking this second door, the three entered a round room of masonry similar to that of the hallway. It was a sort of tall, hollow turret, with a single, elevated window casting a chunk of the morning's wan sunlight onto the junction between the wall and the round floor. Dietrich at this point turned and left, leaving Princess Berthilde and Arsalan standing there and looking at an object situated precisely in the center of the circular chamber. It was a large, green, metallic object, and it was oddly shaped; it was nicely curved on one side like a saddle, but on the other side was jagged and mangled. The greenness of the object was itself astounding; it was an emerald hue, beautiful to behold. But what made this object more astonishing was that it was floating five feet above the floor. Arsalan stared at it in amazement.

"Do you know what this is?" asked Princess Berthilde.

"I'm not sure," whispered Arsalan.

"You don't recognize it?" asked the princess.

Arsalan shuffled over to the emerald artifact and gingerly touched it with his fingertips.

"It looks familiar," he said, "but it can't be what it resembles to me."

"You are looking at a piece of your World's Leaf," said Princess Berthilde.

"Here?" Arsalan gasped. "How could it come here?"

Princess Berthilde replied, "When I first heard about its collapse, several months after it happened, I commanded my court to acquire a piece of the rubble. I wanted a piece that displayed magical properties to be part of my collection. I sent a team of delegates to your empire. A piece like this was difficult for them to locate, even harder to purchase. Haggling for it was a nightmare, but I bought it at great personal expense."

"You..." stammered Arsalan, "you bought it?"

"Yes!" said the princess with a demurely proud smile, wiping away a few tears. "And I had it shipped here. The most difficult task was to bring it to my kingdom. It can be moved from side to side, you see, and even upwards a bit, but it cannot be pressed downward fewer than five feet from the ground. No man, animal, or stone, no force or weight, can press it down any lower. It floats solidly as if on invisible rock, not yielding one inch downward. Its magical properties have not deteriorated one bit since I had it stored here. We even have measured it, and its height is precisely the same. Isn't it amazing?"

Tears welled in Arsalan's eyes as he brushed his fingers across the metal object's surface. He then pushed it slightly, and although heavy, it floated away from him by a few inches.

"Yes, it is. It still works! This is the junction between the branch and the stem," he said, "and it still floats. It still defies gravity as if I had charged it yesterday."

"Yes," she said calmly. "You made this with your own hands, Mr. Ozdikmen. You made its abnormally smooth and continuous surface, without seam or rivet, that reached from the base to the zenith of your structure. You held those secrets of how to render such metal. You made it hover. The rest of your structure failed for some reason still unknown to us, but this still floats, refusing to fall. I come here often, when I am feeling despondent, when I am thinking my way through problems. I wonder how you can achieve such things, and I know that if you and other magical architects are able to accomplish these impossible feats, even despite your failures, I can surmount my own puzzles and conundrums, my own affairs of the heart. Don't you see? This piece stands as a stubborn testimony to your brilliance. So long as it floats, I believe in you, Arsalan, and I have believed in you for years. This piece of eternal magic is why I do not dismiss you and why I still have faith in you."

Arsalan gently wrapped his arms around the object to embrace it, to feel its heft and solidity, and tears began to stream from his eyes, which he closed. He remembered how breathtakingly beautiful the World's Leaf looked from a distance in the sharp desert sun, crisp against the blue sky, how grand and otherworldly it was. It was unlike any structure that ever had been built. But he could not help also remembering its awful collapse, and the terror and mortification and waste it caused. Arsalan heaved with sobs for a moment before wiping his eyes with his sleeve.

"I'm sorry," he said. "I'm sorry for crying in front of you like a boy. But the failure of this structure was one of the worst events of my life. I feel I will never outlive its infamy. A portion of my heart thinks you are foolish for spending your money to preserve a symbol of such spectacular failure. But another area of my heart is enthralled and grateful to you for preserving a part of its former beauty in some small way. Most of all, I am grateful for you for not losing faith in me, after everything that has happened."

"I feel I understand you too well now to lose faith in you," said Princess Berthilde. "Let us agree that you will not explode in a drunken rage at the merest sign of doubt in your abilities while I ensure that you will be trusted and treated with respect and the honor that is due to such a legendary magical architect."

"Thank you, Your Majesty," said Arsalan. "I promise to conduct myself in a way more befitting of my status. And I also vow to repair your structures that Conrad the Ineffable has built with such solid and enduring craftsmanship as you have never seen, and if you are even in the slightest disappointed with my work, I will refuse all payment."

"Oh, no," said the princess. "I couldn't agree to that. You will get every coin that is due to you for your work. Besides, I think your agent will have something to say about your overly honorable offer."

Arsalan nodded, "Hm, that is true. You are an insightful and mature young woman, Your Majesty."

"Let us leave here and return to the others," said the princess. "We can return here together again if you like. But now there is much work to be done."

Princess Berthilde and Arsalan returned from their cloister and proceeded to the grand ballroom, where the princess assembled every noble, servant, and official working for the Royal Throne of Bavaria in her palace. The ballroom was a lushly decorated hall, as large as the nave of a cathedral. Onto every wall, ornate golden wallpaper was applied, and expansive paintings of wars and nobles standing in haughty poses were hung. A tremendous mirror covered one end of the ballroom. It crowned a great fireplace as large as a cellar doorway, and it sat beneath a ceiling adorned with a biblical mural of cherubs ascending to heaven. Many doors led into this opulent hall, and through them two hundred people filtered and were soon gathered there in every uniform, down to the chef and the stableboy, standing at dutiful but confused and curious attention. Princess Berthilde stood in front of them at the grand fireplace and solemnly announced that Arsalan the Magnificent had been commissioned to repair and to rebuild Conrad the Ineffable's old structures in the kingdom, and that while Arsalan was here, he was to be treated with all due authority, respect, and deference befitting someone of his illustrious stature. At the mention of Arsalan's name, many of the servants and officials gasped with awe and surprise, but at the princess' insistence upon his treatment within her court, many nobles cast uncomfortable eyes to the floor, as if wondering if the magical architect was to be treated with more honor than they themselves would be afforded. In the end, though, all bowed in agreement and in unison said, "Yes, Your Majesty."

Afterward, Siegfrieda and Arsalan met alone. Their exchange was awkward and unemotional, but Siegfrieda offered her apologies, along with a stilted explanation of her perceptions and motivations, all which Arsalan accepted. Arsalan likewise offered his own, which were accepted in kind, and a truce was then drawn between them that was cool to the touch due to the absence of deep understanding between them. But Arsalan attempted to warm it by promising the best building work she ever had seen, a promise which she accepted with a staring and cautious nod and a hint of curiosity. Later, in private over lunch in their connected rooms, Bayram applauded Arsalan with a clap that was not unironic.

"Bravo, my friend," said Bayram. "You saved the day again after almost ruining it."

"It was you who saved it," said Arsalan, "thanks to your way of talking. Otherwise, I'd be thrown onto the street. Thank you, my friend."

Bayram responded by smiling and holding his palms up to face the ceiling. They then clinked their glasses of wine and ate lunch.

The road to Fürstenfeldbruck was a day's ride. He traveled west from Munich with his horses and carriage, accompanied by a small contingent of royal guards, and a crew carting wood and stone materials using draft horses as large as Solmaz and Aysel. Bayram stayed behind to discuss business with the princess and Siegfrieda, as did Kizil, to be cared for and spoiled by Princess Berthilde herself and her staff of upstanding and attentive staff.

Arsalan and his caravan arrived at the site of the famous turret. It was a tower sprouting upward from the center of Fürstenfeld Abbey, built by Conrad to repair the damage from a fire. It was indeed twenty stories tall, the tallest structure in the city, was gilded with gold paint and decorated with sculptures, and was topped with a rounded roof of exaggerated Byzantine style. The roof had a round base that tapered dramatically to a thin spire, which in turn ballooned outward and upward again into the shape of an onion. This entire peculiar volume was tiled with a bedazzling checkerboard array of black and white plates that formed swirling stripes across its surface. These tiles were sizeable and some of them now were breaking into pieces and falling, and the body of this knobbed roof, which once in its day had rotated slowly on its base, had stopped moving.

The head monks met with Arsalan, the delegation of construction officials, and the working crew. Here, everyone offered greetings and shook hands. Arsalan helped the workers unload the heavy materials from the carts, and when the bulk of that task was complete, he prepared to inspect the roof.

"Excuse me, gentlemen," said Arsalan, "but allow me to conduct an initial inspection."

Arsalan looked upward toward the roof, and he floated up directly toward it, leaving the ground far below, where he heard all the men laughing with wonder and delight at the sight of him flying. He then reached the roof, which was so large that he was able to stand on its rim like someone at the foot of a hill. The complete, dizzying extent of Fürstenfeldbruck, with all its towers and buildings and farm fields and the river running through it, was spread out around him like a grand feast. The noises from the city were muffled and replaced by the blustery sound of chilly wind roaring past his ears. If there was anything of which Arsalan had no fear whatsoever, it was heights; he had conquered that anxiety many decades prior. Arsalan walked around on the tiled surface, closely examining the roof. He saw broken and missing tiles scattered here and there and recorded how many tiles of each color he had to manufacture. He also observed the weird environment of the rest of the roof: the tapering base, the thin spire, and the widening balloon that sat on it by means of magic and which now loomed over Arsalan like the body of a whale. Within that spherical portion, there was also a clock whose face stared out at the municipality like a giant eye. It had stopped working, and its bells no longer rang. Above the clock's face, the bulb was crowned with the golden sculpture of an angel blowing a trumpet; this beautiful object now leaned to one side.

Arsalan returned to the ground to the cheers of the others, and laughingly waved off their excited attempts to ask him what it felt like to fly. He then set about making the new tiles using as a model a slightly broken one he had removed from the roof. The crew watched in fascination as he carved each one using only the invisible magical powers that were issued from his fingers and hands, and Arsalan felt relieved at the opportunity to demonstrate his powers openly once again rather than to conceal them.

Eventually he finished making all the replacement tiles, and he floated back up to the roof with the heavy load of new stone tiles in tow next to him in mid-air. He lowered them onto the roof and then set about with the replacement work. Arsalan spent long stretches of time fastening each one into place, not only with nails but with magical spells, such that no wind or force could move them. He also tested the magic charges on all the rest of the tiles, and he replenished them to keep them in place and for good measure. Arsalan labored with a particular conscientiousness while the sun emerged from behind the clouds and blazed upon his shoulders and back, and he sweated until water dripped from the end of his nose onto his gray beard and his shirt became drenched.

After several days, the tiling was renewed, and it was time to repair the clock inside the bulbous head of the roof. The spire leading from the base to the bulb was hollow yet wide enough to allow a person to climb up through it using a ladder. Arsalan made this precipitous journey and found himself at the internal mechanisms of the clock inside the bulb. He found that it had been powered by magic rather than weights and that all it needed was to be recharged. After doing so, he then sat and observed the various cogs, flywheels, and gears clicking and clacking together around and above him, serenely but fastidiously, to rotate the giant arms of the great timepiece. He then set the clock to the correct time and waited for the bells to ring, a sound which he greeted with glad and celebratory laughter and hands over his ears.

Next on the agenda was the rotation of the roof on its base. Referring to the official plans and diagrams left behind by Conrad, the roof was not attached to the rest of the tower below it by any means of masonry, but simply fit atop it and over its sides like the cap to a bottle. Conrad's spell had caused the roof to hover above the tower at a fraction of an inch and then to pivot on its axis with extreme slowness, such that everyone within every part of the city, at some point during the day, could have a view of the clock from below. To reconstruct Conrad's spellcasting was Arsalan's most difficult task. He had to perform all the correct incantations in the right order for the mechanism to work. Before Arsalan commenced this stage of the repairs, each evening he methodically studied Conrad's plans, which included his abstruse spells. The princess had arranged for Arsalan to lodge in the abbey at night, and there, at their large oaken table by dim lamplight, he dined with the monks on their modest but filling dinners of lamb and bread. Being monks, they did not offer much conversation during repast, and this afforded Arsalan time and privacy to review Conrad's notes and diagrams.

After several days of research, Arsalan was ready to begin. Standing within the top of the tower under the base of the roof, he pointed a wand upward. He recited his chants and performed his enchantments until he was dizzy and started to sweat, and it was after some hours that he noticed the seam between the ceiling and the walls of the tower widening, and then of course it was a few more hours before he could confirm that it was revolving at the correct speed. He marked the roof and the wall with a piece of charcoal at the same spot, and after several hours, when he saw the mark on the ceiling now several feet away from the mark on the wall, he knew he had been successful in conjuring the rotation in the roof.

Arsalan spent the next few days inspecting the tower's roof from the ground and from the windows of the many buildings of the abbey. He adjusted the clock's mechanisms and at the tiles of the roof, just to make sure everything was well. He also charged the spire of the roof that supported the bulb with ample magical charge to make certain it would hold for many centuries. Lastly, he remembered to right the sculpture of the angel on its crown. Arsalan lingered in the abbey for a few more days, observing, testing, surveying, measuring, and asking the monks and officials if they noticed anything wrong with the tower's roof, until the public works officials and the head monks themselves implored Arsalan, with good-natured smiles and many grateful handshakes, to consider his work done. They insisted in the friendliest of ways that they could see no flaw in it, that all was well, that Arsalan should proceed to his next task set forth by the princess, and that they would send for him if they saw anything wrong with the repairs. It had become clear that Arsalan had overstayed his welcome a tad, though he had exceeded their expectations greatly and had impressed them with his extraordinary attentiveness to detail. No, this newly refurbished roof most certainly would not fall to pieces. He knew Teodora and his children would be proud of him if they were to see this.

Arsalan returned to Munich with an accomplished sense of aplomb he had not experienced in a long time. He spoke little and was quietly tickled at the job he had executed, and he knew that his obsessiveness over its minutiae, however painful it was at the time, was a manifestation of passion that surprised even him and proved to be the fulcrum to his success. The first person to greet him at the princess' palace besides the guards and horsemen was Bayram, who smiled glibly and said, "Well done, my friend. I knew you could do it."

"Then you were surer than I was at first," replied Arsalan.

CHAPTER 11

Princess Berthilde received Arsalan in her court with a warm and knowing smile, that of someone who despite her youth was now wise to an older man's strengths and weaknesses, almost like an aunt regarding a nephew. She sat on an ornate chair in a large sitting room, surrounded by her servants and lesser nobility. Siegfrieda stood quietly in the background by a door, shadowy but still unmistakably present.

"Mr. Arsalan Ozdikmen, I have heard wonderful tidings from high officials and the head monks of Fürstenfeld Abbey. They say you have executed a flawless job, and everything has been repaired nicely."

"Yes, I am pleased to concur, but only humbly and after great pains," said Arsalan, bowing, "and I am careful to append my warranty that I am available to repair the roof again if any of my work proves less than acceptable."

"I should take a tour of the abbey to corroborate their reports," said the princess, "but I trust their accounts."

"I appreciate your kindness, Your Majesty," said Arsalan, still bowing.

"And I have some good news for you as well, Mr. Ozdikmen," said the princess, "but I would like to invite you to dinner tonight to reveal it to you."

"I will be honored to be your guest again for dinner, Your Majesty," said Arsalan, "and I am eager to hear what news you bring."

Arsalan was reunited with Kizil in his room by the servants, who quickly left to let the old man become reacquainted with his pet. Kizil missed Arsalan as badly as he missed her, and she became lost in an elated ritual of purring, head-butting Arsalan's hands, and climbing all over his arms and shoulders, while Arsalan did his best to embrace the cat amid her restless jubilation. Afterward, he wrote letters to Asker, updating him on the latest news and with his new address.

That evening, only Princess Berthilde, Siegfrieda, Arsalan, and Bayram were present in the dining hall with a few servants. The four sat directly across from each other at the center of the long table that stretched out from either side of them like a road. Although the atmosphere was now slightly more relaxed, Arsalan remained steadfastly proper, not venturing to take for granted to any degree the more carefree attitude of the princess.

"Now I must tell you the news," said Princess Berthilde, barely able to contain her excitement. "Dietrich! Please summon the scholar!"

"Yes, Your Majesty," said Dietrich, who pivoted on his foot and sped silently out the door. A moment later, in walked Dietrich again, but accompanied by a monk in a dark brown robe, a head of bright orange hair, and eyebrows so thin and blond they were nearly invisible. He was a slender young man, so skinny that his Adam's apple protruded from his throat like a chunk of flint in a bag, and so young that his cheeks still bore the diagonal red blush of a recent childhood.

Dietrich announced, "Friar Heinrich of Andechs Abbey, Your Majesty."

"Your highness," the red-headed monk said as he bowed stiffly, revealing his florid pink tonsure.

"Friar Heinrich, thank you for coming to help us with this small puzzle," said Princess Berthilde.

"Not at all, Your Majesty," said Friar Heinrich. "It was no inconvenience. As a matter of fact, it proved quite an intriguing puzzle for us."

"Please tell us what you told me this afternoon about our cat's mysterious note," said the princess.

"Yes, Your Majesty," said Friar Heinrich. "After extensive research, we have identified the language in which the note was written."

There was a pause, during which no one knew what to say, and Arsalan gingerly submitted an interjection. "And if you don't mind me being so bold as to inquire," Arsalan said, "what is this language in which the note was written?"

"Galatian," said the monk.

"You will have to excuse my ignorance in the branch of linguistics that involves this Galatian language," said Arsalan. "Could you elaborate?"

"It is, or was, an ancient language of Celtic extraction, but which now is extinct, that is to say there are no known remaining speakers of it, although we are fortunate to have some surviving documents written in that language," said Friar Heinrich. "Interestingly, the language was last recorded as being used in your country, Mr. Ozdikmen."

"How interesting. I knew little about the Celtic languages, and less still about the possibility of them being spoken among Turks," said Arsalan. "But have you had the fortune to be able to translate the note from Galatian?"

"We have not had that fortune, sir," said the monk. "Sadly, our scant knowledge of the Galatian vocabulary was sufficient only to identify the language. We have sent a copy of the note to our brethren at an abbey in Rome, where, hopefully, their scholars will be able to generate a full translation."

Princess Berthilde grinned and nodded at Arsalan.

"That is wonderful news," said Arsalan. "I am grateful for your efforts and await the translation with great anticipation."

"It is an honor to serve you, sir," said Friar Heinrich.

"And we thank you, Friar Heinrich," said Princess Berthilde with a wide smile. "You are now relieved."

"Your Majesty," the friar said, and left the room with his austere robe sweeping the ground.

Arsalan turned to Princess Berthilde and said, "Your Majesty, and I am grateful for your help in the solving this little mystery of ours and doubly grateful for your taking such good care of Kizil."

"It was a pleasure," said Princess Berthilde. "She is such a delightful cat."

Siegfrieda had watched this entire gushing performance respectfully but with some amount of detached amusement.

"Your Majesty," she said, "perhaps now would be a good time to proceed to the next item on our agenda of repairs, which is, I believe, the Stadtturm of Straubing."

"Oh yes, of course," said the princess. "So many more!"

The Stadtturm of Straubing served as a watchtower that overlooked the Danube and all roads that led to the Straubing city gate. Construction of the building was completed centuries before, but as houses and buildings in the city grew in height, and as the city's limits expanded, the tower underwent multiple renovations to elevate it. Finally, Conrad the Ineffable had been hired to make the final adjustment to its present elevation, which was so high that city officials doubted their ability to maintain such a tall structure. So, Conrad invented a means by which the tower could be raised or lowered as needed using magic. The building was detached from both the ground and the small, two-floor structure from which it grew. It was re-engineered such that up to half the building's height could be lowered below the surface using a lever located inside the tower so that workers safely could access all parts of the tower's exterior with less fear of falling. After any maintenance work was complete, the tower could be raised again to its full, grand height, or to any lower height that was necessary. Along with many of the other magical structures at that time, the tower's chief magical property had ceased. Its levitating properties were inaccessible, and it was presently stuck at its lowest height. Princess Berthilde revealed to Arsalan her request to repair the landmark, and the famous magical architect duly accepted it.

Repairs began immediately. The way to Straubing was northeast from Munich, a week by horse and carriage. Materials were arranged and procured locally this time rather than transported from the capital. Arsalan was accompanied by another troop of royal guards, and the travelers stayed at small but tidy, comfortable inns frequented by royals as waystations. Once there, Arsalan found he did not need many materials to refurbish the building. He only needed some new steel mechanical parts to replace those that were rusted. Otherwise, reviving the building was the most difficult task. It needed a tremendous amount of magical energy to charge the elevating mechanism, with its many oversized gears and stark shafts and taught chains. Arsalan spent three days recharging it, after which he was exhausted and slept for one and a half. On the day of testing, Arsalan threw upward the lever that was attached to the wall. He heard a roaring, echoing groan from below as the old mechanical parts jumped into action. The floor trembled and Arsalan felt himself become heavier in his legs. The landscape outside the windows broadened and angled downwards to reveal more of itself. The building slowly lifted itself to its full height then gently stopped. Arsalan climbed to the top of the watchtower and stood between the comically pointed spires where the wind whistled past his face and tousled his beard, and he peered over the ramparts at the hazy distance, seeing all the way past the farthest farm fields of Straubing. At the bottom of the tower, the townsfolk stood around the building from the middle of which the massive shaft of the tower protruded, and they cheered with their arms in the air, gazing upward at the majestic watchtower reaching like a great hand toward the azure heavens. When Arsalan finally descended and emerged from the doorway at ground level, they surrounded him and applauded, slapping him on the shoulders and back and shaking his hand. For the rest of the night, they celebrated his achievement at a local beer garden, after which a smaller group of singing, laughing men helped a staggering, inebriated Arsalan to his room where he slept until noon the following day. Arsalan remained another week, measuring the magical charge, calibrating the engine, testing the building's range and speed of movement, then raising and lowering it time and again to make certain that it would continue to work after he left. Yes, this tower, too, was solid and would not fall.

So, again Arsalan returned triumphantly to Princess Berthilde's palace where she, Bayram, and Siegfrieda waited for him, along with lovely little Kizil, who snuggled in his arms. Princess Berthilde was overjoyed, Bayram was glad, and Siegfrieda's frigidly doubting heart seemed to be warming to him with small smiles and friendlier eyes. One night after dinner, she made a point of catching up with Arsalan and walking with him along a balcony overlooking the gardens outside, where she expressed her softening sentiments toward him.

"Well, Mr. Ozdikmen," she said, "you are either the most gentlemanly brute I ever have met, or the most brutish gentlemen, but I cannot be sure of which. In any case, I know I had my doubts about you, and I apologize to you for that. I was ignorant of all this magical architecture business myself. And hearing so much of the culture turning against it, I was influenced by the naysayers, I admit. But you've proved yourself twice now, and for that I am glad."

"I understand your primary concerns were the health and well-being of Princess Berthilde," said Arsalan. "She is young, and you wished to prevent her harm, disappointment, or humiliation. You also wished to spare your kingdom waste or fraud. I have a daughter about the same age, and I had taken the same precautions to protect her as you have the princess. And insofar as one's home is one's own kingdom, I should have been as cautious and discerning as you to prevent financial dissolution."

"And I understand you were not successful with the latter," said Siegfrieda.

"No," said Arsalan. "Fame and success coming so early in one's life have these effects on one's sense of judgement, and I will rue that till the day I die. I envy royals. You handle wealth and power with such panache, and you pass this wisdom from one generation to the next without much interruption. My father was a cloth merchant, and—bless his wonderful soul—he had no such wisdom to grant me. In terms of money, he only knew how to sell cloth and how to handle the modest wealth he was able to achieve."

"And your daughter?" said Siegfrieda. "What happened to her?"

"Her life was threatened by an impetuous suitor, a spoiled prince who wanted her as an expensive plaything," he said. "I did my best to defend her, but she was strong-willed, and she made her own decision to disappear in order to protect herself and not to be a burden to me."

"That is saddening," said Siegfrieda. "I wish we could help find her."

"I appreciate your sentiments, but she is too far away. I simply wish her to be alive and well," said Arsalan. "All the same, my failure to protect her using my own means is my most profound calamity, greater even than the collapse of that building. Such is the reason I dare to say I have as much interest in protecting your lovely princess as you do. You have my word."

Chapter 12

That summer, Arsalan kept busy with three more of the princess' projects: the Marienkapelle Cathedral in Würzburg whose red stone exterior had ceased glowing at nighttime, the Reverse Aqueducts of Nürnberg whose water had stopped flowing upstream from the river to the castles on the hills, and the Circular Ramparts of Nördlingen, which normally revolved around the perimeter of the city like a caravan to deter invaders but had halted. Arsalan labored all the sultry weeks on these structures, his face red and beading with sweat and his eyes steely with impassioned concentration. He spoke little and worked tirelessly and paid limitless attention to every detail of his tasks, to every nail in every corner and every keystone in every arch, and he did not stop until his repairs demonstrated sufficient evidence that they were incapable of failure. Many were the townsfolk who witnessed the fiery Arsalan waging his wars on disrepair and decrepitude, on immobility, on rust, cobwebs, and moss, on broken switches and cracked stonework and squeaking gears. Some wished to ask the old magical architect why he was performing repairs rather than manifesting brilliant new buildings, but others shushed the questioners, saying that only a magical architect could renew such wonderful buildings and mechanisms and that they should be grateful that none other than Arsalan the Magnificent himself had availed himself to such tasks. So, there they stood, audiences of awestruck onlookers surrounding him like the leaning seats of an amphitheater, staring with widened eyes and pursed lips at the fantastic conjuring that was being performed before them by the bearded old wizard from the tip of whose majestic, reddened nose droplets of perspiration trickled as he waved his arms and spread his fingers in his fervent spellcasting.

At nights he would retire to his temporary beds in the inns and guesthouses, beds that although comfortable never seemed quite fitting, never seemed quite right. Each of them was always different, slightly off, cold, unfamiliar. Of course, by this time in his life, Arsalan could sleep comfortably enough on anything at all, but he realized that, aside from his functional and crudely fashioned bed in the cabin at Sliven, he had not had a bed to call his very own for quite some time. He recalled his luxurious old bed in his palace in Kirklareli. It was a sumptuous, canopied bed in which he and Teodora could become wonderfully lost, swimming in a blissful pool of satin and silk until late mornings. He recalled how after the febrile storm of love of a previous night they would awaken in each other's arms, and as the dawn's pink light filtered through the shutters and tenderly illuminated the radial fibers of their irises and the pores of their skin, they would look deeply into each other's eyes for prolonged periods when wishing each other a good morning, while outside the distant calls of the muezzins echoed across the city to call the pious to prayer. Arsalan would never heed their call while looking at his wife in the mornings, for at those times he felt he was already deeply lost within prayer.

Arsalan realized at this point how acutely he missed Teodora. His anger and shame finally had abated such that he experienced a renewed yearning for reunion with her. His feeling was like a severed nerve whose end had not ceased sensing what it had lost, one that could heal if only it could find its mated end. Arsalan found himself missing Teodora's hair, her face, her voice, and her eyes, at least as he remembered her then, and he felt his breath and heart quicken. Somehow an ember from the deeply familiar ashes of his love had been rekindled, or had never fizzled, and now was glowing—a faint orange speck in pile of gray ash that was being swept away by the actions of his labor, bit by bit, to reveal a fire that had never been extinguished completely. It was Teodora's deep, assuring familiarity he missed the most, the way the presence of her face, her voice, her body, and her mind had made its imprints on his soul that no one else had made. Even when Grozda had come near him, he could not help but encounter a subtly fearful revulsion toward the new woman for her inability to fit Teodora's strongly entrenched but emptied impressions.

As autumn began to make itself known with its first chilly breezes and flotillas of clouds sailing overhead in the luminous teal sky, Princess Berthilde, overjoyed at the completed work thus far, commended Arsalan and asked him if he needed to take leave for a time.

"I have been enjoying the work that you have been supplying me, and for which I have been most grateful to receive. I would like to continue all your work until it is complete. However, there has been one matter that has been on my mind of late, a matter that I would like to put to rest in my heart," answered Arsalan.

"And what matter is that?" asked the princess.

"My former wife, the Lady Teodora of Brzeg," he said. "If you remember, our marriage was never formally annulled. I feel I should go to visit her to finalize the annulment, or to see if she is willing."

"How long would it take to annul a marriage that has been discarded years ago in a foreign country?" asked Siegfrieda, who had been standing nearby. "Would it require the officiation of a governing body to formalize it?"

"I suppose it is more the case that I have feelings regarding her I have never settled," said Arsalan. "She left in a hurry, with no paperwork signed. I did not feel I had the right to follow her. The matter of our marriage was left unresolved, even by her abandonment. I want to see if I can get that sorted somehow now."

"Is it not a long way to Brzeg?" asked the princess. "If I remember correctly, it requires two weeks of travel there and another two to return. Are you sure you want to make that journey? Do you know if she is still living and willing to see you?"

"I do not know," said Arsalan simply, "but I know it will not take me that long."

Siegfrieda had been standing there and conferred with the princess quietly to one side, then returned.

"Mr. Ozdikmen," said Siegfrieda, "we see your heart is still deeply affected by your wife's leaving you. Perhaps there is some way to help in the matter that could save us all some time and trouble."

"I did not mean to make my affairs of the heart those of your court. You are kind," said Arsalan. "What help you may offer in this regard I would highly appreciate."

"Allow us to send a letter ahead of you. And wait at least to get a response from the Lady before you depart," said Siegfrieda. "We don't want you to head there blindly."

Princess Berthilde drafted an official communique to send to the royal court in Brzeg notifying Lady Teodora of the intended visit by Arsalan, who now was under the employ of the court of Bavaria. The letter explained in general terms the rationale for the visit, which was to assist their magical architect in ascertaining the true legal status of his marriage to the Lady. The letter was transcribed onto the most opulent parchment by their most talented calligraphers in their finest ink and sealed in a gold envelope with a large blot of red wax on the outside. The letter was spirited off by official post to Brzeg. A month later, one returned in the official stationery of the Duchy of Silesia. The wording was frosty and officious and not written in Teodora's own hand, to be sure, but it was indicated that she nonetheless accepted the request. The letter also made the point that Teodora now held the title of Duchess since her father's passing. The Duchess of Brzeg would receive the magical architect whensoever he would arrive.

Arsalan arranged for Kizil to stay with the princess once again while on his journey. Again, he would miss his lovely red feline, and he spent a night cuddling with her and telling her his plans and when he would return.

"You must be a good and brave kitty until I return," said Arsalan, scratching her face to her delight. "I will miss you tremendously. Don't be afraid of Princess Berthilde, though, please. She is a wonderful young woman, just like my daughter. I will be back."

The next morning at dawn, Arsalan stood in the cobblestone courtyard of the princess' palace with only a backpack of his belongings slung onto his shoulders. He wore his thick traveling clothes, a hat, his boots, and a scarf. Princess Berthilde, Siegfrieda, and Bayram were there to see him off.

"You still haven't revealed how you are going to travel to Brzeg alone with only your backpack in less time than it would take you by horse," said Siegfrieda.

"I am, after all, a wizard," said Arsalan. "I will fly there."

The three were speechless. Although they knew abstractly that magical architects should be capable of such feats, magical architects typically proved to be so judicious in the demonstrations of their powers outside of the act of construction that it did not occur to Arsalan's friends that he simply could fly like a bird whenever he wished. And this was precisely what he did; Arsalan raised his arms and floated ten feet into the air.

"Your Majesty, again I am grateful for your granting me leave. I will return in due time. Please be well, and I respectfully request, please, for you to take good care of Kizil, and make sure she gets some exercise. I do dare to say that she is fattening under your lavish care. I will be eternally grateful," said Arsalan.

"I promise," said Princess Berthilde. "And please do take good care of yourself. And do return safely. I will be worrying for you."

"And I as well, Mr. Ozdikmen," said Siegfrieda.

Arsalan bowed, as well as one could affect a bow while floating in midair, and then he turned and flew away, with remarkable ease and panache, northeast toward the rising pink sun, over the vermillion rooftops of the princess' complex of palaces and buildings and above the trees, until to his friends he was a small black dot in the orange sky. Arsalan flew oddly—not horizontally like a bird, but standing upright, perhaps even leaning forward a little—and he flew just over the treetops, not too terribly high from the ground. It was a glorious morning for flying. The blazing, peach-colored sun rose before him, and the seas of trees sailed below him like a procession of soldiers to war. The frigid wind roared past his head, and his cold face became ruddy and swollen, his eyes narrow. His scarf flapped behind him, and the lip of his thick, broad-brimmed hat also shook above his eyes. Arsalan was shooting forth faster than any horse running at full speed, but not so fast that he could not control himself. At times he flew higher, at other times much lower, just above the road he was following, with the rocks and puddles speeding under his feet blurrily, until he saw travelers ahead of him, whereupon he ascended to avoid them, and the travelers saw a shadow, something strange and manlike, flit past them over their heads like a huge bird before it vanished into the distance.

Arsalan flew at this pace for six long hours, passing one small town or city after another: Landshut, Deggendorf, Zwiesel, Železná Ruda, Klatovy. Their concentrated hives of bristling red steeples and roofs expanded beneath him in all their quaint and gleaming splendor. Here and there between the gables in small lanes, a child would look up and would stare at Arsalan; pointing, the child would tug on the mothers' dress, distracting her from her errands, but in her irritated confusion, she would not see the flying man. Arsalan would be gone by then, in a flash, and the mother would think the child had seen yet another bird or cloud. In seconds, Arsalan would be exiting the city limits of that town that dotted the route to Brzeg with so many others, like delicate spider's eggs tangled in strands of silk, lying along endless branches of settlements. Between each city and town lay expanses of green forest, some laced with oranges and reds. The trees stood shoulder to shoulder like congregations of people, bending this way and that in the wind as if sharing whispered gossip. Arsalan paid keen attention to his route that often was lost beneath their branches then found again. At these times, he flew at a lower altitude to make certain of his route until it became clearer, then he would blast forth again at increased height with all due haste. Farm fields soared beneath him in their patchworks of greens and browns dotted with folk and horses, as tiny as game pieces, bent over their plodding work. None of them noticed him as he sailed over their heads, except one woman who stood to wipe her brow with her sleeve and whose gaze followed him in wonder has he passed far overhead.

At noon Arsalan stopped over a forest just outside the municipal limits of Prague. He recalled the proper wizardly method to come to a safe halt. He decelerated until he stopped entirely in midair, hovering over one spot on the ground, to which he then descended gradually and gingerly to his feet. He landed on a soft bed of pine needles, which felt soothing under his boots. The sudden lack of the sound of rushing wind disoriented him, and since his legs had not supported his weight all day, they were wobbly for a few minutes before he recovered his balance. Arsalan would have flown directly to the middle of town, but he did not wish to draw a crowd. He would arrive innocuously, on foot, like a common traveler, and he would look for the nearest inn for lunch.

Walking this distance was more of a chore than he had anticipated. Casting his flight spell for hours had exhausted him, and one's progress on foot, by contrast, was so much slower and more plodding in any case. He was able to make his way past the city gates and into the midst of the town, but once there he found it difficult to summon the energy to look for a suitable inn. Although Prague was one of his favorite cities and had been there many times in the past, he had not visited it in such a long time that he almost lost his way through it. Eventually, after some weary searching, he found that his favorite inn he remembered from years ago had closed and was replaced with a leather shop. Nearby, there was a shop selling bundles of sausages, where he purchased a few, along with a bottle of wine. He brought these to the Charles Bridge, where he sat on the low wall. Arsalan combined the meats with some fresh bread he had brought from Princess Berthilde's palace and ate them as he sat, staring at the river as it flowed and sparkled lazily beneath him, while he occasionally washed his food down with the wine. He was famished from his flight, and once he finished his lunch, he was ready to fall asleep in the warm sunlight that glimmered over the languid river, painting the bridge and the genteel crowds that promenaded over it with pale, golden light.

At length, he caught himself dozing off. He was not a young man anymore. The extreme itinerary of the day had taxed him, but he knew he had to continue if he was to reach Brzeg by sundown. He placed his uneaten food back in his backpack and shouldered it again. At this time, Arsalan did not feel it was necessary to find a private place from which to launch himself into flight again, so he decided to do so right there from the Charles Bridge. He raised his arms and flew off into the air soundlessly, like a kite thrown aloft. Bystanders gasped and watched him with slack jaws. They did not yell or cry, but simply witnessed him, as if they were dreaming. Arsalan flew over the bridge and down the length of the limpid blue river as if carried by its waters until he left it and headed northeast again over the rooftops. He disembarked from the city of Prague, a bit too soon after such a long absence from it but vowing to return to find a better inn for lunch and beer.

Arsalan careened forth with a particular intensity, high above the tree-tops, his eyes directed forward. Eschewed now were any signs of leisure or flamboyance in his aerial techniques. He rocketed stiffly forward like a knife through bread. The reddening sun shone onto his back, lighting the long way before him and projecting its lengthening shadows. He had to hurry to Brzeg before nightfall, when he would not be able to see anything well enough to fly safely. Beneath him glided the cities of Nehvizdy, Třebestovice, Hradec Kralove, Nachod, Klodzko, countless farm fields and villages and groves and woods, and three expansive blue lakes that glittered in the fiery afternoon sun. He recognized Nysa and Grodków from above and, bearing north and slightly west, saw the limits of modest little Brzeg with its numerous, spired cathedrals reaching endearingly toward the sky.

Arsalan now was too fatigued to care if anyone saw him approaching from the heavens for a landing. He simply wished to stand on solid ground once more to rest. He located the Brzeg Castle, where he remembered Teodora's family lived, and landed directly in the courtyard, stumbling to a halt on his toes. It was now five o'clock, and the sun was lowering, casting blue shadows and ruminative orange light against the white building's arcaded balconies and bannisters. The little chateau was only three stories high under its red eaves, and here its balconies surrounded the courtyard on three sides, with a wall, covered in ivy, in the back. The windows were dark, and the courtyard desolate, which puzzled Arsalan. In fact, he felt somewhat disappointed that no watchguards marched forth to challenge him. Eventually, he wandered over to the wall where he found a stone bench. There he sat, leaning backwards and stretching his legs in front of him and placing one ankle on top of another, for nearly an hour as the sun set and as he chewed on the rest of the sausage he had purchased in Prague.

After a time, a man appeared on the third-floor balcony above. He wore a bright blue suit of a servant of the castle, and a white wig. He stopped for a minute or more, glaring down from his height at Arsalan. From his position, he yelled toward Arsalan.

"You, there!" he hollered. "Excuse me!" And this he repeated as he walked over to a set of stairs, disappeared into it, and descended, finally emerging from a door at the bottom. All the while, the servant was exclaiming, "You, there! Excuse me!" without variation and in such an irritating tone of voice that Arsalan refused to answer him until the blue-coated servant was standing right in front of him, glowering at him.

"Who are you," asked the servant, "and what business do you have here? And who let you in?"

It was apparent that the man was mistaking Arsalan for a traveling vagrant who somehow had found a way over the rear wall and into the courtyard just to sit there. Arsalan looked down at his own clothes which, to be fair, were indeed worn here and there. Then the old man stood and bowed.

"Arsalan the Magnificent," said Arsalan the Magnificent, "wizard and magical architect, at your service."

"Oh, really?" said the man, whose skepticism was not so easily dispelled. "And is the Duchy of Brzeg expecting Arsalan the Magnificent, wizard and magical architect, this evening?"

"Yes," said Arsalan, and he handed the man the letter he received from the Duchy of Brzeg.

The man read it impatiently and said, "Why, this was mailed to Munich, postmarked two weeks ago. From whom did you steal this? How would you come from Munich so fast? Where is your horse? Or did you fly here like a bird?"

"As a matter of fact," said Arsalan, "I did fly here like a bird. And if you don't show me to Duchess Teodora, I will fly in to find her myself."

The servant of course scoffed, but Arsalan angrily snatched the letter from the other man's hands and floated into the air. The man's mouth shot open as if smote by a fist, and he twirled around wildly as he watched Arsalan levitate, in a rather graceful arc, over his head all the way to the balcony of the third floor.

"You have left me no choice!" yelled Arsalan from the balcony. "I will find her myself!"

"Wait!" said the man, capitulating finally and holding up his hand. "I believe you. Come down, and I will bring her to you. Please, wait down here."

Arsalan returned, alighting to the stone tiles of the courtyard's ground, and the blue-suited servant hurried inside the castle with Arsalan's letter in his bunched hand. By this time, there were several more servants who, while simply passing by on their normal errands on the other balconies, had stopped to watch the strange events unfolding before them. They all wore the same blue uniform and white wig, and they stood next to each other in their spots, murmuring to each other and gesturing toward Arsalan. Somehow none of them dared to descend to confront him themselves but decided instead to keep watch over the stranger from the safety of the surrounding balconies. Arsalan stood in the courtyard alone, waiting for something to happen, until dusk ensued. The evening slowly drank the light and color from the sky, and the stacked rooms of the castle glowed yellow and orange and white against the darkening blue of the starlit nocturne. Arsalan dared not barge into the castle but waited stubbornly outside for its occupants to decide how they wished to react to his presence. He already had reserved plans to stay at an inn that night if this visit to Teodora was not welcome.

At some length, a procession of guards and servants emerged from the main, wide archway in the middle of the building toward Arsalan, carrying lanterns, and they surrounded him and held their lanterns up to his face until his eyes were blinded with light. Arsalan politely held his hands up to motion them away a bit. On the second-floor balcony in front of him, he saw a figure emerge from the doorway of a lit room. It was a woman's figure, clothed in the layered dress of royalty. Her face was obscured in shadow, but Arsalan could hear her voice as she said, "Let me get a good look at him, gentlemen."

Arsalan said nothing, but simply returned her gaze.

"Arsalan," she said, "that is you after all."

"As surely me as ever I will be," he replied. "My condolences for your father's passing."

"Thank you," she said. "And you have aged."

"Time and hardship do that to a man," he said.

"Meet me in the reception room," she said, and she turned and reentered the room whence she had emerged. A chief guard said, "Come this way, Mr. Ozdikmen." The whole procession escorted Arsalan through the main archway, then turned into another door set within the stone walls of the tunnel and proceeded up a staircase. Arsalan found it funny that the entire crowded troupe went through the trouble of accompanying him up the narrow set of stairs where they barely all could fit. The crowd then went into a dark hallway which led to a room with plain white walls lined with iron lanterns. Here guards and servants quietly conferred with each other until it was agreed that most of them should leave, allowing a smaller handful to watch the visitor until the Duchess arrived. Once the larger body of the crowd had left, Arsalan could see more clearly the finer details of the reception room. Its furniture was weighty, ornately carved, and lacked upholstery. The floor was tiled with glossy stone squares.

The atmosphere here was more relaxed than that in Princess Berthilde's Bavarian castle. The servants chatted with each other, shared news, and generally did not stop their activities due to Arsalan's presence. They cast puzzled and suspicious looks his way every so often, and they seemed to be talking about him in their own language, which he felt was rude. Arsalan had been in this castle only a few times some decades ago, and he had forgotten how loudly they spoke. They irritated him with their constant chatter. If they had been Arsalan's servants, he would have disciplined them.

But all at once they stood at attention and bowed toward a door where Teodora entered.

"Duchess," they all said in unison.

Teodora wore a marvelous dress of blue and white with a short jacket and hat both lined with ermine fur. She of course was older, and she carried herself in a much statelier manner than Arsalan had remembered from before. Her back and head were erect, yet she looked nervous and sheepish, and Arsalan could tell she was attempting to conceal her discomfort with an air of regality. She grasped her hands in front of herself, and her eyes darted from her own toes to Arsalan's face as she approached, trying to gauge his state of mind and mood.

"Teodora," said Arsalan. "Or should I call you Duchess?"

"The former will do," she said, and then turned to her servants and ordered them to wait in the adjoining room, and to shut the door behind them.

"I see you received my letter," said Arsalan.

"Yes," she said. "You wish to ascertain the state of our marriage, which was never formally annulled."

"I daresay you left in such a haste," said Arsalan, "that it was impossible to arrange such paperwork. And you have been on my mind lately, quite a lot."

"I'm sorry," she said, and then there was silence. It was such a simple statement, and Arsalan thought she had more to say. She opened her mouth, then closed it, then she raised her arms toward him and approached him. The two gravitated toward each other like magnets, and they fell into a tight embrace. Teodora began to breathe heavily into his shoulder, and her breaths moistened into sobs, and she began to tremble and to weep into his clothes.

"I'm sorry!" she whispered. "I'm sorry. I was sick of your irresponsible behavior. When you became bankrupt, I…I panicked. I was, after all, still a Lady. I was used to wealth, and I would not stand to be deprived of it. I was fearful of descending into poverty through no fault of my own. I came here to save myself. I didn't realize that I left everything behind! Everything else that was dear to me! I didn't pause to consider that there were people I left behind who missed me! I was young and foolish! Forgive me!"

"Why didn't you respond to our children, at least?" said Arsalan.

"Fear. Pride. Stupidity. Shame," she said. "I thought since they had grown, I could flee safely. But they still needed me. And you still needed me. I didn't consider that you were hurting, too, and needed my love and support."

"Yes," said Arsalan. "Especially Defne."

Teodora's eyes clenched shut, and she hid them in his shoulder.

"Do you blame me for her disappearance?" she asked.

"I was afraid you would blame me," he said.

"I did," she wept. "But I also know that if I had been there, I could have protected her and could have guided her. I'm sorry."

They finished their long embrace and found two chairs across from each other. Teodora sat primly at the edge of hers.

"There are things I have been wanting to tell you," said Arsalan. "I was a stupid and extravagant young man. I had every worldly possession so surely at my disposal that, try as I might, I was not able to cherish it all. I did not have the capacity. I think I took you for granted. I treated you as one of my beloved trophies, one of my accomplishments, but I don't think I tried well enough to know your heart. I did not see that I had made you resentful of everything else we possessed and to which I had devoted my attention. You are royalty, and I should have treated you as the royalty that you were. You did not have to leave your family to marry me. You could have lived a rich life here, in your family's castle, with a noble Silesian man, just as easily. I understand why you fled back here."

"I can't say anything you have said is wrong," she said, "but I have had years to think about it, and I can regard the past with a clearer understanding, and my anger over it has left me, leaving only regret."

"What becomes of us?" said Arsalan. "What becomes of our marriage?"

"As you know, since my father's passing," she said, "I have become a Duchess. This has less importance than it used to have since the Prussians took control, but still, I have responsibilities. This may prevent us from reuniting."

"I understand," said Arsalan. "Have you had any suitors?"

"There have been some ambitious lesser noble men who have called on me," she said, "but I see right through them. Members of the upper nobility aren't interested in me. They are only interested in young maidens, and women with greater rule. I have not been seeking anyone. I have too many affairs of state to manage."

"I understand," said Arsalan.

"And you?" she asked.

"A farm woman took a liking to me on her own initiative, but when she learned I was a magical architect, she retracted her interest," he said. "Otherwise, I have chosen to remain alone. I feel I have failed in love so badly that I do not deserve a second chance."

"I see," pondered Teodora.

"You are too firmly ensconced in your new life, which would have been your old life had I not interloped," he said. "Reunion, it seems, will not be a possibility for us."

"It doesn't seem so," she said. "Especially now that you are the de facto magical architect of Bavaria."

"That is temporary," he said, "until I am able to renew my reputation, which has been proceeding well."

"I'm glad for you," she said. "What did you do with yourself after I left?"

"After you left, and the children left, I sold the chateau and moved to a cabin in the Balkan Mountains, at a place called Sliven. There, I was living alone, when Bayram found me," he said.

"You sold the palace? And you were alone for so many years?" she said. "Was that some sort of penance?"

"I was seeking absolution from my foolish behavior," he said. "And believe me when I say I think I have changed for the better."

"I certainly hope so," she said, "In any case, I feel I have done the same."

"I don't know how to proceed with our marriage," he said. "Tell me what you would like me to do."

"I don't know," she said. "I feel I still love you. I feel my heart never left you."

"I do still love you, too," said Arsalan. "An old burden is lifted from my heart to know that you are no longer angry with me and do not hate me."

Teodora gently placed her hand onto his, blanketing it with her warmth. His hand had been interlaced thoughtfully with his other on his lap as if in solemn prayer. He had been gazing into his lap during the conversation, and when he saw her pale hand over his knuckles he smiled and gazed up at her.

"Let me rebuild myself," said Arsalan. "Let me reconstruct everything I had, and when I have reconstituted my fortunes, I will return to you, and we can speak again of our future, if there is to be any."

"I agree," Teodora said. "There is much to sort in our lives, but I will wait for you."

"I hope not to take too long," said Arsalan.

"My future here in this Duchy is long," Teodora said. "Let fate decide when you are done. I will not take action toward annulment."

Arsalan dwelt in her castle as her guest for three days. They took many long walks and carriage rides together on the grounds of her properties. Arsalan made sure to behave reasonably and maturely around her so that she always felt comfortable around him, neither begging for her affection nor mourning his past mistakes too woefully, although they did shed tears together over their missing daughter and son. Arsalan told her everything he had learned from life on his mountain in the Balkans in clear and frank detail, and he described how it had changed him. He could tell all this affected her and helped heal the fissure between them. In Teodora's gazes and gestures, she indicated a new warmth toward him in subtle ways, although she remained cordial, and she seemed to keep her heart at a careful and respectful distance. The affection Arsalan felt toward Teodora was restrained, self-assured, comfortable, and warm, like old but freshly laundered clothes, different from the zeal and passion of his youthful days when he desired her like fashionable new attire. His feelings toward Teodora now seemed even more assuring than the strange, dark, electric allurement he had experienced toward Grozda, a magnetism that, now that he reconsidered it, had proven disconcertingly insistent, opioid, pheromonal, vaguely unwholesome, like the aromatic call of pungent, purple wine when the heart is in tumult. Grozda was a good woman, but not even she had been convinced of the merits of their mutual attraction.

Finally, Arsalan had to return to his work in Bavaria. He wished Teodora goodbye and promised to write to her, and they embraced. By now, the servants and guards had become friendly with him, and they also gathered in the courtyard to wish him good luck. Even the servant who had challenged Arsalan in the courtyard became affable to him and wished him well. Arsalan raised his arms again and lifted himself into the air, to the warm applause of the crowd, and he flew slowly southwest as if held along by a string from the heavens. When he looked back, he saw Teodora wave a white, gauzy handkerchief at him before lifting it to her face.

Arsalan flew back to Munich in a relaxed haste. He did not stop to rest or to eat. He simply retraced his route, confidently and assuredly, barely paying attention to the minute world of trees and humanity and buildings that sped below him in a boundless, dizzying blur. He arrived at the courtyard Princess Berthilde's palace, galloping along the cobblestone ground to a halt, and he bade hello to the guards and horsemen, who by now had seen enough of his demonstrations of magical prowess to be used to the sight of him flying in from the sky like a falcon. Indeed, Arsalan felt as unweighted and free as one. A stone had been unearthed from his heart, letting in light and fresh air that had not graced his soul in years.

CHAPTER 13

"Welcome back, Mr. Ozdikmen," said Siegfrieda to Arsalan, who was being escorted down a hallway to his room by a servant. "I see you made your journey there and back well enough."

"Yes, I have, Madam Siegfrieda," said Arsalan. "Thank you for asking."

"I wish to live to see the day when we non-magical folk are able to take such speedy voyages to the far ends of the Holy Roman Empire," said Siegfrieda. Arsalan interpreted this comment as her honest attempt at casual and friendly humor, at which she did not prove perfectly adept without sounding somehow sarcastic, but for which she deserved some credit.

"Well, I must say," said Arsalan, "the feat is more exhausting than it seems."

"Well, after you've rested," said Siegfrieda, "Princess Berthilde has some good news for you, which she would like to reveal to you over dinner tonight."

"Thank you, Madam. If I may be so bold as to ask, what does the news concern?" asked Arsalan.

"We've received what we think is an accurate translation of the note that was left in the collar of that cat of yours," said Siegfrieda. "The text came all the way from Rome, so I'll be as interested to hear it now as you, especially after such a long wait."

"Oh yes," said Arsalan. "I would like for all of us to hear it. And speaking of Kizil, is she well?"

"Oh yes, we had the servants return her to your room for you. She is such a lovely creature," said Siegfrieda.

"Thank you," Arsalan said, gladdened at Siegfrieda's apparent attempt at mending relations between them.

He entered his room, pack in hand, where Kizil had been sitting on a couch and staring out the window. She leapt to the ground with a soft thud and then into his arms in a fluffy maelstrom of affection and exultation. They missed each other truly, and he petted her as they looked into each other's eyes, his large and brown and hairy, and hers twinkling and coinlike and filled with cool jade like the surface of a pond in a forest, closing in slits of delight as she received his caresses on her head and ears.

That night, Arsalan dined again with Princess Berthilde and Siegfrieda. Dietrich waited on them again, and Bayram joined them a little later with profuse but unnecessary apologies. While Arsalan was gone to Silesia, Bayram had gone away on business and just had returned. The four of them were like family, it seemed now, and Arsalan realized how fortunate he was to be on such good terms with a member of high royalty for whom he was performing such fulfilling work, and to have such friends as Bayram who emerged valiantly from nowhere after so many years and over so many miles to shepherd Arsalan from his exile. Even during the most glorious days of their youth, Arsalan had not known Bayram to be such a noble and loyal friend. Indeed, it seemed they had grown closer. Even Kizil was there as well, on her precious stool topped with a violet cushion of soft velvet, placed carefully by a table garnished with a small bowl of rich meats. Arsalan's mood had been lifted by the results of his visit to Teodora. To have expected circumstances to be any better for Arsalan at that moment would have been unreasonable. He was filled with a shy sense of serene and gracious vitality. Princess Berthilde sensed this in Arsalan, and she took the opportunity to question him about his expedition to Brzeg while trying not to seem too nosy. However judicious Princess Berthilde attempted to be, though, Siegfrieda cast her cautious but calm glances while nonetheless allowing the innocent young princess to continue.

Arsalan did not mind the princess' inquiries at all. None of her questions pained or annoyed him. Such dark shadows and moldy cobwebs had been exorcised from the corners of his heart that he now bore no shame in pointing out where they had lurked. In fact, he took some pride in it. He told Princess Berthilde all his feelings toward Teodora, all the gnawing doubts, regrets, and sorrows he had harbored that had been resolved in their three days together, and all the ways he recalled he had loved her. Arsalan spoke hopefully, but humbly and realistically, of his future with Teodora, once his work in Bavaria was complete. At this Princess Berthilde, in her blushing youth, listened with fascination. The depths of feeling of which older adults were capable toward each other had remained incomprehensible to her before, and she was enchanted by his stories of rekindled love. She began to giggle and to sigh, and she remarked that one day she hoped to experience a passion like that. At this point Siegfrieda began to touch the princess' arm reassuringly, reminding her that of course she would find a love like that one day, but that now she was still a maiden.

After dinner was finished and the servants were cleaning the table, Princess Berthilde, who had become lost in her intoxicated, romantic reverie, suddenly exclaimed, "And I nearly forgot! The mystery of our dear feline friend is solved tonight! Dietrich! Do summon Friar Heinrich! We must not keep him waiting."

Dietrich did so, and out came Friar Heinrich again, with his festively bright orange hair and rubicund complexion contrasting against his somber, brown, woolen habit. He stood coolly at attention by the table.

"Your Majesty," he said.

"Good Friar Heinrich," said Princess Berthilde, with the frisky air of someone ready for a good parlor game after supper, "We have heard the good news about your translation you have received from Rome. Please enlighten us, if you may be so kind."

"Of course, Your Majesty," said Friar Heinrich, drawing a scroll from his pocket. "This translation indeed has come all the way from that glorious capital where the most capable scholars of philology of our order have evinced a rough but coherent message, which reads in our language as follows."

Princess Berthilde grinned from ear to ear and shifted herself excitedly in her seat, as if about to hear a thrilling tale from a bard. Arsalan sat back in his seat and held Kizil in his lap, gently petting her, and listening curiously but not quite as breathlessly as the princess. Siegfrieda and Bayram similarly gazed at the monk with open but unexpectant expressions, anticipating nothing.

Friar Heinrich cleared his throat theatrically and recited the words in a high, lofty, and somewhat stilted voice, which he perhaps used often in prayer:

By the gods of day, by the goddesses of night,

By these words let the guise of our cat take flight

To reveal from within, to reveal for us all,

The girl who is hidden within to stand tall.

Let her beauty be uncloaked from the fangs and the furs,

From the tail and the eyes of green jade and the purrs.

Let the maiden within unfurl and breathe air,

and walk on two legs again, pure and fair.

All those present were silent for a long, breathless moment, but it was obvious that no one had any idea what the message meant. Even tall Dietrich in his bright red coat, who rarely said anything unless addressed by his masters, seemed to wince to himself in confusion.

"My," said Princess Berthilde, "what a beautiful and strange little poem! What does it mean?"

"With much chagrin I must admit, Your Majesty," said Friar Heinrich, "I do not know."

"All that scholarly translation work and none of your order could determine a meaning?" said Siegfrieda.

"We only could hazard a guess," said Friar Heinrich. "It sounds to me and others of my order like an incantation, a spell of some sort, but one blasphemous, like one woven by a practicing witch, or at least one who fancied herself or himself capable of some sort of devilish magic. I shall pray for this person's soul tonight."

"What do you think it means, my good Arsalan?" asked the princess.

Arsalan was pensive, and his eyes seemed moist, but he tried to maintain a distant and scholarly air to distract himself and everyone from what he was feeling.

"My guess is similar to our good Friar's" said Arsalan. "But I am curious. You have translated the passage beautifully into your lovely German tongue. What do the words sound like in the original Galatian?"

"In the original Galatian?" stammered Friar Heinrich. "Oh, well, now that you mention it, sir, they did supply me with a fairly good pronunciation guide, with which, I disclaim, I do not possess expert mastery."

The friar fished in the deep, brown pockets of his flowing robe and produced another set of papers that he rattled and shuffled in his thin, bony hands. After a moment of this anxious activity, he seemed to find the correct bit of information on a corner of a sheet of paper that he turned sideways in front of his face. In fits and starts, he slowly began to pronounce syllables and consonants of a guttural and spitting nature, filled with peculiar and twisting diphthongs like clashing colors mixing on a painter's palette. As Friar Heinrich progressed, with his brow furrowing unsurely, he struggled less and less with the deeply alien phonemes and fell into enough of a fluency to reveal to himself and his audience patterns of rhythm and rhyming in the charmingly odd language that were pleasant to the ears. By the time he was finishing the passage, it was as if he understood his own words, and when he was entirely done, he simply looked up from his paper and smiled at his audience.

"I believe I have done my best justice to this most mysterious tongue," he said.

Just then, Kizil began to meow loudly. Arsalan looked down at her, and Kizil was staring into Arsalan's eyes and seemed extremely agitated.

"What is it, my dear?" asked Arsalan quietly.

Kizil seemed to enter a seizure of some sort. She became confused and restless, and Arsalan tried to console her, hugging her. Princess Berthilde looked disturbed and anxious and called out the cat's name. Everyone at the table stood. Kizil's body seemed to blur and to change shape, as though seen through thick glass. Arsalan no longer could tell what he was holding, and he pushed his chair backward and placed the blurring animal on the floor in front of him and held his hands in front of himself helplessly. The dark, smudged image of the cat seemed to be squealing in horrific pain. The screams deepened in pitch, and the mutating thing became larger and appeared to grow longer limbs, which, obscured as they were, resembled fins or wings. Finally, the wailing assumed the sound of a human voice. Arsalan stood and walked backward from the bizarre occurrence at his feet, and he continued to hold his hands up in confusion and dismay. He looked to the others helplessly, and they returned his expression. The women held their hands to their mouths and steadied themselves on chairs as the moaning phenomenon writhed on the floor before them.

Princess Berthilde yelled to Dietrich, "Do something! Get help!" But the chief servant was speechless.

"What is happening to my cat?" screamed Arsalan. "What is this? Did you cast a spell on my cat, monk? Did you?"

Friar Heinrich squealed and held his wrists to his face like a small child, "No! It's the Devil's work! It's the Devil's work! It was the spell! I tell you magic is evil! Lord, save us!" The friar then ran from the room, wailing in horror.

Finally, the distorted monstrosity reached the size of a person, and eventually resembled one. The figure of a young woman, nude and panting heavily as if in pain, faced the floor, her face obscured by a head of long, reddish-brown hair. The entire room was aghast. Guards, who had gathered at the door, rushed into the room with swords in hand.

"Princess Berthilde! Are you alright?" one yelled.

"Yes, but there's a...there's a...." said the princess, pointing with her shaking hand to the woman on the floor.

The figure on the floor coughed and retched, and she pushed herself up a little and turned her head to face Arsalan. Her face, covered in strands of wet hair, was now recognizable to him. It was Defne.

"Father..." she croaked.

Arsalan gasped, held his hand up to his mouth, and then to his chest. He looked at the others as if expecting some hope of an answer, and then down again at the woman who resembled his lost daughter Defne. He was utterly dumbstruck. He tried to speak, but only a whimper was issued from his hairy throat.

"Defne..." he managed to whisper finally, before he fainted. He collapsed to one side and was prevented from striking his head on the table only through the intervention of a nimble guard.

"Everyone," wheezed the prostrated woman, "I'm sorry. Please help me."

"Well, what is everyone waiting for?" screamed Siegfrieda. "Get the poor girl some blankets!"

Arsalan awoke, finding himself in a bed covered heavily in sheets. A candleflame fluttered by his bed as a servant oversaw him. Arsalan blinked several times in the dim candlelight and turned his head to take in his surroundings. The servant, noticing, grabbed Arsalan's wrist and began to shake it.

"Mr. Ozdikmen!" he implored. "Mr. Ozdikmen!"

Everyone rushed into the room, including Bayram and Siegfrieda.

"Arsalan," Bayram said in a voice that, thought soft, was also hurried and suspicious, "do you have any idea what happened tonight?"

"No," Arsalan said, too disoriented to notice the subtly interrogating tone of Bayram's questioning. "Where's Kizil? Where is my cat? What happened to my poor Kizil?"

"Kizil is no longer with us," said Siegfrieda.

"Is she dead?" asked Arsalan. "Did she run away?"

"Did you plan this?" said Bayram. "What sorcery was this?"

"I have no idea, Bayram," said Arsalan weakly. "I thought I saw my daughter. I thought I saw Kizil turn into Defne. Was I hallucinating? It was such a painful dream."

Bayram and Siegfrieda looked at each other.

"I want to see my cat," begged Arsalan. "I spent too much time away from her on my travels. Please bring her to me."

"Come with us, Arsalan," said Bayram.

They pulled him out of bed, and, with the help of the princess' many good servants, guided him down a hallway to another bedroom where they found Princess Berthilde herself tending to the mysterious young woman who had appeared in the dining hall. The woman was lying in bed, her long auburn hair spread out on the pillows. She was dressed in the princess' own clothes, since they were almost the same size, and the princess had more than enough to spare. Arsalan blinked several times more when he saw the young woman, and he was reminded that she indeed was Defne, and none other. Dazed, he knelt by her side opposite Princess Berthilde.

"Defne?" he said, weeping. "Is this really you? Am I dreaming?"

"No, you are not dreaming, Father," she said. "I am Defne."

"How can this be?" he said. "Where is Kizil?"

"I was Kizil," she said. "I was the cat."

"I simply do not understand," said Arsalan.

"When Prince Ergin threatened to kill me if I did not marry him," she said. "I knew you in your state would not be able to protect me from him indefinitely, even with your powers. I knew I had to protect myself. I sought out an old sorceress who lived in the woods at the edge of town, and I paid her to cast a spell that would turn me into a cat. That was the only way I knew how to hide that was truly safe. The note in my collar was the spell to revert me to human form. But the old woman only could cast spells in her native language, the language of the Galatians. She was the last remaining speaker, as far as she or anyone knew. Thus, I was transformed into a cat, and I wandered through the woods for days. It was only through luck, or perhaps fate, that I found you, preparing to leave Kirklareli, and I ingratiated myself to you so that you would keep me, and so that you and I could care for each other."

"I have never heard of such magic," he said. "I only knew of my own type of magic. I did not know that people could be transformed into animals and back again. You were Kizil all along? And all the love I was giving to a cat I was giving to my daughter whom I thought I had lost?"

"Yes," she said. "I was Kizil all along. And I saw how much you loved me and Asker and Omer and mother. I saw all the pain you were experiencing, and I tried my best to console you and to keep you company in your despair and loneliness."

Arsalan's love and sadness poured from him like a calving piece of a glacier that had fallen into the sea, causing an uncontainable swell of emotion to radiate in every direction, washing everything before it in its fury and tears. He embraced her, and he buried his face in the pillow beside her and bawled until his torso hurt.

"Oh, my dear daughter," he howled through his tears, "I thought you were dead! I can't believe I have you back!"

"My dear Arsalan Ozdikmen," whispered Siegfrieda, "you never cease to be a source of surprises."

It took some time for everyone in the palace to overcome the shock of the events of the night when a cat allegedly transformed into a woman in front of the princess. Many of the servants who had been in the room that night visibly trembled when they saw Defne again later; the porcelain teacups they carried on plates tinkled and shook in their hands when those servants brought them to her and Princess Berthilde. They regarded her with wonder and fear and left the room hurriedly whenever they were dismissed. Siegfrieda herself admitted to being beset with nightmares of the incident that awoke her with a scream and a start, and Dietrich observed Defne with a cool and wary confusion.

After a thorough examination of her, the court physician gave Defne a clean bill of health, though when pestered for an explanation of how human transmutation into cats and back could occur, the stodgy old physician gazed at them as if they had gone mad. He had never heard such ludicrous nonsense. As far he could see, Defne was a perfectly normal and healthy young woman, and he was in no position to entertain belief in those types of weird reports. She was in fine shape.

Princess Berthilde and Siegfrieda had no choice but to accept the new presence of Defne if they were to continue to employ Arsalan for his services. This was not entirely difficult. Not only did Defne not pose any problems, but also due to her charmingly innocent and humble nature she proved to be a blessing. Remarkably, she and the princess got along like sisters. Princess Berthilde enjoyed having Defne wear her luxurious royal clothing and even had a few new dresses tailored for her. Defne was rather embarrassed to be the recipient of so much affection and privilege, but Princess Berthilde would hear of nothing less. She had gained a new friend who had blossomed into human being from her favorite pet, an occurrence that until then only had been the stuff of the fantastic dreams and fairy tales to which she had been accustomed. But Siegfrieda, still deeply disturbed by the sight of the mutating cat, regarded Defne warily. After a time, however, even she was comforted by the camaraderie between the two girls. Defne turned out to be excellent company for the princess, who had been somewhat lonely in her royal duties in the absence of her parents.

Once, during their sessions together, Princess Berthilde paused and asked Defne, "What was it like to be a cat?"

"I almost died of starvation, but after my father found me and cared for me, I loved being a cat," mused Defne. "But I couldn't understand everything that was said. I could only understand things generally and could sense how people felt. It was like listening to things through heavy cloth."

"Would you ever want to be a cat again?" asked the princess.

"Oh, no," said Defne. "I only became a cat to hide from Prince Ergin. Now that I am safe and far away from him, I no longer need to hide. Besides, there was a lot I was missing in human life."

Princess Berthilde's court spent the next few weeks celebrating the arrival of Arsalan the Magnificent's lost daughter. Arsalan, of course, spent every moment he could find next to his Defne, and sought to renew the special bond that they once had had. Of course, the bond had never been broken but only had been converted into an unfamiliar form and recovered. Still, it brought Arsalan great joy to be with her and to converse with her for the first time in years.

One night, Arsalan brought Defne out to his carriage in the courtyard.

"Do you remember this carriage, Defne?" asked Arsalan.

"Oh yes, of course," she said. "That is the carriage you and I rode to the mountains. I recall having a good time then."

"When you and I came to Bavaria," said Arsalan, "I decided to take all our most precious belongings with us. I left only my farming tools behind in the cabin. But I want to show you something. These are things I never sold when I became bankrupt."

Arsalan dug into the boxes he had been storing in the carriage and dragged out a large case, which he unlatched and opened, and in the dim, orange lantern light of the courtyard, they both peered inside. Arsalan reached into the case and pulled out a bundle of paper tied with string, which he untied and unwrapped to reveal like a blooming flower a pair of embroidered shoes sitting within. Defne covered her mouth and gasped with surprise and delight.

"You saved them!" she said. "You saved my favorite shoes!"

"I saved them all," he said. "All ten pairs. I've been storing them for years, waiting for your return. Little did I know you were right next to me all along!"

"Father!" she exclaimed, and she hugged him.

"There is more," Arsalan said, and from the depths of the box he proceeded to unearth several of Defne's old satin dresses, unfurling them one by one, one sky blue and coral, another yellow and white, and several others of pink, tea green, and creamy light orange, as they shimmered in the fiery lamplight. With the unraveling of each one, her eyes widened and teared. Finally, he opened another box, which contained all her books, pens, quills, ink, and stationery. Defne was overjoyed, and she thanked him profusely.

"You never opened these boxes before when we were living on the mountain!" she exclaimed quizzically.

"I wanted to keep them clean and secure," he said. "I wanted you to use them again."

"Thank you!" she said.

"Defne," said Arsalan, "you were trying to talk to me all those years as a cat, weren't you?"

"Of course," she said. "I was trapped inside a cat's body, and I wanted to speak to you, but, of course, that was not possible. Although it was nice to be a cat with you, I desperately wanted to resume my life as a human. It would have been tragic to lose my life at the jaws of a fox or a hound, or to spend the rest of my life as an unspeaking and unintelligible pet."

"You assumed great peril to cast yourself under a spell like that, especially for so long, with no guarantee of coming back," said Arsalan. "You could have perished."

"I know," said Defne. "I'm sorry, Father."

Arsalan's eyes filled with tears.

"I'm sorrier," he said sincerely. "I'm sorry I made you feel you had to resort to changing into a cat to save yourself. And I'm sorry for treating you meanly when I first encountered you as a cat. I did not know. My own daughter I scolded and tried to drive away."

"I know you didn't know," she said. "That's why I tried so hard to convince you to keep me. Once I turned into a cat, to my horror I realized I made an enormous mistake. I did not know how to hunt or to live as a cat with no one to care for me. I began to starve. I became sick. I was desperate for your care. Finding you again was a miracle."

"It took much bravery to do what you did. You said you would return as a woman, and you did to some degree. You made a potentially serious mistake out of desperation, and you emerged from it alive and stronger," he said.

Defne smiled and embraced her father for a long time.

"I missed being your daughter," she said, shedding more tears onto Arsalan's broad, warm, rounded shoulders. "I was scared I would never change back."

"You always will be my daughter, regardless of any circumstances," said Arsalan. "I love you always."

Defne carried the boxes of her belongings into the palace where she spent hours showing them to the princess, who marveled so much at the exotic designs of the books and clothes that she almost seemed envious. Princess Berthilde finally began to sense the type of privilege Defne had enjoyed as the daughter of a wealthy man, and her regard for Defne, which was not low before, grew even more. At the same time, her sorrow toward Arsalan also grew, for now she began to sense the enormity of his loss, both financially and in terms of his dignity.

The next day, Defne approached Arsalan with bright eyes and a smile.

"I just realized," she said excitedly, "that with the stationery I should write Mother a letter!"

"Of course!" he said. "I should have thought of that!"

The two of them wrote letters, both telling Teodora in their own words of the fabulous news of Defne's return. Arsalan's letter focused more on the general fact of her return and prepared Teodora with many disclaimers for the strange nature of Defne's own tale of events. To his daughter he left the burden of explaining the details of her transformation into a cat and back again. Arsalan was not sure if Teodora would believe Defne's story. Would the fact of Defne's return enthrall her mother, or would the fantastic explanation upset her? At least Teodora would recognize Defne's handwriting and stationery; that much was unmistakable. To make sure it was received well, Arsalan made sure to proofread Defne's writing. Her years as a cat had made her forget her spelling and punctuation, and even more so her penmanship, and he made many corrections, resolving, when all his work in Bavaria was done, to resume her education.

Both letters were placed in a single, ornate envelope, sealed with a Bavarian seal, and sent to Brzeg by express post. Four weeks later, they received a letter from Teodora that, to Arsalan's relief, seemed to overlook the weird details of magical transmogrification and to address only the fact of Defne's return, and she promised an official visit in a few weeks to Bavaria, both to see Defne and as an official diplomatic visit to the princess. Until then, Defne and Teodora were reacquainted through a flurry of many dozens of letters.

During those weeks of waiting for Teodora to arrive, the atmosphere gradually changed in Princess Berthilde's palace. Arsalan was away to repair the dome of St. Ulrich's and St. Afra's Abbey in Augsberg, which magically played soft choral music from its tower without the presence of singers. When he returned, he found that the princess had become, quite swiftly and without much explanation, occupied with an affair of state, and that she grew increasingly inaccessible. On the few occasions when Arsalan and Defne spotted the princess in the hallways, she was frequently surrounded by a crowd of older statesmen and nobles who adhered to her side and muttered softly but agitatedly into the sides of her face. Princess Berthilde would be listening intently, looking downward. She abruptly would notice the father and daughter, would make a point of stopping and apologizing for being so unavailable, but would promise to talk to them again once an important matter had been resolved. She did not explain the nature of the matter, but it was clear to both Arsalan and Defne that it exerted strain on the princess, as she looked worn and burdened, and the crowd of elegantly dressed statesmen and nobles were eager to sweep her away to another meeting to discuss the mysterious issue.

"Don't worry too much, my dear Defne," said Arsalan in the wake of the agitation. "She is a ruler after all, and must attend to affairs of her kingdom, and she does have more with which to concern herself than magical architecture and clothing."

"But Mother is coming in October as part of an official visit," said Defne. "Wouldn't the princess want to know that?"

"Has the princess received a request from your mother to come?" asked Arsalan.

"I don't know," said Defne. "I do hope the princess is well. I wish I knew what circumstance is so grave that we have no chance to talk to her."

"If it becomes more important than architectural repair," said Arsalan, "then it will supersede my services and we should plan our exit. We will go to Brzeg to see your mother."

"Will it come to that?" Defne asked.

"I certainly hope not," said Arsalan. "I wish I knew what it was so I could offer my help."

"I want to help the princess, Father," said Defne. "She has become like a sister to me now."

"That may be beyond your power," said Arsalan. "In any case, you and I have discussed plans to continue your schooling, and I have accumulated enough gold to see that it happens. Do not fret. I still will care for you."

In that vein, Defne spent much of her time rereading her books. When she had finished them, she borrowed her father's books on magic, history, geography, and language. Eventually, she began to read tomes from Princess Berthilde's own voluminous collection, which dealt almost exclusively with magical architects, particularly Arsalan himself. Defne was keen to show Arsalan the accounts contained in them of his accomplishments; though vague and quaintly worded, they were still flattering.

Days passed, and then weeks, until the day when Arsalan found himself waiting for his next assignment from Princess Berthilde but receiving none. Inquiries to Bayram yielded nothing. In fact, Bayram was just as concerned and frustrated. Arsalan took this news heavily, as he knew Bayram could evince news from anyone under most circumstances, and where he could not do so meant that there was genuine trouble afoot. But Bayram was not one to wait in one place for long. Often he was absent, and when he reappeared, his presence was fleeting and his attention preoccupied, and he whispered to Arsalan not to settle too comfortably in the castle, as he was looking for more work for Arsalan and himself.

Arsalan, though, began to feel he had formed too enduring an attachment to his work in Bavaria, to the princess, and to Conrad's legacy, which he had felt privileged to repair. Yet, he felt he would be betraying everything he had accomplished to abandon it all at the first sign of unease. Besides, Teodora had promised to arrive. For these reasons, he was determined to reestablish communication with Princess Berthilde in some fashion. He waited here and there in the hallways to catch sight of her and Siegfrieda, and he called after them, but the two women were too breathlessly wrapped in their secretive matter with their advisors to pay attention to anyone else. When they disappeared around a corner or into a room again, Arsalan wondered why he was still allowed to live at the palace at all if his services were not being sought. Perhaps, he thought with a hint of wonder, they had forgotten he was still there, or that he had become a tolerated fixture of her court, one as accepted as any of her ornate artworks of heroes and gods that silently observed him with their weird and condemnatory gazes as he wandered the halls and waited outside of rooms.

Then the day came when Arsalan and Defne knew precisely what they should do. They would confront Princess Berthilde forcefully and would demand an explanation. They knew they probably would be leaving anyway, and in trying to ascertain the truth from her in this manner they only would be hastening their departure instead of extending the process indefinitely and awkwardly.

Arsalan and Defne searched for the princess, but everyone they asked stated, rather abruptly and in a way that was somewhat rehearsed, that Princess Berthilde had retired to her quarters to consider a matter of grave importance, over which no one besides her advisors had the business to address.

"I think I know where she is," whispered Arsalan to Defne.

At last, Arsalan approached Dietrich, who was busy inspecting the dust on a piece of wooden furniture with a hand gloved in white. He drew his fingertip across the varnished wooden surface and looked at his extended digit with sharp disdain.

"Take me to the turret," said Arsalan to Dietrich.

Dietrich regarded Arsalan for a long time as if to test his resolve, but Arsalan did not break his stare. Arsalan was flatly serious, and Dietrich knew what Arsalan meant.

"What I do next, I do for the princess," whispered Dietrich.

Dietrich led Arsalan and Defne to the enormous wooden door with fixtures of black, hammered iron, and he unlocked it with a loud clack and opened it. He led them down the bare stone hallway to the next, identical door and opened it as well, and once again he pivoted on his foot and left without a word.

In the center of the room still hovered the mangled chunk of green metal, and to one side of it sat the princess on a plain wooden chair. Her arms were crossed in front of her, and she was bent over them in thought.

"Princess," said Arsalan in his low, gravelly whisper. "Why consult an unresponsive architectural artifact for advice when its creator practically lives in your palace?"

"I'm accustomed to it," said Princess Berthilde after a long silence.

"If I may be so bold as to inquire, what has been bothering you, my dear princess?" said Arsalan.

Looking at the stone floor in front of her, she opened her mouth but could not find the words.

"I..." she stammered, and no more.

"Perhaps in my old age I can offer you some needed wisdom or advice, for it would be the most work I have done in the past few weeks, and I do wish to make myself useful to your court. If I cannot do so, I will be forced to quit and to find other work," said Arsalan.

"I...no...please don't," said the princess.

"Like a sister you have become to me," said Defne. "I care about you. If there is anything wrong, please, you can share it with me."

Princess Berthilde put her hand over her face and shuddered with sobs.

Defne held the princess' shoulders while Arsalan looked on, his forehead wrinkled in sadness and concern.

"There's an insurrection," whispered Princess Berthilde. "One of my generals is trying to usurp my throne. I'm trying to stop him, but I don't know how. I don't know what to do."

Defne cast a shocked look at her father, whose face turned grave.

"I'm just a girl," said Princess Berthilde, turning her face like a full moon directly toward them in this open declaration, her eyes wet and filled with terror. "I have no experience with which to counter this type of threat. I'm an impostor. I don't belong on this throne, and he knows it. Everyone knows it. I shall be gone from here by the end of the year."

"Who is this general who lays claim to your throne?" asked Arsalan.

"His name is General Gunther Maximillian von Ansbach," the princess said, "and he is a shrewd and overbearing personality. He has been soliciting ties of allegiance from other generals and factions of the Bavarian army and has been successful in obtaining them. He subscribes to the new political stance that opposes belief in magic and magical architecture. He uses this public sentiment to his advantage, arguing that royals fritter too much time and too many finances on what he sees as not magic, but a form of chicanery that is explainable through ordinary, material laws of engineering. He has been promising that if or when he assumes control of Bavaria, he will dismantle all its magical architecture to investigate it and to reveal its secrets as forms of charlatanism."

Arsalan swelled with indignation at this news.

"That," he said, pointing to the green hunk of metal hovering in midair, "is not charlatanism."

"That I know," said Princess Berthilde, "and that you certainly know as well. But there are many people who are not as certain and are easily swayed by false arguments and shifts in public opinion. I tell you this news now, but I should have told you sooner had I not been so embroiled in my attempts to combat him. It would be best for you to consider leaving here to protect yourself and Defne."

There was a prolonged, stunned silence, but finally Arsalan whispered, "But my work, Conrad's work, it will be undone."

"Yes," said the princess. Her voice was strained, and she began to weep again. "But it's inevitable. I haven't the power. I spent too much time worrying about buildings and magical architecture, and not enough time worrying about my people. I'm going to be deposed. It won't be violent. I will be well. Von Ansbach is still civilized in that respect. He will allow me to surrender peacefully. I wish my father were here. I wish he could tell me what to do."

"I imagine your father would want you to stand your ground and to defend your kingdom," Arsalan said.

"He was not able to teach me how to do that before he died," sobbed Princess Berthilde.

"When my life was threatened by Prince Ergin," interjected Defne, "I hid from him, and I did so in a way that was itself filled with risk and danger. I lost many friends and years of my life from my strange exile. But there was no other way for me to counter him. You, however, have ways. You have power over much of your remaining army to stop him. I would not be able to bear to see you flee the same way I did."

"Von Ansbach has said if I surrender without a struggle, I will be allowed freedom, whereas if I fight, I will be jailed," said Princess Berthilde.

"And you believe him?" said Arsalan. "You should be saying that to him!"

"I tried," the princess said, "but he sees my words as hollow."

"But your actions need not be hollow," said Arsalan.

Princess Berthilde's head slumped into her hands.

"Your Majesty, I see you have not the willpower to fight," said Arsalan. "The general already has sapped your soul with his words. But it need not be this way. I will stay to help you fight him. I pledge my loyalty to you to this end."

"But you are prohibited from using your powers to hurt other people," said Princess Berthilde.

"Yes, and I hold true to that, but there are other ways," said Arsalan.

"I will help you, too," said Defne, "in whatever way I can do so."

The three heard the door issue a loud, echoing clack, and it slowly swung open and produced Siegfrieda, who stood primly but cautiously in the doorway. Suddenly it occurred to Arsalan to wonder why Siegfrieda had not been executing her job as an advisor to Princess Berthilde well enough for the princess to oppose the threat from a treasonous, upstart general. He knew that in his own land the punishment for such an act of treason from a general was swift imprisonment. Why had Siegfrieda not encouraged the princess to pursue such a speedy and resolute outcome? Perhaps Princess Berthilde had not the taste for blood or killing, he thought, and perhaps Siegfrieda either shared this trait or was herself not as experienced in such matters as she had advertised, and perhaps her current demureness revealed a sense of sheepish shame. Arsalan found himself staring at her with narrowed eyes before realizing it, and he lowered his gaze to the floor and addressed her properly with the word "Madam."

Siegfrieda nodded in acknowledgement to Arsalan. "Her Majesty's presence is requested in her parlor with her advisors," she said softly.

Arsalan offered his forearm to the princess, who used it to stand from her little chair.

"I must go now," said Princess Berthilde. "I will consider your offer."

"And my offer stands indefinitely," said Arsalan.

CHAPTER 14

"It's time to go, Arsalan the Magnificent," said Bayram to Arsalan in their quarters. Bayram was packing the last of his belongings hastily, marching this way and that around the room to retrieve this or that item and stuffing it in his bags. "The jig is up, as they say. We can't say we didn't see this coming. We sensed the warnings. But in that time, you earned your small new fortune. You're back on your feet. And you even got your daughter back, in the strangest of ways, of course, but she was restored to you. How fortunate is that? You should be grateful! But now it's time to leave. I have a job for you in Czechia, I think. An opera house. It'll be grand."

"No," said Arsalan, who stood in the middle of the room. His gaze was cast to the floor and his arms hung defiantly at his sides. "I will not leave."

Bayram's mouth worked to issue the right words that Bayram's brain could not form. He was at a loss. He walked around Arsalan as if inspecting a defective piece of machinery that suddenly had stopped.

"What is wrong with you?" said Bayram. "Are you simply being quarrelsome? Do you always choose the least reasonable option? First you don't want to come here. Now you don't want to leave. When will you see reason when it is necessary? There will be war here! Armed strife! You will be jailed. Defne will be jailed with you! Is that what you want?"

"I have too much invested in Bavaria," said Arsalan. "My soul is invested in these structures. Conrad the Ineffable's soul is also invested in them. I can't let some pompous, ambitious general come to tear them to shreds because he wants to be Emperor."

"You will be torn to shreds if you stay! What else will you do?" said Bayram.

"I can oppose them with my powers," said Arsalan.

"You're prohibited by creed from using your powers for military purposes," said Bayram. "I know you've taken your vow so closely to heart that you couldn't kill even your own chickens!"

"I'm prohibited from using my powers to hurt people or to allow them to come to harm," said Arsalan. "This does not exclude military purposes."

"What are you going to do?" said Bayram. "Are you going to build a bunker? A barricade? Are you going to dig trenches or to erect a hospital? What else can you do to exclude hurting the enemy?"

"There are methods of countering a forceful enemy that are cleverer than murder," said Arsalan. "I will use whichever of these methods will defend Conrad's structures best from destruction. The souls of the magical architects are in those buildings. This is about preserving history and culture!"

"This is about money!" yelled Bayram. "It always has been only about money! Never anything else! Your entire career has been about making obscene amounts of gold by doing things few other human beings can do! If no one were paying for your talents, you and your kind would be using your powers to take over the world! And why would anyone want to take over the world, Arsalan Ozdikmen? Hm? Think! Yes! The reason is still money! That's why! But you are civilized wizards. Yes? You use your talents for enlightened and humane means. Magical architects and ordinary people are all the better for this arrangement. Correct? But still, the outcome is an exchange of specialized craft for money!"

Arsalan was silent, and Bayram grimaced and winced at his feet, and struck a more conciliatory tone.

"Arsalan," said Bayram, "you are one of the greatest magical architects who ever have lived. And you are my good, dear friend. I can't stand by to watch you place yourself in such peril. You still have so much more of a future ahead of you, even at your age. Your lot is improving. Let's continue, you and me, together. We make an invincible team."

"I understand that I can't force you to stay here with me," said Arsalan. "So, if you want to flee, the freedom is yours. But I can't go with you."

"And your daughter?" said Bayram.

"She is staying with me," said Arsalan.

"Suicide!" rebuked Bayram. "Stupid, selfish suicide!"

Bayram nervously gathered the small remainder of his papers and clothing and books and threw them into his bag. He grew officious and cold and wobbled his head as he spoke.

"I have business to do. I have people to see," he said. "I have money to make. I must go! I have…"

Bayram turned to Arsalan, as if in abrupt realization.

"Good luck to you, my friend," said Bayram. "I hope to see you when all this is over. Then we'll have a good chat over some strong, sweet tea and fresh, hot flatbread. It will be my treat."

And with that, Bayram fled. Arsalan looked out the window at his agent jogging hurriedly across the plaza toward the stable, his bags over his shoulder and in each hand. His balding pate gleamed reddish brown in the sunlight. Arsalan could not recall a time when he had seen Bayram more afraid, and Arsalan felt ashamed of his friend even as he understood him. Yes, Bayram was bold and capable and resourceful in his dealings with people when matters were civil, but he avoided physical danger like one avoided leprosy and experienced no shame in outright flight from it. This aspect of Bayram's personality perplexed and hurt Arsalan the most. He thought that, after all the endeavors and adventures they had undergone together, Bayram would stand by his side. But Arsalan too easily would forget that Bayram was a businessperson whose ultimate purpose was profit, and that avoiding violence was the cheapest and most effective means of combating it. Even so, Arsalan wondered why Bayram even bothered to carry a dagger if he never used it.

Bayram's departure did little to disturb Princess Berthilde or Siegfrieda. Both women understood the danger he was fleeing, and they were too concerned about the looming military insurrection to think any more about architectural repairs. Also, they were already so accustomed to Bayram's businesslike comings and goings that his leaving again was hardly distinguishable from them. Still, they would have preferred to see him off properly and to thank him for his services in front of everyone than to offer their gratitude and goodbyes to him individually and behind closed doors, and in the overly rushed and stiffened fashion that Bayram offered them each.

Bayram's abrupt exit was offset just as quickly by another person's entrance, that of Teodora, Duchess of Brzeg, whose caravan arrived in October, quite on schedule and as stated in her letters, and with modest fanfare. Despite the attempts of Arsalan and Defne to remind Princess Berthilde of Teodora's stated intent to visit, the princess had been too preoccupied with her issue of civil insurrection to absorb the news. This caused her terrible embarrassment. The trumpets were sounded, the guards and servants streamed out to greet the official guests, and Dietrich entered Princess Berthilde's room to announce the arrival, to which she responded with a gasp, wide eyes, and a slack mouth. The princess readied herself frantically and raced down the halls to the reception area at the palace entrance, where Duchess Teodora was kept waiting outside for the princess, fiercely disgruntled but maintaining her composure. Once Princess Berthilde emerged to greet her, the older Teodora was reminded of the princess' youth and inexperience and was more able to suppress her annoyance beneath her smiles. Teodora reasoned that she at least could fulfill her primary desire of seeing her daughter, an opportunity for which she was grateful.

Arsalan emerged from the palace seconds later, visibly flustered, and he locked eyes with Teodora. Seeing the crowd of officials and the other nobility at the palace entrance, he composed himself, and he and Teodora commenced addressing one another with all the gingerly and somewhat playful courtesies of someone pouring a glass of hot tea into a delicate porcelain cup. Arsalan then found the opportunity to come close to Teodora, where he whispered apologies into the side of her face for the princess' unpreparedness. This Teodora began to dismiss with waves of her hand.

Soon Defne burst through the doors of the palace and, with no official decorum whatsoever, screamed, "Mother!"

Immediately, Teodora cast aside her guise of regal propriety. She ran to her daughter and hugged her, overcome with the sweet, sad joy of the miraculous reunion with a loved one deemed forever lost. Arsalan joined them. Embraces, tears, weeping, wrinkling smiles, cries of emotion, and declarations of sorrow and remorse filled the palace entrance where mother and daughter were reunited. Most of the officials who looked on were unaware of the context of their meeting and were beset with embarrassment and awkwardness as they stood and waited, shifting their weight from one foot to the other. Siegfrieda, however, watched the scene with distant confusion, while the princess smiled in wonder and wiped away a few tears.

It took a while for the grand reunion to seem real to Teodora and Defne and not a dream. Gradually, mother and daughter's faces and mannerisms, once estranged from one another for so long, became less strange to one another, and the renewed familiarity refilled the painful gaps that the mother and the daughter each had left in each other's souls upon their separation. Many hours later, at their formal state dinner, Defne was seated next to her mother, almost with their shoulders touching. Princess Berthilde and Siegfrieda were across from them, and officials from both courts lined either side of the long table. Arsalan flanked Duchess Teodora on her other side and sipped his soup with a slight smile on his face, a smile of bemusement or perhaps quiet delight.

Duchess Teodora and her officials were debriefed on the situation involving the insurrectionist general who wished to capture the Bavarian throne and to disassemble all magical architecture within the kingdom. To this Duchess Teodora reacted with deep dismay, but the solution to her part of the problem was clear and immediate. Defne must leave Bavaria at once and return with her to Brzeg, and Arsalan, too, of course, if he wished.

"Mother," said Defne, "I've decided to stay and to help Princess Berthilde fight General von Ansbach."

At this Duchess Teodora reacted first with a look of blank shock, and then a scoffing snort.

"And how do you plan to help Princess Berthilde?" she retorted. "Are you going to be her military advisor?"

"No," Defne said. "Father has decided to help the princess with his powers, and I can't abandon him. Besides, we all know he can defeat them."

"He can't use his powers to hurt others, my daughter," said Teodora. "We all know that, too."

"He won't hurt others," said Defne, "but he can use his powers for blockades and other nonlethal defenses."

Teodora looked at her plate intently, and her face turned red with suppressed anger and panic.

"That's your father's decision, and he is capable of doing so, even though it's perilous," said Teodora, "but it doesn't mean you have to stay. Even if you did, how would you help him?"

"We just found each other again, Mother," said Defne. "I can't abandon him."

"You're placing yourself in harm's way!" whispered Teodora. "That is insanity! Come back with me!"

Defne avoided her mother's gaze but shook her head in the negative.

"I have faith in Father and in Princess Berthilde," Defne said.

Turning to Arsalan suddenly, Teodora fumed, "Did you convince her of this?"

"It was her decision, and I could not dissuade her," he said. "She is a grown woman."

Duchess Teodora violently stood upright from her seat, pushing her chair backward and startling everyone at the table into stunned silence. The servants, pitchers in hand, looked up in alarm and concern. Teodora breathed heavily for a moment, realizing the uncouth scene she was making, and in a more controlled voice spoke to Princess Berthilde and Siegfrieda.

"Haven't either of you had the sense to send this poor girl away to someplace safer until your civil strife is ameliorated?" she said.

"Duchess Teodora, I am honored to make your acquaintance as the mother of one of my dearest friends," said Princess Berthilde. "It is certainly not my wish to bring your dear daughter to harm. All the same, I trust your husband's assessment of her sense of judgement, and I am humbled and comforted to have her at my side in these difficult times. In any case, trust me when I say that when the situation becomes untenably violent, I will send her into safety."

"I hope you will understand if I demand that my daughter be provided with safety and protection much sooner than that," said Teodora.

"Like the protection she had from you three years ago?" posed Arsalan.

He had stood with an erect posture and a face red and stern. He waited for an answer, breathing visibly, but then sat and continued eating from his plate. Teodora, with wide, white eyes, searched the tabletop for an answer, but to her abashment could not find a proper retort. Arsalan sighed.

"I'm sorry. It has been a long time, my dear," said Arsalan in a low and conciliatory voice, "and although certain things have not changed, such as my love for you, and Defne's love for you, other things have changed, such as such as Defne herself. Her transformation into a woman makes her the one who decides for herself how to live. Accept this as true. Her childhood is already behind her."

Duchess Teodora, stunned, and no longer wishing to be the center of attention, dropped into her seat. By Arsalan's words she was suddenly pushed into a realm beyond shame, one of abrupt, pensive realization, like the solemn toll of a bell to which we now was silently listening. The others at the table, the princess and her advisor, the nobles, the officials, glanced at her with concern, but, reading her calm face, began to refill the air with murmured talk of affairs of state.

Princess Berthilde and Defne watched her with worry. A while later, Duchess Teodora excused herself and retired to her room. There, Arsalan later found her, sitting on a couch and staring out the window through gauzy curtains at the glittery sky.

"I'm sorry," said Arsalan. "I was unfair."

Duchess Teodora turned to look at Arsalan as if noticing for the first time he was there. Her face still held the same expression of open understanding she had assumed over dinner.

"No," she said. "I should thank you. I needed a renewed perspective. You were right. Defne is old enough to decide her own fate."

To Arsalan's relief, it was clear that she was not sulking, but reflecting. Arsalan sat next to her on the couch and held her hand.

"Bavaria's nights are beautiful. The stars are not quite as splendid as in Kirklareli, but still pleasant," said Arsalan.

"I've decided to stay to help you and Defne," Teodora said. "Princess Berthilde is charming and intelligent, even wise in some ways, but she is still young. She needs my help with diplomacy."

Arsalan regarded her with impressed surprise.

"What about your own court?" he said. "How long do you expect to stay here?"

"As long as it takes to support Defne, and you," she said. "I should admit that I am nothing but a figurehead at home, as devoted I am to the people of Silesia. The Habsburgs administer most everything vital. They will not miss me in the time I am gone. I again was selfish and presumptuous just now at dinner, Arsalan, and I apologize. I should realize that things have changed and in fact that I have helped change them."

Arsalan did not wish to exacerbate the conversation by agreeing with her, and he maintained a polite silence.

"Tell me something, Arsalan," she said. "Defne told me the way she had evaded Prince Ergin was to have herself transformed into a cat. Was she serious?"

"I'm afraid so," said Arsalan. "I found her as a cat and cared for her for all these years without even knowing it was Defne. A god or goddess was looking over us, surely."

"I thought she had gone mad when I read her letter," said Teodora. "I had never heard of such magic."

"Neither had I," said Arsalan, "and as such, I didn't know how to corroborate her story without seeming an accomplice to madness."

"I suppose there is more than one type of magic in this world besides yours, and that we shouldn't be surprised to find it," she said.

"Perhaps it's all one type," said Arsalan, "all from a single source. Perhaps the mystics and poets are correct, and that the greatest magic of all is devotion and love, as trite as how such a truism sounds."

Teodora looked at him for a long time, and after a while kissed his cheek and laid her head on his shoulder. Arsalan received this affection bashfully and blushed.

CHAPTER 15

It was not long before a courier arrived at Princess Berthilde's palace with an official communique from General Gunther Maximillian von Ansbach. It reiterated his previous offers for a peaceful surrender on the princess's part in exchange for freedom and safe passage out of Bavaria. This set Princess Berthilde into another bout of fright and anxiety. Arsalan advised her to attack his forces and to punish him once and for all for his impudence, whereas Siegfrieda was more cautious and warned of von Ansbach's sizeable army, composed of factions formerly loyal to her but now turned against her. A little more than half her own army had been compromised, and an outright military engagement between them may cause untold suffering for the people of Bavaria, she insisted. Arsalan and Siegfrieda were now at odds, and they became frequently angry with each other and quarreled until Siegfrieda threatened to have Arsalan bound to his quarters and Princess Berthilde would scold Siegfrieda for her own presumptuousness. Siegfrieda demonstrated increasing impatience and mystification at Arsalan's influence over the princess but could do nothing about it so long as Princess Berthilde valued his council. Teodora advised Princess Berthilde to impress upon the general that the Duchy of Brzeg was present in the Bavarian court on diplomatic matters, and that any act of aggression toward the Bavarian court while members of the Silesian delegation were present would be considered an act of war on the Hapsburgs. It was in these confusing circumstances, given all the pieces of advice that were being tossed around her head, and given the somewhat useless pieces of advice being bandied about by her other supposedly more expert advisors, that she decided to speak with the general directly. To this idea both Siegfrieda and Arsalan could find agreement in their strong opposition, as they insisted that direct negotiations with insurrectionists only served to embolden them and would grant them an air of legitimacy that they did not deserve and that he would use to further his advantage. Defne offered the idea that an offer to appear for negotiations could be used as a trap to arrest the general, but Teodora mentioned that the general, being aware of this, might choose not to appear, unless he could direct the armed factions under his control to initiate an attack upon his detainment or harm by the princess. It took a moment for the princess to work out whether all this meant she should invite the general to talks, but after that moment it was agreed that since the tactical advantages possessed by the princess and the general were nearly equal, a political summit probably was the best course of action.

Princess Berthilde, to the great angst of all her advisors who clung to her sides and pestered her with council, finally sent an official invitation to General von Ansbach to a summit in the town hall of Ingolstadt, halfway between Munich and the general's home of Ansbach. After the communique was sent, Princess Berthilde retired alone to a balcony overlooking her tranquil, elegant estate. From then on, she was often seen on the balcony pacing up and down its length in attempts to soothe herself and to steel herself against the possible outcomes of her invitation. Here Arsalan found her, and she stopped her walking and greeted him with a sharp sigh and a forced smile.

"I must calm my anxiety," she declared to him. "I must conquer my fears." As she said this, she began to pace again slowly while examining the tiles of the floor beneath her toes. One arm was behind her back, and with the other she gesticulated like a professor giving a lecture. "I must assume a detached and bemused air in my dealings with the von Ansbach. Don't you think? I must treat him as if he were merely a wayward child who needs to be inculcated with reason before being given a stiff punishment." Arsalan regarded her not without some concern.

"That sounds like a good strategy," he said. "We will support you in this."

"I simply cannot allow him to intimidate me any longer!" she said, shaking her head and looking at him with wide eyes, "or at least to allow him to perceive me as intimidated. I am not! I must display strength, but I also must show that I am civil and benevolent. Don't you agree?"

"Yes, your highness," he said. "I agree. Put your fears to rest. You have us to bolster you."

The princess received a swift and terse reply of acceptance from the general. A procession was hastily arranged, and all who could give the princess any degree of adequate support or council was stuffed inside the convoy's many carriages, which was thickly flanked on all sides with armed soldiers on the backs of massive warhorses bristling with keen, bladed weaponry that gleamed in the sun. Beginning at dawn and riding into midday, Princess Berthilde rode in her carriage, her weary face staring solemnly out her window while the sound of the horses' clopping hooves resounded through the jostling cabin.

Princess Berthilde and her company, including Arsalan and Defne, Teodora and Siegfrieda, and all her other advisors whose white, wigged heads nodded and turned this way and that as they quietly conferred with one another, all sat at a great oaken table in the sturdy town hall of Ingolstadt. The ceilings were high, the walls were lined with dark wood paneling, and the windows, which were thrown open to let in the fresh autumn air, were tall with many panes, allowing a commanding view of the town center and its plaza and tinting the large, bright meeting room with the yellowish light of the October day. It was clear that this room was fashioned to discuss issues of more local and municipal concern. Ingolstadt's mayor, a short, thin man with an elegant goatee who had greeted princess and her entourage with as much fanfare as his little city could afford, now stood nervously aside with one hand on a table, appearing to antici-pate his role as host of the talks with unmistakable trepidation.

The company waited in tense boredom, filling the silence with uneasy, mumbling talk. The general apparently had decided to arrive fashionably late. Just as one of the princess' advisors whispered to her that the general, to their great relief, had forfeited the negotiations, there came from the doorway the an-nouncement of General von Ansbach's arrival. The announcer's own words were interrupted by the entrance of the general himself, who threw open the doors to the meeting room with a grand, sweeping motion from his own arms, caus-ing the doors to slam rudely onto the walls. Until this point, Princess Berthilde only had read von Ansbach's name on paper and was not prepared for what she saw. Von Ansbach was an unusually tall figure with broad shoulders, bedecked in all the military regalia one would expect—badges, insignia, epaulets, and a sash—granting him the overall appearance of a well-groomed rooster. He was accompanied from behind and on either side by two stern officers who looked like more miniature and ordinary versions of himself. At his hip, a gleaming, sheathed saber hung, on the handle of which he placed his white-gloved hand as one would on the head one's favorite hunting hound. A military coat of red swept its long tails over his white pantaloons and black boots. It was his enor-mous head that was most arresting; it was one of a younger man, perhaps in his late thirties, whose precociousness had propelled him upward through the ranks of the Bavarian military to his present and most impressive position. His face was lineless and smooth. He famously had spurned the wearing of wigs, preferring to sport his own hair, which consisted of boyishly golden, blond locks pressed into curls. General von Ansbach was shockingly handsome, almost exaggerated-ly so. His face held all the most ideal proportions of classical Greek statues; his jawline was chiseled, his nose was boldly aquiline, swooping down to just above two full, pouty lips and a jutting chin. His irises, as azure as the sky, were large and beautiful, and they shimmered such that they seemed to float several feet in front of his face, but they were blank of all emotion, which gave him an uncanny appearance. No one in Princess Berthilde's entourage knew what to make of him. The general stood erectly in front of the princess' council and chose not to sit.

"Princess," said General Gunther Maximilian von Ansbach in a deep, throaty voice.

"General," Princess Berthilde said.

"I will not sit, for this will be brief," he said. "First, any attempts to harm me or to arrest me today with be met with immediate military force enacted against your armies, and my stated plans to take your throne will be enacted."

"We already thought as much," said Princess Berthilde, sustaining a grave composure. "Stand if you wish. But tell me. What are you trying to accom-plish by committing this treason that is punishable by imprisonment or death? You must know your efforts will fail, and that I simply am humoring you today. So, use this opportunity to sing to us your vaulting ambitions before they are vanquished."

"Your boldness is entertaining," said General von Ansbach. "I differ in your assessment of me as a traitor. I do consider myself, and most objectively am, a patriot of Bavaria, and a more fitting ruler of it than you or any of your court. It is my view that you are causing damage to our nation and our throne, and I demand your immediate and peaceful abdication; or, if you were considering any military action, your surrender. Your father was a great king, but he left behind a daughter who was much too young for her inherited station and has proved to be an ineffective and immature leader. You fritter too much of your time on trifling personal pleasures such as clothes and books about magic. Worst of all, you spend too much of the kingdom's coffers on what is commonly known as magical architecture, which consists of nothing more than charlatans' tricks of ordinary engineering. I pity you for being so captivated by such chicanery. You must stand aside and must allow someone with my experience and capabilities to lead the kingdom more efficaciously."

Arsalan's face silently reddened with fury as the general's comment about charlatanism, but he respected the princess' role and said nothing out loud. Otherwise, he could see right through von Ansbach as an intelligent but shallowly ambitious brat, and he found himself despising the general even more deeply than he had expected. He turned to look at the princess from his seat at the long table, and he worried that she would lose control of the negotiations. But Princess Berthilde was still surprisingly in command of some verve.

"Someone of your appearance cannot be said to have spent any less time and effort on his own clothing, General. Perhaps my only mistake of which I am guilty is paying you too much for your suit and make-up," she said.

A wave of snickering wafted among the crowd, from the princess' own entourage, from the mayor's delegation, and even from some of the guards. Arsalan found himself smirking despite himself. General von Ansbach turned to listen to the twittering laughter and nodded stiffly, acknowledging the success, and even the truth, of the jest.

"Indeed, maybe you have paid me too much, which may be counted only as one of your many oversights," he said. "In fact, it is perhaps this inattentiveness that allowed me to assume control of half your military from under your nose while you were trading fairy tales and playing dress-up with your new playmate who claims she was a cat."

The room dropped into silence. Princess Berthilde reacted with a look that was at first confused and injured, but then infuriated. Defne stood halfway from her seat, her fists clenched, her mouth open, ready to protest, but Teodora grasped her forearm and pulled her down again. General von Ansbach's face for the first time assumed an expression, one of mockingly feigned surprise. His eyes grew wide, and his lips pursed, and his head tilted to one side as he nodded.

"Oh," he jeered. "Did I strike too intimate a truth? How did I know that? While you're trying to determine how, listen to this. I will take over control of the Bavarian throne, and once I do, I will dismantle every piece of your allegedly magical structures, brick by brick, stone by stone, to see how it was assembled, and I will expose to the eyes of reason the ancient, fraudulent trickery of these alleged wizards who have milked money from royal thrones for far too long. It is inevitable. The era of sorcerers is finished."

Princess Berthilde stood, and her voice quavered with fear and rage as she spoke.

"If my reign and the age of sorcerers are ever to end," she said, "they will end not by you but long after your death."

Impassioned, Teodora then stood.

"And let me remind you that any military action against the throne of Bavaria while I, Duchess of Brzeg, and my delegates are present there also will be considered an act of aggression on Silesia," said Teodora.

"Then the Duchess of Brzeg should leave!" said the general. "And if I have any quarrel with Silesia, I'll confer with the Habsburgs who are the true rulers of that country. Besides, there need not be bloodshed. Make this simple, Princess. Lay down your arms, and allow my usurpation of your throne to happen, peaceably, with no casualties. I promise you the most peaceful transfer of power in Bavarian history, and the end of the age of spurious claims of magic, and the beginning of epoch of reason."

At that precise moment, a bizarre, abrupt, and dreamlike event occurred. General Gunther Maximillian von Ansbach's clothes fell from his body. His outward apparel—his red coat and white pants and black boots—transformed into loose dust and poured from his limbs and body and onto the ground like grains of dry sand poured from a bucket. No longer supported by cloth, his medals also dropped and bounced onto the hardwood floor with light clanging noises near where his sash and epaulets also collapsed like dead animals. Everyone in the room, startled and confused, held their hands to their noses and mouths, either from shock or to guard themselves from inhaling the dust. General von Ansbach took several seconds to realize what was happening. He was left standing in the middle of the room in his beige linen undergarments and a pool of dust surrounding his feet, and he was looking at his forearms as they were covered in patches of red powder that once were his coat. Whether he exercised absolute control over his reactions, or whether he was genuinely incapable of surprise and humiliation, no one could tell. His gaze remained clinical and unperturbed as he turned his forearms this way and that to inspect them.

"Fascinating," said von Ansbach. "One of your alleged wizard's illusions, I see, and eventually explainable through natural philosophy, no doubt. Who knows what chemical you secretly applied to my clothing as I was standing here? You should have paid more attention toward resisting me militarily and politically, like an adult, before committing this parlor stunt. In either case, your attempt to humiliate me has failed and only will result in hastening your overthrow. Goodbye, Princess. I extended a chance for a peaceful surrender, but now I will see you on the field of battle for however briefly it will last."

Arsalan stood.

"What I did to your idiotic uniform," the old wizard said, "I will do to your defenses and weapons, I will do to your guns, I will do to your bayonets, I will do to your reigns and tackle and carts and equipment and artillery. Let me submit that I am fully capable of doing it to you, and your men, if I choose to be less than humane. You will have nothing with which to conquer anything, and you and your treasonous armies will be naked and defenseless and standing among piles of dust along with the dust of your broken aspirations. You will not take the throne of Bavaria, and you definitely will not touch the works of Conrad the Ineffable."

General Gunther Maximillian von Ansbach, however, who had not recognized Arsalan before he stood and spoke, now centered his frightening attention solely on this strange, old, courtier. Von Ansbach's stare was icy and keen with silent hatred, as if he wished to swat Arsalan like a fly, and for a brief instant Arsalan wondered whether attracting the general's attention had been a good idea.

"So, you are the old Turkish swindler who considers himself a wizard," von Ansbach said.

"Be careful with your words or I will disintegrate your undergarments, too," said Arsalan.

"You will be the first one I will send to prison," said the general, "for life."

"No prison can hold me," chuckled Arsalan. "I am Arsalan the Magnificent, and I will build the penitentiary that will imprison you so inescapably you will forget what sunlight looks like."

It seemed General von Ansbach paused, factoring how to respond. Despite his audacious skepticism toward magic, he was gauging how seriously he should consider Arsalan's threats. Lacking a timely retort, von Ansbach decided he rather would exhibit impatient aplomb. He turned on his socked feet and marched back out of the room, upright and proud, and left the trailing, granular particles of dust, scraps of lint, and stray threads behind as he strode in his wrinkled undergarments, ignoring the military decorations that lied on the floor behind him. His two anonymous minions, however, were slightly less concerned about their pride, and busied themselves with stooping and retrieving the dropped items from the pools of dust while throwing confused, and bitter glares this way and that at everyone else in the room as they hurriedly retreated behind the general.

The princess' political congregation then amassed at the window facing the stables, where they watched with laughter and amazement as General Gunther Maximillian von Ansbach, with this tall, sheer back as straight as a board, mounted his armored warhorse in his linen undergarments and rode off with his entourage.

CHAPTER 16

"His attack was inevitable!" screamed Arsalan at the delegation. In the exhaustion that followed the tense and commanding presence of von Ansbach, the team felt compelled to speak their minds; royal and diplomatic protocol were momentarily disregarded, giving way to an open and heated argument. Many of the other delegates, even in their impressively uniform numbers, had proven themselves useless, and had retreated to a side-room for lunch, leaving only the princess, Siegfrieda, Arsalan, Defne, and Teodora to set matters straight.

"It was time to send him a message that Princess Berthilde was not to be intimidated," said Arsalan. "How better to show him than to let him know that you have not just an army but wizards on your side?"

"Her Majesty never authorized such a display!" yelled Siegfrieda. "You were out of your bounds!"

"Then why am I here?" asked Arsalan, gesturing to himself. "Why am I part of your advising committee? Why should we sit and allow this general to walk all over the princess?"

Princess Berthilde, who had been pondering the gravity of the challenge, now held her hands in the air in a bid to silence everyone.

"Your move was simply unexpected," said the princess plainly. "I wasn't sure how to respond to it. But you have a point, Arsalan. I was struggling to respond to the general's arrogance. I was being too coy. I was underestimating him. He needed an immediate and threatening warning."

"We could have persuaded him with reason, I think," said Siegfrieda.

"I don't think so," said Teodora. "He is not like others. The general seems not to have normal feelings. I could see it in his face. His drive to assume power is unfettered by conscience or reason."

"His scorn of me was not just evident but wounding," said Princess Berthilde. "I don't understand it. It was almost magical, hypnotizing. I almost believed his terrible words about me and my rule. He even made it seem sensible. I wanted to acquiesce. He made me question my worth as a princess."

"No! Don't listen to him!" said Defne. "You are intelligent and wise for your age. You are honest and pure of heart. Your parents tragically left you behind to rule and you have met that challenge wonderfully. Yours is not a position anyone would have wanted to inherit. Don't believe the general. Just defeat his forces and imprison him."

"Defne is right," said Arsalan. "General von Ansbach has an empty, selfish heart and would make a terrible leader. Yet at the same time he possesses powerful charisma. He shouldn't be underestimated. You are a strong young woman, but this is someone the likes of whom no one has met before. You urgently need our help."

Bunching his fists, Arsalan then added, "Bayram would have been able to spar with him, though. He would have known exactly what to say. He has a way with words that is unrivaled. Why did that coward have to flee so readily?"

"Bayram is a businessman, Arsalan, not a politician, and certainly not a military strategist," said Teodora. "You know him too well to expect anything otherwise."

"We all should learn the art of negotiation from Bayram, though," said Princess Berthilde. After a pause, she added, "How did von Ansbach know?"

"About what, Your Majesty?" asked Arsalan.

"How did he know what I had been doing with my time, with you, and with Defne?" asked the princess. "He wasn't wrong. And he made me feel guilty for it."

"That's how he manipulates others," said Arsalan. "He gets under their skins with bold and tactless words. But as to how he knows those details, I don't know."

"Spies," blurted Siegfrieda. "Or perhaps not even spies, but gossip-traders. We have a large staff, and it's conceivable that information was gleaned from them. We haven't been terribly circumspect in our endeavors, you know. Perhaps we should have been more careful."

"If I don't surmount this challenge," said Princess Berthilde, "I will be remembered as Bavaria's worst ruler."

"That is why you must defeat him," said Arsalan, "because history is written by the victors, and your honor, in the eyes of your people and descendants, is at stake."

"That may be," said Teodora, "but it is the welfare of the people of Bavaria that should concern us all the most if he assumes power."

"And the welfare of the people of the surrounding kingdoms when he makes war with them, too," said Defne.

CHAPTER 17

Impending war, and its grim tidings, echoes, rumors, soon broiled on the horizon. The delegation returned to the palace in Munich where Princess Berthilde gathered her military strategists and held council. General von Ansbach's forces, the strategists reported, already were marching through Gunzenhausen and Schwabach and Nuremburg, and it was suspected that von Ansbach's forces would gather to engage with loyalist forces at Donauworth and Ingolstadt. Soon there came the news that Princess Berthilde's forces had been routed there and that General von Ansbach's army was heading southward toward Munich where they met battalion after battalion of Princess Berthilde's defensive forces desperately attempting to stifle von Ansbach's advancement. General von Ansbach repeatedly sent officious and vaguely deriding communiques to the princess demanding her surrender. The princess and her friends stared out the windows with lined foreheads expecting the fire and sulfur of battle to appear already on the night's northern horizon and to hear the marching of boots and hooves. The nights were increasingly cold with dreadful winds and the encroaching massacres they portended. Arsalan's family and friends' white breaths flowered before their worried faces as they stood on balconies facing northward, gazing with trepidation at each clear and twinkling evening sky.

But there was no stopping the apparatus of von Ansbach's war now that it had commenced its lumbering motions. It was not long before the mass of war refugees arrived, fleeing the unprecedented violence of von Ansbach's campaign. The farmers and millers and blacksmiths and builders and woodsmen, with their donkeys, carts, horses, bundles, and crying children in tow, headed south along the roads toward them. Their haunted faces bore expressions of terror and exhaustion. Many stood at the gates of the princess' palace, pleading for entry and protection, and all were allowed in, some of whom were housed in stables while many others were allowed to camp on the princess' wide and plentiful grounds. The princess made certain to notify all that they should continue their migration southward, as there was no guarantee she would be able to fend off von Ansbach's hostilities.

The weight of war's approach sickened Arsalan. Despite all his threats to von Ansbach, he regarded with disgust the possibility of using his powers in ways that might hurt others. Perhaps Bayram was right, he thought, perhaps he should have divorced himself from the events of this foreign nation once he had earned his salary from them. After all, this was not even his own nation, and he was not even among his own people. But he thought about the structures he had rebuilt so fastidiously, and he recalled how his soul and Conrad's soul and the cultural lineage of the magical architects still suffused them. He thought about his burgeoning fatherly affection for Princess Berthilde herself. Arsalan then smiled to himself, confirming to himself that he would not flee, and that he would defend his dear friend Princess Berthilde with all the powers that were at his disposal.

Princess Berthilde, when not busy with the wellbeing of the refugees during the day, appeared to Arsalan to be deeply haunted by the fact of civil war in her kingdom. She roamed the halls of her palace, sometimes refusing to eat or to sleep, and often hugging herself as if she were freezing. Often Siegfrieda or Dietrich would find the princess in one of the grand, dark hallways in the middle of the night, whispering an imagined conversation with a statue of one of her royal ancestors—a bearded great-grandfather or great uncle holding a shield and a sword and staring out from beneath a helmet with a wild and imperious gaze—and she would be pleading with his stony likeness to tell her what she should do. There Siegfrieda and Dietrich would retrieve her and would lead her to bed by her shoulders. Repeatedly Princess Berthilde, her young, lovely face corrupted with weariness and insomnia, would urge Defne to leave for her own safety, but Defne's sisterly fidelity to the princess was already established as firmly as Roman concrete. Although she professed no formal political or military expertise, Defne insisted on providing emotional support to Princess Berthilde, who indeed seemed to need it increasingly as her anxiety intensified, even as she pleaded with Defne to flee.

One night, the princess went so far as to appear by Defne's bedside in the middle of one wintry night with a suitcase in one hand and a candle in the other. With eyes hard with mad, fiendish panic, the princess explained that she wished to escape with Defne and Duchess Teodora to Silesia, where she hoped to take refuge. Defne of course was startled and disturbed to tears, but she grasped the princess by her arms and forcefully reminded her of her responsibilities as a princess, and that the welfare of the Bavarian people was her duty to preserve. The ruckus awoke Arsalan, Siegfrieda, Teodora, and Dietrich, and the group spent the remainder of the night calming the princess over the candlelight that flickered wildly in the whistling drafts of winter. Eventually, they talked sense back into her, sent her to bed, and shook their heads in despair. Princess Berthilde slept until noon the next morning and ate breakfast with a fatigued and sheepish face. From then on, she remained in relatively normal spirits—until the explosions arrived.

They appeared on the far northern horizon one night, distant, booming eruptions that produced lights bright and pink. Smoke climbed in slanting columns, made visible in the darkness only by more successive, flashing detonations whose terrible sounds rumbled from horizon to horizon. General von Ansbach's forces finally had reached the gates of Munich and were fighting

Princess Berthilde's troops to enter. It would be only a matter of hours or days before von Ansbach would pierce his way to the heart of the Bavarian kingdom to assume his seat in power. The dreadful blasts approached as if they were von Ansbach's own stomping footsteps, terrifying everyone in the palace. Many of Princess Berthilde's own nobles and statesmen and servants began to abscond. Suddenly they had reasoned that their terror of von Ansbach far outweighed their fear of possible punishment for abandoning their princess, and with little compunction they were seen openly running down the halls of the palace and across the grounds carrying baggage stuffed so fully and hastily that corners of garments protruded from inside and sheets of paper fell to the floor behind their heels. Princess Berthilde attempted desperately to convince them to stay, sometimes grabbing them by their arms, but the escapees—her trusted advisors and staff—only would glance at her, over their shoulders and in great haste, with shamefaced and frightened eyes. The princess would realize the futility of her efforts with them and would let them go, for it was a terror she duly shared with them and for which she could find little cause for blame. She stood alone and listened to the echoing sounds of hurrying footsteps and the shouts of friends raucously calling to each other to leave.

Princess Berthilde's generals—those who were not needed at the front but awaited the enemy at the palace--accosted Arsalan in desperation late one night while he was alone in his room. Generals Weishaupt, Heltau, Schröter, von Steinsdorf, Böhner, Weinkamm, von Wolfram, and Ott abruptly materialized at Arsalan's bedside with candles held under their strangely illuminated faces like a host of monks conspiring in murder. They begged Arsalan in hoarse whispers to use his powers to defeat their enemy. Arsalan assured them that once von Ansbach's battalions arrived at Munich, he would shield the city from danger, but that he could not use his powers to kill anyone. The generals and advisors objected to this moral restriction and implored him to make an exception in this case. They argued that if he did not use his powers to destroy the enemy, more loyal soldiers and civilians would lose their lives, and that should weigh more heavily on his conscience than killing at all. To this Arsalan vigorously objected.

"No," said Arsalan. "I cannot kill. I simply cannot."

The bronze, flickering firelight reached into their wrinkled faces and hairy brows like clawed thorns and brambles, and their eyes shone blue and black in the fitful, shadowy glimmering above their gnomish noses. Their expressions became ever more wrought with angst and exasperation, ever more exaggerated in their horror and vehemence, like the pale, plastic faces of ghosts.

"Then we have no choice but to declare the princess unfit for leadership and to declare martial law!" they said. "She is incapacitated with nervous exhaustion!"

Arsalan had feared before that Princess Berthilde's generals and advisors were ineffectual, but now their uselessness became shockingly apparent. They were to Arsalan simply a group of scared, effete, paunchy middle-aged men who had enjoyed peace and prosperity under their former kingly leadership for so long that they had forgotten how to counter a truly formidable nemesis with any effectiveness, and that their expertise lied mostly in the holding of forks and knives and wine glasses. Yes, they had bided their idle time playing abstract war games and exercises on paper maps in parlors, but against a truly diabolical foe such as von Ansbach, who utilized espionage and subterfuge along with brutal military might, they were powerless. Arsalan saw that if they truly wished to commit themselves to such an act as extreme as martial law, they would have done so days ago, stridently and courageously, but that cowardice and ineptitude had prevented them.

"No," said Arsalan. "I cannot allow you to do that, either. Whether you like it or not, Princess Berthilde is the holder of the throne, and we must help her hold it! I will prevent you from taking it from her! Listen to me. I will take control! Follow my lead, men, and I will lead us from this darkness. Have courage, my men, my brave soldiers! Gather all your nearby infantries at the gates of Munich and fight as you had planned and await my instructions. I will show you how to defeat von Ansbach!"

This appeal to their bravery and loyalty appeased them, and their courage was renewed when they found in Arsalan not an obstacle, or even an instrument of their use, but as a leader under whom to serve.

"Yes, Master Arsalan!" they said, emboldened. "We will do so! Together we fight!"

Princess Berthilde's soldiers fought stubbornly at the city gates, stalling von Ansbach's advance. News was heard that tremendous ramparts had been erected and that casualties on either side were low. For several days and nights, they seemed to be at a stalemate. But some booming continued far into each night, pausing only momentarily just before dawn, except for one angry night, perhaps during which von Ansbach grew impatient, when the explosions persisted throughout the dark hours. On this night, Princess Berthilde, finally pushed to her breaking point, awoke from her fitful sleep, screaming like a child, placing her hands on her ears and panting with unmitigated panic. Again, the young princess was consoled by several of her friends, and with a quavering voice she told them of a dream in which she saw populations of people drowning in a great, rushing river of blood.

"I surrender," she whispered. "I want to surrender. I am merely a sixteen-year-old girl. I have no power over this."

Siegfrieda began to say something but was interrupted by Arsalan.

"No!" he commanded. "I don't allow it."

Siegfrieda began, "But you're not in charge here. You're just an—"

"The problem is that one has been in power here!" yelled Arsalan, "You and I speak in the hallway alone! Now!"

Arsalan marched out of the room with Siegfreida stalking behind him.

When they stood alone in the hallway, they turned to face each other furiously, eye to eye.

"You useless coot," said Arsalan. "What good have you been as an advisor all this time? You have far more experience in these matters than the princess, yet you stand by and do nothing while she flounders and panics! If I didn't know any better, I'd say you are one of von Ansbach's spies, infiltrating her court, feeding her fears, and actively undermining her ability to rule!"

"How dare you accuse me of being a spy and undermining her?" Siegfrieda spat. "I think it's you who are the one who has infiltrated her circle of trust and has made a mess around here! Ever since you appeared here, things have gotten out of control. You're not even Bavarian! Why don't you go back to your Ottoman Empire with all the money you've siphoned from our coffers with your fake, illusionistic magic to resume your wealthy life, you parasite? Your job was finished here a long time ago!"

"If you really valued the princess' rule," said Arsalan, "you would do everything in your power and experience to help her, including welcoming the help of someone with demonstrated magical powers like me. But you have not done so. You only have tolerated my presence with gruff condescension and have stewarded the princess' descent into helplessness. So, tell me, have you let your kingdom go to hell because you are incompetent or because you are deliberate?"

"It's because von Ansbach is inevitable," said Siegfrieda. "I don't want the princess to go mad, but I do see her reign was doomed from the start ever since her parents died. We tried to keep things quiet and peaceful to prevent something like this from happening because we knew Princess Berthilde was weak."

"And that's why von Ansbach recruited you, isn't it?" said Arsalan. "You secretly believed that, and he exploited your fears and misgivings, and now here we are. Am I wrong?"

Arsalan was bluffing, of course, to some extent. He was not even certain of his assertions, but he thought now he had nothing to lose to voice his suspicions openly, if only to gauge her reaction to them and to see if there was any truth to them. But even if there was no truth to them, Arsalan intended for his accusations to dislodge from her the real reason through their sheer bluntness. And indeed, there was a flicker of fear in her eyes, and her mouth opened to speak, but, whether due to fearful defensiveness or justified mystification, she could find no words, and her lips twisted and turned into so many expressions of anger and frustration that he thought she had invented a few of them.

Arsalan's next reaction surprised even himself. He laughed out loud. His amusement at Siegfrieda's reactions gave way to a sudden remove from all the despair and dread that surrounded him. He realized that Siegfrieda's expressions, whether they indicated a genuine ire at being falsely accused when simply exhibiting incompetence or were an attempt to conceal her guilt beneath such a feigned reaction, were natural, and that neither case should matter to him. They both led to the current situation of utter pandemonium that had to be managed in the most efficient way possible. He also realized the only person who could manage the situation was himself. Bayram was correct in that Arsalan was in fact not of Bavaria and not of their court. Arsalan saw that this applied even more so now to the current state of emergency, where he was under even less obligation to abide by their normal protocols than before. Additionally, as a magical architect, he could not say that he was a man of any ordinary society whatsoever, and that the only society by whose rules he was obliged to abide were those of the magical architects. Now was the time to use his powers to solve the present crisis in a way only a magical architect could do, and with no apologies.

"You're right," said Arslan to Siegfrieda. "Although I love the princess like my own daughter, I'm not Bavarian, am I? And everything has gone to hell already. It doesn't matter now if you've been his agent, even if unwittingly. That damage is done. I'll let Princess Berthilde handle that matter after I defeat von Ansbach and assure her position on her throne."

And with that, he exited the hallway and reentered Princess Berthilde's bedroom, where Defne, Teodora, and Dietrich were consoling her. Siegfrieda, although shaken and irritated by Arsalan's boldness, followed him and stood in the doorway with her fists by her sides, fuming.

"Call all your generals, servants, and advisors who are remaining in the palace, all those who haven't fled, into your ballroom," said Arsalan to Dietrich, who nodded, and within minutes it was done. Arsalan, Defne, Princess Berthilde, Teodora, Dietrich, and Siegfrieda faced the staff of the Bavarian palace. Their numbers by this time had been reduced dramatically by means of attrition to a mere twenty individuals, including her remaining generals, some of the advisors, and the main servants under Dietrich's command. The reduced crew all stood much closer to Arsalan than the former crowd had stood when Princess Berthilde had made her announcement in the ballroom months earlier, when there were so many attendees that those in the back had resorted to leaning forward and standing on their toes with their hands cupped at ears to hear her.

"Thank you for assembling tonight," said Arsalan to his little audience. "I cannot commend you enough your bravery and fealty for remaining. As you know, I, Arsalan Ozdikmen, am a wizard, hired to build structures for your beloved princess, but I have been forced by these perilous circumstances into the uncomfortable position of having to assume interim control of your armies until such a time as I defeat General von Ansbach. I do not take control of your throne, and I will not do so. Princess Berthilde remains the Princess of Bavaria, and I will allow no man or woman to challenge that, not any of us, and not von Ansbach. As a magical architect, I swore a vow never to use my powers to hurt other human beings or for military purposes, but now I believe this is a restriction I am forced to bend somehow, but carefully. If I am to use my powers for lethal force, then it will be only a matter of time before some other nation hires another magical architect for their military use, and from there it will be an arms race, and the creed and promise of the magical architects will be ruined, and the political stability of the world will be thrown into turmoil. But know at least tonight that I will keep you all safe," said Arsalan.

"Arsalan!" cried a voice echoing from outside a door, and Bayram ran inside, out of breath.

"Bayram!" hollered Arsalan angrily. "A fine time for you to show up again!"

Bayram, seeing the crowd gathered before Arsalan, took a moment to catch his breath.

"Your Majesty," said Bayram, bowing. "And Lady Teodora! I apologize for my rude entrance."

"Duchess," Teodora corrected him. "And it's no matter during wartime."

Bayram ran to Arsalan's side. "Forgive me Arsalan, for I've had a change of heart."

"Evidently, if you're going to run into peril at its gravest point. But now it's too late for apologies," said Arsalan. "We could have used you earlier, but what's done is done. I'm in charge here for now."

"I approached General von Ansbach, posing as the princess' emissary," said Bayram, "and I negotiated a peaceful surrender on her behalf."

"What?" bellowed Arsalan. "Turncoat! Traitor!"

"No! I'm saving you all. It's the only way, Arsalan!" said Bayram. "You may have noticed that von Ansbach's forces have not tried hard to make their way into Munich for the past few days. I convinced him to allow her more time to make her decision to surrender. I've bought you all time, my friends, time to fly! He's letting you go so long as you flee southwards to another kingdom! Take this chance and save yourselves!"

"Arsalan" said Princess Berthilde, "Bayram's right. It's time for me to quit. My heart is tired."

"No, she does not surrender!" screamed Arsalan.

"Who gave you the authority to speak for her?" said Bayram.

"And who gave you the authority to speak for her?" Arsalan retorted.

Bayram twitched and fidgeted irately but could find nothing to say. His hands made fists and his brow became furrowed. As Arsalan and Bayram glared at each other, they approached each other in front of the crowd and stood nose to nose and toe to toe, with their faces as gray and weary and stern as iron.

"Well, then it looks as though we need to come to an agreement, my friend," said Bayram.

"Yes, and these are my terms," said Arsalan. "Tell General von Ansbach I will treat with him and his men directly, tonight, at the city gates."

"Should he expect a surrender?" asked Bayram.

"Yes," said Arsalan, "but don't tell him the surrender will be his own."

Bayram stared at him for a long time, trying to maintain a furious visage, but he recognized when Arsalan could be convinced no longer, and he found he could not stay angry with his old colleague. An insuppressible but warm smirk slid across his face.

"Very well, old friend," said Bayram, and he turned and left.

The advisors smiled and patted Arsalan warmly on his shoulders and arms, and the generals, who seemed relieved and pleased, stood at attention and said that they were ready for his direction, and that they were now prepared to fight to their own deaths to defend Princess Berthilde's throne. The servants bowed, and Teodora regarded him with a look of renewed and somewhat astonished admiration.

CHAPTER 18

As Bayram had negotiated, a ceasefire was decreed between the two sides to make way for negotiations. The northern gate of the city of Munich was now quiet but bore all the evidence of the ongoing battle. Torches, fluttering in the cold winds, were lit all around the makeshift but imposing wooden ramparts that surrounded the city gate. The edifice surrounding the gate, stretching between two sturdy towers, had most of its windows smashed and shot. Pockmarks, large and small, marred the smooth masonry of the entire structure. On the ground, the offense's bulwarks were parallel with those of the defense, and between them a wide aisle yawned, one in which was strewn stone rubble, craters, and small fires that exuded fatigued little spires of smoke. Every rampart, window, battlement, and parapet bristled with the ends of rifles and arrows and cannons. Tense soldiers hunched behind them, their hats poking into the air, their faces obscured in shadow and fear, and both sides ready to exchange a ferocious barrage of artillery at the merest provocation.

In the corridor between the two fortifications, nervously rushing soldiers placed a simple wooden table and two chairs. A single sheet of parchment was placed on the table, along with an ink bottle and a quill. The anonymous soldiers retreated hurriedly to their bulwarks, and a few moments later General Gunther Maximillian von Ansbach emerged, again in full military regalia including his feathered hat, strutting with his straight back and high head, and finally sitting in the chair closest to his own men, his legs, sheathed in his spotless white trousers, splayed widely. There he waited, until, from somewhere within the ramparts guarding the city gates, there emerged Arsalan, dressed in his somewhat mismatched clothing he had not bothered to change during the entire extent of the onslaught. He shuffled toward the table with a look of gruff impatience on his hairy face. There, he plopped himself down at the table across from von Ansbach, leaned back, crossed his legs and arms, and offered the general a wry smile.

"So, they sent the Turkish magician to treat with me," said von Ansbach. "That makes two Turks! One to negotiate your surrender and one to sign the agreement. I suppose Princess Berthilde has run out of Bavarians to do her work for her."

"Maybe," said Arsalan, "except that we will not sign that paper."

"So, then tell me, Arsalan the Magnificent," said von Ansbach. "Why did you bring me all the way out here, exposed to enemy fire? Do you plan to dissolve my clothes again? Go ahead. I still won't be ashamed. I still will be General. Do you plan to assassinate me? You still may do that as well, for my commanders will carry out all my instructions on the event of my death."

"You are an idiot for not heeding my warning," said Arsalan, "and I am an idiot for not doing this sooner instead of warning you about it."

At this moment, General Gunther Maximillian von Ansbach's expression changed to one of horrified surprise. He stood upright, as if jolted into position, his chair tumbling backwards, and then slowly, like a board, and as if hinged at his heels, his body was lowered to the ground, where he eventually lay, struggling and crying for help within his own uniform, which had been stiffened to the rigidity of wood by Arsalan's spell.

Next, General von Ansbach's bulwarks and ramparts wholly disintegrated, all at once, turning into hissing particulate matter that flowed to the ground in large, flattening pools like dry sand. Behind the dissolved barriers stood the soldiers who had been hiding with their weapons in hand and who, now to their great shock, found themselves exposed. Just as immediately, however, all their weaponry—their rifles, sabers, artillery, and crossbows—also disappeared from their hands into palls of dust that poured to the ground or blew away in the breeze. Those soldiers, too, fell victim to Arsalan's magical puppetry. Against their will, they stood stiffly at attention and were lowered to the ground like mannequins, although ones who writhed ineffectually within their hardened clothing, grimaced, hollered in frustration, and then were placed to one side of the road or another like pieces of lumber. First, dozens, then hundreds, of von Ansbach's soldiers were subdued this way as Arsalan nonchalantly strolled behind enemy lines, freezing all their uniforms into stiff, straight poses and destroying everything else that was made of wood, metal, canvas, or leather. The enemy hardly had the speed to act against Arsalan's rapid spellcasting; they raised an arm to shoot or to strike, a knee to charge, and within an instant they were grappled by their own uniforms as their tools of war were disintegrated in their very hands. Many soldiers, witnessing Arsalan's approach from afar, did find the chance to fire on him, but their bullets bounced off what seemed to be an invisible wall that encased him, one that was so impenetrable that Arsalan hardly seemed to notice the bullets. Many other soldiers, quickly and smartly reasoning from the fates of their comrades, dropped their weapons, removed their uniforms entirely, and ran away, completely naked even in the cold darkness rather than to be captured in the same disturbing way. Horses, newly freed from their reins and carts, were frightened by the chaos and fled, nearly trampling the escapees. A soldier from far away fired a cannon toward Arsalan, but the cannonball bounced away, far up into the night sky, never returning to the ground. To this Arsalan took irritated notice and dissolved the cannon at once into a pile of rust. He restrained all the soldiers who stood near it, and then continued with his campaign against the enemies directly around himself. The braver soldiers attacked Arsalan directly with sabers in attempts at melee; their blades pounded against a transparent shell and could not reach the impassive old wizard inside who ignored them to continue with his business, until such a time when he finally turned to them to immobilize them.

"None of you have any idea how merciful I am being to you!" screamed Arsalan as he performed his work. He cast a spell to magnify his voice to horrifying volumes that echoed resoundingly over the landscape like the curses of a god. "What I'm doing to your guns and cannons I could be doing to you! But no! I cannot hurt! I cannot kill! I should not be doing any of this! I hate this! I hate war! I should be making beautiful buildings. Do you hear? I should be constructing beautiful structures! But I can't do that now because you idiots want to fight and to steal and to main and to kill! Well, fight me then, cowards! Fight me, you wretched weaklings!"

Utter mayhem reigned among the enemy ranks at the north gate to Munich. Apoplectic commanders screamed orders, their swords in the air, their horses rearing on their hind legs. Soldiers ran in every direction, some attacking, many deserting, while others, when confronted with Arsalan's terrifying powers, dropped to their knees and pleaded for mercy. Screams, explosions, commands, whinnies, and crashes all collided into a symphony of bedlam. To make more of his point, Arsalan detonated several of their carts holding gunpowder charges in fiery blasts, making sure they were far enough away from anyone to do any injury. Finally, the enemy was able to scramble a retreat. The remaining soldiers fled northward as fast as they could manage, but Arsalan simply took flight and pursued them effortlessly, like a bird of prey. From his airborne trajectory he froze and immobilized the running rebels one by one until, miles down the road, even the commanders were subdued by his thaumaturgy and were laid out on the ground, panting violently from the exertion of their attempted escapes.

Finally, Arsalan returned to the scene of battle at the north gate, where debris was scattered, fires still were burning, and enemy soldiers lay moaning on the ground for help and mercy. Arsalan toured the carnage and regarded own work with resigned factuality tinged with a deep sense of shame, knowing fully that he had tested his lifelong vow of nonviolence if he had not broken it outright. The princess' soldiers emerged from behind their barriers and, a little stunned by the swift and businesslike routing of the enemy, commenced their cleaning operations. During the extent of the battle, Princess Berthilde's forces had followed Arsalan's orders not to fire a shot or an arrow, not to kill or harm the enemy, but simply to capture the harmlessly immobilized enemy rebels as prisoners of war as they were rendered prone. This, of course, was as easy as moving logs. The task proved only a matter of time and of ignoring the curses and pleas of the captives as they were lifted onto carts and freighted away to jail. Soon Princess Berthilde's soldiers found they had not enough space in their prisons for the rebel fighters and were forced to resort to root cellars and stables. In any case, examination by the army's medical staff revealed to their amazement that although many of them had suffered superficial scratches and bumps from their harrowing experiences with Arsalan and were suitably shaken, the wizard's tactics against them otherwise proved entirely nonlethal. In fact, after the prisoners' uniforms magically loosened in their jail cells, the pain and fear and humiliation were lifted from them, and many of the rebel soldiers began to realize the fortune of their predicament and to laugh to each other with some relief.

Of course, this laughter was not shared by the instigator himself, General Gunther Maximillian von Ansbach, who, upon Arsalan's orders and Teodora's urging, was placed in his own windowless cell deep in Munich's most secure and forbidding bastille. The bastille was a foreboding, octagonal stone tower of many stories and immense blocks of rough white masonry, blossoming at its top into a guard's platform with toothy battlements. Von Ansbach, however, was imprisoned in its cellar, just above the catacombs, where no sunlight reached. There, he was isolated from his commanders, his rebel soldiers, and any sight of the sky. Two dim lanterns hung on a wall outside his cell. In the semidarkness, Von Ansbach was lounging with calculated nonchalance in the corner of his rocky cell as if on his reading couch at home when Princess Berthilde and Arsalan entered to see him.

"Hello, Mister von Ansbach," said the princess.

At first, von Ansbach did not move. Arsalan noticed how tremendous the man's frame looked in comparison to the cramped, dimly lit cell in which he sat, like a mythical creature caught in a cage. After a second, von Ansbach responded to the princess' words with just a look. He had been gazing through some spot on the far wall opposite him, and when he heard the princess' words, he slightly turned his head and stared at Princess Berthilde with his glittering blue eyes. They were so calmly lacking in emotion that it still made one's spine shiver.

"General," he corrected her.

"Not anymore," quipped Arsalan.

Von Ansbach, still and silent, continued to stare at them both.

"So," said Arsalan, "I don't suppose you still doubt magic. Do you?"

"If you came here to gloat, trickster," said von Ansbach, "you're wasting your time."

"No," said Princess Berthilde. "We came here to ask you what you had in mind for your remaining army."

"And why would I divulge that to you?" said von Ansbach. "Whether I told you or not, my faction still has its plans, which you will discover soon enough anyway, particularly when they become successful."

"Telling us would save us all time," said Arsalan. "Your forces will be defeated anyway."

"Don't be so certain of that," said von Ansbach. "In addition, once my forces prevail, they will come to free me from here. That is what I await now, aside from the greater mission of overthrowing you."

"Your plans seem far too bold," said Arsalan.

"I otherwise remain silent about the details of my plans," said von Ansbach. "Don't waste my time."

"Time? Don't fool yourself," laughed Princess Berthilde. "You'll have all the time you ever can imagine having."

"You are such a weak and pathetic leader," said von Ansbach. "A mere child. If it were not for your friends, you'd be sitting here instead."

"Isn't it true of all strong rulers," said Princess Berthilde, "that they succeed due to the support of their subjects and allies?"

Von Ansbach sighed, as if to conceal with feigned impatience the twinge from her sharp retort.

"In that case," he said, "a true ruler would not attempt to question me directly but would delegate that role to a professional interrogator."

"Don't lecture me on leadership anymore," said Princess Berthilde. "You've caused needless killing, devastation, and turmoil in the very kingdom you wished to rule, my kingdom, which I rule. And you were defeated. You are a traitor, a disgrace. And now you're trying to dismiss me because you're ashamed to look at the victor in her face. You should feel fortunate that I haven't executed you yet."

"Do so, but I tell you I have no shame. And I know you don't have the taste for violence anyway," said von Ansbach.

"Maybe," said Princess Berthilde. "But don't think I hadn't planned to employ an interrogator, at least." She stepped aside, and Bayram entered.

"Forgive me, my friends, for I was a coward," uttered Bayram, "and I underestimated you all. Here is where I correct my mistake."

Everyone smiled to themselves in anticipation of what would happen next. Bayram produced a stool and sat in front of the iron bars of von Ansbach's cell. Bayram sat on the stool, leaning back and crossing his legs.

"Mister von Ansbach," said Bayram, "You and I have much to discuss tonight."

Everyone else left the room, leaving Bayram alone with his victim, the giant general who sat in a dark corner. Bayram's trickery, manipulation, and questioning lasted long into the night. He paused for sleep, and resumed the next morning, and then continued deep into the night following. At midnight that night, Bayram emerged with bloodshot eyes and stooped posture.

"There will be an attack of large scale," he said, "but he won't say where. I can't get anything else out of him. He's frightfully stubborn and has no conscience. Never have I met anyone like him, so unnerving he is in his callousness."

"Allow me," said Duchess Teodora, who plunged into the room and shut the door behind her. Everyone raised their eyebrows at her quiet confidence but waited outside for the results. The night passed, and it was obvious that Duchess

Teodora was not going to be as kind as anyone else had been. She did not allow von Ansbach to sleep and had the guards cast cold water on him and scream at him to keep him awake. Teodora then proceeded to question von Ansbach with a low, quiet voice and an intimidating and deliberate air.

Next to the room that housed von Ansbach's cell was a jailer's chamber where the rest of the company would improvise their strategies for grilling the traitor. A small, coarse table sat in the middle, decorated with pieces of paper with plans and notes hastily sketched on them. Around the table were chairs, side-tables, and a small iron oven, and not much else but a narrow, barred window at the top of a wall. The room was as cheerless, frigid, and dankly stony as any of the cells, and this atmosphere began to depress everyone except the jailers who, brutal and healthily muscled with their pink, shaved heads, assisted in the operations without complaint. The jailers' hoarse screams from the cell next door frightened the aristocratic company who waited for Teodora's results as they sat around the table with gloomy expressions. Though none of them liked von Ansbach, none of them were comfortable being accomplices to torment, and over time, they began to become as unsettled by Teodora's punishing interrogations as by von Ansbach himself.

"I daresay," said Defne, "that we have become a gang of jailers and torturers now, haven't we?"

"Now you see the anguish and carnage to which your father had been so adamant not to make any contribution," said Bayram.

"These are strange times, my child," said Arsalan. "Ruling a kingdom can be unpleasant. However, we committed to helping Princess Berthilde, didn't we?"

"I am merciful. He's not receiving even half the punishment he would be receiving in any other kingdom," said Princess Berthilde.

Finally, at noon the next day, Teodora emerged, appearing tired but resolute.

"The attack will be to the south of here, and will involve all his remaining battalions, twelve in all, but he still will not reveal the location of the attack," she said. "He is definitely intransigent, but not invulnerable."

Finally, after days of being denied proper sleep, von Ansbach fell into a deep slumber. It was partially purposeful and intended to demonstrate his defiant insouciance. Still sitting in the same position as before, von Ansbach leaned his great head against the wall and commenced snoring raucously, infuriating everyone.

The one whose patience was finally worn to a breaking point, to everyone's surprise, was Siegfrieda. For the days during which von Ansbach was interrogated, she busied herself with this or that small task and listened quietly and soberly to all the developing news. But after Duchess Teodora had reported her progress, Siegfrieda finally and angrily blurted, "Conrad's Castle!"

Everyone was startled from their dazes. Siegfrieda was sitting at one end of the table drinking hot tea from a wooden cup. She was hunched over the tea in the cold, and both her hands were surrounding the cup as if in prayer.

"Conrad's Castle! Can't you see?" Siegfrieda squeaked. "He's going to attack the Castle!"

"How do you know?" asked Princess Berthilde.

"It's to the south. It's a symbol of the reign of the magical architects that he can destroy to break our spirits! It's simple math!" Siegfrieda said. "What could be farther south in Bavaria that would be worth attacking anyway?"

The notion took everyone by surprise by its simplicity. Arsalan observed her with a keen look that did not go unnoticed by Siegfrieda, who flinched and looked in the other direction.

"And that's why I have you as an advisor, my Siegfrieda," said Princess Berthilde.

Siegfrieda leapt from her chair and exited their room and entered the room with von Ansbach's cell.

"Wake up!" yelled Siegfrieda, throwing the tea in his face.

Von Ansbach again moved little, only opening his eyes to stare at the new interrogator.

"That's it, isn't it?" said Siegfrieda. "It's Conrad's Castle you're attacking, isn't it?"

Von Ansbach observed her with an eye of cool suspicion but remained silent.

"Tell them!" said Siegfrieda. "Just say it!"

Again, von Ansbach maintained his silence, but there was a slight smile bent at the corner of his lips.

"Stop your smug grinning, you demon," said Siegfrieda, and between the bars of the cell she threw her wooden cup at his forehead, hitting it squarely, but von Ansbach still did not move and did not flinch.

"Siegfrieda!" screamed Princess Berthilde. "That's enough. You're getting nowhere with him."

"I am tired of you," said Siegfrieda to von Ansbach. "I am tired of you, abusing the darkest portions of others' hearts and dragging kingdoms into chaos and despair. I want you to die."

Von Ansbach began to convulse as if wanting to cough, silently and oddly. Still staring at Siegfrieda and saying nothing, he revealed his seizures as laughter, low and mocking, which grew until it was heard by everyone who crowded into the room to see what was happening.

"Siegfrieda, no," said Princess Berthilde. "You're letting him torment you. Don't succumb to his instigations."

Siegfrieda began to weep, and she turned to the princess to embrace her.

"I'm sorry," said Siegfrieda. "I'm sorry I wasn't a better counselor to you throughout this ordeal."

"I understand," said the princess, puzzled. "This conflict has torn all our hearts to pieces."

"What do you suggest we do?" asked Arsalan in a low voice, standing in the doorway. He stared intently at Siegfrieda.

"Since we're not precisely sure yet of his plans," said Siegfrieda, wiping her tears. "Send scouts southward. Send for news from that area. Have we located the remaining battalions? Where are they? We need to learn this from our own generals."

"Do so," said the princess to Dietrich, who had been standing nearby. "I request a conference with my generals immediately."

"Yes, Your Majesty," said Dietrich, and he bowed deeply, turned, and left.

After the princess left for her meeting, Arsalan helped Siegfrieda retrieve her cup from the cell where von Ansbach still was sitting and leering at them.

"You weren't the only one, Siegfrieda," said von Ansbach in his deep voice. "They were legion. You yourself knew. Eventually, some of them will help me escape, and there's nothing you can do about it."

"As far as anyone is concerned," said Arsalan to von Ansbach, "you are insane, so be silent."

Arsalan looked at the jailed man for a long moment in grim sadness. Arsalan then guided Siegfrieda back into the jailer's room where he poured another cup of hot tea for her. They were alone. There at the table they sat silently together in the dim cold by a lantern, their breaths steaming before them. They stared at the bleak wooden tabletop for anything their minds could grasp for distraction and comfort, but all they could find were stains, crude graffiti, and notches from the blades of knives. Arsalan looked around him, as if to search for eavesdroppers, and back at the tabletop.

"I wasn't wrong to accuse you," uttered Arsalan to Siegfrieda, "but I was wrong to blame you. You were manipulated by him. He exploited your anxieties about Princess Berthilde's rule. Didn't he?"

Siegfrieda looked at him with an honest but slightly fearful expression, and then she looked down again at her tea.

"He approached me," said Siegfrieda. "He knew of my skepticism toward magic. He spoke to me in private long before his insurrection. He asked me to help him topple Princess Berthilde's rule, and I refused. I was stern in my refusal, but in truth, I was also terrified of him. You know the spell he has on others. I knew that the princess would react in fear if I told her what had happened, so I kept it from her. But von Ansbach persisted with me, and he promised me a seat in his new government. He told me that his takeover was inexorable, and he boasted that if I assisted her in resisting him, I would be tortured in the most unimaginable ways if he achieved victory. Finally, I became angry, and I ordered him to be imprisoned at once, but my guards already had been compromised by him and were fearful of him. They were hesitant to touch a general in any case, but of von Ansbach case they were singularly petrified. It was then I learned that he already had built deeply prevalent alliances within our court through menacing threats and promises of power. It was the threats that were most effective, which is probably why you saw so many of our palace flee in abject terror upon his approach. No one wanted to serve him, least of all me."

"You did not give him information?" asked Arsalan.

"No," said Siegfrieda. "Others must have, though, which is why I said as much."

"He told you about Conrad's Castle. Didn't he?" said Arsalan.

"He did not hide those intentions from me," she said. "It was one of his many threats. He was successful in terrorizing me with these threats, and as a result, in my service to the princess, I dithered, and I tarried, and I hesitated at crucial junctures. My judgement was clouded. I didn't report von Ansbach's intentions. I was too far into my fear of him. Thousands of Bavarian subjects probably have died due to my reticence. I should be jailed. I should be exiled. I probably should be executed. I secretly might have betrayed a young woman who is like a daughter to me."

"It does not sound exactly like that," said Arsalan. "Although your discernment was clouded by terror and doubt, you seem to have been as much a victim as anyone else. It is not my role to bring you to justice under Bavarian law anyway, especially to accuse you of being a traitor under such nebulous circumstances. I wanted only to help Princess Berthilde fight her enemy. The rest is her responsibility."

"But you, quite boldly and successfully, have assumed interim control over the throne," said Siegfrieda. "I would have understood if you exposed my treason, demanded my punishment, and jailed me."

"Now that von Ansbach is jailed and the princess is once more in command, there is no need to share your secret with anyone," said Arsalan. "You did not wish to betray the princess, but you were coerced into inaction through terroristic means. The princess still loves you and needs you. The stability of her court depends on you in many ways. The costs of your imprisonment outweigh any benefit. You need to resume your responsibilities and to do good henceforth.

I know you are a shrewd and capable advisor under better circumstances."

"I am not sure I am believing what you say," said Siegfrieda. "You trust me so? You are always so adamant at how swift and merciless justice is in the Ottoman Empire for those who fail their leaders for whatever reason."

"I say that many times in impatience, but I am nothing like that, and I never was," said Arsalan. "And we are not in the Ottoman Empire. I have lived too long to be unmerciful or accusatory. I am forgiving, and I cannot eradicate this tendency in myself. Perhaps I am not forgiving so much as resigned and jaded. I hate seeing others suffer. I care more about sparing others anguish than about strict law or morality. I sense your inner conflict and remorse, and I cannot stand to bring the law to your neck during such a fog of war, as they say in Prussia."

"But I am afraid she will reason what I have done to her and will draw judgement on me," said Siegfrieda.

"She is an intelligent young woman who sees things clearly," said Arsalan, "but only when she wants to see them clearly. Even if she could discover what you have done, she would not want to believe it. And even if she were to believe it, she would seek to understand. Live up to her expectations of you from now on, and everything will be well. Most importantly, do not doubt again her ability to rule."

"You have my promise. I have regretted my actions, or rather, inactions, all along. It made me miserable. I hate von Ansbach," said Siegfrieda, and she sobbed, then collected herself again. "Forgive me for all the unkind things I have said about you. Forgive me for all my disparaging comments about magic. Not only are your powers real, but you are a good man, I see now; brusque sometimes, yes, but humane."

"Of course I forgive you for your comments," said Arsalan. "You have been generous to have me as a guest in your palace for so long. Anyone who can tolerate me for that long is worthy of esteem."

"You have saved us, Arsalan," said Siegfrieda. "You have helped us more than I ever would have liked to admit."

"Although we're not finished yet," said Arsalan. "There's still the Castle."

Chapter 19

Reports returned from the loyalist generals, through their own reckoning and their scouts' reconnaissance, that the remaining rebel battalions were now concentrated to the southwest and southeast of Munich. Early in the insurrection, the loyalist generals had presumed those battalions to be rebels when communications with their commanders had ceased and could not be restored despite all attempts made in good faith. From then on throughout the conflict, their positions had been monitored, but no armed engagement occurred with them. The wayward battalions remained quiet, and the loyalist forces wished to avoid the unnecessary deaths of their own countrymen. They needed to devote their resources to the more immediate combat from the north. Now that the northern threat had been thwarted, there were indications of the rebel battalions' setting out from Kempten, Murnau am Staffelsee, and Rosenheim, from which their trajectories indeed appeared to converge at Lake Starnberg. Siegfrieda's inside information was fortuitous, for before the mobilization of the rebel battalions from the south had begun, the princess' loyal generals already had surrounded Lake Starnberg with massive reinforcements, whether the enemy were to attack Conrad's Castle or to feign such an offense for some other hidden goal. The princess' generals surmised that after the rebels' planned victory at Lake Starnberg, the insurrection would proceed northward to take Munich and to free their leader who sat brooding in the bastille. Since von Ansbach had failed to consider Arsalan's awesome defensive power, he had not sent both factions of his armies to take Munich at once from the north and south.

All this conjecture caused Arsalan to pace nervously up and down the halls of Princess Berthilde's gilded palace, in the dark, with his hands at his sides. It now was clear that von Ansbach's tens of thousands of soldiers, whom he could not fight all at once, were nearing the magical architects' venerated Conrad's Castle with the intent to dismantle it with their cannons and bullets and trebuchets, and this news filled him with quiet rage and horror. Teodora found him there in the hallways in the small hours of the morning. She said nothing, but looked at Arsalan in pity and appreciation, and she took his arm and led him outside to a balcony where he could invigorate himself with the fresh, frigid air. His hands shook within hers from either the chill or his fury and dread at the coming battle. That night, Arsalan looked long at the stars, and Teodora gazed at them and then at him in loving curiosity. She sensed precisely what he was thinking and feeling, so she asked him nothing, granting him the respectful tranquility of silence.

"I want to see Conrad's Castle," muttered Arsalan. "I want to see it one last time before it is destroyed."

Teodora remained quiet but her face became somewhat worried, yet understanding, and she clung to his arm more closely.

"I know Siegfrieda was compromised by von Ansbach," said Teodora. "I knew it as soon as I met her."

"As did I. You said nothing?" asked Arsalan.

Teodora shook her head and looked to the floor. "I couldn't prove my suspicions at that time, and besides, it wasn't my place as a diplomat," she said.

"I questioned her, and she told me her story. She was not entirely truthful. She made herself seem like just another victim, which she may have been to some degree, but I feel she was less so. In any case, it doesn't matter. Say nothing about it," said Arsalan. "She and I came to an agreement. She understands that I suspect more than she said and that I could have chosen to act very differently. We can trust her from now on. There is no need to disclose it."

"Yes, I could sense the conflict in her," she said. After a moment, she added, "If you go to see Conrad's Castle, you must promise me you will keep yourself safe."

"I promise," he said.

"Will I have to come with you to make certain?" she asked.

"Maybe," he smiled.

The next morning was wild with glaring sunshine that burned like magnesium, and the azure dome of the sky was as dry and solid and pure as glacial ice. It was a day that illuminated every window with stark whiteness and sent whipping winds down the halls of the palace in mischievous drafts to rattle chandeliers and to slam doors shut, a day when the arctic air hummed with electricity, causing everyone's hair to stand on end. Snow covered the ground without anyone noticing it falling the previous night, so embroiled had they been in their own grave and convoluted human affairs. Now they were vaguely surprised to find themselves in the very center of winter, amid its bright and otherworldly citadel of opalescence.

On this windswept day, a new stranger arrived without any forewarning. News flew in from the palace gates that a bearded young soldier of Turkish extraction was demanding to see his father, the great Arsalan the Magnificent. The order was given to escort him to the waiting room, for he was alone and weaponless, except for his enormous, ivory, Arab mare, whose expensive leather bundles housed a scimitar. The newcomer was dressed in an exotic uniform and spoke loudly and brashly and repeated the name Arsalan to everyone he met, asking each person if they knew him or had seen him.

At this news, Arsalan, Teodora, and Defne looked at each other in wonder, then hurried together down the halls to the red waiting room. As they approached, they heard a hoarse and forceful voice, accented in heavy Turkish, ordering the polite servants to bring him to his father immediately. Arsalan, Teodora, and Defne burst into the room and saw the red backs of the servants, including Dietrich, surrounding a figure in the center of the chamber. As the servants turned to notice Arsalan's entrance, they exposed the stranger to Arsalan's eyes. The newcomer wore a thick woolen cap and was dressed in a rich fur coat over a red jacket and a white sash, and his blue pantaloons were loose and ballooning at his thighs. His face was tanned and handsomely creased and wore a heavy brown beard. The stranger detected Arsalan and immediately turned to him.

"Father?" the stranger inquired. His voice changed at once from one of gruffness to one of innocence and wonder.

"Asker?" said Arsalan. "Is that you?"

"Father!" he exclaimed, and he ran toward the old man, and grabbed his arms. "My dear father, you have aged, but I still recognize you. Yes, it is me. Don't you recognize me?"

"Not with that beard!" laughed Teodora.

"Mother!" Asker said. "I can't believe my eyes. You are all here! Defne!"

Defne screamed Asker's name, and her eyes welled with tears, and she jumped to him and embraced him.

Jubilatory embraces ensued, laughter blossomed, kisses were exchanged, and tears flowed. They spent an hour in their celebration until they calmed themselves enough to trade tidings. It happened that Arsalan, Teodora, and Defne all had been writing letters to Asker, and when the young man heard the news of Bavaria's civil war in which his family had become embroiled, he requested leave and sped to Munich. After four years, he had paid his debts with his military salary and now enjoyed the rank of Lieutenant Commander.

"Let me look at you," said Arsalan, grabbing Asker's face. He had blossomed to resemble Arsalan more eerily than they had predicted, only taller. To his visage Teodora had contributed hair of brown, cheeks flushed with red, and eyes lightened to a hazel and rimmed with the beginnings of fine, handsome lines that crinkled when he smiled.

"You are quite the soldier now, aren't you? You have matured into full manhood. You make me so proud," said Arsalan.

"You have seen conflict and pain," said Teodora, also looking into his face. "My son, I'm sorry for leaving you all."

"I understood, Mother," said Asker. "I was already grown then, and I had my own path to forge in any case. There were more terrible things I later saw in war, but I never doubted we would see each other again."

At this moment, Princess Berthilde entered with an impatient air, her hands clasped in front of herself.

"And whom do we find visiting us today at a time like this?" she snapped. Everyone in the room turned to face the princess, bowing and formally addressing her, revealing tall Asker in his exotic apparel. The princess stopped short as if startled and looked at him from his face to his feet and back again.

"Hello," she said.

"Your Majesty," said Asker, bowing like a reed bent in the wind. "It is an honor to make your acquaintance, and please forgive the impertinence of my sudden arrival. I am Lieutenant Commander Asker Ozdikmen of the Ottoman Imperial Navy and son of Arsalan the Magnificent. I have come to visit my father after many years of separation and perhaps to assist him in his efforts with my own military knowledge."

Princess Berthilde seemed flustered and spent a moment to search for her next words, but she eventually forced them out of her reddening face.

"Oh, yes, of course. I have heard much of you," said Princess Berthilde. "You are welcome to our palace. We all hold your father in the highest esteem and gratitude for helping us combat our opponents during our civil strife. Without him, we would be defeated certainly. I am honored to accept your assistance, especially since I have had so many of my own military staff abandon me."

"I regret to hear of your difficulties," said Asker, "and I am honored to lend whatever expertise I may possess."

"How many leagues did you travel to come here?" asked Princess Berthilde.

"I departed from my station in Greece several weeks ago when I heard of my dear father's endeavors, and that he had been reunited with my mother and sister. My heart was overjoyed," he said.

"Then you must be famished and weary," said Princess Berthilde. "You must join us for dinner. But I must apologize that it will not be our usual royal and formal fare, as even most of our chefs and servants have absconded, though a few have returned."

"Certainly," said Asker. "And how silly of me nearly to forget this. As a token of gratitude toward your hospitality toward both myself and my family, I have brought the Bavarian court a gift from our empire, which you may add to your already fine collection. I am sorry it is only this one item, which is all I safely could carry on my long journey."

And Asker reached into one of his soft suede packs and produced a bundle of cloth, in which was a bright wad of rustling paper, from which was born a beautifully gleaming object of porcelain and silver. It was a grand pitcher, as tall as one's calf from the floor, tapered toward its top and wide at its bottom, with an elegantly thin dispenser arching from one side. Its cap was delicate and polygonal, its neck fluted and pleated, and its plump body was decorated all around in geometric floral motifs and images of racing horses. Princess Berthilde gasped.

"My, you shouldn't have gone to such trouble," she said. "It is gorgeous. Thank you."

She motioned to Dietrich, who delicately took the artifact in his white-gloved hands and bowed politely to Asker and left.

There was a brief silence during which Princess Berthilde regarded Asker in subtle fascination. Finally, she said, "Dinner will be at six. Please kindly join us." She bowed, turned, and left gracefully, followed by her entourage of red-coated servants, leaving the family of four alone in the room.

"Nice work, Asker," said Arsalan, patting him on the back, "but be careful with your courtesies. She may be ruler of Bavaria, but she is still a young and impressionable woman."

"It's for her court!" countered Asker.

Across Teodora's face crept a touching smile, which she attempted to soften by gazing downward.

A servant helped Asker and his newly reunited family carry his bags to his room. Asker, as he had indicated breezily in his letters, walked with a slight limp. This saddened and concerned his family, but Arsalan assured them that his injury was for the cause of the empire. This was an explanation that hardly consoled them. Nonetheless, Asker seemed to have become accustomed to the slight inconvenience of his gait and appeared to go through every means to ignore it. In fact, his way of accommodating for his limp was to hide it with a swagger that was notably manly, particularly when it was coupled with the stories of the keen danger Asker had seen in battle. Asker stood with a straight spine and shoulders thrown backward and his head held aloft while he swung his arms and shoulders with exaggerated confidence. Once in his room, Asker eventually but briefly showed his family the scar that remained on the back of his left leg. The raised, pink tissue was long, shiny, and as thick as a snake, and all regarded it with gasps, pity, horror, and Teodora's squeamish touches, but Asker laughed and assured them that it looked better now than it once did and was diminishing. He then told them the rousing story of how he received the injury from a rifle blast from a marauding pirate, whom he subsequently killed with his bare hands. Asker related the violent and harrowing tale with such smiling forthrightness as to seem callous or sardonic. His three family members were shocked and went pale at hearing his recount, and they told him not to continue his detailed description of the grisliness. They assured him they were simply glad he was alive and that they appreciated his service to his empire. From then on, his parents, with poignant, moistened eyes, often would hold him about his shoulders and would pat him on his back, sometimes using these means to help him from a chair. Otherwise, they regarded Asker's commanding air and jumpy, energetic walk with silent love and amazement.

"Why, this room is certainly fit for a maiden, isn't it? With all the lace and gauze and all," said Asker about his quarters, as if to change the subject. "Say, I hope I didn't frighten her with my arrival."

Teodora approached Asker and caressed the side of his face again.

"Asker, my dear son, I have missed you so much," she said. "I didn't want to say this in front of the princess or her servants, but there is one thing you need to know, even at your age."

"What is it, Mother?" asked Asker.

"Stay away from young noblewomen," she said. "We're far too much trouble. Besides, she's far too young."

The royal dinner that night was as modest and functional as Princess Berthilde had promised, but to famished Asker, who had traveled hundreds of leagues through the wintry cold and many dreary inns and boarding houses to be there, it was a sumptuous feast. Assured that most royal protocol was being disregarded in the execution of wartime duties, Asker, as quietly and as politely as he could manage, tore into his food like a carpenter's saw through fresh wood. Princess Berthilde could not help noticing Asker's hunger and stifled a giggle. Such small barbarities were of little matter during desperate times such as this. After dining, the glasses and dishes were quickly removed by the servants to make room for the plans and maps, which were unceremoniously splayed out on the table. The generals and advisors sat among Arsalan and his family and friends. Beside Princess Berthilde sat Siegfrieda, eating her sausages quietly and thoughtfully, but also engaged in listening to the excited conversation. Siegfrieda was sure to add a pointed question or two about the generals' tactics, pausing only to sign a few documents and send a few people off on errands. Asker was already in deep debate with the ten generals who sat around one end of the table. With the corner of a map in one hand, he was waving the other hand in the air and was pointing to a spot on the paper at which several of the generals were peering through their spectacles and nodding their heads. Princess Berthilde leaned toward them to absorb what they were saying and made a point of squinting and furrowing her brow to show that she was following it all just as well. Teodora and Defne sat together, quietly making comments to one another, and there was Bayram, measured and observant, and whispering sometimes to Arsalan, who sat quietly at his side and said nothing.

Arsalan was following the discussion but felt somewhat detached from it. In truth, he was exhausted. However vehemently he wished to defend Princess Berthilde from being overthrown, the grimness of war depressed him and drained him of energy. He was accustomed to building great things, and war appeared in every way to accomplish the opposite; to obliterate, leaving nothing, no prize or creation except ruin, casualties, flames, and despair. He was elated that his dear son had appeared in such a timely fashion after so many years, not just because he had missed Asker dearly, but also because, with his son's vibrant stamina and knowledge of military strategies, his son could bolster their efforts and could let Arsalan rest for a time.

Arsalan watched Asker from afar and wondered at the ability of his son, a lieutenant commander from a foreign navy, to discuss matters of war so assertively and capably with the local generals, although Arsalan was unsure if this was due to his son's precociousness or due to their relative ineptitude. In any case, it became obvious that the rank of General was where his son Asker was headed. Arsalan felt so profoundly proud of his son that a tear beaded in his eye, which he stealthily wiped away with one of Princess Berthilde's many embroidered napkins. Arsalan was honored to have a son like this, even if his son had chosen as his life's path one of a warrior.

At the meeting, it was decided that Arsalan and Asker would travel with the generals to assist in fighting von Ansbach's forces at Lake Starnberg. This, however, would not be the end of the discussion, as neither Defne nor Teodora nor Siegfrieda nor Bayram could be dissuaded from accompanying Arsalan to defend Conrad's Castle from the traitorous rebels. Arsalan became momentarily angry at the four of them, particularly Defne, for wanting to put themselves in harm's way to achieve such a difficult victory, but he hardly could say he was surprised that they would insist. Just as soon, with a begrudging smile, Arsalan found it impossible to thwart any of them. His heart warmed, and his spirits rose, and they all seemed to share an irresistible, collective sense of optimism, that together nothing could defeat them, or that, whatever the outcome, he at least would let nothing harm them.

The very next morning the company set off for Conrad's Castle. The pearly, windswept morning presented a watery, rosy sunrise blushing on the horizon. Everyone found their warmest clothing to wear for the journey and bound themselves up to their necks. Their breaths blossomed like white bouquets from their faces. Bundled in layers of wool and fitted with snow-flecked boots that crunched the frozen ground, they clumsily boarded the caravan of carriages destined for the southern trek. Arsalan's family sat in one carriage, and the princess, Siegfrieda, and Bayram sat in another. Arsalan cast a spell on the cabins to keep them warm. Elite guards with bayonets, rifles, and spears flanked them riding tremendous white warhorses with muscled necks and steaming nostrils. The sharp sun emerged from behind a continent of clouds above and at once the frosty landscape was ablaze with painful sunshine. The journey lasted several hours, passing by many small villages. Their progress was occasionally slowed by drifts of snow, which Arsalan blew or melted away from the wide road with his spells. As they approached their destination, they saw more and more the presence of Princess Berthilde's loyalist forces marching to and fro in the frigid morning. At last, the company caught sight of the metallic surface of Lake Starnberg, miraculously sapphire in the winter sunlight, and frozen here and there into circular gray slicks that edged into each other like water lilies.

Princess Berthilde's battalions were setting up barricades and camps along the shoreline, and campfire smoke rose in twisting gray pinnacles here and there in the distance. The gorgeous lake peeked out at them tantalizingly from between prickly, puce groves of bare trees and hid again as Arsalan's crew rode along.

They proceeded to Münsing with the lake to their right with the presence of the Bavarian army everywhere along the shore. Here the travelers turned west, and at noon the team reached Ammerland, where they descended from their carriages and took in the spectacular view of Lake Starnberg. A shelf of marbled, milky ice extended before them from the banks of the lake and stopped some distance away where its edge was licked by gentle waves. The troop of soldiers greeted Princess Berthilde and her team with strict, upstanding protocol, salutes and all, and bade them to board one of many large boats tied at a pier commandeered nearby, where the ice was still in the process of being pierced and broken by soldiers wielding pikes and sledgehammers. One by one, the friends boarded one of the boats lying in the newly freed waters, and suddenly they were on strange and unsteady territory. The floors of the boats swayed unfaithfully below their feet, and with wobbly steps they were quick to plop themselves into seats with the polite assistance of the experienced military boat hands who served them, all except for Asker, whose balance was impeccable. The young soldier could stand wherever in the boat he chose as if his feet were pinned to the wood and with his tall figure standing as vertically as a heron. Eventually, he sat at the bow, facing outward with a bold, flinty gaze.

Finally, the boat was launched from the back with a pole, and four soldiers, two on either side, began their labors of rowing using long oars. With firm strokes and warbling splashes, the boat crawled like a tortoise across the playful surface of the lake. This pace made Arsalan impatient, and he quietly cast another spell to make the boat lighter for their efforts. The dark field of water that surrounded them was studded with countless pyramidal wavelets that bounced in the icy breeze, and a toothy air bit at the ears and noses of Arsalan and his friends as they progressed. Their destination in the center of the lake was a small, gray, distant form, which gradually gestated into the vague shape of a castle. Arsalan had visited Conrad's Castle before, but through a different route, much earlier in his life, and, of course, under entirely different circumstances, so it looked somewhat unfamiliar to him. Nonetheless, his heart rose as he approached it again.

The boat softly seesawed as it approached the crew's giant terminus. At this point, the glaring sun slid behind a sober bank of clouds, casting everything in shadowless gray light, and everyone blinked in relief and surprise. The castle's immensity soundlessly unfolded and pivoted before them as the boaters wended their way toward it. It was a towering cubic structure constructed from massive blocks of granite. The castle floated motionlessly two stories above the lake's surface, exposing its flat, stony base, which spread like a vast ceiling over this area of water, to anyone who ventured near it. The bottom of the castle was covered in a thin layer of green moss and mildew. Here, one could sense the fearsome mass of the structure above, and one was afraid to row beneath its shadowy bottom for fear of being crushed. Here, the amplified sounds of lapping waves echoed loudly off the mossy stone ceiling almost as a warning.

Peering outward from the walls were many tall, narrow arched windows of all sizes, some lofty and kitelike, some compact and intimate, and each filled with kaleidoscopic stained glass and intricate stone tracery and topped with a pointed arch that protruded from the wall like a surprised eyelid. Arsalan was quietly dismayed to see gaps and cracks in the glass of the windows, as if children had thrown rocks through them. Here and there on the stone walls, more moss and mildew grew, sometimes in small, bulbous tufts. At each corner of the castle was a turreted tower that exceeded by many stories the height of the multitude of all the other roofs, which were collected above the walls of the structure like playthings poking out of a toybox. All these tiled peaks vaulted upward in narrow spires and acute triangles that, like lances and cleavers, sought to lacerate the sky. At the base of each turret was a single block of amethyst of wondrous volume; in each, one could become lost in the marbled, diaphanous depths of the violet minerals as if looking into the eye of an ocean. Arsalan once in his youth had witnessed them shining with a lavender light that illuminated everything around and below the castle, but today they were inert, hibernating in darkness.

On one side of the monumental edifice, facing southward, was the entrance, deeply nested in a set of concentric archivolts. A pair of somber wooden doors, as thick and as tall as the oaks from which they were crafted, awaited no one. Rimmed with riveted black steel, the doors sat impassively on a ledge, making no concessions to the beckoning waters below in the form of stairs or a ramp one might ascend to enter the castle. Here sat the evidence of the true function of Conrad's Castle. It was a fortress of ultimate refuge for the Bavarian royalty in times of attack. Magical spells had strengthened the walls and windows and roofs from the fiercest and fieriest blows any army could deliver. Within the impregnable walls of this castle the royal family would conceal themselves and could wait out a siege for over a year. Inside, it was reported, were stocks of water and grain, and gardens of rich soil, stables, and pens for livestock, all sufficient to sustain the survival of a sizeable community for many months.

However, for some generations, Bavaria had enjoyed a peace that dulled its vigilance, and the fortress fell into gradual neglect. The castle's gardens were not maintained, and the windows were cracked from weathering. The fortress and all its rooms, courtyards, balconies, and stables sat empty and forlorn, their halls echoing with the roars of raw wind for long stretches of time. Eventually, the population of Bavaria began to doubt even its magical nature, and the importance of the castle in their eyes was reduced to that of a quaint cultural landmark. The means of entering the castle had been forgotten, such that the present company had had to research old notes and documents before arriving. The key to entrance consisted of certain a few magic stanzas of rhyming poetry in Latin shouted at the castle loudly enough to echo from its walls. The castle was to respond to the magic words by extending a staircase down to greet them. How this would happen mechanically no one was sure, except Arsalan, who had studied the mechanism in detail but did not have the patience to explain it to anyone.

Since Asker had developed a particularly loud and hoarse voice from years of hollering orders to his men, the crew chose him to deliver the incantation. He stood, cupped his hands around his lips, and let the words fly. The princess held her ears as he did so, for his voice was roaring. Curiously, though, there was no response from the castle. It sat, stolid and stony and staring at them with disdain.

Asker and Arsalan reviewed the poem, which they had written on a piece of paper, and it was decided that Asker should try again, as perhaps he had mispronounced his Latin the first time. Asker boomed the poem again, this time with noticeably improved pronunciation, but still with no movement from the castle. A third time Asker screamed, and then a fourth time, until his voice reached a shrill pitch in frustration. He fumbled some of the words and his face turned red, before he finally gave up, quite out of breath.

Arsalan put one hand to his face and peered at the note like an exasperated scholar, and everyone looked over his shoulder, giving points and suggestions that were increasingly desperate and useless. For a moment, Arsalan was at a loss. There they stood, feeling stupid and hopeless in the drifting boat, until the oarsmen, in their long blue coats, began to yawn and to rub their hands together in the cold while gazing to the sky in despondent boredom. Members of the company began to sigh and to mutter to themselves, burying their hands in their pockets. Finally, Arsalan in desperation decided to try the password himself, warning everyone to cover their ears before he used a magic spell to magnify his voice. Arsalan put his hands to his mouth and issued the poem so explosively that the water rippled beneath him, and everyone else in the boat not only covered their ears but also shut their eyes and lowered their heads, as if weathering a thunderstorm. Arsalan's voice boomed so menacingly that it seemed to arrive from everywhere at once, as if from the mouth of an invisible giant from whom there was nowhere to hide. Still, remarkably, exasperatingly, the castle refused to answer. It was apparent to Arsalan that the spell for the recognition of words had dissipated, and he needed only to bypass it.

"To hell with the poem," said Arsalan. "I'm giving it a kick."

Arsalan lifted his hand and cast a spell, whereupon something beneath the castle doors began to stir. There was a disquieting rumble, abrupt and thunderous, that resonated over the water. An enormous stone slab extended from the masonry beneath the doors. A hidden mechanism pushed it outward, farther and farther, until it was a giant plank parallel with the water's surface. No sooner had it reached a certain length than it began to slant downward toward the boat just enough to kiss the water's surface with light ripples. At this point, it paused its automated movements, but after a few silent seconds, and with the sound of grinding rock, the slab sharply articulated itself into an elegantly ascending staircase with broad, shallow steps. After the show was over, the company in the boat turned to each other and nodded, impressed, their previous impatience and despondency dispelled.

"Sorry for the wait, my friends," Arsalan said, "but we're now free to ascend."

It took some time for the rest of Arsalan's friends to convince themselves and each other that the magical staircase could be trusted with their feet and would not spring suddenly into movement again to eat them or to dump them into the freezing water. The oarsmen, who had been awestruck by the monstrous display of motion and thunder while toiling to keep the boat away from the stairs, calmed themselves well enough to approach the staircase and to usher the company onto the wide, bottommost step. Onto it each friend stepped especially gingerly, as if to test its solidity; they thrusted their weights downward through the balls of their feet to see whether the apparatus would shake, but it remained earthily stable. After everyone had debarked, the oarsmen searched, almost in vain, for something onto which to moor the boat, eventually finding a small metal peg, which they had to pull up into position from a hole in the stair with their own manual strength. It was rusty and stubborn, and it took all four of them and several metal tools and much stifled grunting and cursing to pry it loose from its base, but Arsalan, after having been lost in thought for those few moments until finally noticing their plight, stepped in and fixed it with his magic at the last moment.

The company then directed their attention to the long flight of stairs upward to the soaring doors. As gradual as the staircase was, it was still two stories, so they breathed heavy sighs and commenced their trek upward. Each of the men took a woman by the arm and safely escorted her up the staircase's length. Arsalan led Teodora and Defne by either arm, Bayram led Siegfrieda, and Asker, somewhat to Teodora's annoyance, somehow ended up assisting Princess Berthilde. The four oarsmen remained by the boat, but to avoid the freezing winds that were blowing across the surface of the lake at them, they eventually would wander up the stairs to the castle. There Arsalan later would find them loitering just inside the doors.

Arsalan did not bother even to utter any magic words for the heavy timber doors. He simply lifted his hands and pulled them open with a spell. The colossal doors rotated outward ever so slowly on their silent hinges, yawning toward them, and Arsalan found he was forced to use a fair bit of energy for this task. The rest of his friends gasped at the sight of the towering things spreading to greet them like the hands of a god.

Reticently, they wandered inside to discover the courtyard, as wide as a royal lawn, with a stone path cutting directly through a field of tangled brown grass from the entrance to another entrance in a high wall opposite them. Among the brambly grass were simple stone fountains, one on either side of the footpath. These at one time had trickled with water but were now dry and spotted with lichen. A second stone walkway crossed the first through its middle, intercepting the two fountains and surrounding them with circular paths. The company found themselves flanked on their left and right by great stacks of colonnaded balconies that reached ten stories skyward, leaving a limited square of gray sky visible.

They proceeded inward to the entrance in front of them. There was another set of arched double doors, resembling in every way their giant cousins in front except that they were much more human in scale. For these the company used a set of keys to open a clunky lock that was beginning to rust. They were oversized, iron skeleton keys that clanged officiously in Arsalan's hands as he fumbled with them. The working key released the lock with a whine and a squawk, and the doors squealed open. The royal company ventured halfway into the main hall. It was as ornate as Arsalan recalled, but dim, illuminated only by the ashen light that drained in from narrow windows high on the walls on either side. In this light the hall looked scarcely familiar to him. Arsalan could discern colonnaded ambulatories on either side, wall spaces garnished with spears and glaives that hung in parallel lines and militant crosses, a great aisle proceeding down the middle of the chamber, and arches—some broken and some rounded, some high and some decumbent—vaulting in every direction, such that every door, window, entryway, and opening had one as its eyebrow. Dark wood paneling lined the walls up to the windows. The floor consisted of black and white tiled squares fraught with a sheen of dust and pebbles. Old furniture, covered in generous white linen sheets, stood in the room in tense stillness like the ghosts of animals. On the far, opposite wall, a stained glass rose window, embellished with tracery, glowed at them with a gray light that was stagnant and dusty. The baroque room was redolent with the air of moldering neglect and forsakenness, like a luxurious oubliette. The company stood and stared in confused but reverent silence for a good while, not quite sure what to do next.

Perhaps a little too hastily, however, the silence and stillness were broken by guards and soldiers who arrived by boat behind the princess' company and proceeded to inspect the castle with respectful but hurried steps. The newly arrived military personnel lacked the luxury of time to wander in reverence through the castle as one in a museum first before putting it to its intended use. With mops and brooms, they cleaned the dust from the floor of the main room with great swishes and sweeps. With flourish they yanked all the linen from the furniture and put the desks and tables to use as bases of operations where they lit candles and lanterns, began to sign stacks of orders with quivering quills, and ran from one to another with maps and papers, coordinating their wartime maneuvers. Arsalan and his company were somewhat sad to see the cobwebs of history swept away so unceremoniously even as the six of them were brusquely reminded why they had come to the stronghold in the first place.

Arsalan wished to see the rest of the castle before it was entirely populated by the din of human activity again, though this did not seem entirely possible, as the fortress was vast and convoluted and still contained many corners unattended and undusted. He slowly broke away from the commotion and meandered down hallways and through dim chambers, balconies, cellars, and stairwells. The castle's interior was so mazelike that it was a genuine puzzle to try to remember his way back as he progressed. During his previous visit in his younger years, he had not gone much further inward than the main hall and its surrounding chambers, and, even so, his memory of those was unreliable. His recent studies of the castle had not helped; he had uncovered many different floor plans that contradicted each other, and no one, not even a student as ardent as Princess Berthilde herself, was confident of the fortress' true arrangement.

So, Arsalan improvised by wandering, leisurely and aimlessly, up stair-wells and down corridors and through long sequences of adjoining chambers. Each sandy, lonely, atticlike room was in the same undisturbed condition as had been the main hall, save for the occasional pigeon or gull Arsalan disturbed in its hiding place; Arsalan would round a corner and would be met with a sudden, wild fluttering whose reflective white feathers would broaden the interior with light and sound. Curled scraps of plumage would be lying on the floor among a buckshot of dried feces and strings of grass, accompanied by a moist, festering odor of life. Arsalan would gaze upward to find a gaggle of pale gray sea birds or purplish brown pigeons peering down at him accusingly with their frightened, darting glances and their nervous, dribbling coos. The birds would pace back and forth, melting into the shadows around them. They would take refuge on a ledge by the glass window that had cracked open to allow them to make their homes there. Arsalan gazed at them in adoration and pity and let them be. He knew that eventually they would have to be dismissed from the premises, but not quite yet; their unperturbed existences here harmed no one, and he wandered onward.

At length, Arsalan found himself in a wonderful kitchen. There was an expansive window of many panes of frosted glass. Hanging from rafters were progressive sequences of differently scaled cauldrons, pots, and pans, growing or diminishing beautifully in one direction or another. In one wall was installed an enormous brick oven featuring a solid iron door. Its craftsmanship was superior, and Arsalan enjoyed feeling its heft and swing as he opened it and closed it again. Though it was being handled perhaps for the first time in decades, its smooth, dependable hinge produced only a whisper of a sound, and its lock clanged shut sincerely as he pulled the lever down. It was during these times that Arsalan rekindled his innate, childlike love of materials, especially those that were used in sturdy and well-crafted mechanisms. Ah, to be simply a magical architect again! But soon he became self-conscious and realized he was tarrying. He looked around to see if anyone had been watching him. No one, of course, was there. The complete silence and isolation now weighed strangely on him, reminding him that he had wandered too far away from the rest of the group and his mission, and he headed back.

The return trek was not straightforward. He recalled the succession of rooms and hallways he had traversed to arrive at the kitchen, but soon his path diverged from his remembered route in some subtle way he could not determine. He had been tricked by rooms and corridors that resembled those he had seen but which were slightly dissimilar; doppelganger rooms and devious corridors that led him far astray. Soon Arsalan found himself in rooms that seemed utterly foreign to him, with strange, red-cushioned furniture and elaborate tapestries he had never seen before, and he finally conceded he was lost, abandoning all conceit of any knowledge of his way. He proceeded to rely only on his immediate senses to guide him. After a time, he found himself in a corridor with windows facing the grounds of the fortress. He was on the fourth floor, and he noticed that beyond the spires of the watchtowers the sun was already midway through its afternoon descent to the horizon, and looking down, he saw the windows to the main hall, which were now lit with warm firelight. Arsalan knew he needed only to go directly downward and toward the hall. Of course, the architectural layout of the fortress would not allow this to occur in such a forthright fashion, but through innumerable twists and turns that led him harrowingly off course. Arsalan found himself hurrying through rooms whose décor was so elaborate and unfamiliar as to seem sinister. To his great relief, he found himself on the second-floor balcony of the courtyard, where he could see soldiers walking back and forth between the front entrance and the main hall in the blind fulfillment of their duties. From here, he magically flew down, and they looked up at him in wonder and laughter, and they greeted him.

"Excuse me, gentlemen," said Arsalan. "I don't mean to startle you, but I'm returning from a little tour of the place."

Arsalan then entered the main hall again from the courtyard. It was still dark in the main hall, only now because dusk had arrived. But a large, merry fire had been started in the grand fireplace, which before had sat unnoticed in the shadows, and its orange blaze now shimmered on the edges of the silhouettes of all the officers who made it their job of sitting, standing, and milling from one place to another with papers in their hands. Someone had produced bottles of liquor and cider, and dinner, which had been brewed over the fire from barrels of food the soldiers had hauled in, was being served in the adjacent dining room, where there was the clanking of silverware on porcelain, which someone had found in some cabinets. Supper under these circumstances was served and partaken in a way that was refreshingly casual. Candles were everywhere but seemed only to compress the thick darkness back, where it surrounded the fluttering orbs of light in heavier densities. The business occurring in the stubbornly murky chambers was brisk and official but murmured, as if in respect for the frowning, lugubrious castle interior. The candlelight, the lamplight, the dancing fireplace, the half-seen faces, the dampness, and the lingering reverberations of voices beneath the vaulted stone ceiling all bestowed upon the proceedings an air of unreality. Princess Berthilde and Siegfrieda were in constant conversation with the generals and advisors while Asker and Bayram drank at a side table with two generals. Asker was offering his fervent opinions on where along the lake and within the castle they should staff soldiers for their best defense. At these assertions the generals were listening with keen interest and nodding heads.

Teodora and Defne materialized at Arsalan's side, nearly startling him.

"Where have you been?" said Teodora. "We were worried about you!"

"I'm sorry," said Arsalan, "but I was inspecting the grounds."

"That sounds awfully official," said Teodora. "Are you sure you simply didn't get lost?"

"A bit," he said. "The layout is confusing. I suggest you don't venture into other parts of the castle. It can swallow you. In any case, I believe the magic has dissipated somewhat from the fortification. I can tell by the way it has begun to deteriorate. I might have to refortify it with newer spells."

"Is that something you can do?" said Teodora.

"By myself, I'm not sure," said Arsalan. "I can start tonight, but I'm not certain if I have the capacity to reinforce the whole stronghold."

Princess Berthilde and General von Steinsdorf, who had heard their conversation, joined them and said, "Please do, Arsalan. We don't have that much time before the rebels may push their way here."

"Are you sure you want to be in this castle, the one they are targeting, and not safely located in Ammerland?" asked Arsalan.

"I have thought about it," said Princess Berthilde, "and I have reasoned thusly: This is the most secure position in Bavaria. If they conquer this fortress, they will be able to march on Munich, and the result will be the same, so I may as well fight from here on the front lines with my army."

Arsalan smiled.

"I will start my spellcasting immediately," he said, "but after I have supper, if you don't mind."

"Not at all," said the princess. "Please join us. We were about to partake."

Arsalan sat at the great oaken table and ate quickly, chomping healthy portions of lamb and washing them down with gulps of diluted ale. He did not speak much, but Teodora, his daughter, his son, and all his friends chatted animatedly around him, as if confident he had a plan in mind to save them from destruction. Their frosty breaths swirled in the shadowy, golden firelight from the hearth as they chattered. Arsalan did not join the conversation. He was too preoccupied with his plan, and at the same time with the sinking reckoning that he had, in fact, no suitable plan at all.

CHAPTER 20

That night after dinner, Arsalan started the process of inspection and re-fortification of the outer walls of the castle. He did not plan to accomplish much in the failing winter daylight of his first day at the fortress. In a dark side-room, he opened his pack of magical architect's tools and found his lighting pendant, his charge detector, and his other equipment. He had not used the lighting pendant in many years since he usually had elected not to work at night, but tonight it would be essential. The pendant was a circle of pyrite hung from a rawhide necklace, and when he donned it on his neck and flicked the pendant with his finger, it glowed brightly enough to illuminate a room like daylight. He placed his other tools in his leather tool belt, which he wore around his waist under his slightly protruding belly. Arsalan laughed gently at the comical sight of himself in a mirror and marched outside.

From the courtyard, Arsalan launched himself upward and drifted over all the walls and roofs of the fortress, proceeding to the east wall and down again. There, with the vertical cliffside of the east wall before him, he floated as if on an invisible scaffold, his pendant painting a circle of golden light on the stony surface. Each block was as massive as those of the Great Pyramids, and the masonry was unparalleled in its smooth, regular geometry. The seams were as thin as hairs, such that one could not fit so much as a playing card between them. There was so little mortar surrounding a single block that Arsalan guessed the amount could fit into a teaspoon. When he looked closely at the mortar, however, he detected crumbling and pitting in places.

From his belt he produced his charge detector, which was a short wooden rod. He applied it to one of the blocks in front of him, and it glowed with a weak lavender light. Arsalan was puzzled and distraught, for he knew the magic in the blocks should last for centuries, and the castle was built only as long ago as Conrad's youth. The other blocks surrounding this one yielded the same reading. Arsalan sighed and thought for a long time. Beneath him, the lake yawned like a black pit, and far away on the indiscernible shores he could see the lights of the army's campfires and the glowing yellow windows of civilian houses. A cold wind sliced at Arsalan's reddening nose.

Arsalan brought out his charging wand and began to recharge the hardness spell on the first block he had inspected. He took measurements as he did so, and he found that to supply the block with the energy necessary to withstand the blows of cannonballs and boulders thrown by trebuchet required an hour of time. He then charged a second block with the same required charge, and then a third block. In the third block, there were also fine cracks, which he repaired. After this, Arsalan was exhausted, and he realized that at this rate he would never finish recharging and repairing all the blocks of the immense fortress in time for a bombardment from enemy forces.

Troubled, Arsalan returned to the main hall and reported this fear to Princess Berthilde, who listened worriedly. She shared reports that the insurrectionist forces already had started their assault on the battalions stationed at the southernmost tip of the lake and were making slow but steady progress northward along the western bank. Arsalan shook his head and grumbled angrily to himself. He walked over to the flaming fireplace to stare into it. His friends and family heard both sets of news and became disturbed, sitting nervously in the darkness there in the main hall, murmuring questions to each other. They had better sense than to ask Arsalan what he was going to do. He gave every indication that he did not know, though there was one option, one last resort, that he was loath to take.

At length, Arsalan turned from the roaring fireplace to his friends, family, and the generals and officers. The fire was so hot it had caused sweat to bead on his forehead and his eyeballs to become bloodshot.

"It seems I need to try to call reinforcements," said Arsalan.

"But all possible reinforcements have been summoned," said Siegfrieda, "and they are on their way."

"Not these yet," said Arsalan. "Please excuse me."

Arsalan returned to the side room where his baggage still sat on the floor. Placing his toolbelt, tools, and pendant aside, he dug deeply into his suede packs. He rifled past his few changes of clothing and the rest of his tools in his search for a new item. He looked over his shoulder from side to side as he did so, making sure no one was watching. He drew out a small bag, from which he then extracted his wooden jewel box, which he placed on a table. The box's patterns of writhing ivy and serpents glimmered in the candlelight of the room.

As if handling an explosive, he faced the box and gingerly opened it, revealing only a small, smooth, sphere sitting in an indigo cushion of undulating velvet. The orb was made of featureless white marble whose flecks of silicate glistened subtly. Arsalan did not remove the item from the box but simply stared at it. After a few moments, it began to glow faintly with a light that pulsed with white and blue, and it brightened as the minutes passed, like an iron being heated in a fire. After a while, it was throbbing with luminescent color, illuminating Arsalan's face as he continued to gaze into it intently. Soon, the entire side-room pulsated with mysterious light and color until Arsalan saw nothing else. In the luminescence he saw other faces emerging, which he recognized as the faces of other magical architects. The faces familiar to him were aged or old, but there were other faces young and unfamiliar. One by one they formed, and they stared back at Arsalan with alert sincerity and concern. Soon some of the faces disappeared, only to be replaced by others. Arsalan sat staring at the glowing ball for a long time until all the ghostly visages had vanished, and the thrumming light faded to darkness, leaving only phosphorescent sparkles that danced across the surface of the spherical stone.

Arsalan blinked and rubbed his eyes, and he began to hide the talisman, when he saw Defne standing in the doorway.

"Father?" she said timidly. "I'm sorry. I saw strange, flashing lights, and I wanted to see what was happening."

"I didn't mean for you to see this, my daughter," said Arsalan.

"What was it?" she asked.

"One of my secret possessions, a magical architect's secret. It is perhaps one there is no point in trying to preserve now, for you will see its effects soon," he said. "It is a beacon. Upon becoming a magical architect, one is issued one of these beacons. In times of true desperation, when there is absolutely no other option, a magical architect uses it to call all other magical architects to his or her aid, and they receive the mystical signal through their own beacons, regardless of distance. All magical architects vow to heed the beckoning of another magical architect when they receive the signal. One must drop whatever one is doing and must fly immediately to the beckoner's aid, using one's own beacon as a compass."

"Indeed, you've never told us about this, but I do remember seeing it when I was a cat," said Defne, walking over to the marble ball to look at it more closely. "How often is this used?"

"Hardly ever is it used," said Arsalan. "Perhaps once in a generation. One does not disturb all the living magical architects in the world from their important work for trivial matters, and the preservation of Conrad's Castle is not a trivial matter. The last time one was used was when the late Cyrus the Calm beckoned all to his aid to prevent the breach of the Golden Levees of the Tigris, eighty years ago."

"Do you mean all the magical architects of the world will arrive here?" asked Defne.

"I can say only that they must do so, or they will be expelled from the Guild," said Arsalan.

"When will they arrive?" said Defne.

"In one or two days, by air," said Arsalan.

"Then you must tell Princess Berthilde," said Defne. "She will be overjoyed to receive so much aid."

"Yes, I know she will be," said Arsalan, "but eventually there will be the issue of compensation. The magical architects need to be paid, and I hate to force this type of expense onto her."

"You mean they will not be doing this just for a noble cause?" she asked. "People here might die if the magical architects don't help us."

"Yes, they are doing it out of the goodness of their hearts," said Arsalan, "but they are human beings, and they do need to be compensated for their efforts, ultimately."

"Father, there is one thing I've wanted to ask you all these years," said Defne. "If magical architects are such masters at manipulating materials, what keeps them from counterfeiting their own gold and never needing to work?"

"Elemental conversion is extraordinarily difficult," said Arsalan. "Some of the old masters achieved this. But the primary reason is economic. If everyone produced their own gold out of, say, stone or sand, then the price of gold would plummet, and the markets would deflate. For this reason, magical architects also take a vow never to counterfeit any form of official currency, or any rare material that could be used as such."

"So many vows and restrictions, merely in order to keep you from conquering the world," said Defne. "But I'm certain Princess Berthilde will be more than willing to pay for their services under circumstances such as these."

"They, or I should say, we, are a self-interested and quarrelsome lot," said Arsalan, "but once they arrive, I will manage them,"

Arsalan paused, allowing Defne to gaze curiously at the beacon before he placed his hand on the box's lid, as if to shut it.

"I truly wonder how this magic works," said Defne.

"Not even we magical architects are certain," he said. "We just know that it works, and we know how to make it work for our uses. Isn't that so selfish and ignorant of us?"

"Do you think humankind ever will discover the mechanisms behind it?" asked Defne.

"Hopefully, one day," said Arsalan. "If human beings can temper their egos and can channel their ambitions more into understanding and friendship. All this magic is wonderous, but it is worthless if we just use it for more competition and quarrel, and especially worthless when compared to the value of our family and friends."

"I miss the days when we were children, in our chateau," said Defne.

"Oh yes, I'd give anything to have that back, to have my three little treasures, so I can reverse my mistakes and can prolong our happiness together," said Arsalan.

"Yet somehow through our recent adventures together, Father," said Defne, "somehow I feel it was based on something that was tenuous all that time, like thin ice."

"Yes, I know what you mean," said Arsalan. "Do you know what the strangest thing about it is?"

"What, Father?" said Defne.

"I miss Kizil," said Arsalan. "I know you were her. But I miss having a cat. I miss you as a cat. It's confusing and odd, and I don't know how to think of it. I miss our time together."

"I was happy being your cat for that time," said Defne, "but, like being a child, it was temporary, and I had to return, and I had to accomplish other things as an adult."

"Yes, I was forced to say as much to your mother," said Arsalan.

"You still love her," said Defne.

"I never stopped," said Arsalan.

"She never stopped either," said Defne. "I know it. I can tell. And if you had not returned from exile, you would never have been able to redeem yourself to her."

Arsalan gazed lingeringly at the beacon, and he closed the lid to the box.

Ultimately, Arsalan decided not to tell Princess Berthilde yet that all the world's magical architects would be arriving at her doorstep to help her in her dilemma. He wanted it to be a wonderful surprise if they appeared, but more importantly he did not wish to disappoint her if anything would prevent them from doing so. For the first time in his life, Arsalan felt he must use the beacon, and despite all his prior, lifelong preparation for its use, he knew what might occur next was still abstract and uncertain to him. The next day, he remained quiet, and he busied himself in charging one block after another of the exterior castle walls, making slow but assured progress. The sky was overcast but still light; a featureless ceiling of gray had been flung under the blue, casting everything in a dour but detailed light that served only to highlight every flaw, every wrinkle, crag, or crack. Under this dispiriting light, faces became old and deadened, eyes became baggy and filled with shadows and weariness, and stone surfaces looked as rough as shorn metal. Occasionally Arsalan would pause his work to inspect the desolate heavens. His eyes would narrow against the invisible glare, waiting for his allies to manifest from the clouds or on a horizon as a distant black dot or a smudge. But all the dark flecks on the slate skies that day turned out to be gulls and pigeons flying to roost in the broken windows of the castle. Along the shores, the miniscule motes of soldiers, sharply visible by their bright red coats in the monochrome day, walked to and fro among barricades and encampments, and a traffic of boats passed each other as they ferried messengers and decision-makers from Ammerland to the castle steps and back again. Did they realize precisely how dire their situation was? Arsalan neither fretted nor grumbled but continued with his labors. Eventually, he grew exhausted from working in the cold, and he wished to preserve his energies; instead of continuing to float outside the castle walls, he arranged to be suspended there by means of a rope and pulley. This hardly was an improvement, as he tended to swing in the frigid winds that blew him from side to side, and in the end, he saved none of his energies.

Toward the end of the day, he heard the first boom, velvety and distant and ominous, calling to him over the water. After a silent interval, there was another, then a third. In the evening, when he returned to the great hall, the air was fraught with whispers and discussions, electrified with angst and alarm. Some arguments erupted among the generals before being muffled again like blankets over a sudden fire. The news was that von Ansbach's headless forces indeed were making gradual progress up the western shoreline of the lake. Behind their vanguard were battalions using tremendous teams of draft horses to haul large boats, cannons, and trebuchets by cart.

Arsalan rested in a dark corner of the great hall, lost in contemplation. He could feel himself drifting again, as if pulled by some oceanic current, into the familiar depths of shame and regret, a compulsion he fought to resist. He sat in a simple chair with his arm over its back, and he sipped a glass of ale and said nothing, only watching the muted, anxious activity in the room with growing sadness.

Princess Berthilde approached Arsalan and asked, "Arsalan, what did you mean when you said you were calling reinforcements?"

"I have means to call other magical architects to our aid from afar," said Arsalan. "Last night I performed the magical summoning procedure, but because I have never used these means before, I'm not sure if the summoning will be successful."

"Other magical architects will come to our aid?" asked the princess.

"Theoretically," Arsalan said. "But I would not rely on this possibility. Proceed to fight the rebels as if it will not come to pass. And do not tell others what I have said to you. I do not wish to give them false hope."

"Arsalan," she said, "I want you to know that whatever comes of us, and of Bavaria, and of the castle here, I will be eternally grateful for all you have done. You were not obliged to stay to endure this conflict. You could have taken your money with you to some other job. If you left now, I would understand. But don't worry about me. I will stay here to fight, whatever the cost."

"Like a daughter you have become to me," said Arsalan, "a feisty one, a wise one, an intelligent one, a vulnerable one. I could not abandon you, or the works I have preserved. I have stayed willingly, and I hope my efforts lead to some success."

"And like a father you have become to me," said Princess Berthilde, "a feisty one, a wise one, an intelligent one, a vulnerable one. If my own father were still alive, he would sing your praises to every royal across Europe."

Arsalan absorbed this compliment with poignant and humble appreciation.

Later that evening, at the grand dining table, Arsalan and his family sat and stared at their sumptuous meals with glum faces. All their appetites, save Arsalan's, were suppressed by worry. Defne shoved her food around from one corner of her plate to the next, while Asker glared off into the shadowy room with his fingertips placed thoughtfully below his nose.

"I tell you," whispered Asker to his family across the table, "these are some of the most incompetent generals I've met in my career."

"I know," said Arsalan, slicing a piece of lamb. "That's why I'm helping them."

"There's no helping them," Asker said. "I give advice time and again, and they never understand. They don't know how to do their jobs. They only know how to give orders for wine. We're dead if we stay here."

"What will we do if von Ansbach's forces prevail?" said Teodora.

"I will spirit us away, of course," said Arsalan, buttering a slide of bread. "We're in little danger of dying here. We may lose this battle, and the princess may lose her kingdom, but none of us in this castle will lose our lives."

"When should we leave?" asked Teodora.

"If the situation does not improve by tomorrow," said Arsalan, slicing a vegetable, "we will leave the next day."

"Good," said Asker. "I need to return to my post. My leave is soon finished."

"Where will we go?" asked Defne.

"With me back to Silesia," said Teodora.

"Will we be safe from von Ansbach there?" asked Defne.

"Perhaps," said Asker, "but there is no guarantee with von Ansbach."

"And that is why we must stay," said Arsalan, before biting into a piece of meat.

"Damn!" said Asker. "That makes too much sense."

"Asker," said Arsalan, pointing a fork at him, "you know better than to curse at the dinner table like that."

They retired to their rooms, which were a collection of side-rooms not far from the main hall. They were afraid of venturing too deeply into the castle. Arsalan could not sleep, and he walked out into the courtyard to gaze at the stars, finding only a featureless layer of black clouds. The massive front doors were closed and locked, and guards stood watch. After taking a few deep breaths of the frosty air, he nodded an acknowledgement to the men, and he was about to retire to his room. At the last moment, Arsalan noticed, in the highest window in the northeast watchtower, a faint light glimmering with the pale luminescence of a single candle. It illuminated the side of the window and a portion of the interior wall.

"Say," said Arsalan to one of the guards, "whose light is that in the window there in the northeastern tower?"

"We do not know, sir," said the guard. "We guards have been noting it since we arrived. We have been assuming it is one of you."

"No. None of us are there, as far as I know. Can you send anyone to investigate?" asked Arsalan.

"We dare not, sir," said the second guard. "The castle layout is deceptive, and we are afraid we would become lost within it."

"Have you done anything about it?" asked Arsalan.

"We only can redouble our watch within the occupied areas of the castle to make sure nothing nefarious occurs from within," said the first guard. "So far, no such things have occurred."

"Curious," said Arsalan.

"Yes," said the second guard. "The locals here say they often spot the light in one or another tower on certain nights, and they assumed that it was the royal family here on business, though the royal family has had no dealings in the castle for decades."

"Well," joked Arsalan, "be sure to keep watch out for wills-of-the-wisps."

Finally, Arsalan retired to his side-room, where he lay on a couch to sleep, and drew his covers over him. He noticed a candlelight approaching his room from a doorway. The candle was held by Teodora, who stood in the entrance, gazing at him for a long time. Arsalan sat up from his sleeping position and returned her gaze curiously. Teodora entered and placed the candle on a table and sat on the couch next to where Arsalan was lying. Arsalan and Teodora looked at each other's faces for a silent, pregnant interval. One half of Teodora's face was hidden in flickering chiaroscuro while the other was painted in buttery orange candlelight, and it seemed as through Arsalan was looking at the face of the beautiful woman with whom he awoke on certain mornings years ago in Kirklareli when the sun shone on her while the bells and voices rang outside their window. But here he was staring at both her lovely side, full of strength and radiance, and her dark side, filled with passion, drama, and mystery, and Arsalan realized he adored both masks as one woman, and his heart ached for her kiss again. Teodora lay next to him on the broad couch and continued to look at him and to touch his face. She drew the covers over them both, and she embraced him, and thus they both fell to sleep.

The next morning, Arsalan was too tired to work, and it did not seem worthwhile to continue his labors at the same rate. In effect, he quit his efforts to charge the castle walls. He and Teodora carried wooden chairs out into the hard, frigid, colorless morning. The enormous wooden doors now were open to the stony sky and the dark lake that burbled beneath it. Arsalan and Teodora placed their chairs on one of the broad stairs and sat. Arsalan leaned back while holding hands with Teodora, and they both waited for something to happen. The two saw soldiers and advisors run past them from boat to door and back again while casting the couple confused looks along their hurried ways. Arsalan just gazed at the sky, squinting at the glare.

Eventually, Bayram wandered outside and saw them.

"What are you doing out here?" he asked.

"What were you doing in there?" asked Arsalan.

"Not much, to be honest," said Bayram. "My negotiation skills have not been much use over the past few days."

"My case is hardly different," said Arsalan. "Pull up a chair."

"Something tells me you have a plan in mind," said Bayram, sitting next to them on the stair.

"Shouldn't you have one?" said Arsalan. "Let's start thinking about our next job."

"What about Princess Berthilde?" asked Bayram.

"She has committed to staying and fighting," said Arsalan, "but I used the beacon two days ago."

"Will they arrive?" said Bayram.

"I certainly hope so," said Arsalan.

"When?" asked Bayram.

"Today," said Arsalan.

"And if not?" asked Bayram.

"Then I'm getting us all out of here," said Arsalan. "Probably like we should have when you left."

Bayram nodded embarrassedly.

"It was worthy of you to stay and to try to help," said Bayram.

"Sit with us for a while," said Arsalan. "Let's enjoy the view from here while it lasts."

The staircase on which the three sat was enormous. It sloped gradually from beneath them to the waters like a long, shallow hill. After every ten stairs, there was a wide landing. Here and there on the landings were officials and officers discussing business in close and hushed terms. Arsalan could not imagine what more there was to discuss. Either his old magical architect colleagues appeared, or Princess Berthilde would be deposed by an insurrectionist general with a powerful army. There was not much else to consider. Perhaps the conversers were debating plans of escape again. As powerful as Arsalan always imagined himself to be, he now felt he did not have the stamina to defeat multiple battalions of soldiers all at once while using the same troublesomely intricate, nonlethal means of immobilizing them as he had in Munich. There were too many men to tackle, and Arsalan would tire before he could subdue all of them without committing a mistake that would prove fatal to himself or to someone else. Of course, if Arsalan went on an indiscriminate, murderous rampage against the enemy, the war would be over in an hour. But this tactic, of course, was out of the question for him as a magical architect, and for perhaps the thousandth time in his life, he became disgusted at himself for considering the idea even for a second.

At length, Teodora mentioned how she had to prepare her belongings for leaving the castle, and Bayram muttered something similar. Each stood and left, leaving Arsalan to sit there in his miserable tranquility and to stare out at the lake. The sky grew whiter, and the air warmer and more glaring, and this coaxed Arsalan halfway to sleep. Above him, the cloud cover wore thin, exposing a shriveled, misty sun that shone like a smoldering moon.

In the reverie of his half-sleep, Arsalan seemed to dream of something strange; a covered gondola appeared on the surface of the monochrome clouds and descended like a goose, landing on the surface of the lake with a splash. Arsalan was startled awake by the crash of water, whether it occurred in his dream or in the real world. He opened his eyes and sat upright. Indeed, there, where he thought he had hallucinated a boat had landed, was the actual gondola, painted violet, topped with a purple cover embellished with fleur-de-lis motifs, gold trim, and tassels. Its bow and stern were finished in elaborate coils. The craft still rocked from the impact, and now it seemed to move under its own power across the lake toward the bottom of the staircase, carving a quiet white gash of a wake in the black waters. By now, even the soldiers and officials, who had been conversing on the steps, took notice.

When the purple boat reached the bottom stair, a platform emerged, and two young men walked out onto it, wearing old-fashioned pantaloons, stockings, and folded boots, frock coats, and hats of violet and cobalt blue. One produced a bugle and played a sharp little tune of pomp and circumstance, while the other announced, in a most loquacious manner, the arrival and emergence of his greatness Marcelle the Marvelous, wizard and magical architect.

Marcelle emerged from the shade of the cover and, not without some struggle, stepped out onto the platform. He was dressed similarly to his entourage, only with a cape, a fine cane, a trifold hat with an exaggeratedly large plume, and a white goatee. Marcelle had aged most gracefully and handsomely. He was trim and limber. As he stepped onto the stone stair, he removed his enormous flowerpot of a hat and, with a practiced flourish, bowed deeply to whomever happened to be standing nearby. The few bystanders who were standing there regarded Marcelle and his pale, blading, gray crown with an almost affronted astonishment.

"Marcelle the Marvelous, wizard and magical architect, responding respectfully to his summons, at your service!" he said in his breathy voice.

After some time with no response, Marcelle returned his ostentatious hat to his head and looked uneasily around. He continued, "I would like to confer immediately with one Arsalan Ozdikmen the Magnificent, also wizard and magical architect!"

A soldier who happened to be descending the stairs at that moment simply motioned to Arsalan, who lazily sat in a wooden chair at the top of the staircase and who, from Marcelle's squinting perspective, was a silhouette. Arsalan simply stood and shouted, "Marcelle! What took you so long!"

"Arsalan?" said Marcelle. "Arsalan! Yes, come closer. Let me see you! It has been some time! You must forgive me. We made a wrong turn at Munich."

"There was only one way from Munich," said Arsalan, swaggeringly descending the staircase, "and that's south!"

"Arsalan," said Marcelle, laughing in his measured, apprehensive way, "look at you. You are an old man like me, but you haven't changed one bit in your personality! Still as salty as ever! Come here, old friend!"

Arsalan burst into laughter, and they embraced.

"Where's Fernando?" said Arsalan.

"He..." said Marcelle, and judging by his tone, Arsalan was afraid to hear awful news regarding Fernando's health, until Marcelle continued, "he stopped at Cologne to procure some wine."

"That drunk! Worse than me!" laughed Arsalan. "Come in! We'll wait for him."

Arsalan paused for a moment.

"Oh, and I suppose I should add," said Arsalan, "thank you for coming all this way."

Marcelle's face brightened placidly, and he gazed at Arsalan.

"My old friend, Arsalan," he said, "of course, I willingly would take this adventure to assist you. Maybe once we go inside, you can brief me of the circumstances."

Just then, there was the rumor of explosions that murmured over the lake from the south and Marcelle turned to listen.

"The bells of war are ringing," said Arsalan.

Just then they both heard another splash in the water near them, and for a moment, Arsalan thought it might be a cannonball. He looked, and he saw what resembled a horse carriage, bedecked in yellow and orange trim, sitting on the water's surface. The carriage was floating on a set of pontoons that had been attached onto where the wheels would be. This new vessel was rocking where it had landed. A door opened, and a full-bearded old man, dressed in an outfit like Marcelle's but in crimson and gold, thrust his head and arm out. Though stouter than Marcelle, he resembled the Frenchman closely enough to have been his cousin. It was Fernando.

"I have procured the wine!" he shouted to Marcelle in his cackling voice. "Arsalan, you old scoundrel! Is that you?"

"As truly me as I ever shall be," said Arsalan.

"Wonderful! We have some stories to tell!" screamed Fernando. "I hope you don't mind that I've brought along my best journeymen!"

"Not a problem, my friend. We need all the help we can muster," said Arsalan. "Apparently, Marcelle has done the same, and the castle can fit many!"

Both Fernando's and Marcelle's journeymen busied themselves by mooring their odd vessels to the bottom stair. There were three journeymen to each master, and they all seemed so young that Arsalan felt guilty drawing them into what he knew would be the line of fire. They said little, except among themselves, and remained polite, helpful, and observant.

"Oh, where are my manners!" said Marcelle, turning toward his three young folks. "Allow me to introduce my talented journeymen, Jean-Jacques, Renard, and Natalie."

The two young men bowed, and the young woman curtsied. They all had dark hair and fair skin, and Arsalan realized that Natalie's dress was so like her male colleagues' suits in color and fabric that her difference in gender was scarcely noticeable. Fernando, in kind, introduced his own crew: Miguel, Francesca, and Luciana, who were attired in similar outfits, matching Fernando's in color and style. Once the six youngsters learned that they were standing in front of the one and only Arsalan the Magnificent, they stared at him in wonder, bowed and curtsied some more, and addressed him with especial deference.

Eventually, Arsalan became embarrassed. He felt he was not dressed nearly as well as his friends and their journeymen to warrant such admiration; immersed in his arduous business for so long, he had devoted no thought at making himself presentable. He wore a Bavarian wool frock coat over a linen shirt and vest, and his old Turkish pantaloons, all which struck Arsalan as slovenly and mismatched by comparison. Then again, he thought, perhaps his colleagues and their helpers had little idea of the sort of mess in which they were involving themselves. He strove to put his young admirers at ease and to distract attention from himself, and he bade the new visitors to enter the castle. They followed him, and the six young men and women twittered to each other and gawked at the stone citadel that expanded before them as they ascended the long staircase. Finally, as they crossed the threshold of the towering doors, and as Arsalan was preparing to introduce the eight newcomers to Princess Berthilde, they encountered a tall, old woman who had appeared in the middle of the courtyard, dressed like the grandmotherly version of Grandfather Frost. After a second, all recognized her as Anastasia the Austere, and they quieted in astonishment.

Anastasia was now elderly but still just as tall and austere, and her hair, once cuprously orange, now was as white as the fur trim of her coat. Her long, wintry coat of blue and white embroidery and furs was astounding, and it reached to the ground like a conifer. She wore a conical hat decorated on either side with horns that twisted upward to meet above her head. Her blue eyes shone from within her gray face, which was graced with a lovely cobweb of wrinkles. She was surrounded by guards who had been questioning her, and whom she was facing without the slightest bit of fear or concern. Anastasia did not smile but waited for the crowd who just had strolled in through the doors to say something, while Arsalan and the rest were far too surprised to utter anything at all. This silent staring back and forth went on for long enough, and it was Fernando who found the wherewithal to break the tension.

"Anastasia!" Fernando said. "You have arrived!"

"Yes, obviously," she replied in her thick, guttural voice. "I was summoned. It is good to see my old students again. Now what seems to be the problem?"

"Thank you for coming," said Arsalan. "We just were making our way to the main hall where I could brief everyone. Would you like to come along?"

"Of course. That's why I'm here," she said. "You look well; in fact, you look better than I had imagined from the news I had heard."

"Thank you," said Arsalan. "Where is your flying vessel?"

"I didn't bring one," she said.

"Through such a cold atmosphere?" said Arslan. "You must be freezing."

"We're magical architects, Arsalan," she said. "We can warm ourselves. Besides, you should know that in my country this is considered fine weather."

"Did you bring any apprentices?" said Arsalan. "The more the better, you know."

"No," she said. "I don't have any at the moment."

"Well, let us proceed inside," said Arsalan. "I don't want to keep you all out in the cold, anyway."

Arsalan and his newly arrived comrades burst in through the main hall doors. Their arrival had the air of a carnival that had breezed into town. Everyone, all the generals and officers and advisors in the hall, arose at once in amazement at the visitors. Arsalan's own family recognized them at once as their old friends and began their greetings, handshakes, and introductions to the rest. Princess Berthilde, who had been indisposed in another room, eventually wandered into the hall, and upon seeing the newly arrived magical architects, almost completely lost what little regal composure she had had. Her eyes widened in shock, and she placed her hands over her mouth, and she gasped and nearly squealed. When introduced to the legendary magical architects, whose stories she had read throughout her childhood, she trembled and stammered. To her they were immortal gods descending from empyrean realms of various mythoses, and she struggled to assemble the right words to say to each of them. Fernando and Marcelle's magnanimous gallantry put her more at ease. That they had brought along journeymen as young as herself as intermediaries between herself and godliness calmed her even more. Anastasia, by contrast, did nothing to dispel her own mystique. She stood amid the fray like a silent obelisk and greeted Princess Berthilde with all the curt inscrutability of a high priestess.

Before the crowd could begin even to address the reason for the summoning, they were interrupted once, twice, and thrice by more noises from outside. Gustav the Golden arrived in a sled. Like Anastasia the Austere, he was tall and old, and his blond hair had grown white and long, and he wore a long robe of yellow wool and tan furs beneath his forked beard. He brought two apprentices, a young blond boy, and another boy with black hair and a complexion as pale as paper. They were serious and quiet, speaking only to each other and in whispers, and they followed Gustav everywhere he went. Immediately behind him came Jawahir the Spellbinding in his blindingly white robe that matched the short, grizzled beard on his tanned, lean, wrinkled face, and he brought no fewer than five people with him, three bowing young men and two women with heads wrapped in shawls.

Dimitra the Blue was next, wearing her woolen robe dyed her signature cobalt color and complaining about the cold. "How do you people stand this temperature?" she blurted outright. Though her hair was now as gray as pepper, she still sported an irritable temper, and she tended to complain most bitterly in her loud and husky voice about everything.

Then Fahim the Fathomless entered with a flourish in his black robes and turban like a beautiful purplish onion. Fahim had the habit of always smiling and, though not always the most talkative, offered gentle laughter at others' commentary as his characteristic sign of concurrence. His coy mannerisms were ticklishly mysterious and often made others guess what he was thinking.

Gonashvili the Giant thudded to the courtyard ground like a boulder, carrying nothing but a toolbelt and a shoulder bag and wearing little more than leather pants and a loose woolen sweater. Although close to eighty years of age, with his white hair closely cropped to his head, he somehow seemed even larger than he was in youth. He did seem to have gone somewhat deaf, though, roaring everything that he said at the top of his lungs. His bulbous ears protruded from either side of his face like shelf mushrooms from a tree, and he took in his surroundings with a relaxed and unassuming gaze.

Kirakosyan the Colorful suddenly appeared in the room, laughing and startling everyone. She had sneaked in invisibly and wished to make a surprise entrance. The wrinkles around her eyes and mouth nearly divided her face in half, like a globule of dough cut by a string, as she laughed uncontrollably at everyone's shocked expressions, rattling all her multicolored necklaces, bracelets, and shawls as she shook.

Ramūnas arrived. He was a stern but polite young chap in trim, modern, black garb. He strode in as if to join a business meeting and succeeded in avoiding any attention until he was standing in the middle of the crowd, suddenly causing everyone to turn their heads. He sported short black hair and a fair, shaven complexion, and although not very tall, he quietly attracted attention with his impressively deep voice and his tendency to keep his arms at his sides.

Soon after him came Majdouline, an intelligent woman with shining eyes and a head and body bound in swaths of paisley silk. She was a large woman with an expansive personality. Her voice was beguilingly musical, and her laughter often mingled with her words. Unlike Ramūnas, her laughter was heard before she even had entered the castle, and she entered the main room with loud salutation and a wave of her hand.

She was followed by a mysterious figure in a shadowy green cowl. The figure removed the hood from his head, revealing himself to be Tafari, another new young master from Ethiopia, whose doleful eyes gazed out from beneath his prominent forehead. He was dressed tightly in woolen robes and nodded his head in restrained respect to everyone he saw. Tafari spoke little and in polite, reedy whispers that others often had to pause to hear.

The parade of arrivals of each wizard was like the impossible appearance of fairy tale characters from one's dearest childhood bedtime stories, and this sent Princess Berthilde into unrestrained hysterics. So overwhelmed was she with amazement that she began to hyperventilate, and Siegfrieda had to take her aside, instructing her to pant deeply into a little cloth bag, which expanded and contracted feverishly like a lung.

"My dear Majesty, compose yourself," Arsalan heard Siegfrieda say as she scolded the princess. "These are artisans, not royalty. However powerful they are, you are the ruler of a nation. Remember that!"

Princess Berthilde nodded and gathered herself and reentered the main hall. By this time, the magical architects were discussing the whereabouts of Sigrid the Lucent, and hearsay was that she had been seen along the way.

Eventually, a guard discovered Sigrid standing on a roof outside. She was inspecting the tiles and poking here and there with a wand. When the other magical architects emerged to look, they spotted her, and called her to coax her down. Sigrid at first glared at them in cold vexation, then begrudgingly succumbed to their pleas and descended gracefully to the ground among her colleagues. She was just as petite as always and dressed in a man's purple suit and matching purple shoes, and with stockings striped with red and blue. Her hair, now white and thin, was pulled into two pigtails on either side of her head. She gazed at everyone with her penetrating eyes of gray ice and bowed to the princess, who giggled in disbelief.

"Where's Ubaldini?" someone asked, and all the magical architects simply looked at one another quizzically, shrugging in their outlandish attire like members of a circus who had lost their ringmaster. As if in response, the man in question arrived only moments later, riding a white horse through the air. He was followed by a caravan of five other people riding various breeds of horses and donkeys that towed flying carts like Saint Nicholas' caravan. They all landed directly in the courtyard, the horses' hooves clapping on the ground and their fleshy lips sputtering and neighing as they reared their mighty heads, causing all the lofty, untouchable magical architects, as well as the generals, guards, and officials who had crowded the courtyard to look, to scatter in every direction to make room. The horses' plain wooden carts contacted the stone floor with painful smacks, and all was done. Ubaldini the Ingenious had made his triumphant entrance before his intended audience, which appeared to fill him with satisfaction.

Ubaldini was dressed much like Marcelle and Fernando, only in emerald green. He was recognizable to Arsalan as Emilio of his youth; the man's long nose and chin protruded above and below his white Van Dyke beard, which was trimmed and curled daintily beneath cheeks that protruded like small, pink apples. He dismounted his gallant steed and yelled only one word.

"Arsalan!" he barked, throwing his arms in the air.

"Emilio, my brother!" replied Arsalan, doing the same.

And the two ran to each other and clasped in a long, brotherly embrace with laughter and tears. Arsalan's friends and family and all the magical architects smiled at the heartwarming display, though those of the Bavarian court looked on in patient confusion, knowing not what to make of their close friendship. Finally, the two old men parted and stared at each other.

"You look terrible!" said Ubaldini.

"Not as terrible as you smell!" said Arsalan, and they both laughed coarsely.

"There are a few folks here I'd like you to meet, my dear friend," said Ubaldini, and he motioned to the rest of his company who were dismounting their own horses. Arsalan recognized them as his own apprentices and assistants from long ago: Sunduk, Estani, Etci, Ibrahim, and Sevket, and even old Doruk.

Doruk was grayer and balder, and his face was as serious and as hangdog as before. He looked at Arsalan with his turtlelike gaze and said, "Hello, sir.

It's good to see you again."

"Doruk! You've come! I cannot believe my eyes!" said Arsalan.

"Believe them, sir, for I stand right before you," answered Doruk factually. At this time, Arsalan's former journeymen and apprentices approached and stood around Arsalan, who felt confronted with guilt of how he had treated them when he last had seen them. They all now were tall, fully grown men, and they regarded Arsalan, once fierce and fearsome in his youth but now more grizzled, shrunken, and grayed, with a look of begrudging forgiveness and affection.

"My boys," he said, "I am so sorry for how I treated you."

"Master Arsalan," Sunduk said, with his moody eyes and reserved manner, "we understand what happened. Let what has been done lie in the past. We are here to fulfill the oath of the magical architects."

Arsalan's tears came to his eyes, and he embraced each one and shook his hand.

"You all work for Ubaldini now?" asked Arsalan.

"Of course," Doruk said. "We did need a new master with whom to work. It is good, the work. We are paid well."

At this Arsalan did not know how to respond, and he looked at the ground before him in misty wonder, unsure of what this meant.

"Very well," said Anastasia. "Now can we discuss why we've all been summoned here?"

"Of course!" said Arsalan. "Everyone, into the main hall we go!"

By now, everyone was in good cheer, and they shuffled inside the main hall. It took only moments to realize the presence of so many bodies would warm the room, and soon the door and a few windows were thrown open for fresh air. All in attendance began to chatter, like birds having stopped on an island in their migratory path, until it was too noisy to hear oneself speak. It was midday, so servants did their best to pass food around the room to their new guests. Fernando waved in the air a bottle of the wine he had bought in Cologne. "Drinks, everyone, to celebrate!" he proclaimed with a grin, though he did not mention what it was they were supposed to be celebrating. Perhaps it was Arsalan's return from his exile, or perhaps it was simply that all the magical architects were together for the first time in many years. But the reason seemed to matter little, as Fernando, Ubaldini, Marcelle, Kirakosyan, Gonashvili, and Dimitra were extending their glasses and mugs to receive the pouring from his dark red bottle, which splashed with joyful carelessness over the rims of the receptacles and all over their knuckles. Anastasia, while in her seat, and despite her air of somberness, also received some in an enormous stein she had found somewhere; she shook her receptacle and nodded her head for more, to the laughing delight of Fernando, who filled it to the brim. Anastasia then downed the whole drink in one gulp and slammed the stein on the table and glared at the ground intensely, as if the wine were setting fire to her soul. Only Sigrid could be seen holding a glass in the air while not drinking anything from it, apparently too deeply occupied with the way the light sparkled through it. The Muslims in the room, of course, and most of the journeymen, apprentices, and assistants, all genteelly abstained from drink, and they instead chose to watch their imbibing comrades and masters with well-mannered embarrassment. Even Arsalan, who certainly was no stranger to alcohol, was quietly aghast at his carousing friends. All, however, partook of the lamb and bread in great, healthy portions; everyone's hands tore loaves of wheat bread apart like the heads of wolves at a kill. The road to Bavaria from all the great magical architects' respective corners of the world had been long, and everyone was famished. Even Princess Berthilde, descending from her starstruck spell, was able to settle her mind well enough to notice how human the magical architects all were, and commented as such to Arsalan, who replied "You see, my child, they're no different from me, and I was considered the greatest."

"This is marvelous to see, all of them here like this," whispered Siegfrieda to them both. "I had no idea how many of you all existed. But I think it's time to remind them why they were summoned."

"Don't worry. I was waiting for them to get settled," said Arsalan.

Moments later, Arsalan, Princess Berthilde, and Siegfrieda slid to the front of the room, between the colorful, chatty assembly and the great hearth whose mouth roared with fire. When his comrades saw Arsalan, they cheered, chanted his name, and raised their drinks in a toast, but Arsalan smiled nervously and made the hand motions of fluttering wings in front of his face to quiet them, and they quieted to listen.

"My friends," he began, and they all cheered again, drowning out any possibility for Arsalan to finish his sentence. He turned and looked awkwardly at the princess as if to assure her, and she returned a gaze of bewilderment. It was apparent they all were so weary from their long journey that they now were in more of a delirious mood for jesting and cheering than a one for accomplishing anything important. So, again, he waved them down with a queasily courteous smile, and tried to utter a few more words, which still were hopelessly lost beneath the commotion.

"Silence!" bellowed Teodora from the rear, and abruptly the ruckus stopped. Seeing her word heeded, she sat again.

"Thank you," said Arsalan. "I want to thank you all, my most distinguished comrades and colleagues, for assembling here today. The reason I have summoned you all here is grave. The great kingdom of Bavaria, led by Her Majesty Princess Berthilde, is undergoing an insurrection, a civil war declared by a faction of their army loyal to a general who opposes the belief in or use of magic."

The crowd booed and hissed.

"Yes! Yes!" he said. "We all know this movement, which is devoted to the opposition to thaumaturgy. It cropped up some years ago, whence we know not, and it has increased of late. It is proving more and more difficult to convince others of the reality of magical architecture. The world is turning against it, even as our monuments stand as a testimony to its power. Those who oppose magic will stare directly at our constructions and will deny that it is magic that enables them to stand. Well, the insurrectionists of Bavaria go so far not only to want to depose their dear princess because of her affection for magical architecture but also to threaten to tear down all magical structures within Bavaria to show just how false it supposedly is."

"No!" yelled Dimitra, standing, with her finger in the air. "That's veritably a crime!"

"I share your sentiments, Dimitra the Blue," said Arsalan. "Yes, I do share them. Bavaria is the home of our late, beloved Conrad the Ineffable, one of the greatest magical architects ever to have lived, a man who personally was our mentor. This kingdom is the home of many of his constructions, which I personally have repaired and have returned to working status, and I wish never to see them destroyed."

"What do you need us to do, our good friend Arsalan?" asked Anastasia.

"Here, where you stand, and where many of you have stood on many occasions in the past, is Conrad's Castle, our master's greatest work," said Arsalan. "It serves as a defense bastion for the Bavarian royalty, as you may know, in case of attack. The rebels are on their way to siege it and will be here any day now, and their objective is twofold: one, to depose the princess, and two, to eliminate Conrad's Castle as a symbol of the viability of magic."

"But should it not hold against their attacks?" asked Gonashvili.

"It should hold," said Arsalan, "but in its present state, it will not hold. For reasons unknown to us, and perhaps for reasons related to the World's Leaf..."

Arsalan's words tapered, and he paused for a moment to wipe his forehead. The crowd was silent with sympathy and anticipation. Princess Berthilde and Siegfrieda placed their hands on his forearms to offer their strength.

"And for reasons related to the other structures I have had to repair," he continued, "Conrad's Castle's magic has drained, and there is not enough magical charge in its stonework to withstand an onslaught of cannon fire. I have attempted to recharge the stonework to its full complement, but it is arduous work, and I lack the ability to restore this enormous fortress to its full strength in time for the attack."

"When do we start?" asked Ramūnas.

"Immediately," said Arsalan. "We have no time to spare. The rebellion's forces may arrive here at any day, any hour."

"But we're exhausted, Arsalan," said Marcelle. "We just have flown hundreds of leagues to come here."

"We can work in shifts," said Arsalan. "The most tired of you can rest while the least tired of you can work, and then you can exchange. There must be a way we can do this."

There was quiet grousing.

"May we address the issue of compensation?" asked Gustav in his deep, lilting voice. "Some of us have had to pause our projects elsewhere to be here, and it's costing us much."

The crowd grumbled in accord with Gustav.

"Compensation," said Arsalan. "Of course, you will be paid, but I don't think now is the best time to address this. I..." Arsalan stammered a bit and looked to the princess for assistance.

"You all will be paid," said Siegfrieda, holding up her hands. "Have no doubt. We will be deeply grateful for your efforts, but let us not become bogged in negotiations at this point. There are human lives at risk here, and we would not call you here if it were not as serious as that."

With this reasonable beseeching the crowd could find no cause to disagree, and they grew grudgingly quiet.

"Come, my friends," said Arsalan. "Did our masters before us argue about payment when they rushed to the aid of Cyrus the Calm when he called them to repair the Golden Levees of the Tigris? They saved tens of thousands of lives that fateful day. Did they quibble about sleep and compensation when Aldus the August summoned them to quell the Fire of London? In that same vein I implore you to devote your energies to protect the livelihood and justice of your fellow men and women in this most savage of insurrections. Come, my dear comrades. Who will accompany me at this moment in our desperate labors to save the good folk of Bavaria from tyranny and to save the soul and work of Conrad the Ineffable from wanton obliteration?"

One hand shot upward like a spear, and it was Ramūnas'. Another rose, and it was Anastasia's. Majdouline, Gonashvili, Doruk, Tafari, and Dimitra raised theirs. Sigrid raised hers as well, but in a rather bored fashion, and only after finally noticing what was happening around her. Almost all the young journeymen, apprentices, and assistants volunteered to start right away, whether because they possessed more energy or because they wanted to seize the opportunity to prove their skills. The older masters, who had grown tired and effete and tended to feel somewhat entitled to ease and privilege, chose to retire for the night and would rise in the middle of the cold, dark morning to relieve the first shift of workers.

Arsalan joined the first shift, starting promptly after the rowdy, impromptu luncheon with his magical architect colleagues. The members of this shift followed Arsalan as he floated over the east wall again. Once they were hovering in front of its massive, sheer wall of bricks, he provided them with brief instructions. The recharging began and, stone by stone, it proceeded more quickly than Arsalan ever could have done by himself. He watched them charge each block, and he saw each stone glow its lavender color when inspected for the charge. Occasionally Arsalan would intervene to reinforce his instructions or to add a piece of information he had forgotten to mention, but soon all his helpers were on their own ways, spread out across the wall like a crew of window-cleaners. On occasion, Arsalan and the others would hear explosions rumbling from far away, and they could see columns of smoke rising in the south.

"We must persist, and we must hurry," said Arsalan said to them. "Von Ansbach's forces are almost here."

The second shift of magical architects, including Ubaldini, Fernando, Marcelle, and the rest, arrived to relieve the first of duty, but Arsalan, Anastasia, and Sigrid continued far into the lightless night with them. Silently, the blocks glowed here and there with purple light, with the slight silhouette of a person in front of it, before going dark again. Arsalan, with the support of his friends, now seemed energized, his wizardly stamina heartened by their presence. However busy his work was, though, he still had the mind to see if there was candlelight in the window of the northwest tower, but curiously on this night there was none. The second shift of workers was able to progress to the north wall, and somewhat to the west wall, before Jean-Jacques the journeyman called to Arsalan from the roof that his wife Teodora bade him return to sleep. Arsalan smiled to himself and thanked the young man.

Arsalan, lying next to Teodora on his wide couch, fell into a fathomless sleep. He lost all references to time, place, and circumstance and drifted into a dark gray universe of slumber. When he awoke, it was midmorning, and he sputtered and panicked. "The walls!" he exclaimed. "I must continue. Von Ansbach's forces are almost here! I've overslept!"

"My love, relax," said Teodora. "You worked too far into the night. Your friends have been working throughout the night, and Princess Berthilde's forces have been successful in keeping the enemy at bay."

"Thank heavens," said Arsalan, tossing his covers aside. "But I must go out to look."

On his way out, he met Ubaldini and Marcelle at the long dining table. They were leisurely enjoying a hearty breakfast of crepes and croissants, which their journeymen had prepared over the perpetually churning fire. Jawahir had joined them and was looking at the delectable but unfamiliar morsel at the end of his fork like a jeweler inspecting a diamond.

"Arsalan, my brother!" hailed Ubaldini, butting a piece of bread. "Come and join us for breakfast. It's lovely, and you worked more fiercely than anyone last night."

"What's the status of the wall reinforcement?" Arsalan blurted.

"Goodness! Listen to yourself!" said Ubaldini. "You have become practically German! Sit! Everything is fine. We completed the roof as of this morning!"

"So, are we ready for an onslaught? What about the floor beneath?" spouted Arsalan.

"Gonashvili is working on that. It will be as solid as earth when he is done with it!" said Marcelle. "Please, have some tea and bread, at least!"

"Thank you, my brothers," said Arsalan, relaxing a bit. "I must apologize. It has been a few tense weeks."

"You have been through more than that, my friend," said Jawahir. "You lost much and are striving to regain your fortune. Lesser men in your position have been driven to madness by their despair!"

"Thank you, and well received, Master Jawahir, but don't remind me," chuckled Arsalan. "I'd rather have a piece of that crepe, if you don't mind."

"By all means my friend!" laughed Marcelle, who pushed a precious little plate of goodness over to him like a gift. Arsalan pushed a fork into the syrupy layers and pulled out a triangular prism of soaked bread. It was positively delightful to Arsalan's palate, and he was reminded of how hungry he was, and how he had forgotten dinner last night. Before he knew it, he had finished his plate, several croissants, and a large draft of lukewarm tea. After this, Arsalan was released from his gustatory trance and gazed at Marcelle, and then at Ubaldini, who looked at him with strangely tense and expectant eyes.

"My god you French and Italians know how to cook!" he said. "Almost as well as the Turks!"

They all laughed, and Arsalan wiped the corners of his bearded mouth with a kerchief.

"Now that I have some energy, and if you don't mind, gentlemen, I need to inspect our work," he said.

"You will be pleased!" said Ubaldini.

Arsalan walked out to the courtyard and floated out to the outer walls. The freezing morning was bleak and tense, but his friends appeared to be administering the finishing touches on their work. Arsalan joined a team of shy journeymen in their task of inspecting the charges on a group of blocks, all of which, when touched by the magical architects, gleamed bright lavender in the colorless gloam of the morning. Arsalan was astonished by the strength of the charges, and he went about inspecting many on his own, with the same wonderful results. Even the roofing tiles were fully powered with the rigidity spell.

Eventually, Arsalan caught up with a gaggle of magical architects who were concentrated around one of the blocks of amethyst crystal, this one at the base of the southeast tower. Gustav was there with his two journeymen, and with Sigrid and Fahim, and they all stared at the giant crystal with somber and perplexed faces.

"The crystal is irate with us," said Sigrid. "It has been neglected for so long that it refuses to cooperate."

"We've sunk as much energy as we can muster into this thing and it still won't light," complained Gustav.

"Is there anything in Conrad's notes that might give us a clue?" said Fahim.

Arsalan placed his hand on his breast pocket, then on the other, then on his waist pocket, then the other. Soon he was patting his clothes, up and down, searching for a note or a piece of paper hidden somewhere on his person. Finally, he wrenched his left arm into a rear pocket and yanked out a wad of disorganized, hastily folded parchment, which he unfolded and shuffled before them. Gustav rolled his eyes as Arsalan then repeated the same exercise to find his reading spectacles, which Arsalan at length located in his breast pocket where he had begun searching in the first place.

"It says," said Arsalan, "there is a lambency spell especially for crystals. Try this."

Arsalan read the words to the spell aloud, which Gustav repeated with his wand directed to the translucent purple stone. A second after the spell was recited fully, Gustav started to turn to Arsalan to lodge another complaint, just before the eyes of all six people were blinded by the abrupt flood of intense violet light that blew from the center of the enormous crystal block. Arsalan could feel the hot radiation on his hands and face as he turned away and clenched his eyes and shielded them with his forearms.

All six floated some distance away from the intensely glowing crystal and spent the next few minutes shaking their heads, blinking their eyes, looking at each other, and smiling. Dots and smears of phosphorescent color drifted through Arsalan's vision. Finally, he could see well enough to approach Gustav and to slap him on his old shoulder, for which Gustav glared at him in irritated reproach.

"Gustav, my old mentor," chuckled Arsalan. "Don't look so angry. You did it!"

Arsalan and his six comrades then continued to the other three crystal bases, where they met other magical architects loitering while trying to solve the puzzle of how to light them. Using the same technique, the magical architects managed to activate them all, and now all four dazzling crystals shone from the corners of the castle like lanterns. The rippling waters of the lake below were now electrified with purple glimmers, just as older magical architects had remembered in their youths. In fact, they had forgotten just how intensely bright the crystal lamps were.

Arsalan returned to the main hall and immediately noticed a difference in the atmosphere inside. Whereas, for the first few days and nights, their candles, torches, fires had lit the murky and cavelike interior of the castle with notable strain, now every inch and corner of every space in the castle was illuminated with a mysterious and sourceless light, one that shone as if it were being cast from many invisible lanterns. The previously cryptlike hallways, once filled with shadows and trepidation, were now alive and awake with a friendly but unpeopled light.

All those who had been dwelling in the castle were shocked. Clearly the element of lighting had been missing all along, but they had reasoned it was because they had not brought enough torches and lanterns with them due to the hurriedness of their war efforts. No one had been able to recall that Conrad's Castle could illuminate itself, and that this ability was bound with the amethyst lamps outside. In any case, everyone's spirits were elevated, and the magical architects celebrated their completion of the reinforcement of the castle with a large dinner that night, followed by more revelry. Some generals and advisors joined them, but in a more distracted fashion since their civil war remained to be fought and quelled; many of them resorted to enviously peeking inside the dining hall at the strange, mythical artisans who dined there. The magical architects seemed to them always mirthfully removed from whatever grim concerns involved ordinary folk and their scurrying and worrying, their muscle, blood, sweat, and strain. They appeared to sit in bemused detachment, living their lives according to their own whims and eccentricities and harboring few ostensible worries. The sole and inevitable exception to their lack of concern was, of course, the issue of payment for their services. This typically exposed its unlovely head near the end of any of their meetings, which were otherwise superficially charming and delightful affairs full of boastful storytelling and flattering commentary and garnished with clinking glasses and bubbling laughter.

Arsalan was quiet for most of the dinner. His close friends and family sat around him, and for this he was grateful, but he noticed himself becoming bored with all the talk. He recognized his old colleagues' bold and hyperbolic manner of speaking as a characteristic of the magical architects from his life before, but it did not impress him anymore. He found himself stifling a few yawns behind the back of his hand or with his food and drink. He was, to be fair, also still exhausted. Several times, Teodora or Defne touched him on his arm to see if he was well, to which he nodded enthusiastically, just before drifting into ennui again and becoming lost in the deep luster of the dark oak dining table. Arsalan was glad when, eventually, the conversation turned to him and roused him from his daze.

"A toast," Ubaldini was saying, holding a wine glass in the air, "to the triumphant return of Arsalan the Magnificent! And to his noble cause of assisting the Bavarians in their civil war, and their preservation of magical architecture!"

"Hear, hear!" everyone cheered, some striking the tabletops, and almost everyone drinking. Arsalan quickly stood, bowed, lifted his glass, and drank.

"And a toast," said Marcelle, "to the reuniting of Arsalan with his lovely wife, Duchess Teodora of Silesia! May they live many happy years together ever after!"

There was more applause. Arsalan was flattered and gracious, but also embarrassed at having the state of his marriage be addressed in a toast. He flashed his broad smile while bowing again.

"And a toast to you all," said Arsalan, his glass aloft again, "for heeding our most desperate call for assistance! Without you, a Bavaria free of tyranny, and with all its magical structures preserved, would have been impossible. Thank you!"

"Hear, hear!" they chanted in a warm rejoinder.

"I second the thoughts of Mr. Ozdikmen!" said Princess Berthilde, also attending. Next to her sat Siegfrieda, who seemed as thoroughly tired as Arsalan, though no one seemed to notice.

"I have admired your work all my youth," continued the princess, "and it is a deep privilege to have every one of you come to assist us in our hour of need. Never in my wildest dreams would I have imagined this to happen. We are deeply indebted to you and to Arsalan."

Her words were so movingly sincere in contrast to the magical architects' glib bravado that the crowd grew momentarily quiet in tense embarrassment.

"Your praise is well received, your kind Majesty," said Kirakosyan, her curly white hair bobbing as she spoke in her ebullient way. "But on that note, would this be a good time to address the issue of compensation?"

Arsalan rolled his eyes, looked away, and shook his head. With complete dread he had been sensing this moment approaching, and he wanted to leave, if doing so were not so rude. There were a few murmurs of agreement among the magical architects, but most of them were too reticent to broach the issue themselves. It became obvious the magical architects' sudden quiet was due not only to their humility at the princess' warm remarks as much as their awkward desire to address the issue of money. Nonetheless, the princess clearly was not prepared to have the issue broached so abruptly.

"Well," Princess Berthilde said, "we would be glad to discuss this matter after dinner."

"Yes," said Siegfrieda. "Let's not disturb the levity of this fine dinner conversation."

"Of course!" said Ubaldini, pouring himself another glass of purple wine. "Why rush matters? The night is young, and we haven't seen each other like this in years! Arsalan! You still haven't told us about your adventures in repairing Conrad's old structures. Tell us more! Which ones have you fixed?"

"Yes, well, not to bore everyone in too much detail," started Arsalan, "but with great pains, I repaired the Turret of Fürstenfeldbruck, the Stadtturm of Straubing, the Marienkapelle Cathedral in Würzburg, and the Circular Ramparts of Nördlingen."

"All in one year?" said Ubaldini. "Incredible! So, you now fancy yourself more of a repairperson?"

"Not particularly, of course," said Arsalan, "but after my commissions dried up after my disaster in front of the Sultan, I found it difficult to refuse the work. In fact, as I've stated before, I was honored to continue Conrad's legacy by refurbishing his constructions."

Neither Arsalan nor Princess Berthilde felt entirely comfortable having the conditions of their agreement probed and aired in front of a crowd of listeners. The princess was aware that Ubaldini's characterization of Arsalan's work in Bavaria diminished Arsalan's stature in front of the others, and it was not clear if Ubaldini was mocking him or simply being tactless. So, to ameliorate the matter, she offered her own clumsy commentary.

"Yes," said Princess Berthilde, "and he has been critical in helping us fend off General von Ansbach. Arsalan fought him off at the gate of Munich and captured him!"

There was a stunned silence. It lasted long enough that the princess herself looked around to see what had gone wrong.

"What do you mean when you say Arsalan fought off von Ansbach at the gates of Munich?" asked Marcelle.

"I mean," said Princess Berthilde, "he used his magical powers to subdue hundreds of rebel soldiers! And he subdued their general!"

Arsalan felt his stomach drop into a pit. He knew the other magical architects would disapprove of his using his powers for military action, and he was preparing himself for their opprobrium. He wished Princess Berthilde had been more discreet with her revelations. Yet, he knew that the actions he had committed were not a containable secret, and that the Guild would hear of them eventually. In fact, he was oddly relieved the princess had blurted the truth so innocently since it would spare him the anguish of wondering when the Guild would discover it. He even had entertained a secret, perverse desire for them to hear it just to upset them from their smugness. Arsalan had been through too much agony over the past five years to be cowed by a furor over his bending of some rules. This weird, carefree sentiment registered on his face, and he found himself unable to conceal a sardonic little smile.

"You..." said Gustav, "You used your magic powers for aggressive military purposes."

"Yes," said Arsalan.

"You killed people with your powers?" asked Jawahir.

"No," said Arsalan. "I merely immobilized them by using the cloth-stiffening spell. And I disintegrated all their weapons. No one was hurt, I assure you. And certainly no one died due to my actions. I took great care."

"This is surely unprecedented," said Fahim. "It was bad enough that you almost killed hundreds of people with your collapsing building, but to engage in these types of activities clearly violates the magical architects' vows."

"Not so clearly. If I had not done what I did," said Arsalan, "then General von Ansbach would be occupying Princess Berthilde's throne, and he would be dissembling all of Conrad the Ineffable's structures, one by one. And there was no guarantee he would have stopped his violence once he assumed power."

"Arsalan," said Ubaldini, "I don't know what to say."

"Say the vow," said Arsalan.

"Excuse me?" asked Ubaldini.

"The vow," said Arsalan. "What's the vow you all are mentioning? Recite it."

"I will use my powers to harm neither man nor woman nor child," recited Majdouline, "nor will I allow harm to come to them through willful neglect. I will not use my powers to cause deliberate pain in any living thing. I will use my powers to construct dwellings and structures for the benefit and protection of humankind and toward a society prosperous, peaceful, and wise."

"Correct, Majdouline," said Arsalan. "Thank you. Now, I ask you all. Did I harm anyone?"

"We don't know," said Ubaldini.

"I know," said Siegfrieda, "and he didn't harm anyone, nor did he allow anyone to come to harm."

"He ordered our loyalist armies not to harm those who were immobilized," added the princess. "There were no casualties."

"The vow was intended to keep magical architects' powers out of military use," said Ubaldini.

"Gonashvili uses his powers for military use all the time," said Arsalan. "Think of all the defensive bunkers and forts he has built!"

"True," said Gonashvili, "but I just built defensive structures. I didn't assault people directly."

"Yes. I meant that we should not be using our powers to attack others directly!" said Ubaldini. "You can be disbarred from the Magical Architects' Guild for that!"

"I wasn't attacking others," said Arsalan. "I was defending others. I simply was not allowing others to come to harm through willful neglect. How else am I supposed to do that with my powers?"

"You defend them with a force shield! You cast an invulnerability spell on them! But you must not attack others!" said Dimitra.

"The spirit of the vow is strict, my friend," said Jawahir. "There is a reason it must be upheld: to prevent a race to magical armament."

"I know the reason and there was no danger of that," spat Arsalan. "Princess Berthilde will not ask me to be her military magician, and von Ansbach does not believe in magic at all. But in this case, we must remember that the preservation of human life is more important than the preservation of an antiquated vow."

At Arsalan's apparent insult of their venerated oaths, the argument exploded. On one side, Arsalan stood, pointing and shouting at his detractors. Surrounding him for support were all the Bavarian generals, Siegfrieda, Teodora, who was shouting just as vociferously, Defne, and of course Asker, who, being a military officer, entertained no qualms with Arsalan's interpretation of his vows. On the other side of the table, all the elderly master magical architects stood screaming and gesticulating like shopkeepers furious at having been robbed. The assistants and the younger masters sat silently, unsure of what to say, and looking to others for cues. Princess Berthilde was beside herself with horror at seeing all her childhood heroes and gods hollering at each other with reddened faces over glasses of alcohol. She held her hands in front of her, looking from one side to the other, and pleaded for everyone to stop, but her voice was inaudible beneath the din; her mouth and throat tensed and moved mutely.

Arsalan was brought on the defensive at Dimitra's point, which the other magical architects used repeatedly against him, and to which he reacted rather instinctively by throwing liquor into his glass and swallowing large gulps of it between his sentences and pointing at his opponents with a finger extended from a hand that held the empty glass. Suddenly, Teodora intervened, and held his arm down as he attempted to bring another glassful of liquor to his face. Arsalan paused, and he peered into the glass at the swishing pond of sweet, bloody liquid that was about to pour into his mouth for the fourth or fifth time, and he realized the harm he was inflicting upon himself. Arsalan did not drink it but placed the glass loudly on the tabletop.

"You useless, effete snobs! How dare you turn on me like this? I don't need to argue anything with you," he proclaimed with a red, spitting face. "Throw me out of the Guild. I've been to Hell and back and nothing more can harm me. I'm going for a walk! You all are going to get your money, and you're going to get the hell out of here! Thank you!"

CHAPTER 21

After a furious and theatrical wave of his arm, Arsalan stormed out of the room. His team of advocates, headed by Teodora and Siegfrieda, continued their haranguing of the elderly master magical architects. "Now look at what you've done!" Arsalan heard Teodora say, "You've insulted my husband and everything he has done for this kingdom, and possibly for all of Europe!"

Even after hearing his wife's heartening defense of him, Arsalan felt it best not to be drawn back into the dispute. He was shaking with rage and wished to quiet himself. Soon he found himself wandering throughout the winding hallways of the castle, now lit fully and comfortably from every angle by invisible sources of light. Arsalan thought he would retrace his route that he had taken a few evenings ago, but he could not recall it. The rooms and hallways he saw around him were different from what he remembered. Even when he tried to make his way back toward the dining hall, he discovered the rooms and hallways were different even from just moments ago, as if they had been altered in his brief absence and inattention.

Arsalan realized he foolishly had allowed himself to become lost within the castle. Its mazelike interior had captured him in his careless daze. He was only a little concerned, as he always had the castle windows as a means of escape. Otherwise, he hoped the challenge of negotiating the passageways and rooms would distract him from his indignation at his colleagues.

But this did not have the effect he had intended, for after a while of playing a game of navigating through the castle's labyrinth, Arsalan started to believe he was losing his mind altogether, and for this he blamed his own ire. He stopped in a small, cozy salon and sat on a couch; it had red velvet cushions, a deep brown finish, and a high, straight back. Next to it, a brick hearth somehow was lit with a little fire whose flames pointed upward like a dragon's teeth. Arsalan warmed himself by it, holding his head in his hands, despondent, exasperated, and lost. He leaned forward on his elbows for a while, and then leaned backward, but he could not find comfort in any position within the unnatural right angle of the couch's seat, so he rose and moved on. Now with calm purposelessness he resorted to meandering through whichever rooms and hallways were presented to him by the castle. Because he could not retrace his way back, his progress through the fortress' entrails was always in some way forward into perdition, from one luxurious but eerily desolate chamber to another. Every path or bend he took revealed an entirely new room, with novel, elegant maroon furnishings and wood paneling and red carpet and wrought iron candelabras, all designed and arranged in slightly differing ways, or yielding a mysterious corridor leading to a strange chamber with many new doors from which to choose. Sitting rooms, bedrooms, dining rooms, wine rooms, staircase landings, libraries, studies, kitchens, and pantries followed each other in pointless and confounding sequences that recurred neither in one direction nor the other.

Arsalan started to feel smothered by the limitless configurations of furniture and walls and carpet. To his relief, he eventually discovered a stairwell down which a faint, fresh breeze wafted from above. By his reasoning, he was in one of the four towers of the fortress. The staircase wound its way up narrow passageways, and the landings on each floor had a door into yet another well-furnished room of one sort or another. Arsalan decided that once he reached the top of the tower, he could fly out a window and back to the courtyard, where he could make his way back to his sleeping quarters without having to greet any of his insufferable colleagues.

Upward and onward Arsalan climbed, until he was almost to the topmost floor of the tower. He glanced out a window and saw that he was far above the highest roof of the main complex of the fortress. It was a murky night, but he could see campfires and windows lit with golden light on the lakeshore and beyond in the distance. The broad roofs of the fortress below him formed their own gloomy geometric hillscape, and their planar surfaces were highlighted here and there by weak glimmers of yellow light emitted from the fortress' countless windows. Climbing a few more levels, Arsalan's legs weakened and wobbled, so he leaned against a wall to catch his breath. As he was resting, he heard what he thought was music, echoing down the bare stone staircase from the floor above, as if a group of musicians were playing together there. Yes, it was delicate, delightful, and poignant, and the music lifted and pained his heart simultaneously.

Gently, Arsalan ascended, rounding one turn and then another. He slowed to a furtive creep, stalking his way toward a subtle candlelight that radiated from the door to the room on the final landing. Here, he could ascend no further; the staircase was terminated by a wall of brick. In front of him to his left was the open doorway that exuded the light, the beautiful music, and the wonderful little breeze. The sonata was quiet, as if it were being performed from far away. Arsalan was almost afraid to look inside. He could not imagine who possibly could be here, imprisoned in the mystifying and inescapable depths of the castle yet unbothered enough to play music.

Arsalan peeked around the jamb of the door like a small child. In the room he saw a desk, and many side-tables, covered with papers, books, scrolls, and models of buildings and geometric figures. By the window stood a gilded brass telescope whose gaze was directed out an arched window swung open on its hinges. From here the light draft was inhaled by the room, softly rustling the papers on the desk. Bookshelves stuffed with old tomes stood on either side of the desk and lined the walls of the modest chamber from floor to ceiling. The fresh, wintry air from outside mingled with the moldy smell of the old books and sent the subtly pungent mixture toward Arsalan. The music was audible from this very room, although no one was present to produce the noise, with the sole exception, perhaps, of the translucent old man who stood at the window, peering intently through the telescope.

Arsalan turned back around and hid again in the stairwell outside. He rubbed his eyes and face and shook his head as he was accustomed to doing when he was inebriated. After blinking a few times and trusting his eyesight again, he peered into the room a second time. The semitransparent man was still there, standing at the telescope. Through the stranger's body the telescope, the windowsill, and the outside sky were visible as if through colored glass. The man had shifted his position slightly, and he seemed to be recording something in a book with a quill. Arsalan saw the feather shaking as the old man wrote, and he noticed that none of those instruments the ghostly man held shared his translucent qualities. They all were opaque and seemed as real as the room itself.

From the ethereal old man's face drooped a pendulous white beard, and he was dressed in a set of blue robes, all as translucent as the man himself, like a projection of sunlight through a stained-glass window into a darkened room. There was a diffuse glow about him, and grains of luminous dust seemed to swirl languidly within him as if suspended in liquid illuminated by firelight. There was something familiar about the blue robes, and about the stance and shape of the old man. By this time, the music piece had ended, and another started, a lively, dignified tune that put Arsalan more at ease. Arsalan now reasoned that if he had encountered a ghost, at least it was an educated and civilized one who would mean him no harm. In fact, at this moment, when the ethereal old man turned around to face the desk, Arsalan finally recognized him as Conrad the Ineffable.

Arsalan now stood openly in the doorway with his mouth agape. Never in all his years of magic had he seen anything like a ghost. He had busied himself chiefly with materials and substances, and the ghostliest phenomena he ever had witnessed, besides magic itself, were invisible force shields and his beacon. Arsalan could not say if he ever had believed in spirits. He had never given it any thought.

The translucent Conrad spied Arsalan standing in the doorway.

"Good evening!" Conrad said, "And please come in, why don't you? You've been lingering outside long enough!"

This Conrad's voice was certainly different from before; gone were the pained, hoarse, breathy mutterings Arsalan strained to hear. This voice was now fluid and mellifluous, brimming with soothing conviviality. Arsalan, dumbstruck, wandered into the room, his eyes fixed on the apparition that for all purposes was Conrad the Ineffable.

"Excuse me," Arsalan said in his low, gravelly whisper of respect while trying to maintain his composure. "I don't mean to bother you. But I became lost, and I saw your light, and I heard music, and I came to see what it was."

"Ah!" said Conrad, and he reached onto the desk and lifted a small wooden box. "Yes, Partita Number Three in C Minor. Isn't it wonderful?"

"Yes," said Arsalan.

"And isn't this wondrous?" said the incorporeal Conrad, holding up the box. "All of Telemann's music, recorded into the substance of this small container. I just decide what music I want to hear, and the box emits it! They don't make many of these anymore nowadays. After all these years, I know exactly how to craft these instruments, but I still don't know precisely how they function."

"Yes, I have seen such a thing," said Arsalan. "The dome of St. Ulrich's and St. Afra's Abbey in Augsberg. It plays choral music."

"Yes, I know that one!" said Conrad. "In fact, it may surprise you to know that I made it, and I conjured the music spell upon it. Yes, tell me, friend. Do you worship there? Does it still play the music?"

"No, I was not raised as a Christian," said Arsalan. "But I do know that the roof still plays music. For a long time, it sat in disrepair and did not play, until I was hired to restore it."

"You say you fixed it?" asked Conrad.

"Yes," said Arsalan.

Conrad keenly regarded Arsalan this time.

"Do I know you from somewhere?" said Conrad.

"Of course you do, Master Conrad," said Arsalan. "Don't you recognize me?"

"I have known many people in my life," said Conrad, "but you are the first to appear here in my room for a long time. You will have to forgive me if I cannot recall you."

Arsalan walked closer to the shimmering apparition of Conrad.

"I am Arsalan Ozdikmen. Arsalan the Magnificent they call me," he said. "I was your student at the Magical Architects' Guild in Florence."

"Arsalan!" whispered Conrad in astonishment. "Why, I haven't seen you in years! You surely don't look the same! You have aged wonderfully! Here, come closer and let me look at you, my dear journeyman!"

Arsalan approached Conrad and looked directly into his face. Conrad placed his luminous, glasslike hands on Arsalan's shoulders. They had weight and force but were strangely cold. Conrad returned Arsalan's gaze with an expression Arsalan was not accustomed to seeing on the old man's face when Conrad was flesh and blood, when he was gruff, irritable, and taciturn and stomped from one private door to the next. Conrad now regarded Arsalan with a gentle, mischievous benevolence in the crinkles of his eyes that made Arsalan wonder with envy what marvelous things Conrad had seen in the intervening years.

"My!" said Conrad. "Look at you! You've turned into a fine old man!"

"It has been many years, Master," said Arsalan. "And you certainly have changed as well."

"How many years?" said Conrad. "I am almost afraid of knowing."

"Twenty-seven," said Arsalan. "It has been that long since your—"

"No, has it been that many already?" said Conrad. "Twenty-seven years since we have seen each other?"

"Master," said Arsalan, "I don't mean to upset you, but I must tell you the truth. It has been almost three decades since your funeral. It was grand. All the magical architects and all the heads of state were there in Florence to pay their deepest respects. It was one of the largest funerals in history. Even both Popes, Catholic and Orthodox, put aside their differences long enough to come and to give their benedictions."

"Is that right?" said Conrad. "Well, well. I must say I am duly flattered and humbled."

"You don't recall?" said Arsalan.

"I am afraid not, my friend," said Conrad.

"I don't understand," said Arsalan. "Are you not a ghost?"

"To tell you the truth, my friend," said Conrad, "I don't know. What is a ghost? What makes a ghost? I know not."

Conrad turned and walked back to his desk and gazed at the objects on it. He picked up a model of a bridge and held it up for both of them to see.

"We know what a bridge is. We know which materials are used to construct it. We know its mass, its strength, its stresses, its tensions, its weight. We know something about magic; how to cast it, its duration, its effects on matter, as though it were merely another mundane form of energy, like heat. We know little of the intricate means by which magic works, but it works for us, dependably, like a road or a lantern. But about ghosts we know nothing. Long have I pondered as I have dwelt here about the nature of my continued existence in this state," said Conrad, lifting his forearms and twisting his hands, "and I have not been able to arrive at a satisfactory conclusion. I certainly don't mind my existence, mind you. I never grow hungry or tired or ill. I am free to contemplate the nature of the world as I wish. But what am I? I suppose it is one of two possibilities. Perhaps I am a ghost, born directly from my body after death, and perhaps I am the only agent keeping this dear castle of mine from deteriorating completely. Or perhaps I am a separate being, perhaps Conrad's essence, a duplicate of my consciousness, if you will, imprinted into the stuff of this castle when I poured my magical powers into its construction and operation, and perhaps it is the castle that is keeping me from dissipating. That of which I am certain, in either case, is that I love this fortress. It is my greatest work of magical architecture, and I am afraid, unwilling, unable to leave it."

Conrad caressed the stone jamb of the arched window with his wrinkled, translucent hand. Then he looked at his hand and chuckled to himself.

"Did you know Telemann's parents tried to dissuade him from pursuing music?" said Conrad. "How foolish of them! Had they succeeded, we would have missed one of our greatest and most prolific composers. My parents similarly tried to prevent me from pursuing my career. They didn't want me to pursue magic when it was first discovered that I had the power. But what else is one supposed to do with telekinesis? There was no other choice. To make me a lawyer would have been a waste of their money. Maybe they were able to predict that I would be haunting a fortress as a wraith. I tell you, my dear Arsalan, I have thought my entire life about the nature of substances, and I have come to a hypothesis. Do you wish to hear it?"

"Yes, please," said Arsalan.

"Perhaps," said Conrad, staring out the window, "perhaps matter at its most fundamental, when you dissolve it into its most miniscule particles, is itself nothing more than bits of magic solidified. Maybe there is no difference between magic and matter and energy. We think of matter in terms of its weight, mass, force, and rigidity. Perhaps these qualities of matter are epiphenomena of spells cast by something higher."

"Interesting," Arsalan nodded. "But is that knowledge useful?"

"Probably more than we realize," said Conrad.

Arsalan was not certain where to proceed with Conrad's subject. "Have you noticed that your castle has been revived?" Arsalan asked. "It is illuminated from within now."

"Yes, I have noticed," said Conrad. "In fact, I was observing that just now before you walked in. I see lights in the windows and reflecting on the water. Did you fix it?"

"We fixed it. I used the beacon," said Arsalan. "I summoned all the magical architects here to repair the castle."

"The beacon?" said Conrad. "What dire circumstances prompted you to use it?"

"Your castle will be under attack soon," said Arsalan. "Bavaria is undergoing civil war, waged by an insurrection that opposes the belief in magic."

"Oh dear," said Conrad, and he sat in his chair. "This explains the presence of all those men I see from my window, and the explosions from far away."

"Yes," said Arsalan. "And the magical architects are here to reinforce the castle from the enemy's cannon fire. The opposing force seeks to demolish all works of magical architecture, especially this one, as a symbol."

"Oh my," whispered Conrad in shock, looking at the desk. "Oh my. These are horrid tidings indeed."

"Yes, Master, they are, and I am sorry," said Arsalan. "We will try our best to preserve your fortress."

"I knew this would happen someday," said Conrad. "It's my fault."

"I don't understand," said Arsalan after a shocked pause. "How can you have caused this?"

"I didn't cause this directly," said Conrad. "But I believe I have committed a mistake, one tiny infraction in my secrecy, which, once breached, laid the groundwork and fostered the situation into being."

"Is this a secret you can tell me, Master?" said Conrad. "I can keep the secret, if you confide in me."

"No one can keep a secret if it involves power," said Conrad. "But you may as well know it. You are, after all, a master magical architect, and I believe the secret has been revealed already."

Arsalan found another chair in a corner, and, afraid to take his eyes away from Conrad lest he vanish, pulled the chair to the front of the old man's desk.

"I leave the decision to you, Master," said Arsalan.

"This relates to what I was saying just now, about all substance being made of magic," said Conrad. "If everything is made of magic, then every one of us is made of magic, since we are made of substance. And if all people are made of magic, then it is not outside the realm of possibility that all human beings can control magic to greater or lesser extents."

"All people," said Arsalan. "Not just magical architects?"

"Correct," said Conrad. "It may not be the case that some of us can wield magic and others simply lack the ability. Consider that even among us wizard folk, the degree of power to use magic varies from one individual to the next. There are those of us whose abilities are less, and they go on to be lifelong assistants to magical architects. Some of them become master magical architects with many other assistants' help. Who is the boy who became your assistant? What is his name?"

"Doruk," said Arsalan.

"Yes, Doruk, one of the finest assistants I have known," said Conrad. "Sensible, judicious."

"Yes," said Arsalan. "The greatest. He has corrected my thinking on countless occasions."

"Yes, well," said Conrad, "the diminutiveness of magical potency does not stop with him. I have found that everyone can use magic. All people are wizards."

"What?" said Arsalan. "In what way?"

"They whom we call ordinary folk," said Conrad, "individually, they too possess telekinetic powers, but to a degree so weak that it is undetectable by our instruments. But in large groups, in numbers sufficiently great, and when their minds are directed in a single direction or toward a single purpose, their faint powers are combined and augmented to equal the power of a master magical architect."

"Really?" said Arsalan, who for the first time wondered whether it was possible for a ghost to go mad with isolation and loneliness. "How do you know this?"

"I have conducted research into this for most of my career," said Conrad, "clandestinely. You are surrounded by it. This is where I stored it, not the Guild in Florence. These books, they're not just Cervantes and Chaucer. They contain details of my experiments and findings. In short, I have seen that the amount of magical charge a magical architect must expend to cast a durability spell on structures is inversely proportional to the surrounding population. The charge is always higher in areas where the population is lower, and lower where the population is higher. But this assumes a certain amount of favorability the population feels toward the structure. When the population likes and believes in the structure being built, the buildings endure longer, and if the population is skeptical of the structure or harbors unfavorable sentiment toward it, the building deteriorates faster."

"I suppose I would have to read your findings," said Arsalan. "Help me understand the implications. Why would you keep this a secret?"

"Don't be so naïve. You're no longer an apprentice, old man," said Conrad. "All these wonderful, ancient magical structures that have endured for so many centuries, such as the Obsidian Obelisk of Kush, balanced on one tiny point, why might they do so?"

"Because it's famous throughout the world," said Arsalan, "and the people there worship it."

"Right," said Conrad, "and when Saint Adolphus the Faithful built his cathedral, which was imbued with enough charge to last a thousand years, in Bukhara, where it was universally despised by the locals for being unsightly and heretical, do you know how long it lasted?"

"Five hundred?" said Arsalan.

"I understand if you don't remember this little footnote of magical architectural history," teased Conrad. "One hundred fifty-eight."

Arsalan was pensively silent.

"You say you've had to repair my church," said Conrad. "Were there others?"

"Yes," said Arsalan. "Many."

"And you say there is an insurrection in Bavaria that opposes magic," said Conrad.

"Yes," said Arsalan.

"Have other structures dilapidated?" said Conrad.

"Yes," said Arsalan. "Jawahir's Egg, and my own, the World's Leaf."

"The World's Leaf?" said Conrad. "Oh, that sounds intriguing. I wish I could have seen that one!"

"Yes and no," said Arsalan. "It was my best work, the world's greatest, and it crashed to the ground in front of everyone on the day of its grand opening. If you had not died already, there is a chance you would have been killed there."

"That is excruciating to hear, my dear Arsalan," said Conrad. "What was the sentiment surrounding the erecting of the structure?"

"Mostly curious and positive, but there were murmurs of incredulousness and skepticism," said Arsalan. "I could not explain it. I had not heard such suspicion directed toward my work before, or toward any magical architect's. I thought it was because the building was so daring in its design and engineering, so different from anything constructed before. I ignored them."

Conrad sighed, held both his ghostly hands in the air in mild despondency, and dropped them on the armrests.

"Tell me, Master," said Arsalan. "If this is true, and you say it is because you accidentally revealed this secret, then how did you do so?"

"When I made this discovery," Conrad sighed, "I shared it with another master, one older than me at the time, Banaszak the Black, if you remember. He was arranging his retirement back to Lodz where he was to live his remaining days."

"I believe I saw him once, from a distance, when I arrived," said Arsalan.

"Yes, well," continued Conrad, "when I made this discovery, I too did not understand the full implications, until I conferred confidentially with this elderly master. His face became grave, and he implored me to tell no one. He quickly reasoned that if so many of our structures rely so heavily on magic to stand, and if the general population has some magic effect on them, then our magical buildings, and our very livelihood, are subject to compromise by something as potentially beyond our control as negative public sentiment. The buildings stand so long as the populace believes in them, and the buildings crumble when the populace disbelieves in them. This was an extraordinary weakness. Banaszak told me that the population must continue to revere the buildings and to believe they will stand, but they must not know that they have any power over the buildings."

"Did you or Banaszak tell anyone else?" asked Arsalan.

"No, of course not," said Conrad. "We swore a pact of secrecy, one that Banaszak took to his grave, and one that I have upheld, until tonight, with you, in this case."

"Then how do you think this secret was compromised?" said Arsalan.

"Well," said Conrad, "Banaszak and I spoke at length about this problem many times. The problem was that elderly Banaszak had grown quite hard of hearing. I often had to raise my voice or to talk directly into his ear. We had not thought of inventing hearing-stones then, pebbles that louden the sound that comes to one's ear. In any case, we were talking like this one afternoon, and I noticed that my office door was ever so slightly ajar. A beam of daylight shot through. It was a hot summer afternoon there in Florence. In the middle of our conversation, I had the inkling that I should ensure there was no one outside listening. I stalked over to the door, looked out, and indeed there was someone."

"Who?" said Arsalan.

"Emilio," said Conrad.

"Ubaldini?" said Arsalan.

"Yes," said Conrad. "He was still just a little boy, and he was startled and flustered, and he made an explanation that he was passing by on some errand. I asked him if he was eavesdropping, and he said no. Of course, I could see clearly in his eyes that he was lying. 'What did you hear just now?' I asked him. I became angry. 'Nothing' he said, shaking his head, and he became frightened. I looked at him sternly and warned him against spying on things that he had no business knowing. He swore that he had not snooped. I think I frightened him well enough. From that time on, I kept a stern eye on him, and it seemed to have worked. But I always worried that I let loose this awful secret that day to him."

"But Emilio was just a boy then," said Arsalan. "Do you think he knew or understood?"

"Clever children always can put together the pieces to a puzzle, given enough time," said Conrad. "And Emilio was perhaps the cleverest of them all."

"It is difficult for me to comprehend how that small incident can lead to this," said Arsalan, motioning out the window, "a full-scale military insurrection against magic. Besides, Emilio, as a magical architect, has as much impetus to keep the secret as you or any of us. If he reveals it, then all our careers are doomed."

"I'm not trying to convince you to be suspicious of Ubaldini," said Conrad. "I can't be certain of what has happened since that small incident. But once a secret is compromised, one cannot retrieve it. He may not have misused the knowledge, assuming he understood it, but a second or third person may have done so."

"Is it possible that others may have discovered this independently?" said Arsalan.

"Most probably not," said Conrad. "The effects are too subtle to notice unless one conducts extensive numerical research, as I have done."

"Then all my life has been wasted," said Arsalan, "wasted on something that can be torn down in an instant. This is still true and has not changed, ever since the collapse of my tower. All my work is for nothing."

"No, my friend," said Conrad. "It's not in vain. Your magic is real. It is as real as everyone believes it to be."

"I prefer to believe in things that remain true whether I believe in them or not," said Arsalan.

"Magic is real," said Conrad. "It's simply not real that we possess a monopoly of it."

Arsalan thought for a moment. "All the world's living magical architects are downstairs," he said. "You must come with me to explain this to them. We can work together to solve this problem."

"Alas, my dear friend," said Conrad, "for various reasons, it appears I simply am unable to leave this room."

"Well, I will go to gather them up and I will take them here," said Arsalan. "You will tell them what you told me. They and I had an argument, but we've had plenty of those in the past. They should understand."

"You all will get lost," said Conrad. "Frankly, I'm not certain even how you found me here."

"Why is your castle so deceptive and labyrinthine, my Master?" asked Arsalan. "Why does it seem to confound me every time I walk through it?"

"Another secret of mine," said Conrad. "There are more rooms and hallways included in the castle than can fit in it at any one time. The rooms shift in and out of position, and they replace each other. The chambers that cannot fit in the castle exist in another space, like ours, resembling ours, but on the other side of now, so to speak."

"But why?" asked Arsalan.

"To confuse enemies!" said Conrad. "This is a defensive fortress after all. If they storm in here with their swords and battering rams, they will become hopelessly lost. Of course, it has the additional function of keeping my study here out of harm's reach. I'm not sure if you will be able to find it again if you tried."

"Your lights are visible from your window here on certain nights," said Arsalan.

"Are they, now?" said Conrad. "Well, I should have figured as much. Well, the next time you see my light on in this window, fly up to see me! No ordinary person would be able to reach me unless they have an exceptionally long ladder."

"I understand now why they call you the Ineffable, my Master," said Arsalan. "The level of your recondite knowledge astounds even me."

"Again, don't fawn so much, friend!" said Conrad. "You are not a boy apprentice anymore. You are a master. You will unearth these enigmas in due time. In fact, here. I will save you some trouble. Take this book. Don't worry. It's a copy, one of many. It outlines all my most abstruse principles. It's about time someone else sees these. I thought they would die with me. What would be the point of that?"

Conrad, laughing, produced a book from a shelf nearby and handed it to Arsalan, who leafed through it quickly. It was unadorned and filled with scribbled notes on yellowed paper.

"Of course, take good care of it," said Conrad. "When you're finished with it, bring it back here to me, and we can have another nice chat. It does get lonely up here sometimes."

"I am honored," said Arsalan. "And I will be privileged to return. I must go back to the others now to fend off the enemy. War soon will come here."

"Remember one thing in your tactics against them, and this is something I have realized only in my old age," said Conrad. "The preservation of human life is more important than the preservation of a vow. Or a secret."

Arsalan smiled slyly. "Yes," he said. "I think I see now. Thank you."

Arsalan placed the book in his coat and embraced Conrad the glimmering specter. The little old man's embrace was eerily cold, but Arsalan did not mind, as his heart was exalted now with calm warmth.

"I must go by way of your window, if you don't mind," said Arsalan.

"Indeed, I don't mind," said Conrad. "I wouldn't want you to get lost again." And he kindly opened the window more widely, and the wintry night's raw, frigid air flew into the room as if down from the peak of a hoary mountain beneath a starry dome, and all the paper on Conrad's desk shivered, and all the pieces of paper poking out of the books and stacks on his shelves quivered. Arsalan raised himself into the air, turned to a horizontal position, and gingerly floated out the window. Once outside, he turned to look at Conrad again, who now was leaning casually on the windowsill like the women in Florence.

"Oh, and I'm sorry. Sorry for being so surly when I was alive, so to speak. I was sick and old and miserable," said Conrad. "You'll see for yourself soon enough as you grow older. It won't be long!"

It had not occurred to Arsalan that he might have needed an apology from Conrad about this. Arsalan from his childhood had become accustomed to Conrad's bad temper as simply his nature in the way one recognizes stone as rough and rigid.

"Apology accepted," said Arsalan. "Farewell, my friend."

"Take care, Arsalan the Magnificent, and good luck!" said Conrad, waving, then pointing. "Oh, look at that beautiful night sky!"

Arsalan turned to see the sky. Indeed, the pall of dense clouds no longer was blockading the glistening universe. The clouds were breaking into clusters and clots, allowing the godly, violescent Milky Way to peer through at the Earth with its silent, terrifying gaze of a million shining eyes. Arsalan turned back to Conrad to return a comment, but the old man was already gone. The light in the window was dark, and the room seemed suddenly empty and bare.

"Why, you old elf," chuckled Arsalan.

CHAPTER 22

Arsalan felt he should waste no more time. He calmly began to float down toward the courtyard. At the last moment, however, he diverted his trajectory to the roof of the arcaded balconies that surrounded the yard. There he stood, twelve stories above the water, with the wintry winds whistling through his beard, staring out at the black lake as if into a bottomless hole. He allowed his ruminations and emotions to play out their drama on the stage of his mind, and he studied them, allowing them to coalesce in the most natural way possible. Several issues that troubled Arsalan chose to orbit one another like dance partners in his mind, uniting like weak magnets, forming a simple but undeniable constellation: Ubaldini, Conrad's secret, and magic depletion. A fourth thought came, and it was of The World's Leaf. A fifth thought came, which Arsalan barely dared to entertain, and it was of the rivalry between himself and Ubaldini, and his friend's jealousy toward him, which, although sublimated into Ubaldini's creative work, always had seemed present. There was the assumption of Arsalan's apprentices and journeymen. And now, there was Ubaldini's desire to take the lead in condemning him for possibly breaking one of the magical architects' vows. Arsalan rolled his thoughts over and over in his head to see them from different angles, to see if they would break apart, but they continued to adhere to each other and to present to him the same gnawing conclusions.

Arsalan descended finally to the courtyard and entered the doors to the main hall. It was late, and Arsalan ignored the few military strategists who were busy with their documents, maps, and diagrams, pushing little tokens this way and that on their broad tabletop maps as if playing a board game. Arsalan proceeded directly to his side-room. He pulled out his reading spectacles and Conrad's notebook and leafed through it. It was divided into sections with labeled bookmarks. There was a bookmark on which the label "On the Nature of Ordinary Wizardry" was written in Conrad's tightly woven Latin cursive. There, in this section, was Conrad's summation of his research into the subject, and into the problem of magic depletion. This section had an appendix consisting of all his conversations with Banaszak the Black, and the encounter with a young Ubaldini. Evidently, Conrad had been deeply worried about this breach of secrecy.

Arsalan put the book in his coat. He then turned and went to the dining hall, where he still could hear the voices of his friends, colleagues, and family members discussing the matter of Arsalan as if he were an abstract problem.

Opening the door, he saw everyone there. No one had left, but the tenor of the conversation had changed. It had become calmer but more officious. Ubaldini and the other magical architects now sat at the table as some sort of committee, with papers spread in front of them, except for Sigrid, who sat on the sill of the clerestory of tall, narrow, arched windows that looked out at the night. Bayram, the princess, Siegfrieda, and Arsalan's family sat to one side looking unhappy but quiet. Apparently, they all had been brought to some sort of tentative and uncomfortable truce so that they could discuss matters more rationally. Upon seeing an expressionless Arsalan standing in the doorway, everyone looked up in suspense.

"Ah, there he is," said Ubaldini. "Hello again, my brother. I hope you've calmed down this time. We've finished negotiations regarding our payment and have come to an agreed salary for each of us. Now we've begun discussing the matter of your future within the Guild given your involvement in military affairs."

Arsalan stood and stared at him.

"Don't you have anything to say for yourself? Anything more to say in your own defense now that you're quieter?" said Ubaldini.

Arsalan continued to stare at him.

"Dear God, my brother, you concern me," said Ubaldini. "You have become mute in your anger. Don't you realize your future as a magical architect is at stake? Why don't you say anything?"

"You sabotaged my building," said Arsalan, in a low, gravelly tone.

Arsalan observed the initial response of his old friend and rival. Ubaldini reacted with plain, dumbfounded shock, and there was a glimmer of fear in his eyes. Suddenly, Ubaldini laughed in his merry, flutelike way, which was now breathier with age. His laugh was nervous and stiff.

"What?" said Ubaldini. "My brother Arsalan, you must get hold of yourself. You've been too riled this evening. I apologize for stoking the emotion with my initial accusations, but I think you've become mad or desperate. We all know you've been working hard for the princess, but this matter of becoming involved in her political and military affairs must be discussed."

"You were always jealous of me," said Arslan. "All along. You overheard Conrad the Ineffable discussing his secret with Banaszak the Black. Although it is difficult to prove outright, I suspect you used the secret principle against my building."

Ubaldini threw his hands in the air and leaned back in his chair.

"Please enlighten us all," said Ubaldini. "What on earth is this secret principle of which you speak?"

Ubaldini stared Arsalan in the face boldly. Arsalan could tell Ubaldini probably was bluffing, daring him to reveal it. The price for exposing it was high for the entire livelihood of the magical architects, all of whom were present, but since Arsalan suspected its effects were already at play, fear of its ramifications was no longer an issue.

"The principle that ordinary people unknowingly possess wizardly abilities to an extremely low degree, and that if one can sway public sentiment with rumors and fears, the combined effect of their disfavor toward a magical structure can deteriorate it or can topple it outright," said Arsalan.

Ubaldini's laughter was warmly incredulous, and he looked around the room for confirmation of his disbelief but found none. Everyone else was too flabbergasted at the drama to come to any conclusion. Arsalan produced Conrad's notebook, opened it to the correct page, approached the dining table, and threw the book onto it in front of Ubaldini, which stopped his laughter. Arsalan pointed to the text.

"Just now I wandered the halls of the castle and found Conrad's old study and found this book," said Arsalan. "It is Conrad's. Look at the handwriting, and the seal."

Ubaldini's eyes gazed at the book and then looked back up at Arsalan.

"So, I see. You know you cannot win our first argument, so you stalk off in a fury. Finding a miscellaneous old book off one of Conrad's shelves—a most fortuitous coincidence—you think you can use the contents of the book in a desperate attempt to distract everyone from our initial accusations against you with accusations against myself. I must admit, it's a brilliant strategy, opportunistic, but frantic, for these accusations are not only serious but also bizarrely farfetched," said Ubaldini. "I'm afraid you suffer from nervous exhaustion, my friend. Faced with these circumstances, I'm afraid we do have the right to petition to have you deemed unfit for active service within the Guild, at least temporarily."

Tears began to stream from Arsalan's face. Anastasia took the book and began to read it.

"It does mention the findings here, Ubaldini," said Anastasia, "but even if this principle is true, Arsalan, how can you prove Ubaldini used this knowledge against you?"

"Would you perpetrate such atrocities against your closest friend?" said Arsalan to Ubaldini. He walked around the table, sat by Ubaldini, and looked at him squarely in the eyes. "Look into your heart, my dear old friend. I believe you spread worrisome rumors about the World's Leaf as I was building it, and I believe those rumors caused the general magic depletion in the structure, such that by the time it was finished, it was ready to drop. If another magical architect had drained the magic directly from the structure, there would have been indications. This would have been the best way to sabotage a structure without leaving a trace. How else would magic simply become depleted from a structure like that? And unless you had told anyone else about the secret of magic depletion, you were the only one alive then with that knowledge. Can you look into my eyes while telling me this is not true?"

All eyes were on Ubaldini. He looked uncomfortable, his face reddened, and his eyes dropped. The mouths of all the magical architects in the room went slightly slack.

Ubaldini stood and walked away. "Don't look at me like that, Arsalan! You're making a fool of yourself!" he snapped.

"You can't do it," said Arsalan. "You can't tell me it's not true."

"I don't know," said Ubaldini, walking over to a tapestry hung on a wall and examining it, as if planning to escape into its woven, idyllic scenery. "Maybe this thing, this secret, is true, and I had nothing to do with it. Why would I want your building to fall? What would I have to gain? Maybe public sentiment turned against your building because they were afraid of it. Maybe they were rightly fearful it would fall. I mean, look at its design. It was so weird. So outlandish. It was spindly and weak. It couldn't stand under its own weight. Magic was the only thing holding it up! Like string and glue. It was a precarious construction! Who would trust their lives in that thing, much less their higher education?"

"You were jealous of me!" said Arsalan. "You wanted that building to fall because you wanted to see me fail!"

"And what's wrong with failing once in a while, oh, Arsalan the Magnificent?" yelled Ubaldini. "You seemed so incapable of it. Everything you did succeeded. Everything you did was grander and more soaring than anyone else's. It was always Arsalan having done this and Arsalan having done that, bigger, wider, more inspiring, ever since you came to the Guild, ever since. It was enough to make your closest friends sick!"

"Why would such success make one's closest friends sick?" said Arsalan. "Why would one's friends not share the joy of their friend's success? Why would they succumb to the poisons of envy and jealousy instead?"

"Because you were younger than all of us!" said Ubaldini. "We had worked so diligently for years to attain such knowledge and skill. Then you arrived, and within weeks you had matched us, and within months you had exceeded us!"

"It was true, Arsalan," said Marcelle. "We did find it difficult not to be jealous of you."

"So, you admit it," said Arsalan. "You sewed rumors among the people of the Ottoman Empire about my construction, just to see if it would poison my building!"

"Maybe I voiced legitimate concerns about your construction," said Ubaldini. "Maybe I was a voice of reason!"

"Then why didn't you come to me with your concerns?" said Arsalan.

"Why did you have to gossip with others?"

"Maybe they weren't concerns," said Fernando. "Maybe they were wishes. Weren't they, Ubaldini?"

Ubaldini was silent for a moment.

"All I wanted was to be as great as you, Arsalan the Magnificent," said Ubaldini. "All I wanted was to catch up to you just once. But you were unstoppable. You were so busy with all your marvelous structures that you did not have time even to come to the Guild to teach any of our new apprentices. You demonstrated no interest even in sharing your knowledge! You wanted all the glory of the magical architects for yourself! You were so selfish and irascible!"

"You wicked backstabber! You degenerate cur!" screamed Arsalan. "I lost everything because of your skullduggery! I lost my wife, my children, my house, everything! Long years of loneliness, despair, and disgrace! How could you do such a thing?"

"Because maybe you deserved it!" screamed Ubaldini.

Arsalan's deep wrath was now fully stoked. Red-faced, he lunged at Ubaldini and grabbed him by the collar. Arsalan attempted to strike Ubaldini in the face, but it was obvious that Arsalan was not a fighter and had never been one, aside from the abuse he had enacted on his own apprentices years ago. Arsalan pummeled his opponent with blows, though ones that turned out to be harmless slaps, making Ubaldini scream with alarm and annoyance. Ubaldini defended himself while trying to throw half-bunched fists at Arsalan, but it was just as evident that Emilio, too, had never used his hands for anything other than his own magical instruments. Ubaldini's flailed wildly, missing almost every target. Everyone in the room rose in disbelief and panic at the two floundering, effete, old men.

Asker leapt into the fray, attempting to wedge himself between the two fighters.

"Father! Don't do this to yourself!" he implored. "This is disgraceful! You know you can't fistfight, and you only will hurt yourself! Stop!"

He grabbed both brawlers by their collars and tried to separate them, until Asker's own face became the recipient of Ubaldini's misplaced slaps, which the seasoned soldier bore with the irritated countenance of someone being splashed with cold water.

Abruptly, however, the melee ceased. To Asker's surprise, the two old men now stood still. Their arms were raised, and their legs were splayed for battle, but they remained frozen in place. The two fighting men grimaced and grunted angrily in their attempts to move within their clothing, which was now as rigid as wood. Asker, confused and a little disturbed, released their collars and took a step backward, staring at the two men and at his own hands.

From the crowd of onlookers, Anastasia the Austere stepped forth with a hand raised.

"How disgusting!" Anastasia rebuked. "To think that I have been forced to use the cloth-stiffening spell to keep two grown wizards from boxing and brawling like a pair of farm boys! Look at yourselves! I have been the witness to your rivalry for too long, both as apprentices and as master magical architects. How many times have I had to intercede between the two of you to settle your differences at the Guild? Do you recall? How little you've changed in this regard!"

"You will not shame me, Anastasia. We are boys no longer!" growled Ubaldini. "Release us and let us settle our differences our own way, or I will cast the same spell on you."

"You dare not!" cried Dimitria, pointing her finger. "Or I will constrain your team of assistants!"

"We do not condone Ubaldini's actions to which he has confessed," exclaimed Marcelle, standing next to Fernando. "But we will not allow you to punish his assistants for his actions!"

"Marcelle is right," said Arsalan. "I put them through enough hardship when they were my assistants. Keep them out of this!"

"Everyone, stop your threats!" Teodora commanded. "And release my husband!"

Teodora made sure to place herself directly between Arsalan and Ubaldini. She gazed into Arsalan's eyes, which were now brimming with tears, then she glanced at Anastasia, who, with a wave of her hand, reluctantly released the spell. Arsalan and Emilio then began to pant, their chests heaving. Their fighting had tired them, and the constricting spell had prevented them from catching their breath.

Arsalan turned his dewy eyes to Ubaldini.

"You ruined...my life..." said Arsalan. "You took my business, my apprentices, my livelihood."

Defne stepped forward.

"No, Father, you ruined your own life," she scolded. "After the World's Leaf fell, you could have worked harder to demonstrate to the world that your powers were still sound. You could have treated your apprentices in a kinder way. You could have found more work abroad. And even if you could not find more work as a magical architect, you could have used your wealth more wisely. You could have invested it in property or banks. Instead, you continued to spend it as if your income was unaffected! You were unwilling to adjust your approach toward your finances! If you had changed your ways, we could have survived the World's Leaf! We could have survived anything together! The collapse of one building should never have mattered! It should never have sundered your life to shreds! You planted the seeds of your own downfall!"

There was a long silence.

"She's…" panted Arslan. "She's right. My daughter is right."

"And you, Ubaldini," said Teodora, turning to face the other old man. "Obviously what you did was unconscionably underhanded, diabolical, destructive."

"And in doing so you have begun to ruin magical architecture for all of us!" growled Gustav from the crowd.

"Yes," yelled Jawahir. "It was probably because of you that the great Egg of my namesake fell!"

"Yes, but I didn't know," wheezed Ubaldini. "I didn't know it would work on the World's Leaf so effectively. I had no idea it would come crashing to the ground so readily. I thought the building simply would fall apart here and there. I was horrified at the news of the collapse. And I didn't know it would start a cultural trend of distrust toward us magical architects. I was wracked with such horror and remorse for so long. I've ruined us all. This is all my fault. I don't belong in the Guild anymore. Please, cast me out."

Ubaldini began to sob, and he hid his eyes in his gloves.

"I'm sorry, everyone. I'm so sorry," he said. "I am a devil."

To the sobbing man's surprise, Arsalan chuckled.

"You're also a terrible fighter," offered Arsalan.

Ubaldini snorted insuppressibly despite his sobs.

"You're hardly any better," he muttered smilingly. "I deserved a better thrashing than that."

Anastasia and Teodora, with mouths agape, rolled their eyes.

"Oh, honestly, you two!" exclaimed Anastasia. "Confront the situation squarely!"

"Arsalan, let me redeem myself to you, to everyone here," said Ubaldini through his snotty tears. "Let me help you rebuild the World's Leaf."

"It's too late," said Arsalan. "No one will fund such an undertaking. Besides, maybe it was too vaulting and unsound. Besides, I'm tired of thinking about it. It has become the death of me."

"No, Arsalan," said Ubaldini. "You simply are trying to devalue what you have lost. That building truly was beautiful. It was the most elegant structure I had seen in my life. It brought tears to my eyes! I will fund it. It will be at my expense. We can rebuild the public's trust in magical architecture. That way, all our structures will be restored!"

"I simply don't know, Emilio," said Arsalan. "You'd have to restore my trust in you first."

Ubaldini, downcast, looked at the floor.

"What does this mean now?" asked Ramūnas. "Is Arsalan at fault by Ubaldini's accusations, or is Ubaldini at fault by Arsalan's accusations? Are they both wrong?"

"We are all wrong," said Anastasia. "We all have been arrogant and self-absorbed. Look at us dining as if we are attending a ball and demanding payment for services during the height of a civil war. Look at our infighting and jealousy. Look at our ostentation. Are there other ways magic can be used for the good of humankind rather than simply for the construction of majestic palaces for the aggrandizement of the supremely wealthy while the poor and middling go huddling as refugees of war in encampments during the coldest clutches of winter?"

"You speak the truth," said Fahim. "It is those people we should be helping. I feel ashamed of us."

"I would be lying if I said I had not been motivated or poisoned by jealousy," said Dimitra. "Enough to try to impair rivals in small ways in my youth. What will it gain for us to punish Arsalan and Emilio when they are manifestations of sicknesses within our own culture as magical architects?"

"Underneath, we are an awful breed. It's a wonder even our own spouses can stand us," said Fernando. "I know my wife thinks I'm intolerable."

Many grunted in agreement and looked at the floor. Anastasia looked up at Sigrid, who sat in the clerestory and seemed to be observing her own thoughts as they played outside the window through which she was staring.

"Sigrid," said Anastasia. "You've been quiet, or at least much quieter than most of us. What are your thoughts?"

Sigrid turned to look down at everyone.

"My wife thinks I'm unbearable, too," she said. "But she still loves me."

Sigrid then returned her gaze to the window. No one was quite sure what to say to this, so they remained silent for a moment. Only Bayram smiled to himself.

"We need to reassess ourselves, our roles as magical architects. We are not heroes and heroines. We are not gods and goddesses. What should our priorities be? Where do we go from here?" asked Kirakosyan.

Just then thunder rolled throughout the castle, as if someone had dropped a boulder from the sky onto a cobblestone street. The walls quavered and everyone looked at each other. Another blast occurred, followed a few seconds later by another.

"They're here," said Arsalan. "The rebels have broken through our ranks, and they have arrived."

"My friends," said Ubaldini, "I do not know yet how we magical architects should define ourselves in the future, but I know what we should do now."

Ubaldini picked up from the table the invoice for his service fees, signed by himself and the princess. He looked at it closely and sadly, then disgustedly, and then he tore it in half, and ripped the two halves into shreds. He opened his hand and let the pieces of the parchment snow onto the tabletop.

"I'm sorry, my dear Princess Berthilde, for the confusion," said Ubaldini, "but I waive my fees to you. Everything I do now to protect this castle and the people of Bavaria I do at my own expense."

Before anyone knew, Gonashvili followed suit, crumpling the paper in his ogrelike hands, as did Kirakosyan, Dimitra, Anastasia, and all the rest, except Sigrid, who realized she had forgotten to sign hers, but made her invoice burst into flame and ash anyway. Gustav looked at his invoice not without a little regret, shook his head, and turned the paper to dust in his hands while wiggling his fingers.

Princess Berthilde and Siegfrieda gasped. Arsalan, Teodora, and Defne gazed at them in astonishment. Bayram was shocked. Asker grinned. The booms outside did not cease but increased in their mounting menace. Defne and Teodora hugged one another for comfort, as did the princess and Siegfrieda. Asker seemed to be assessing the situation with removed fearlessness.

"Everyone, let us proceed to the main hall," said Arsalan.

There in the main hall, the magical architects were briefed as to the latest developments in the conflict. Princess Berthilde's soldiers had fought valiantly, but Von Ansbach's rebel forces had pierced the defenses stationed at the southwest corner of the lakefront and now were launching boats equipped with cannons from their captured beachhead. There were ten in all now on the lake surrounding the castle, assailing the fortress with cannon fire, but without much effect. The spells cast on the outer stone walls had worked beautifully so far. The stairs were retracted already, and the front doors shut. All was sealed off from the outside.

"Masters, journeymen, apprentices, assistants, what have you," said Arsalan, "I understand your doubt and outrage at me when I revealed my involvement in this conflict, and I regret my embroiling you all in this one. We, by definition, pride ourselves on our refusal to become engaged and political and military affairs of any sort, but there does come a time when inaction becomes malefaction. At these times, even magical architects must take a stand against injustice, against threats toward our own lives and livelihoods, but most pressing, against the lives of millions of innocent civilians threatened by an entirely unnecessary conflict. I ask you to assist me in ending this war.

We will use solely painless and nonlethal means, and I assure you they work. I ask you to do this for Conrad's Castle, for Conrad himself, for Princess Berthilde and the good people of Bavaria, and for magic and the culture and soul of the magical architects. If here is any man or woman who objects to engagement in this struggle, make yourself known now, and your decision will be respected, and those who fight will bear no ill will against you. And those who fight will accept whatever punitive or disciplinary action is enacted against them by the rest of the Guild, even if it is disbarment."

Everyone faced Arsalan in a silent ring of somber faces, but no one made a sound.

"And who volunteers to aid in this struggle?" asked Arsalan.

Everyone, large and small, man and woman, old and young, in every manner of dress, raised their hands, like a pledge given by all the deities of Mount Olympus. Even Bayram raised his, as did Teodora, Defne, and Asker. Had there been a cat or a dog nearby, it probably would have raised its paw in allegiance. Anastasia stepped forth.

"Lead the way," she said.

Arsalan quickly gave them their orders. Each of the most powerful magical architects, who also happened to be the oldest, would team with a journeyman or younger master. Each of the pairs would fan out from the castle in an expanding circle. Force shields would be established around themselves, and the attacking pairs would skim the surface of the water to avoid cannonballs and gunfire. The attacking wizards would approach the rebels and would dissolve everything that was wood, leather, stone, glass, or metal, save the boats, leaving the soldiers weaponless in their immobilized watercraft. After this, Arsalan would lead the mighty team of wizards into battle against the rebel forces. Doruk and his team of apprentices would guard the castle.

Marcelle and Jean-Jacques would launch from the south, Fernando and Luciana from the southwest, Jawahir and his journeyman Ghalib taking flight from the west. Gonashvili, arriving alone, would be accompanied by Ramūnas from the northwest. With Anastasia, Majdouline would fly. Fahim would launch from the north with Sigrid, and from the northeast, Gustav and no fewer than both of his loyal journeymen. From the East, Kirakosyan and Tafari would attack. Arsalan and Ubaldini would launch from the top of the castle and would attack boats coming into position from the southeast corner of the lake. Teodora, more frightened than Arsalan had seen her in many years, embraced Arsalan with tears in her eyes and kissed him on his face, pleading for him to do his job well and to keep himself safe.

"Of course, my love," he said.

The magical architects took their relative positions in the courtyard, put their hands together, reaffirmed their commitments, wished each other luck, and launched themselves all at once into the sky like a set of firecrackers. Immediately afterward, Doruk activated the force shield that protected the castle from assaults from above. Asker then raced up the stairwell through the pillared balconies, then found a hidden service ladder to the roof, where he intended to watch the action. Teodora implored Asker to be careful, but he replied he would be fine, as he climbed the masts of ships frequently. Doruk floated up and stood on the roof next to him, and the two men stood where Arsalan had perched earlier that night, looking out to the west.

"Yes, be careful, little Asker," said Doruk. "You wouldn't want to fall with that limp. These aren't the stone blocks your father had lying around the workshop."

"I'm fine, dear Doruk. Thank you," said Asker, staring out into the darkness. "What can you see from here?"

"I can see their lights, sir," said Doruk. "And some of the boats are illuminated by the crystal lamps, but beyond is opaque."

The flying wizards each wore a lighting pendant around their neck, and they were visible as points of light making their way through the solid volume of blackness. They twirled out from the castle like the ends of growing vines, and they swirled around the boats like dragons and falcons. They saw the little soldiers staring up at them from their boats; the soldiers' faces, illuminated by the dim orange lights of boat lamps, were innocent with fear and wonder. The vessels were small but compact and sturdy, and the magical architects were surprised that the rebels had transported them over such distances on land. On each craft, there were two small, dense cannons, one at the bow and one at the stern, squatting like heavy iron frogs, their heads directed outward and upward. Teams of men continually fed the cannon's posteriors with ammunition and held fingers in their ears as the thick metal tubes pounded the air with flashes of rudely concussive force and light, illuminating the waters around them with bursts of red fire. When the rebel soldiers saw the flying magical architects approaching like hawks, their panicked sergeants ordered the underlings to fire. The frightened soldiers lifted the ends of their rifles in almost every direction in the sky and let loose their rounds, crackling like fireworks, but their wild bullets only ricocheted from the wizards' force shields as if bouncing off rock, and the magical architects saw only flickering stars of bullets rebounding away from their faces like pebbles off glass.

The magical architects' handling of the boats was swift and businesslike. The cannons were reduced instantly into rustling piles of iron filings, spilling all over the decks and into the water. The soldiers' feet slid and slipped on the decks made messy by the effluvium and the men fell on their faces and backsides. Everything the soldiers carried as a tool or as a weapon also disintegrated forthwith into clouds of dust or cascades of dry, spilling particles. Their oars vanished into sawdust that scattered onto the surface of the lake like pools of yellow algae. Within minutes, all ten boats were immobilized and helpless, adrift on the murky lake, and the magical architects, seeing this objective met, flew to their next target, which was the captured lakefront to the southeast.

The flock of airborne wizards in their outlandish, assorted garb from all over the world approached the occupied lakeshore. Their faces were stern. Their beards and heads of hair flailed in the wind. Their arms were outstretched on either side. Their bodies and legs were stretched behind them like birds' tails. They could see the rebel soldiers milling about the shore under the many torches that pushed the darkness away from the waterfront and onto the lake and the surrounding woods, but the soldiers could not see the approaching onslaught until the wizards were mere yards away from their heads. In they swept, the magical architects, like nightmares, like owls of the night into the nests of sleeping, blind prey. Before the rebel soldiers had time to react, their guns vanished in their hands, their swords corroded in their scabbards, and their scabbards dissolved into dirt. Their carts and boats disintegrated into sawdust, their cannons and cannonballs softly burst into clouds of rust, their horses' reins rotted away, and their horses fled in abandon and terror. The soldiers reached into their holsters and pockets to find their pistols decayed and their knives and bullets crumbled. It was only an instant later when the soldiers found they could not move within their clothing. Their wool, linen, and leather stiffened, suddenly and immovably, and the soldiers tipped over and plopped to the ground like felled trees, one by one, as if weighted down by unwieldy suits of armor. There, they cursed, and they screamed for help from their compatriots, receiving none.

The magical architects made their way through the throngs of rebel soldiers. Each squadron, each unit, each battalion was separated from the previous one by darkness and distance and had no way of foreknowing the swift defeat that bore down on them. Eventually, the corridor of rebel forces that had pierced the loyalist front, and that now were meeting their defeats, widened into the rebel divisions that stood beyond the front, away from the lake, where they were checked into place by the loyalists. As the magical architects made their way through the rebels, the loyalists fell in behind them from either side, capturing the immobilized enemy soldiers and lifting them onto carts. The princess' infantrymen cheered for joy when they saw the magical architect's decisive devastation of the rebels. They learned what was occurring and received orders from their leaders to harm no prisoners.

Here, before the magical architects, spread the great, wide sea of the rebel forces; there were several divisions of them with hundreds of thousands of warriors bristling with weaponry and torches, silhouetted sinisterly before red fires that glowed like embers and smoked into the night sky. Arsalan barked his orders: fan out into a circle the size of a courtyard and cast spells as widely as one's magic can reach, subdue everyone, and harm no one. Arsalan and Ubaldini would assume the vanguard, and everyone else would follow their lead.

Arsalan led the charge with Ubaldini at his side, and swath by broad swath the enemy was immobilized, lying screaming but unharmed within their own frozen suits among piles of debris and dust. From far away the rebels attempted to kill the flying magicians with bullets and cannonballs, all which recoiled away in every direction as if having struck transparent stone. Whenever the magical architects happened to fly over fields empty of soldiers, the enemy took their chance and released a fusillade of cannon fire at them. Detonated soil plumed and blossomed into fountains of filth and flames as high as houses all around the magical architects as they flew, but the wizards proved invulnerable to the blasts, and the rain of clods of soil bounced off them harmlessly. The circle of magical architects wended its way through the enemy ranks like a wet cloth cleaning a tabletop, and all the rebels within their radius fell to the ground feebly.

The enemy's withering rout was unequivocal, though the battle had lasted the entire night. Twilight began to make itself known, and the air slowly became suffused with a desolate, gray light like the approach of a slug. The last two battalions surrendered; they raised their white flags in the air and waved them frantically. Their flags were rags hastily tied to their bayonets. They suffered from terror, exhaustion, and cold, and they trembled as they held their filthy hands in the air and cautiously rose from where they had cowered in their foxholes. In the dismal light, one now could see the battleground strewn with living cocoons of men who struggled to move within their frozen suits like the squirming larvae of insects exposed to the sun. Some had stopped trying and remained still, waiting to be arrested, their breaths streaming from their faces.

The magical architects grouped in the field and conferred with the loyalist commanders. This scene, with the mingling of fire and smoke in the background, some of Bavaria's most talented painters would capture, and their renderings would hang in the museums of Europe for centuries.

"How many divisions were there?" asked Arsalan. "Is that their entire army?"

"Unfortunately, sir, we estimated only two thirds of the remaining divisions were present here," said the commander from beneath his boatlike hat. "We could not keep track of the other divisions in the maelstrom. We are not sure."

Arsalan, Ubaldini, and the rest stared at each other in alarm.

In the silence after the raucous battle outside the castle, no one in Conrad's Castle could sleep that long night, least of all Asker, in whose military blood flowed the excitement of combat along with the fear for his father's life and wellbeing. Several times he had descended to the dining hall to comfort his sister, mother, and friends and had returned to his high spot on the steep, tiled roof from which Doruk did not move. Doruk sat there, wrapped in an oversized coat, and silently smoking a pipe. The aged assistant was squinting at the graying southern horizon. It was difficult for anyone to read Doruk's emotionless demeanor, and there was no exception in Asker. Doruk barely had changed since Asker's childhood, as though the older man had been middle-aged his entire life. He had the same drolly bedraggled appearance, with his drooping jowls and wrinkled forehead. A pyramidal wisp of thinning hair stood like the kindling to a bonfire atop his large cranium, which sat on his sagging, lank neck like a globular mushroom on a stalk. But the young man thought he could detect worry through Doruk's expressionless face. Eventually, Asker produced his own pipe and proceeded to smoke in solidarity with him. For anyone looking at the roof, the two smoking men became scarcely discernible from chimney tops.

"Doruk," asked Asker, "were you worried about Father while he was gone for those three years?"

"Yes," said Doruk.

"How worried were you?" asked Asker.

"I thought of him daily," said Doruk. After a time, he added, "But I know he is a capable man. However effete and proud he seems to be, he always proves resourceful and vigorous, and he survives in the end. Not like Ubaldini. He's as brittle as porcelain."

"You know this of Father?" said Asker.

"Of course," said Doruk. "I had worked for him for years. I was concerned, but I knew he would live."

"How long have you known him?" said Asker.

"Since we were in the Guild together, in Florence," said Doruk. "We were classmates."

"Have you felt regret that you could not become a master magical architect like him?" asked Asker. "Do you ever feel envious of master magical architects?"

"Never," Doruk said.

"Never?" asked Asker.

"Not once," said Doruk. "In fact, sometimes, when I witness their behavior, I am quite glad that I did not have such powers. As you can see, such privilege can cause confusion in the soul. You heard how honestly they spoke of themselves tonight. I feel lucky to have the few magical powers I have."

"Really?" said Asker. "Sometimes I wonder what it takes to inherit those gifts, especially when a magical architect is one's own father."

"It doesn't matter," said Doruk.

"What do you mean?" said Asker.

"The most important thing to know, young lad, is this," said Doruk. "Regardless of your level of talent, regardless of your powers, when you are given a task to complete, large or small, devote yourself entirely to making a good job of it, as best you can, every time. Give no guarantees you can't keep and make no excuses for your failures. Adhere to facts and details, adhere to your word, and adhere to the task at hand. Don't hurt anyone. And be glad for everything you have. If you commit yourself to these tenets then everything else will mind itself, wizardly powers, or none. If you can't be a wizard, at least be someone worthy of respect."

Asker nodded his head and furrowed his brow, impressed at Doruk's commonsense insight.

"But I suppose the question is," said Asker, "how does one best judge which task to assume?"

Doruk tilted his head and pursed his lips.

"That's the hard part," Doruk said. "I suppose any task that doesn't harm anyone is one worth doing."

"Didn't you have any suspicions about Ubaldini when he was sewing discord and rumors?" asked Asker.

"No, I didn't, until he asked me to work for him afterward," Doruk said. "There was something strange about his demeanor and his timing. But then again, I needed the work. Perhaps that was my personal blindness."

"Do you harbor any misgivings about him now?" said Asker.

"No," he said. "He spoke the truth tonight. I always can tell when one has spoken the truth. Tonight, I felt he sang it. Forthrightness is redemption."

The two puffed smoke silently for a moment more.

"The one I worry about most of all, Asker, is your brother," said Doruk. "These wizards flying through the sky, they are old and powerful. Their problems are rarified and untouchable. I worry about where Omer is. I worry daily, just as your father does. I can't control any of it, I know, because he is a man on his own path. He is no longer the little boy running between the blocks in the workshop, either. But I still fret."

"I do as well," said Asker. "I hope he and I live to see each other again."

Just then there was thunder, roaring from the east. Asker and Doruk were startled and looked over the roofs of the fortress, over the lake, its shores, and the forests and farms beyond. In the bleak twilight, Asker could see a white light and smoke emanating from a spot beyond the trees. The white light ascended directly into the sky, and as it soared, it reddened and defecated a thick trail of gray smoke behind it. There was little in Asker's military experience to prepare him for such a sight. For a few seconds, his mind intuited calculations and compared wartime experiences and memories. When the climbing star ceased its ascent at a certain zenith above the castle and began to grow larger, there were several more blasts from the horizon near the first one's source, and from these several more shooting stars identical to the first emanated. For Asker, there was no escaping the obvious conclusion.

"Incoming!" screamed Asker. "Doruk, get us down from here! It's an attack!"

Doruk lowered them both down to the courtyard.

"Incoming!" yelled Asker to the guards, pointing to the ominous red light above them. "Take shelter!"

Suddenly he turned to Doruk and said, "How much impact can the force shield above us take?"

"Unsure! I don't know how much impact that cannonball will deliver!" he said, and both the men ran into the main hall.

Asker and Doruk and the guards burst in, gaining the attention of all the generals and commanders from their charts and reports.

"Incoming!" Asker screamed. "Take shelter beneath the tables!"

Everyone did so, but Arsalan and Doruk ran into the dining room where Teodora, Defne, Princess Berthilde, and Siegfrieda were sitting with Arsalan's old team of apprentices and journeymen. He screamed at everyone to dive beneath the long table, and they did. Asker helped the princess scuttle beneath and held her there, just in time for the blast to report from above.

The entire castle wavered, and dust and mortar snowed down from the vaulted ceiling. Everyone in the room shrieked in terror.

"What's happening?" squealed the princess.

"The rebels flanked your forces to the east. They are using incredibly large and powerful cannons to deliver fire to us from miles away. I have never seen such powerful weaponry!" said Arsalan.

"What should we do?" she asked.

"We only can wait it out," said Asker. "Doruk, is the force shield holding?"

"Yes, but I don't know how much longer," he said. "These shields were not cast to resist such forces."

"Can we increase the charge to the spell?" said Asker.

"We can try, but we don't have the power of master magical architects," said Doruk.

"Where is the spell cast?" asked Asker. "Where is the mechanism located?"

"As the base of the southeast tower, to the left of the main doors," said Doruk. "We used a block there as the charge entry point, and the current runs up the side of the tower and out the turret roof."

"We must try!" said Asker.

CHAPTER 23

Doruk, Asker, and Arsalan's five former apprentices stooped as they made their way outside. As soon as they peeked out the door, another projectile struck the force shield that formed a transparent umbrella above the castle. There was a thunderous blast, and the fire spilled like fluid all over the invisible roof above them as if breathed there by a dragon. The inferno lasted a moment before dispersing and revealing again the dreary morning sky. The seven Turks took advantage of the pause between explosions to scamper outward toward the base of the southeast tower accessible in the corner of the courtyard. They took refuge in the arcade of the ambulatory, beneath the first balcony, where they could access the block of stone that was utilized as the focus of the spell.

Doruk, with quick and trembling hands, opened the maw of his leather sack to expose an intricate array of tools, each sitting in its own little pouch, and all of them bristling and gleaming like the dentistry of a deep-sea creature. He chose one instrument after another and handed each to the other apprentices. They all held their tools up to their noses and narrowed eyes, adjusted the tools quickly, and lifted them to point at the block. The stone glowed with a lavender light. More detonations occurred from above, and with each blast everyone flinched, and the purple glow of the stone faltered and flickered before resuming.

"Is the charge good?" said Asker.

"No, it's seriously low," said Doruk. "Each time one of those projectiles strikes the shield, it subtracts energy from the enchantment."

"Can the six of you recharge it fast enough?" asked Asker,

"We don't know," said Doruk. "I think we need the recharger."

"Where is it?" said Asker.

"In the dining hall by the table in my yellow satchel," said Doruk. "I must retrieve it. I was too hasty. I should have taken it out with us!"

Before Doruk could finish his sentence, Asker was bolting recklessly across the broad courtyard. More violent blasts mushroomed above the castle as he ran, shaking the ground beneath him and almost tripping him. He burst into the main hall and ran through it and into the dining room. Frantically, he searched for a yellow sack of some sort. He spotted a tan suede haversack among some other bags, and he grabbed it. It was unexpectedly heavy, and as he shouldered it, he almost fell again.

Defne, who still was sheltering beneath the dining table with the others, saw her brother's feet run by, and she cried out his name.

"Asker!" she said. "Don't go back out there!"

But he either ignored her or was too preoccupied to hear her voice peeping from beneath the table among the din, and he scurried out the doorway. Defne scrambled out from beneath the table and followed him.

"No!" she cried, with anger in her voice, each phrase punctuated by an explosion from outside. "Asker, my brother, you will not go out there! Come back! You are not a wizard! Stop!" Defne became frenzied with indignant and protective love for her brother, and she sprinted forcefully after Asker as if she planned to tackle him.

Outside, where Doruk and the others crouched, they continued their forlorn attempts at rejuvenating their magic spell that held the castle's shield aloft. All six stooped there like fishermen trying to reel in small trout that refused to emerge from a river. Their stone still shone with the lavender light, but it was dimming, and they became frustrated and desperate. Finally, one more explosion bloomed above them, and the stone went dark. Doruk tapped his instrument against the block, but there was no response. Doruk, Sunduk, Estani, Etci, Ibrahim, and Sevket all gazed at each other in shock.

"It's down," said Doruk. "Goodbye, my friends."

Another giant cannonball was making its graceful and inevitable parabola down toward them from the heavens, trailing a blanched, smoking trail of death behind it. The six Turks found a doorway in the ambulatory beneath the arcaded balcony and dove inside. Doruk was the last to go in, making sure all the younger ones saved themselves first. Just then, the main hall doors flew open again, and Asker emerged, running at full tilt toward them from across the courtyard with the sack over his shoulder, and with Defne following.

"Asker, Defne, no! Get back! The shield is down!" screamed Doruk.

Asker, distracted by Doruk, tripped, and he fell, and he looked up at the sky toward the terrible descending thing. Defne apprehended him there and fell on top of him, and she tried to raise him back to his feet.

"Asker, no!" Defne said, and she held her hand up to the sky.

Asker crouched on the ground in a fetal position, hugging his sister. Defne, also hugging him while on her knees, had buried her face in his coat and continued to hold her hand upward, behind her bowed back. The brother and sister both waited for their deaths. Several seconds passed, but the impact did not come. Slowly, queasily, Asker opened his clenched eyes. Across the courtyard, he could see Doruk and the rest peeking out of the door at him in horror. He turned his head, and he saw Defne still on top of him with her hand in the air. Looking through her long hair and over her shoulder, he saw that the giant cannonball floated just above them and was glaring down at them like the face of a demon; it had the diameter of a table, and tongues of flame licked the sides of many holes that were bored into its surface. He could hear the roaring of the fire inside it and could smell the smoke that bled upward from its orifices.

Doruk and his men fearfully emerged from their hiding place. Hesitantly, but with growing boldness in their realization, they stalked over to the treacherous predicament balanced before them: Asker, who was beneath Defne, who in turn was beneath an oversized, flaming cannonball that hovered above her, somehow prohibited from falling to the courtyard's surface by the gesture of her hand.

"She has the power," the men whispered to each other. "She has the power! She's more powerful than us!"

Doruk was careful not to disturb anything. He crawled toward them and took the haversack from Asker and stood back. Asker grasped Defne's wrist and kept it upward.

"My sister," said Asker. "Keep your hand raised."

Defne was still too terrified to look. "What is happening, Brother?" she asked. "Is my hand hurt? Are we burning? I smell fire."

"No, no, we are fine," said Asker. "Come with me, and do not open your eyes."

Asker brought his feet beneath him, grabbed Defne around the waist, and suddenly pulled her out from beneath the flaming sphere, and they began to scramble toward the corner where Doruk had been hiding. As they did so, Defne turned to look where her hand had been directed, and she shrieked in terror at the face of the flaming orb of black, perforated metal glowering down at her. It exuded an evil, malodorous smoke, and the air around it rippled from its ferocious heat. The cannonball thudded to the ground, rolled to one side, and continued to smolder and to crackle from within. The dead, dry grass beneath it gently caught fire.

"What happened?" she asked. "Why didn't it hit us?"

"You happened," said Asker. "You have Father's powers. You stopped it."

"I did? I do?" she asked. "I don't. I didn't."

"Point your hand at it again," said Asker, "and will it to move with your mind."

Defne looked at the palm of her pale hand. It was shaking, and her breath was shivering. She redirected her palm, fingers outstretched, toward the cannonball and furrowed her brows in mild concentration. Suddenly, the iron ball rolled a few feet away from them. Defne gasped and brought her hand to her mouth.

"Did I do that?" she asked.

"I believe so, Sister," said Asker. "Now, command it to levitate off the ground."

Defne tried again, and the thing rose about a foot into the air for a moment. Rudely, from above, there was a vicious new eruption that broke her focus. Defne screamed and jumped, and the cannonball plunked to the ground again, but nothing fell into the courtyard from above them. Asker looked up at the sea of fire that formed a roof above the castle, and then glanced at Doruk, who had extracted the charging stone from his sack and had placed it next to the stone at the base of the tower. Both blocks now shone with solid, bright purple light.

"The shield's energy is now replenished," said Doruk, "but the reserve power won't last indefinitely!"

"You saved us, dear Sister!" said Asker.

"But how?" she said. "Where did I get these powers?"

"From Father, obviously!" laughed Asker.

"But why did I not have them before?" said Defne.

"Maybe you always had them, but they were latent until now," said Asker. "Maybe they were triggered by the magic used to turn you into a cat and back, or by your anger at me! By now, what does it matter, my sister?"

"I wasn't expecting this," said Defne. "I don't know if I want this. I was thinking just tonight how glad I was that I wasn't a magical architect. I don't know what to do now."

"I have a suggestion," said Asker.

Doruk, Sunduk, Estani, Etci, Ibrahim, and Sevket elevated themselves, along with Defne and Asker, to the battlements on the top of the eastern wall of the fortress. Defne wailed a bit as she rose with them, and she hugged Asker and closed her eyes until she was placed safely on the floor of the battlement and between their low, toothy walls. There, she caught her breath, and she balanced and comforted herself with the feel of the solid stone ramparts on either side of her.

"No time to waste, Defne!" said Asker. "Catch that one! Arrest it like you did the first!"

Another projectile was headed down toward them from a great, arced height in the eastern sky, trailing smoke behind it. Defne raised both hands upward and gazed at it with a fierce but uneasy grimace. For effect, she curled her fingers slightly, as if wanting to catch a ball. Miraculously, the cannonball began to slow until it almost stopped above them, but then bounced harmlessly against the invisible ceiling with a comically harmless bang. Defne flinched and lost control of it, and to the men's anxious protestations the ball plummeted stories down into the water's surface, which it met with an enormous but distant splash. The men had peered over the edge of battlement to watch its precipitous descent and dwindling disappearance into the lake. When they saw there was no explosion from the little white plume, they cheered.

"There's another!" shouted Estani, pointing to the heavens. "Try again!"

Surely enough, there was not one but two new cannonballs dropping toward them like pieces of a broken planet. One was farther northward but ahead of the other, which was directly in front of them.

"Bring all your energy from here!" said Etci, making a chopping gesture with his straightened hand to his solar plexus. "Become angry! Order it!"

"Scream your decree!" shouted Ibrahim.

"You can rule it!" barked Sevket. "Think of it as your own fist!"

Defne outstretched her left hand.

"Halt, you, thing!" she said. "Descend no longer! I forbid you! You cannot fall any further!"

Though farther away, the cannonball's deceleration was gradual but unmistakable, in fact almost polite and obedient. It stopped, just above the northwestern turret, and its smoke, no longer blown behind it in windblown wisps, now formed a proper crown of thick, vertical, gray plumage.

"Now order it to stay in place, dear Defne," said Doruk.

She clenched her fingers as if smashing a handful of clay against a wall to stick there.

"Stay!" she squeaked. "I want you not to move from there!" And the cannonball did not drop.

Defne placed her hand over her mouth.

"It worked!" she said, shaking her hands and jumping. "I like this! I want to try another!"

"Then try making it work on that one," said Sunduk, pointing to the second cannonball.

Defne leaped into a pouncing position, feet wide apart, and extended both arms above her.

"Hah!" she exclaimed fiercely. "I prohibit you from dropping!"

More readily than the one before, it was seized into place, several hundred feet above them, and it remained there, burning and smoking as if in patient frustration.

Defne successfully apprehended a third, a fourth, a fifth, and more, until above them hung a crowded array of blazing cannonballs that nearly blocked their view of the eastern landscape. The collection quickly became an overload, and the crew was running out of places to put them all. The hasty amateur spells cast on several of the flaming cannonballs ended up evaporating too soon, and the iron spheres dropped dangerously into the water below. Eventually, what had been to Defne a fun and exhilarating new game became a numbing task of war, and she recognized, even more clearly than when she had been sheltering under a table, the grim and remorseless resolve with which the enemy was trying to murder her and everyone with her. She was staring directly into the face of stark madness. The barrage from above was constant and punishing, like an avalanche of boulders. Defne found it difficult to keep up with the onslaught, and she began to wince with stress. Her arms tired. Her concentration was fracturing and several of the cannonballs pieced her defenses, striking the invisible shield just above them with a deafening blast and a pool of liquid fire spread over a smooth plane. The battlements shook beneath the soles of their very feet, and the team cowered and to cover their ears. Sunduk and his friends cowered unabashedly in one corner of the battlement, and one of them was screaming and crying inconsolably in sheer shock and terror. Defne herself screamed and panicked and burst into tears, and Asker lifted her, soothing and encouraging her, back to her feet to continue. As she stood and resumed her efforts, Asker then began surveying the horizon with his portable spyglass.

"How long must this go on?" Defne wept, bent over in agony, her arms in the air. "I don't know much longer I can continue! This is hell! I didn't agree to this!"

"Have courage! Obviously, we can't stand here playing catch all day," said Asker. "We don't know how many of those cannonballs they have, and we know our shields are limited. We must destroy those cannons!"

"How?" asked Defne.

"We must shoot the cannonballs back at them," said Asker. "Can you do it?"

"But that might hurt someone!" said Defne.

"This is war!" he said. "What do you think they're trying to do to us?"

"I'm afraid I might miss it!" she cried. "There are innocent people whose houses are out there!"

"They all have been evacuated by now," said Asker.

"How do we know?" said Defne.

"Defne, you need to know this isn't like throwing a rock," said Doruk, who had approached her. "All you have to keep in mind is the target and how much you want the object to meet it. There's no aiming involved."

"Really? It's that simple?" said Defne, catching another cannonball.

"If you really want the cannonball to hit the target, there is no missing it. There can be no mistakes!" said Estani, who was crouching on the ground beside her.

"You see those cannons pointing upward like smokestacks from behind the trees? Aim for the tops!" said Asker. He pointed to them, and they were illuminated clearly by the rosy light that was cast from the sun rising behind them.

Defne reluctantly agreed, and she found a slight pause in the enemy fire. Quickly, she chose one of the burning spheres that hovered above them and shifted it into place before her. She concentrated on the tip of the faint, gray smokestack far away and several degrees below the horizon, and with a sneer, she mentally commanded it to fire. Instead of shooting toward its intended destination, however, its trajectory drooped downward—to the horrified gasps of everyone there—where it plunged harmlessly into the lake to join its fallen cousins. Defne screamed and became despondent, but they had her gather another one, and this time Asker stood in front of her with his finger raised.

"Imagine that giant cannon out there," he said, pointing to it, "is Prince Ergin."

Defne became quiet. She had not thought of Prince Ergin for a long time. She had wished never to think of her terrifying experiences with him again, and she had intended with all sincerity to move ahead with her life now that she was separated from him by many years and leagues. But at the mere mention of his name, remembrances long buried were stirred within her that made her vibrate with fear and loathing and rage once again as if she had escaped him just yesterday. She recalled the hysterical desperation that drove her to hide from him in the form of an animal, a self-imposed curse from which she could not free herself for three long years. A hot despisal swelled within her and from its raw material there was birthed a secret desire for vengeance, which she normally considered uncouth and unbecoming of a woman like herself, but here and now seemed strangely delicious and appealing. This malignant vigor tightly coiled itself within her like a spring, and before she could ponder her next move, the cannonball launched itself in an explosive dark blur from the castle and headed in a line as straight as any ruler toward the distant, giant cannon. Within a second, the cannon was replaced by a rocky boom and a mushrooming cloud of vermillion and black that tapered into a treelike column of smoke.

Defne gasped, and she held her hands in front of her mouth, and her eyes widened with white terror laced with fascination. All were silent, and all the men there seemed to have grown mournful and vaguely afraid, save Asker, who was inspecting the blast through his spyglass.

"Direct hit!" Asker said.

"I did that?" Defne asked.

"You certainly did," Asker said.

"Was anyone hurt?" Defne asked.

Asker, not interrupting his focus through his spyglass, said, "No."

"Are you certain?" she asked.

"I assure you I see no casualties," he said.

Four more missiles were shot into the air from the other giant cannons, all at once, and the cannonballs climbed their typical route into the sky near the clouds like chalk drawn up the surface of a blackboard. Suddenly it seemed Defne's panic was transforming into anger; she had grown sick of the relentless fusillade. She sneered with a rictus of desperate wrath. She twirled her hands in the air and assumed control of four of the cannonballs that still hung before them like mindless servants awaiting her command. She sent the four orbs up a wild ascent to meet the other four that were plummeting toward the castle, and each ascending missile met its descending counterpart with a fantastic detonation of crimson and charcoal fireballs that evaporated into dull gauzes of gray. Without even pausing, she magically grabbed all the remaining cannonballs that were suspended in front of them and jettisoned them back to their sources.

"This one is also for Prince Ergin!" she shouted. "And this one is for von Ansbach! And this one's for Lord Kadir! And this one's for the stupid Sultan! And this one is for every man who ever has terrorized or hurt a woman in his life to make himself feel powerful!"

One by one the faraway towers of artillery were obliterated in smoldering, mushrooming clouds of fire and shadow. The smoke became skewed and faint as it mingled with the blustery upper atmosphere. Doruk and his friends looked on in shock, and even Asker was rendered speechless by the monstrous and unalloyed power demonstrated by his sister. His mouth was slack, and he looked at the devastation and at her alternatingly, as if unable to reconcile the two.

Defne was panting through her bared teeth and had begun to sweat. She wiped some of her perspiration off her lip with her sleeve. Her hair was hanging in her flushed face, and she was bent like someone who had won a vicious fistfight. Asker could see her trembling and quivering. Her arms by her side, she watched the distant burning with a look of profound and righteous satisfaction.

Asker became worried, and he turned to her and placed his hands on her shoulders, and he attempted to look in her eyes.

"Are you feeling well, sister?" he said soothingly.

Defne glared at him and smacked both his arms away with her forearms, and Asker leapt back.

"Am I well? Don't patronize me, brother," she growled. "I just won your battle for you."

Asker was taken aback, almost hurt, and he stared at her for a moment. Defne seemed furious at him, but gradually became conscious of herself. She realized how she had acted toward Asker, and her gaze at her brother became less fierce, sadder, and more pleading. Tears streamed from her eyes, her shoulders drooped, and she began to sob and to weep.

"Brother," she said. "Oh, Brother."

She leaned forward and dropped her forehead into Asker's broad chest, and she hugged him, burying her face in his coat. She wept inconsolably, shaking with anguish. All her accumulated terror and rage emerged in her tears and wails. Asker embraced her carefully and quietly assured her. Many new naval recruits he had helped console after their first taste of battle this way, when their first whiff of the breath of death that had ridden by on its black horse and had missed them by inches. Only few wept as excruciatingly as Defne.

"My dear sister," he said. "It's over now. You are the heroine. My dear sister. Everything is alright now. You're safe. We are safe, because of you."

On the battlefield, the magical architects' conversations with the commanders were interrupted by the soft sounds of explosions from the northeast. Everyone saw the bone-colored streams of smoke clawing into the distant sky. They saw the twinkling red and white lights leading the trails of smoke, and they knew that a new weapon had been devised and deployed without their knowledge. They could not see where the strange lights were headed, but Arsalan had a sinking feeling it was Conrad's Castle.

"How strong are the shields on the castle?" asked Arsalan.

"It depends on how powerful those things are!" said Ubaldini.

"Should we make it back there?" asked Dimitra.

"It's too far away! The cannons will hit their target within seconds!" said Tafari.

And it was true; the distant fireworks met their target with a rumble as they spoke.

"This means the remaining rebel divisions are there, launching those missiles!" said Kirakosyan.

"Let's fight our way there and disable the artillery!" said Gonashvili.

"One of us should go back to the castle to help!" said Arsalan.

"There are too many of the rebels, and we need all the help we can keep here!" said Anastasia.

"I'm with Gonashvili. To the northeast with us!" said Fernando.

"We should be able to make a quick job of it!" said Marcelle. "Come on! We're old and tired, but we can finish this!"

All the magical architects raced in the direction of the cannons. It became clear to them that the remaining two insurrectionist divisions had taken advantage of the loyalists' vigilant adherence to the lakeshore and had outflanked the loyalists to the east by a half a mile and under the furtive cover of night, where the rebels set up their enormous artillery. The magical architects quickly met the enemy divisions there a half mile from the lake, where the enemy was waiting with rifles and cannons at the ready. Every landmark bore the traces of their armed presence. The rebels were crouched behind every tree, hill, house, and embankment, within every hole or hollow, and the barrels of rifles and bayonets jutted perpendicularly from nearly every surface like a porcupine's quills. Nevertheless, the phalanx of magical architects tore into their ranks, and cannonballs and rifle bullets rebounded off their magical defenses like snowflakes, and the insurrectionists dropped to the ground where they writhed and wriggled absurdly in their hardened uniforms. The magical architects plowed as forcefully as they could through their foes' throngs in a race to arrive within striking range of the giant cannons, but the adversary's sheer numbers and the berserk fervency of their defense slowed the magical architects' progress to a slog. The colossal cannons fired off many more rounds toward the lake before the magical architects could come near them. The magical architects began to tire, and Ubaldini became impatient.

"This is madness! We should be attacking those cannons by air!" said Ubaldini. "I will dissolve those things myself!"

"No!" yelled Arsalan. "You'll die!"

"We cannot wait! We must protect the castle and everyone in it!" yelled Ubaldini over the noise.

Ubaldini wasted no more time and flew directly into the sky and toward the giant cannons. He saw they were each four stories high and made of massively thick steel. The rising sun's intense pink light glimmered on their smooth, metallic surfaces, and he wondered where and how such immense weapons of war were cast with such secrecy that the princess was unaware of their manufacture. He approached the nearest one and began to cast his dissolution spell on it, but he found that even his magic spell took time to perform its work. A hole was bored in its side, and the opening expanded as dry rust cascaded off its rounded edges, but there was so much dense material to corrode that Ubaldini sensed it would take minutes to disable the artillery completely. He realized he had committed a miscalculation in his efforts, but it was too late to retreat. Every gun and cannon in the area was now trained on him, and projectiles careened toward him in a great cone and off his invisible shields in every direction. His shields were thinning, and Ubaldini was wearying, but he kept on until the hole was a gaping maw. He sweated, and he fought off despair and panic to concentrate on this now unavoidable task.

His focus was only broken by the heat, sound, and pressure of an unearthly explosion that occurred a half mile away to his north. A cloud shaped like a fiery mushroom erupted into the atmosphere. It was unlike any explosion Ubaldini had seen. Another occurred, slightly closer to him and south of the first, and then a third, in rapid succession, and it became clear that something was destroying the cannons one by one without his help. Immediately he flew away to the east as fleetly as a peregrine, just before the cannon he was trying to destroy blossomed into a Vesuvius of flame and smoke. A wave of concussive force struck him, and a piece of debris assaulted his legs, and his world was thrown into blurry darkness.

CHAPTER 24

They found Ubaldini, after an intensive search, lying on a hill among some trees. Over the peals of faraway church bells that rang joyously from village to village throughout the countryside in celebration of the loyalists' victory, the magical architects could hear Ubaldini's faint singing and gentle, merry laughter, weakened and fey with age and injury. Miraculously, he was alive and conscious, but not well. His legs were broken, and the pain made him delirious. He was suffering from shock and had vomited on his clothes. He giggled and joked when he saw his comrades, and they fashioned a stretcher out of some spare canvas and wood and placed him on it. He howled, winced, and contorted with agony when they moved him just the wrong way and secured him to the stretcher with straps, but once in position and hoisted into the air, he began to tell stories of his youth and his buildings. He was not quite sure where he was when they were flying him back to the castle. He simply remarked how astonishingly beautiful the morning sky was as he stared directly up into its immaculate blue and pink dome.

The dining hall table was cleared, and Ubaldini was placed upon it. Ubaldini kept asking where his hat was; it was his favorite, he said, and he was a fool for wearing it in battle, or maybe not. Maybe it was a good hat in which to die in battle. The magical architects ignored his prattling and removed his bloodied leggings enough to assess his injuries.

"Oh, my pantaloons," he protested. "My beautiful green pantaloons. Oh, never mind. I'll have another one tailored. There's that shop in Milan I go to."

Three military surgeons arrived and examined him. The fractures were mostly closed, but numerous. The bones would have to be reset. Splints would be necessary for both legs. Recovery time would be many months, and it was uncertain if he would walk the same way again.

"Wait," said Siegfrieda. "Don't you magical architects know first aid? I mean, you can bend steel. You can do all sorts of things with stone. Why can't you heal a bone?"

All the magical architects looked at each other like schoolchildren who were asked whether they had completed their lessons but had forgotten.

"We never become injured," said Gonashvili. "We always have our protective shields and spells with us at work."

"That can't be," said Siegfrieda. "You don't have accidents at your worksites?"

Gonashvili shook his head and shrugged. Teodora and Defne shoved her way forward to the table.

"Listen," said Teodora. "Sigrid! Come over here."

Sigrid stepped forth.

"You can make stone and metal transparent. Correct?" said Teodora.

"Yes, of course," said Sigrid.

"Can you make Ubaldini's flesh transparent so we can see his bones?" she Teodora.

"I have never tried that spell on human tissue, to be honest," said Sigrid. "Besides, don't you think that's a bit gruesome?"

"It can save his life!" said Teodora. "Try it!"

Sigrid shrugged in her detached way, pointed her fingers at Ubaldini's thighs, focused her gaze, and said something in Latin. Immediately, the injured sections of Ubaldini's legs became translucent, almost transparent, till only the narrow rod of his femur was visible between two portions of visible flesh, connecting them and making his limb look as though an animal had feasted on it for dinner. The sharp fractures were clearly visible, as were the pulsating arteries surrounding them. Most of those in the room fought to control their retching and shock, but all the surgeons stared at it in wonder.

"Now, just cast a spell to reset the bones back into place and to fuse them," said Teodora.

"It will cause him extreme pain," said the chief medic. "He must be sedated."

The surgeons unlocked their little cases and produced containers of opiates in shiny, dark brown bottles. The medicine was potent and expensive, and the thin surgeons handled it as gingerly as if it had explosive properties. With painstakingly delicate care, the correct dosages were extracted and given to Ubaldini to drink, diluted with heavy admixtures of water. He was thirsty and drank the entire draught, and then he asked for a flask of bourbon, a request which the surgeons flatly disregarded. Eventually, Ubaldini grew quiet and relaxed and seemed to sigh with relief, and he fell into a dazed sleep.

Defne and Teodora watched in fascination as Sigrid worked with the head surgeon to nudge the shards of bone back into their correct places according to the anatomy books they had with them, opened on the tabletop next to Ubaldini. Once in place, Sigrid found herself looking to the medics and Teodora for guidance.

"Bone is made of calcium, right?" said Defne. "Use your powers to construct a latticework of calcium around the separated parts to fuse them back into place."

Sigrid nodded, and continued with her work, weaving a lacework of white strands of calcium to envelop the fractures for support. Anastasia looked over her shoulder and assumed the work when Sigrid's eyes grew tired. Eventually, the entire room of magical architects were somehow involved in one way or another, staring down at the operation with keen interest, giving suggestions, making encouraging comments, and taking over when necessary. After several hours, the bones appeared to have been repaired smoothly and seamlessly, as if no injury had occurred, save for the swelling. Ubaldini's lacerations were sewn with sutures, and a disinfectant spell was cast on the wounds. Hard casts, made of dense wool and enchanted with a rigidity spell, were crafted for Ubaldini's legs. After several hours, Ubaldini awoke and found his colleagues beside him. Some were eating, while some were sleeping openly on chairs and benches.

"My friends," he moaned, "were we victorious?"

"Of course," said Fahim, who was slouched in a chair nearby with a bandage on his head, "but it was not without sacrifice. Some of us received scrapes and bruises, but we are fine. You, on the other hand, required all our expertise to restore your good health. Be glad you have such good friends."

"I am. I thank all of you. Where is my dear brother Arsalan?" asked Ubaldini.

"I am here, my brother," said Arsalan, rising from a chair. Ubaldini turned his head and looked at him lovingly.

"My brother Arsalan," said Ubaldini. "I'm so sorry for everything. You did not have to save me. You could have allowed me to die alone. I would have deserved it."

"No, no," said Arsalan, taking Ubaldini's hand. "We would not have allowed it."

"Then I am indebted to you forever, my friend," said Ubaldini.

"We are indebted to you, too, Emilio," said Arsalan. "You rushed out into harm's way like an old fool to save the castle that housed my family and friends. As far as I am concerned, we are on equal footing now."

Ubaldini began to weep with joy and elation mingled with grief. He grasped Arsalan's head and placed their foreheads together.

"I was a buffoon all those years," Ubaldini said. "So many years wasted on ill sentiment. We could have been closer friends."

"It was our exceptional closeness that engendered our jealousy in the first place, my good friend," said Arsalan. "In any case, our rivalry is cast aside now."

Ubaldini was transported to a chaise lounge in an adjoining chamber and was given such attentive care by everyone that he could not help but feel a tad embarrassed. It became clear that he would have no problem recovering from his wounds so long as he rested well, although the pain was so excruciating that the medics were forced to give him more anesthetics. "Please, do not spend so much on me," he said, and he attempted to pay the military surgeons gold, which they felt they had no place accepting.

The magical architects were sore and exhausted, and eventually they would spend weeks recuperating from their strains and injuries. Great volumes of time would be consumed in slumber in various rooms around the main hall and the dining room. The aging wizards had not the stamina to celebrate their victory in any typical way, although Renard found the energy to venture out to the battlefield by the destroyed cannons to look for Ubaldini's hat, which he found by a stream near where they had discovered Ubaldini himself. The old magical architect was overjoyed when it was presented to him, though he made certain to state that such an expedition was unnecessary. Nevertheless, he brushed the dust off it and set it beside his chaise lounge.

Arsalan was astonished and overjoyed at the news that his daughter Defne had manifested wizardly powers, though he had to pause for a moment to consider all the potentially negative consequences. His mood changed dramatically when he heard Asker's report that he had instructed Defne to destroy the cannons. Arsalan became so inconsolably furious that he found it difficult to breathe, and Asker thought Arsalan's heart would fail. A heated argument ensued between father and son behind closed doors, but they were so loud that everyone could hear them anyway.

"She had had no training, no experience, and already you were employing her in violent military operations," said Arsalan. "You could have killed someone! You could have killed us!"

"What was I supposed to do, Father?" said Asker. "They were trying to destroy us! We had to defend ourselves!"

"Could you not have used her powers to continue to collect all the cannonballs until their ammunition was depleted?" said Arsalan.

"We could not assume they had limited amounts of ammunition," said Asker. "They could have continued all day and into the night, for all we know!"

"Could you not have waited? We were almost at the cannons to debilitate them ourselves," said Arsalan.

"I know you weren't at the cannons," said Asker. "You are all so powerful that if you were there the cannons would have stopped shooting at us!"

Defne burst into the room and began screaming.

"Father, stop treating me like a cannon that Asker was firing," she demanded. "I flung those cannonballs myself. It was my decision. I chose to destroy all the cannons, not Asker. If you are to be angry with anyone, be angry with me! We did the best we could do in that situation."

"According to Ubaldini's account and Asker's account, it was one of your explosions that injured him!" said Arsalan.

"I didn't mean to hurt him!" said Defne, tears streaming down her face. "I was trying to protect us!"

"And even if she did hurt him, Father, that's war!" said Asker. "In war, there are casualties! One doesn't head into battle without accepting the possibility of death by any cause, even if from friendly fire!"

Defne stomped out of the room and into Ubaldini's chamber, knelt at his side, placed her head on his arm, and begged for his forgiveness.

"No, no, no, my dear lady," said Ubaldini. "Of course I forgive you. There is not even any real cause for forgiveness in this case. You were protecting others. As I said, I was foolhardy, rushing off like that without anyone at my side. It was something I simply should not have done, though I was trying to defend the castle as you were."

Arsalan and Asker walked in and saw the exchange.

"Arsalan, my old friend," said Ubaldini. "You needn't be so strict with your children. They tried their best. They were isolated in the fog of war, as they say."

After a moment, Arsalan looked contrite.

"Perhaps you're right," he said. "Maybe it's just...maybe it's just my own vows talking."

"I know," said Ubaldini. "Old habits are difficult to defy. But you must remember that although Defne has wizardly powers, she is not yet a magical architect, and has taken no such vow."

Arsalan was silent.

"No," said Defne, not looking at him. "And I don't want to be a magical architect either, Father."

"What?" Arsalan spat. "There is only one path for someone of your power!"

"No, there isn't," said Defne.

"Then what else will you be?" said Arsalan. "What will you do with your magic?"

"I want to be a surgeon, Father," said Defne. "I want to be a medical doctor. I want to help people. I want to heal bones, like we did with Master Ubaldini."

The idea was an astounding epiphany for Arsalan, and he stared at the wall, his mouth agape and his mind filled with the light of wonder. He then turned his gaze to Defne.

"Tell me, Father," said Defne. "Has anyone with wizardly powers joined the ranks of medicine instead of magical architecture?"

"No," said Arsalan. "None whom I can recall."

"Why not, Father?" asked Asker.

"Because typically magical powers are discovered in early childhood," said Arsalan.

"And the child is sent to the Magical Architects' Guild before the child has a mind to decide for himself or herself what to do with those powers," said Asker. "Isn't that right, Father?"

"Yes," whispered Arsalan, adding with a chuckle. "Because what does a child know?"

"And the parents naturally desire wealth and success for their children," said Ubaldini. "And the Guild is the best way for them to guarantee that."

Arsalan again was silent and thoughtful.

"Tell me, Father," said Defne. "If your powers were revealed to you as an adult rather than as a child, would you have chosen magical architecture as your profession?"

"I don't know," said Arsalan in wonder. "I have known only magical architecture, and nothing else. I never considered any alternatives."

"Well, maybe it's time for you to allow me to consider mine," said Defne.

"But there is no guild for magical medicine!" said Arsalan.

"There need not be one, Father," said Defne.

Arsalan sat on a chair and stared at the floor, lost in thought at the developments presented to him. He was quiet for a long time while the other three watched him. Eventually, Arsalan spoke.

"I apologize, Asker and Defne, for scolding you," said Arsalan in his gravelly voice of contrition. "I was seeing things from my viewpoint as a magical architect rather than from yours. Instead, I should be commending you for your actions and your bravery. You and Defne helped us win this battle. It is not easy for me to understand war."

"But Father," said Asker, "you fought in your way so heroically. You are like a military leader in ways of which you are not aware. You would have made a fine admiral."

"That may be," said Arsalan. "Maybe trying times like these bring out the best and worst in people."

"Father, I am proud of you," said Asker. "I am not upset with you."

"And I am even prouder of you, my son," said Arsalan. "You are a fine man and a fine soldier. Thank you." And he embraced his son.

"And I am equally as proud of you Defne, for defining your own way of action at each crucial juncture," said Arsalan.

Defne's eyes became dewy, and she hugged Arsalan.

"Father," said Defne. "I want to visit the wounded soldiers from the battlefield, in the prisons and hospitals. I want to heal them. I want to heal any of those soldiers whom I may have injured."

Arsalan gave a troubled smile. "Let's see what we can achieve," he said.

Princess Berthilde accompanied Defne, as did Siegfrieda, Teodora, Sigrid, and Arsalan. A local cathedral was used as a makeshift hospital for the wounded soldiers, but its conditions were horrid. Even with the pews unscrewed from their bases and set to one side, there was hardly any space for all the patients. Their beds and cots were packed next to each other like crates. Only several straight aisles were maintained between the beds for the medical staff's perambulation. The staff were frantically overburdened; their faces were drawn and grave, and their eyes bore dark, sagging circles. The walls echoed with the groans of the injured for relief from their agony, but it was clear that supplies of anesthetic were grossly insufficient. Moreover, the winter's cold had caused a cough to go around from bed to bed, and many of the injured had fevers. Defne's eyes immediately began to seep tears at the ghastly sight, but she was not deterred. She conferred with the head nurse and asked to be led to those with broken bones. Without further questioning, the nurse led them to one corner where doctors were fashioning splits and plaster casts for many patients.

"Whatever you can do, please do it," said the stout, middle-aged head nurse. "We were entirely unprepared for this level of violence."

Defne and Sigrid set about using the same techniques on the wounded as they had on Ubaldini. Since not all of them could receive any opiates, medics had to rely on draughts of cheap liquor and rags on which the patients could bite to manage their pain. Legs, arms, skulls, and ribs were examined, bones were reset, the wounded cried out in holy agony, and their fractures were woven together, one by one. Defne and her friends worked long into the night. But as they worked, word of her efforts spread back to the castle, and one after another, more of the magical architects appeared, looking aghast and lost. They were willing to help Defne but had no idea where to start in the chaos. First Fahim appeared, rubbing the back of his neck in confusion, then Anastasia, then Majdouline, then Dimitra, then the rest in one large fellowship. Without exception, the blood drained from each of their faces at the sight of the wounded. Even Arsalan could not help feeling woozy and faint at the gruesome sights. In any case, it seemed to them that the bone-setting jobs were already nearly done, so the magical architects tried to recall whatever scant first aid they had learned to use for their own small bumps, scrapes, and bruises through the years. Dimitra shared her disinfectant spell with everyone, and subsequently it was used widely.

Defne persuaded Sigrid to share her transparency spell, or at least the version used for human tissue. Sigrid did so rather reluctantly since its use on stone and metal had been her guarded trade secret. Defne placed her hands on Sigrid's arms reassuringly.

"Sigrid," Defne said. "Have we not reasoned already that it is better to save a life than to save one's profits?"

Sigrid looked sideways to the wounded soldiers whose lives Defne planned to save with the spell. Sigrid then returned her gaze to Defne, smiled, and embraced her.

"Of course it is," said Sigrid. "Of course."

Jawahir shared a way to remove bullets and shrapnel from skin without causing more bleeding, and a way to entice blood to coagulate faster and more solidly. Gustav shared a little magical trick he had discovered to help wounded skin heal faster; he had not thought much of it since it did not work perfectly, but once modified several times over by the other magical architects, it seemed to heal human tissue nearly instantaneously. Of course, warmth spells were cast on all the patients' beds and sheets to keep them comfortable. It came as a surprise to Defne to see the pink sun rising through the stained-glass windows, as she had lost track of time. She and Teodora retired back to the castle to sleep, though it took a long time for Defne to fall unconscious; she was shuddering with shock and horror at the misery she saw and cried into her mother's arms for an hour before she slept.

"My brave, wonderful daughter," whispered Teodora, and she kissed Defne on her head. Teodora stroked Defne's hair long into the morning before she too fell to sleep, and the pale, watery sunlight through the windows woke neither of them.

With her work completed at the makeshift hospital at the cathedral, Defne made a tour of the various places where the wounded were kept, including the prisons for the surviving insurrectionist soldiers where many of them seemed completely unharmed due to the magical architects' nonlethal tactics. The bastille in Munich was nonetheless filled. Injured enemy soldiers occupied several floors with their prone and bandaged bodies and moans of suffering, and Defne saw all of them. Several large halls in Munich also served as temporary hospitals, with most of the wounded having been administered already.

From there, she went north to Ingolstadt and beyond and found the hospitals that had fallen behind enemy lines. These were not as crowded with ailing soldiers. Only the most gravely injured remained. Defne tried her best to align the skeletal fractures and breakages and to facilitate their healing in any way possible. She was accompanied throughout her duties by a continually shifting cadre of magical architects who increasingly looked to her for leadership in the nascent field of magical medicine. They found it difficult to keep pace with Defne's endeavors. After a magical architect tired, they returned to Conrad's Castle to rest and sent another in his or her stead.

Travel between hospitals and prisons was accomplished through direct, magical flight. Defne was brought along through the flying prowess of other wizards, for she had not learned yet how to fly by herself and seemed to have no taste for it. When transported through the air in a boat or a carriage, with an experienced magical architect at the helm, she preferred to shut her eyes and to hug herself until she was safely on the ground again.

"Relax," Teodora would say to Defne as she traveled with her. "Your father used to take me flying all the time. It was wonderful." But Defne's trepidation of aerial transport would prevent her from mastering the art of magical flight for some months.

Defne spent weeks healing the sick and wounded. By the time her tour was finished, she had mastered everything the magical architects knew about medicine, which was not much, but was enough for her to cultivate her knowledge through her own efforts. She also had become accustomed to the sight of blood, injury, and disease such that it no longer frightened her. She saw each new ailment as a challenge into which to delve and to solve. By the end of her duties, she was exhausted, and Princess Berthilde and Siegfrieda, while thanking her profusely, ordered her to rest.

Arsalan and the other magical architects spent time repairing damage to the castle. The destruction was thankfully little, but enough to disappoint them. Still, they were glad they had been able to protect it and had the skill to restore it to its original condition. To Arsalan's dismay, though, he noticed that a large chunk of a wall was blown out of the top of the northeast tower, where he had visited Conrad. Arsalan floated up and inspected the interior. All of Conrad's furniture, in its furtive magical reconfigurations of rooms, had been replaced with an entirely different set. The bookshelves and desk were gone and were replaced with ordinary side-tables and drawers and a bed. Some of the furnishings suffered damage, which Arsalan was able to repair almost without thinking. The lovely little arched window, remarkably, remained unmolested. Arsalan located the blocks that had constituted the damaged wall. Some lay on the roofs below while others were on the ground, in a cobblestone passageway beneath the eaves. He tried his best to put each stone into its original position according to his forensic analysis of its shape, location, and magical charge. After all was refurbished, Arsalan stood in the center of the dusty, empty chamber and tried calling Conrad's name to see if he would return, but nothing happened. Arsalan felt like a sad fool, like a child calling for his imaginary friend. Arsalan secretly and forlornly wondered if the blast had compromised the castle's ability to host the old spirit, and he made a habit of observing the window each night from the ground for the possible manifestation of faint candlelight.

CHAPTER 25

The postwar trials commenced. The insurrectionist generals and commanders who served under von Ansbach were quickly tried and sentenced to decades in prison for their acts of treason. All of Princess Berthilde's advisors were surprised that she had not asked for the death penalty, but she had no heart for it.

"Spending years in dank prison cells is bad enough," she said. "Let them be alive to suffer it."

The commanders and lieutenants were charged according to how fervently they had demonstrated their desire to follow von Ansbach during the war, according to documents, testimonies, and affidavits. The trials were a triumph of slow and deliberate justice. Occasionally, Arsalan, Defne, Teodora, and many of the magical architects were brought in to testify. They did so willingly and factually. They watched the robed lawyers speak with elegant elocution as they presented their cases in front of juries and defendants who sat brooding for hours behind tables within the chilly courtrooms. At certain points during the deliberations, the accused would lose their patience as to the length of the proceedings and the nature of the allegations, and they would erupt into strident histrionics and outraged grandstanding, which were quieted by the intransigent bangs of the judges' gavels. Some of the defendants were unrepentant and swore allegiance to von Ansbach to their deaths as if their insurrection still existed. This only would provoke the kinfolk of innocent wartime casualties, those who had been standing and sitting for long hours in back and along the walls as they waited for justice. Clustering together and whispering into each other's ears, they had struggled to follow the erudite legalisms that had been bandied before them, but when they saw the outbursts of the traitors, they finally saw their chance to vent their simple but suppressed grievances. They joined in the fray, pointing and shouting for justice, justice.

In their persistent questioning, lawyers demanded the names of those who had built the enormous cannons that almost destroyed Conrad's Castle, but none of the defendants would divulge this information. They either became silent or professed blithe ignorance. It was as if they were all stubbornly sworn to some deep secret regarding this matter.

After a time, some of the defendants openly displayed their exhaustion and, leaning forward or backward in their seats, appeared to accept whatever fates would be meted out to them. They sat in slouches of resignation, and it seemed the proceedings became as tortuous to them as any eventual sentence. No less than von Ansbach himself was the least perturbed of them all.

"Sentence me all you want, but I am not a criminal," he retorted, coolly observing his fingernails. "The only reason I am being tried as one is because you are the victors. Believe me when I say that if I won then our roles would be reversed. I would be lauded as a hero for my victory, and you would be tried as traitors." This succeeded in quietly infuriating every one of his accusers and every member of the prosecution and did not help his case in the least.

As the trials made their way down the ranks to the commanders, lieutenants, colonels, and sergeants, the lawyers' questionings became more perfunctory and procedural and less hostile and intrusive, and the sentences handed down grew less severe. By the time the judges and lawyers reached the uncountable masses of colonels and privates, whose associations with von Ansbach were insubstantial and whose services to him were performed only under the threat of death, Bavaria's legal community appeared to throw up their hands entirely, granting all the low-ranking soldiers blanket clemency. The kingdom simply lacked the resources to jail so many hundreds of thousands of unlettered enlisted who had been mechanized into action under the commands of their insanely wayward officers. As an alternative to punishment, the convicted were employed as laborers to clean up wartime rubble and to repair houses and bridges damaged by blasts and bullets, a reasonable alleviation to which they humbly submitted themselves.

During the month of trials, one by one the magical architects courteously took their leaves, eager to return to the normalcy of their own works. Guild members exchanged embraces, handshakes, bows, and promises of writing and invitations for visits. All sensed that the cultural heart of the magical architects' world had altered irrevocably, expanding somehow for the better in subtle but profound ways. The society of magical architects would never be quite the same again.

First, Anastasia the Austere flew off like an eagle on an arctic gale. After her, Dimitra the Blue, Gonashvili the Giant, and Fahim the Fathomless departed, and then others in small clusters. Sigrid had taken a motherly liking to Defne and wished to stay. She had to leave to resume her work, but not without an extended series of warm hugs with the newly discovered young wizardess.

"Come visit me in Reykjavik," said Sigrid. "It's beautiful there, especially in the winter."

"I will," said Defne, holding Sigrid's hands.

The magical architects steadfastly refused all payments offered by the insistently grateful Princess Berthilde. In a good-natured gesture, however, she had servants sneak small amounts of gold into their baggage. Only Gustav seemed to notice the jingling of coins in his bag as he lifted it, and for the first time during his entire stay at the castle his long face broke into a smile—a shy, crinkling, toothy grin that he was not accustomed to displaying.

Among those last to leave were Marcelle the Marvelous, Fernando the Fabulous, Jawahir the Spellbinding, and, of course, Ubaldini the Ingenious, who could go nowhere without help, and Arsalan's former apprentices and assistants. The princess escorted them all, along with Defne, Teodora, and Bayram, back to her palace in Munich where Ubaldini would be rehabilitated. Their caravan was an impressive sight. Princess Berthilde, Siegfrieda, and Bayram occupied one exquisite carriage while Arsalan and his family occupied another. Beside them, Doruk, Sunduk and their associates rode their horses and donkeys while leading Ubaldini's fine white steed by a rein. Marcelle and his apprentices rode their strange purple boat through the air above them, as did Fernando and his crew in their unwheeled carriage. Jawahir and his five associates hovered behind them in the white canopied longboat they had ridden to Bavaria.

Ubaldini was forced to occupy a carriage by himself, in which he winced and grimaced at the slightest bump. Everyone in the company gazed at the wondrous Conrad's Castle wistfully one last time as they left, watching it shrink into the distance. Arsalan was particularly dejected at the act of leaving the beautiful castle. To console himself, he hoped, then thought, perhaps, that he could glimpse a glimmer of light in the topmost window of the northeastern tower in the early morning twilight.

As the caravan of exquisite carriages and floating boats trundled its way northward, surrounded by strapping, healthy guards bearing shining white spears and armor, the people who happened to be at the sides of the road all took notice at the fantastic parade. They cheered, bowed, or threw flowers in their path. This outpouring occurred all along the road back to the princess' palace, through every little town, and through every village. Even the leaping dogs appeared to bark at them in celebration of the princess' triumph. Ubaldini's eye shed a tear at these sights as he leaned his head against the window of his cabin.

When they reached the palace in Munich, Princess Berthilde was elated to find it undisturbed. Tall, straight Dietrich greeted her at the door with a slight smile and welcomed the company inside. Doruk, Sunduk, and his compatriots tried hard not to gawk at the vast, ornate interiors. There, Marcelle, Fernando, and Jawahir made sure that Ubaldini was settled. They and their entourages stayed for two nights and a day of laughing, sharing stories, dining, and exchanging goodbyes before flying off into the morning sky in three different directions.

Ubaldini's recovery, aided by Defne's continuous aid, was remarkably swift. Within a few more weeks, he was walking carefully with a cane. His legs were as fine as any older man's legs could be, and not crooked or misshapen in any way. He looked down at his feet and marveled at his ability to walk again on them, pacing up and down the hallways, with expressions of wonder on his face. He embraced Defne and thanked her so repeatedly that she began to feel embarrassed. Ubaldini's thighs would be perfectly fine from then onward, although on certain cold days they pained him well enough for him to resume the temporary use of his cane. With nervous care, he, Doruk, and their associates mounted their steeds and donkeys, bade their tearful goodbyes, and rode off back to Budapest on horseback, where, before they had been called into action, they had been working on a grand library.

Teodora caught up with her letter correspondences with her court in Brzeg and extended her stay for another month. She wrote to her court that the Bavarian civil war was over, all was well, and she had reunited with her husband, daughter, and son. But it was not long before Asker had to leave to resume his duties in the Imperial Navy. For Asker's family, the thought of separation from him again was unbearable and a source of deep, sincere tears. Arsalan, Teodora, and Defne made the decision to accompany Asker back to the naval port of Antivari, whence Asker would sail to his next mission. From there, Bayram would continue to Kirklareli, and Arsalan, Teodora, and Defne would head northward to Brzeg where they would live while Teodora resumed her duties.

They informed the princess of their plans over lunch one day in her tearoom. Princess Berthilde knew this day would arrive eventually but could not help feeling heartbroken. The news of these plans saddened Princess Berthilde so much that she trembled at first, as if she were going to wilt, but she recovered her newly fortified royal composure and smiled for her friends.

"Arsalan," she said, her voice breaking and wavering. "I simply do not know how to thank you enough for what you have done for me and for Bavaria. I feel you have built me up from nothing. I would be nothing without your help."

"And likewise," said Arsalan. "I feel that you have helped me reconstruct myself, my life, and my family. But you know that when something is constructed or reconstructed on a solid foundation, it may stand on its own, and from then on, its only foe is time itself."

Princess Berthilde smiled broadly and nodded.

"Good," said Arsalan. "I will do the best I can to stand on my own feet, with my family's help, of course. In any case, I still feel I owe as much to you as you feel you owe to me."

"I feel you belong here, though I know you have dealings elsewhere," said Princess Berthilde, handing him an opulently decorated scroll of paper, bound with a ribbon. "Therefore, I hereby appoint you Bavaria's Exclusive Court Master Magical Architect for Life. See? Now I've made it official. You now must return whenever I order you. You have no choice."

Arsalan proudly nodded and chuckled, and they embraced for a long time.

"Like a father you are to me," she said.

"And like a daughter you are to me," he said.

"Will I be able to rule this kingdom without you?" she said.

"You did so before I arrived," Arsalan said, "and you will rule it with even more wisdom and grace and skill than before. I am sure of it."

Princess Berthilde embraced and thanked each one of them, including Bayram, but curiously not Asker. When she came to the strapping young soldier, she seemed flustered and hesitated to embrace him, and instead shook his hand. Finally, the morning came when Arsalan packed his cart and readied Solmaz and Aysel again in the courtyard. Asker prepared his white steed and Bayram his black stallion. The Turks and the Bavarians looked at each other yearningly, one last time, their hearts feeling as if they were being wrenched like wet towels. Suddenly Siegfrieda, who had been prim and stone-faced the entire time after their return to the palace, burst into wild tears and sobbed inconsolably, drying her face with a kerchief. Arsalan and Teodora looked at each other. Siegfrieda accosted each one of them with savage hugs, embraces, kisses to the foreheads, and implorations to them to take good care of themselves. Arsalan was flabbergasted but returned the affection as well as possible with gentle, joyous, magnanimous laughter.

At last, they departed from the royal palace, over the meandering paths of the royal grounds, its dry fountains, and its manicured gardens that were brittle and yellowed in the winter's cold. Defne watched the palatial estate, with Princess Berthilde, Siegfrieda, and Dietrich standing next to each other at its doors, diminish and fold into the distance and over the horizon until they were out of sight. She spent the rest of the morning saying nothing and laying her head on her mother's shoulder as they sat next to each other on the front seat with Arslan.

As Arsalan was driving the carriage, he happened to look over at Asker, who rode to the left to him on his great alabaster steed and stared forward with his bold and flinty gaze. Arsalan had never felt so proud of his son as when witnessing him now in his unfettered, unselfconscious, hale prime of adulthood. But Arsalan also could not help but also notice a strange silver ring hanging from a fine necklace he was wearing, glinting in the pale winter sun as it swung back and forth gently.

"Where'd you get that?" said Arsalan, pointing at the jewelry.

Asker looked down searchingly, distractedly, as though pretending to notice the ring and necklace for the first time.

"Oh, this," Asker said, grasping it with his fingertips. "The princess gave it to me. As a parting gift."

"Hm. A parting gift," said Arsalan. "I see."

"Yes. Impressive craftsmanship, don't you think?" said Asker, holding it up.

"Of course," said Arsalan. "I suppose you will be writing to each other?"

"Perhaps," said Asker, suppressing a slight smile.

"Perhaps, indeed," muttered Arsalan.

Arsalan turned his head to look at Bayram, who was riding his great black steed to the right of him. Bayram was grinning, but he attempted to hide his smile once he noticed Arsalan's gaze. He did not want to make light of Arsalan's little plight, but finally resorted to shaking his head.

"Your future just keeps growing more interesting, Master Arsalan," Bayram said.

"Shut up," chuckled Arsalan, as he smiled knowingly.

Teodora, who had been pretending to sleep on Arsalan's shoulder, finally sighed and patted him on his knee.

Arsalan, Teodora, and Defne spent the remainder of the winter there in Brzeg. Arsalan spent many days sleeping languidly and watching the milky mists of Silesia's winter gather and lurk in the wooded hollows and hills of that mountainous duchy. Arsalan's body was sore and weary from his trials and travels, and he took vengefully languid and recuperative pleasure in doing great amounts of nothing.

It was decided that Defne would attend classes in medicine at the University of Würzburg, in the northern part of Bavaria, next autumn. Acceptance of her application was swift and assured when combined with an official letter of recommendation from Princess Berthilde herself, and no less helped with letters from Arsalan the Magnificent, the Duchess of Brzeg, and the entire Magical Architects' Guild, signed by every member. The point once raised, Princess Berthilde then issued a decree to open all Bavaria's universities to female applicants to ensure the same opportunities for other women.

That summer, before she was to attend school, Defne visited Princess Berthilde while Arsalan took Teodora flying on a tour of Sliven. Arsalan wished to show her where he had spent his years on the mountaintop and the kind villagers who made him feel at home there.

After several wonderful but tiresome days of flight in a carriage, they landed directly on top of the mountain at the site of his cottage. Teodora wandered around the grounds of the cottage, looking at his desolate farm and tracing the outer woodwork of the structures with her fingertips. She was both awestruck at the beauty of the mountaintop and stricken with grief at the isolation Arsalan had chosen for himself, and tears welled in her eyes.

Arsalan cast the spell to unlock the door of the cabin. Teodora entered and peered around inside it for a few minutes. She found she was not interested in lingering there. She disliked the musty smell that had festered inside since Arsalan had left it, and she was quietly aghast at the cramped, rustic modesty of the interior, particularly the bedroom with its coarse, punitive bed, where she knew Arsalan had spent so many cold, lonely nights. To her, the house was a hovel, a prison. Arsalan attempted to elevate her mood by telling her the interesting methods he had used to build the little house, the cellar, and the barn, but, though she listened patiently, she remained similarly unenthusiastic. Feelings of guilt and sadness lapped at her feet like an insistent surf, and she wished to separate both herself and Arsalan from the agonizing past represented there.

Once they were both outside again, Arsalan found the keys to the front door and locked it. He had made sure to leave his box of spare copper and silver coins, which he had never bothered to take with him to Bavaria, inside the house on a windowsill. He placed the keys in a bundle of paper and left it at the door to Grozda's house, while Teodora waited by the roadside. A note, written in several languages, was attached to the package, and it read:

> To Grozda,
>
> *I have reclaimed my fortune and my family in the wider world outside, just as you had predicted. I now no longer need the cabin I rebuilt. I leave it to you in gratitude for your ardent friendship. Please use it for your good family. I will remember you forever.*
>
> *Arsalan*

That evening, Arsalan and Teodora walked alone past Lyubomir's butcher shop. The lanterns inside projected their golden hues through the windows into the contused twilight air outside and onto the dirt road. Both Arsalan and Teodora heard the giant man's boisterous laughter booming from inside. The shadow of an arm or a shoulder would pass by the corner of a window, carving a shadow from the squares of light lying on the well-travelled road. It seemed all Lyubomir's family and friends were there, relating the same jokes and stories to each other that Arsalan had heard for years. Arsalan smiled to himself. He knew from the exuberance of their voices they were well, and he felt no need to disturb them with his unannounced presence and all the insistently friendly obligations that would come with it. Arsalan and Teodora flew on from there to the inn in town, and the next morning, they left for Kirklareli.

Bayram received the two warmly in his modest chateau in Kirklareli, and on the night of their arrival, he had had a sumptuous dinner arranged by his staff. The interior of his dwelling had many tall windows with long curtains, and it was decorated and draped in bright, sunny yellows and grounded with a vivid red carpet.

"I still owe you the tea and flatbread I promised you in Munich!" Bayram jibed.

They talked long into the night. The news of Arsalan's defeat of von Ansbach's forces in Munich had spread far and wide, renewing popular interest in his architectural work. Requests for commissions began to multiply feverishly, the long list of which Arsalan regarded with graciousness and perhaps a little trepidation.

"I don't think I can finish the whole of this in my lifetime," said Arsalan.

"Stop saying things like that," said Teodora, lightly batting his arm.

"Indeed, your exploits have attracted a lot of attention," said Bayram, "including some appeals from governments to use your magic for military use."

"I am not interested," said Arsalan.

"I know," said Bayram.

EPILOGUE

Dearest Mother,

I hope this letter finds you well. I am certain you have understood the reasons for my silence over the years. Only I have not remained so silent. Over the past two years, I have attempted to correspond with Father at our home in Kirklareli, but I have received no reply yet. I do hope he is well and that he is not terribly angry with me for failing to correspond with him after a certain time. To ensure communication now, I have sent this letter to the address of Grandfather and Grandmother in Brzeg in the hopes that it will come into your hands.

You will be glad to know that I am well. You probably could not guess that I am living in the New World, in a city they call Asunción, in the Spanish colony of Paraguay. The fantastic journey that led me to this side of the world I will explain only briefly.

After I left Kirklareli, I dwelt for a time as a monk among the Benedictines in Cyrnos, and then I travelled to Urgell, and then to Barcelona. From there, I boarded a ship across the heaving, silvery seas to the steamy, tropical shores of this continent. I followed other adventurers whom I befriended along the way and ventured far inland to my present location. I made a home among the Spanish colonists and the members of the Guarani people, and I learned the language and religion of these natives, now mingled with the dominant Catholicism. They showed me their alien ways of seeing the face of God. Such a strange, utopian world that has been carved out of the forests and mountains here, unlike even the colonies surrounding it. But of these matters there is too much to tell here in detail. I eventually procured a respectable position in a company that trades in gold and sugar. I am doing well for myself, and I have come under the benevolent tutelage of the other capable businessmen, with prospects of partial ownership. Mine is not the regal lifestyle to which we were accustomed during my childhood, but perhaps that is all for the better. Only God knows what the future may hold for me in this life, which is firmly in his hands.

Nonetheless, of late, an issue has weighed on my mind. As you may know, I left home to flee my creditors after accruing massive debts from my immoderate spending habits. Though I may blame youth and inexperience, and the paucity of financial acumen that was taught to me, I admit that my flight was an act of cowardice, one which perhaps placed an undue burden on my family. After much thought, I have resolved that I do not wish to be remembered this way among those I left behind. I wish to be remembered as a man of honor. With your blessings, I plan to repay my creditors, or you, if you had assumed those debts in my stead. I will do so from my earned income, in full, the amount of which I recall clearly. Any overestimation on my part may be treated as interest earned. I will arrange for its delivery to you once you confirm your need or willingness to receive it. Once received, please distribute the funds as necessary.

Let it be known that this is not simply a matter of balancing expenses. I stated before I left that I would recover our wealth, but that ambition has transformed from one of insolent pride to a more spiritual matter. I am now a man of God, and my repayment to you or my creditors will represent a purification of my soul. I include with this letter a small token of my sincerity in this matter, a rare prize of the mines here, stored in the metal box and locked in a way that only Father may undo with his magical powers.

All else is well. I await your reply in earnest.

Your dear son,

Omer

The letter arrived through diplomatic channels from the Spanish Empire to the Hapsbugs, and eventually to Brzeg, one cloudy, drizzly autumn day, as if emerging from a dream or the mists of time. Teodora discovered the package in her pile of other more mundane correspondences, and she found she had to read the message repeatedly to make sure it was real. The possibility that it was a forgery crossed her mind fleetingly. Though she was overjoyed to receive the letter, its aloof, businesslike tone was discomfiting and puzzling and unlike the writing style of the son they once knew and had missed. The penmanship, however, was unmistakably Omer's. Neither Teodora nor Arsalan knew what to make of it.

In the package, Arsalan found the box mentioned in the letter. Indeed, it was compact and metal, gray and solid, and completely unadorned. The lock had been secured with a key that was not included. Arsalan used Sigrid's transparency spell to see inside the lock, then used his telekinesis to manipulate its mechanism. The lid opened with a pop and lifted itself, revealing a shining bar of smooth, polished gold, or what seemed like that precious metal. Arsalan took the bar in his fingers and examined it, turning it this way and that in the gray morning light. It was cool to the touch and remarkably dense. He had not seen an alloy of gold like this before at all. It shone with a peculiar violet iridescence that splashed across its golden luster.

"What is it?" asked Teodora.

"I'm not sure," replied Arsalan. "I need to analyze it more, but if I'm not initially mistaken, it seems to be some variant of…"

"Yes?" asked Teodora.

"Pyrite," continued Arsalan.

"Oh," exhaled Teodora. "Pyrite. Oh, my Omer. My dear son Omer."

They were disturbed, not at having possibly received counterfeit wealth, but at Omer's possible ignorance of the difference between real and false gold. Still, they were glad that they now had contact with their lost son. In response, they thought for a long time and crafted a reply that was as loving and tactful as any they could produce.

In their letter, they expressed their gratitude, above all else, at hearing from him. They described their harrowing adventures and how it reunited them all and restored Arsalan's wealth and standing. They spoke of Asker's career in the Imperial Navy and Defne's manifestation of magical powers and her entrance into medical school. Teodora, however, broached the issue of repayment most gingerly:

As to the issue of your noble offer to pay your debts, my good son, you may be glad to learn that none of it is necessary. Your creditors long ago accepted your default and have ceased pursuing recompense. It has been some years since then, and they have reasoned your amounts outstanding are no longer worth the administrative costs of recovery. They also have not demanded any such payment from us as your family members; therefore, your debts were not shifted to us. All the same, we would never have demanded repayment from you, our dear son. We only want the best for you, as we always have wanted. We only wish you to be safe, healthy, and happy. Of course, we also would love to see you in person by our side. This would be more splendid than any mountain of riches. However, if you found true happiness, health, and perhaps even wealth in the New World, we can be only glad for you. We realize the mistakes we committed in our raising of you, and for that we apologize from the depths of our hearts. If your decision to remain in such a faraway country is a direct consequence of our errors in parenting, then that is a burden we are forced to bear consciously. Please know, though, that our doors are open to you whensoever you decide to return to see us again, whether you have restored your status as a wealthy man or not. You will be, forever and always, our son. We love you dearly.

Arsalan and Teodora read and edited the letter several times before sending it back through diplomatic channels to the far-flung colony known as Paraguay. They would keep the shining bar of metal in the plain box on their dresser drawer as a keepsake, with Omer's letter beneath it.

They received no letter of reply from Omer. Neither Arsalan nor Teodora were certain of the reason. They read his letter repeatedly for clues. Each time, the bitter aftertaste from his cold, curt officiousness grew more evident, and they sensed his implicit injury and anger seeping from beneath his words. Perhaps the issue of repayment was the only reason Omer had had for contacting us at all, Arsalan thought. They resigned themselves to waiting, as parents of long-gone children often do, perpetually for a reply that had no reason for coming, neither truly forsaking their son nor expecting anything from him.

The news swiftly reached the Magical Architects' Guild in Florence of the disappearance of Prince Ergin. He had vanished mysteriously during a hunting trip with his friends in the forests surrounding Kirklareli. Only his horse and dogs remained, circling aimlessly as if plaintively in search of him. Prince Ergin's friends who had accompanied him were suspected immediately of foul play, detained, and questioned for several days. Eventually, their alibis were corroborated, and no corpse could be found, so the young men were released but regarded for several weeks thereafter with lingering scrutiny. Eventually, it was assumed that the foolhardy Prince Ergin had become lost in the wilderness and had died, perhaps in a river, off a cliff, or at the jaws of wolves. He had left behind only a string of resentful girlfriends, but no wife or immediate family.

The news was a minor but curious footnote among the grander reports of world affairs passed by letter or by mouth from one town to the next, and it reached Arsalan through several close sources only because of his past involvement with the vanished prince. Each source passed the news to him with a tone of distant irony. There were no tears or worries from any of the reporters or from Arsalan. Nonetheless, Arsalan felt somewhat obligated to write Lord Kadir a letter of condolence, but he then thought better of it and threw the half-written letter away.

It was time for Arsalan to address the newly recruited apprentices at the Guild. He stood in the dark office with its high walls that vanished into the darkness of the ceiling, and with books and stacks of papers stacked half as high. It was the very room that had been Master Conrad's. Arsalan donned a vivid blue robe and flat cap. Emerging from the dimness of his office through the ornate oaken doors, he made his way through the arcaded colonnade of the balcony of the fourth floor of the Guild, found the stairwell, and spiraled down it.

Arsalan had told the magical architects to gather the younglings in the rear of the building in the enclosed garden, where he had had a square of soil established. The enclosure was surrounded by an arcade of columns plated with cool green porcelain. A tranquil fountain trickled at one end of the enclosure. When all the recruits had assembled, staring at Arsalan with guileless, expectant faces, the old man gave a bowlike smile and a crinkling, kindly gaze, and he instructed them to help him tend the garden.

The children, somewhat confused, complied with his request, and for much of the afternoon they helped him till the soil and plant seeds and sprouts. They gently nourished the plantings using little decanters filled with water fetched from the trickling fountain. All the while, Arsalan instructed them in the ways of horticulture and gardening, of watering, composting, weeding, and harvesting. He taught them how deeply to dig the holes for planting, how much water to add and how often to add it, and where and at which time of year to plant various types of vegetables.

The children genuinely enjoyed the work. Their minds wandered away from the exciting daily discussions of magic and architecture, and their attentions dissolved into the hazy purity of sun and soil and water. They had forgotten themselves completely. At length, when the molten apricot sun was beginning its reddening descent through the pale afternoon sky behind the roofs of the Guild and the creeping shadows began to make their lengths known from the corners of the enclosure, the children became hot and tired and began to wipe their foreheads and to sit. One boy, after standing thoughtfully for a time while staring at the carefully tilled chocolate soil glistening in the sun, finally found the mind to pose a question to Arsalan.

"Master Arsalan," he said, "I like gardening. It is something my parents do all the time. But when will we begin to practice magic? When will we put blocks together to make things?"

"Young lad, what is your name?" asked Arsalan.

"Pepijn," the boys said.

"Well, Pepijn," said Arsalan, "when a seed, which seems little more than a pebble, is planted in the soil and miraculously sprouts a tender shoot, is that not magic? When that shoot grows into a graceful plant that bears fruit or a lovely blossom, is that not magic? When your muscles work to dig the soil, do you know how your muscles move? Could that be also a form of magic? Feel how your body must work around the forces of nature to conduct labor. It seems toilsome and mundane, but is that also not a form of magic? Your heart races, your breath quickens, your muscles burn a little, and you produce sweat. Are these not types of magic? How does a human being exist, one who can work, can think, can dream, can make music, can love, and can ask questions? Does this not appear to be some sort of miracle? All the forms of rock that we use to build things, stones of one color or another, one texture and pattern or another, beautiful arrays of minerals and ore. What put them together? Regard the way the sun's light, once white or yellow, now reddens against the balconies as it falls. Is that not a type of magic?"

"I think I see, Master," said Pepijn, "but what does this have to do with magical architecture?"

"Before you can appreciate the magic that is employed in making impressive, majestic cathedrals and castles and palaces for kings and queens and gods, those arching, vaulting structures that dazzle the eye and enthrall the heart, one must appreciate first the magic that we see in its everyday forms, encrusted into the minute grains, veins, and fissures of all things, living and inanimate, the magic that lies in pools and puddles in the middle of the forest under mist and moss, the magic of the sun raking across a tree's bark, the magic in a bird's call, the magic in a mother's voice and in the smell of her cooking, the magic in the dappled sun on one's face under the leaves, the magic in the sound and odor of rain, the magic of good friendship and family. You see, magic is everywhere and in everything and in every one of us, and of this the magic of architecture is just one small part," said Arsalan.

"I think I understand," said Pepijn, "but I think I still like magical architecture the best so far."

"And why is that?" asked Arsalan.

"With magical architecture," said the boy, "one can make whatever one needs. If I'm tired in the middle of the woods, in just a few minutes I can make a nice house in which I and my family can sleep for the night."

Arsalan laughed and playfully tousled Pepijn's sandy hair.

"I think you understand what I'm saying more than you realize," chuckled the old man.

After the gardening lesson was over and all the tools were put away and the children were dismissed, Arsalan cleaned his hands and retreated to his study on the fourth floor, where he sat at his broad desk and unfurled a scroll of paper. A light shone on the desk from a high window. On the parchment were the schematics to the World's Leaf, whose design was slightly altered from its previous manifestation. There was a vague noise at the door. It swung slightly ajar as if blown by the breeze, and a narrow beam of sunlight shot through the doorway to the desk. Arsalan turned, stalked over to the door, and opened it fully. Ubaldini was there, wearing his broad green hat and leaning on a cane.

"Good day, my friend," Ubaldini offered with an open, expectant gaze, and he walked into the room with a slight limp. Arsalan greeted him cordially, and they proceeded to the desk to continue their collaboration on the plans for the rebuilding of the World's Leaf. They spent the rest of the afternoon there, pointing here and there at the diagrams, making measurements, adjustments, and notes, and occasionally conversing in spiraling tangents. Eventually, Arsalan grew quiet and somber, and he turned to Emilio.

"Are you certain this can be built?" asked Arsalan. "Are you certain you wish to rebuild it? I understand if we lack the funds and there are no interested customers. I will not be disappointed if it is not possible."

"I do not lack the funds," said Ubaldini, "but I must continue to survey for locations and customers."

Arsalan reflected for a moment, looking first at his old friend and then at the cheerfully elaborate schematics of the structure, filled with notes, lines, and figures, that lay across the desk.

"I know you persist for my sake," said Arsalan quietly. "For that I am grateful. But do not trouble yourself if this is too grand an undertaking. I will remain a happy man regardless. Please know that."

Ubaldini was silent, and he continued to study the diagrams intently, as if he had not heard Arsalan. Teodora appeared at the door.

"We still have the plans, in any case," Ubaldini uttered finally. "We will continue with them when you return, old friend. Enjoy Munich and Brzeg once again and give my regards to the princess."

Ubaldini rose with his cane and approached the door, where he doffed his hat to Teodora and quietly slipped away. Teodora looked long and concernedly at Ubaldini as the man disappeared down the colonnaded hallway outside.

Finally, she turned her attention back to her husband in the office, who now was giving the large folio of plans one last look. Arsalan shook his head slightly before he rolled up the schematics and stored them away in his desk.

"Are you packed and ready for our journey?" asked Teodora. "Defne has returned from Kirklareli."

"Of course!" sighed Arsalan as he put away his pencils and instruments. "My dear daughter!"

Defne appeared in the doorway next to her mother. Defne excitedly held in her hands a cage covered with cloth. Arsalan turned to look at her curiously.

"My daughter," he said. "I trust your journey to our old homestead was fulfilling!"

"Yes, it was," she said, "and I discovered that Lord Kadir is selling our old chateau after the sad disappearance his son who occupied it."

"Is he now?" asked Arsalan.

"Yes!" she said. "You should buy it back from him, Father. In his grief, he is selling it at a greatly reduced price of four hundred thousand."

"Oh my!" he exclaimed, taken aback, "well, now, there's an idea I should consider, I suppose, but perhaps not so soon. It wouldn't feel right to take advantage of a grieving father's despair."

"Don't forget how he came to possess the chateau in the first place, Father," she said. "In any case, it would be grand to have the old place back again."

Arsalan looked at Defne with a curious, sidelong glance, then turned his gaze to the floor, pursed his lips, then nodded pensively.

"Well, let me think about it on our journey to Munich today," he replied. "Along the way, we also can discuss what you've learned so far in your research into magical biology at university. I hear that has been proceeding smoothly."

"Yes, Father," she said, nodding exaggeratedly. "I've learned much."

"Wonderful. Now, is all your newfound knowledge contained in that thing you're holding so enthusiastically?" he asked.

Defne grew a broad, mischievous smile and a glint in her eye.

"Do you remember how you said you missed having a cat?" she said.

"Yes," Arsalan said. "No, you didn't."

"I did," she answered.

Defne placed the cage on a table and removed the cloth. Inside, there was indeed a cat. It had dark brown fur, and it looked around the room with terrified green eyes.

"My," said Arsalan, "where did you get it?"

"I found him. He was lost and hungry in the woods outside Kirklareli, so I took him in and nursed him back to health. He is such a good little kitty, isn't he?" she said, tapping her finger against the wooden cage. But the cat did not respond very affably. Instead, it cowered in the corner of the cage, as if fearful of her, until it was an indistinct mass of shadow from which only its two jade eyes shone. Defne did seem a tad insistent in her affection for the feline, and this did not seem to pacify the animal.

"He doesn't seem to be in good spirits, my daughter," said Arsalan.

"He is still rattled from the flight here, I think," said Defne. "Aren't you, my kitty? Yes, you are."

"Well, thank you, my dear daughter," said Arsalan. "Let's have a look at him. Does he have a name?"

"Yes, I've decided to name him Şehzade," she said.

"Şehzade! That's a fine, princely name for a cat," said Arsalan. He opened the door to the cage and reached inside, but the cat refused to be cajoled out of its shadowy corner. Finally, when Defne neared the rear of the cage where the feline was cowering, the cat leapt out and landed in Arsalan's lap, where the old man was able to embrace it. He began to pet the cat.

"Well! There you are, my little friend," Arsalan said. "Don't be frightened. You are in good hands here, and we will care for you with all the love you can stand."

"Yes, did you hear that, Şehzade?" said Defne, and she approached and knelt before the brown cat on Arsalan's lap to pet it reassuringly, but as she neared Şehzade, the animal growled, hissed, spat, and leapt from Arsalan's lap and sprinted in a fleet blur out the door below the knees of Teodora, who wrinkled her brow. Defne looked out the door at the fleeing cat for a long moment, then turned back to Arsalan.

"Well, I'm sorry, Father," she said, managing her embarrassment with a sigh and a laugh. "I suppose I was a bit too...eager in my choice of a cat."

"Well, no worry, my dear daughter," Arsalan said. "It was your gesture that counted. I think I'm too busy anyway for a pet, what with all the new commissions I'm being extended, and my role here as Librarian. I'll take a cat when I'm elderly and infirm. We either could get a new one or could track down Şehzade from somewhere on the grounds. Let us be off now on our visit."

From some corner of the Guild's courtyard, Şehzade's frightened, electric eyes followed the grand, ornate carriage as it glided into the dusking sky, carrying the Ozdikmen family on their delightful voyage northward. A few minutes later, Pepijn appeared, accompanied by a few of the other newly recruited children. He stooped and gazed at the cat with his child's eyes of daringly observant innocence. He had been playing outside, and his pupils dilated to see the dark cat more clearly in its hiding place behind a column while his grubby nostrils flared slightly with his exhalations.

"Look!" Pepijn said. "A little cat. It looks like a stray. Let's take care of it. Are you hungry, little one? Maybe you were lost in the woods. Don't worry, brown cat. I will build a fine little house for you where you can sleep all day and where you can eat as much as you want, just like a little prince. I know they don't like pets here at the Guild, but I'm sure once they see you, they'll understand. Come now, cat! We will show you all the love you deserve. Because love is magic! That's what Master Arsalan says."

Şehzade reluctantly permitted himself to be lifted by the guileless boy, who seemed harmless enough. The cat looked left and right, as if searching in vain for some better alternative to its present predicament, until finally realizing it was trapped, and resigning itself to its fate as a focus for unsought human affection.

Pepijn did just what he said he would do. He built a wonderful miniature mansion, like an expensive dollhouse, and kept it in his dormitory by his bed. It was four feet high, made of small stones, tiny bricks, little beams of wood, daubs of mortar, and delicate glass windows, like those in his hometown of Utrecht. Every compressed and miniaturized detail was splendidly precise. It was so immaculate and delicate that none of the master magical architects dared to disturb it or the strange, anxious cat who brooded within.

Printed in the USA
CPSIA information can be obtained
at www.ICGtesting.com
BVHW051027250823
668877BV00005B/125

9 781088 191934